THUNDER AND PASSION

Blake reached out and touched her arm. "You're shaking. I thought you said you're not afraid of storms."

"I'm not! Leave me alone!" Another, louder clap of thunder proved her to be a liar.

"Come here," Blake said softly as he pulled her into his arms. "You shouldn't be ashamed of being afraid. I don't like storms either." He held her tense body and nuzzled his cheek against her hair. Slowly Blake lowered his head. Lacey jerked away before their lips met, but he gently pulled her back. His lips moved over hers in a tantalizing caress. His breath was sweet in her mouth, and his warm tongue teased the softness inside her lips and ran over the tiny ridges of her teeth. The physical sensations she felt were unlike any Lacey had ever known.

SUMMERFIELD

LYNDA TRENT

PINNACLE BOOKS   NEW YORK

SUMMERFIELD

Copyright © 1984 by Dan Trent and Lynda Trent

An original Pinnacle Books edition, published for the first time
anywhere.

First printing/December 1984

ISBN: 0-523-42348-9

Can. ISBN: 0-523-43351-4

Printed in the United States of America

PINNACLE BOOKS, INC.
1430 Broadway
New York, New York 10018

9 8 7 6 5 4 3 2 1

To Liza Dawson
for putting foundations under our castles in the sky

SUMMERFIELD

Prologue

Lacey Summerfield edged through the crowd, a burlap bag full of Dr. Summerfield's Wonder Tonic slung over one thin shoulder. Small for her fourteen years, she looked even younger with her red-gold hair in braids, wearing the calico dress that concealed her budding breasts. Papa said folks would rather buy from a child, and she was to pretend to be as young as possible.

She glanced at the colorful red and yellow show wagon where her older brother Billy was singing a rousing chorus of "Oh! Susannah" before a good-sized crowd. Billy had a good, ringing voice. Mama used to say Billy could outsing a bird—but for some reason the people weren't singing along with him today as they usually did. Without Mama's clear, high-pitched tones to keep him company, people seemed to think Billy was singing a solo. He had asked them to join him, but no one seemed to want to.

Lacey dug a small bottle out of the bag in preparation to sell the goods among the crowd. She tried not to think about Mama, who now lay in a grave five towns back up the trail. Billy told her he'd paid for a marker that would show their mother's name and the date of her death, but Lacey hadn't seen it. They had moved on to the next town before it was erected.

Positioning herself beside a plump matron, Lacey waited

for Billy to finish his song and for Papa to start the sales pitch. The woman glanced at her, and Lacey smiled, rubbing the toe of one foot against her other ankle as small children often did.

But when Billy stopped singing, almost no one applauded. Lacey frowned and looked at the faces. None of them smiled, nor did any of the people even nod their approval of her brother's performance.

Papa joined Billy on the platform and clapped the younger man solidly on his broad shoulders. In proud tones he assured the crowd that Billy owed his golden voice and fine physique to perfect health, and the health he owed entirely to Dr. Summerfield's Wonder Tonic.

"What's in it?" a man yelled.

"Now, you know I can't tell you that." Zeke Summerfield grinned as he stroked his black beard. "It's a secret recipe given to me by an Indian chief. He was one hundred and five years old and had already outlived four young wives."

No one chuckled at the joke this time.

Papa's eyes narrowed and swept over the crowd momentarily before he continued. "Two years ago my boy here couldn't carry a tune in a syrup bucket. He only weighed a hundred pounds sopping wet and didn't come as high as my shoulder." Zeke gestured at his tall son. "Now look at him! As strapping a young man as you'll see anywhere."

"He looked about the same to me when I seen you here a while back. He ain't changed a bit."

Lacey let her eyes sweep over the town. All the places they had passed through looked pretty much alike: a jumble of buildings, some old, some new, lined up along both sides of a dusty main street that would be a mire of mud in the rain. The businesses were clumped together in the middle of town, and the houses lined both ends of the street. Still, this one did look familiar.

"That's right," another man chimed in. "You're no

stranger to us. Do you remember a little girl you doctored right over there in that house?"

Lacey followed the man's gesture to the large white house next door to the bank. She was sure she had seen it before and had even been inside—a rare treat she wasn't apt to forget.

"I don't recall, neighbor." Zeke grinned with all the charisma he could muster. "The Wonder Tonic has helped so many people, it's hard to keep track."

"You didn't help her, except to Glory," the first man thundered angrily. "She died the next day."

Zeke's smile faded. "I'm real sorry to hear that, neighbor. These things happen, though, even with the best of medicine."

"She was on the mend. Her ma gave her your tonic to speed her recovery. It killed her flat out."

The tonic had killed her. How could that be? Lacey shifted her weight to the other foot. Between her and the safety of the wagon lay a sea of solemn faces. Lacey didn't know what was happening, but she was sure she would rather be inside.

Suddenly a woman's voice called shrilly, "That's him! That's the man that killed my baby!" The gaunt woman shouldered her way into the crowd. Upon her arrival, a murmur began to spread rapidly, rising in volume like the hum of a swarm of stirred-up bees.

"Now, folks," Billy began, "let's be reasonable about this." He gave them his flashy smile, but the noise increased.

Mama had always been the one to soothe an angry crowd, with her face like that of an angel and a voice to match. What Billy was doing didn't seem to help at all.

The crowd packed in closer to the wagon, leaving Lacey standing almost alone on the dusty street. Billy came to the tailgate as he had seen Mama do and leaned toward the people. At the same time, Papa backed up into the shadowy interior.

Suddenly a man grabbed Billy's coat and tried to pull him forward. More hands reached up, clutching at him. Papa turned and ran for the front of the enclosed wagon. As Billy struggled to escape, his frantic eyes met Lacey's over the heads of the mob, and she saw him frame the word "Run!" Then the hands were upon him, and when Papa slapped the reins on the horses' backs, Billy fell into the crowd.

Lacey was frozen, unable to think, let alone run. Someone produced a rope, and cheers went up as the men handed it down to the place where she had last seen Billy. Shouts of "Hang him!" rent the air. The bright red wagon with its yellow writing was lurching up the narrow street. As Lacey watched, a group of men darted out to intercept it, and Papa veered between two buildings, the frightened horses gnawing at their bits.

Terror sparked Lacey to action. Throwing down the bag of Wonder Tonic, she ran across the boardwalk and toward the buildings in the back of town. Over the screams of the crowd she could hear the horses' pounding hooves and the familiar rattle of the wagon.

"Wait, Papa! Wait for me!" she yelled.

Zeke looked her way, his face pasty with fright, but he didn't, or couldn't, slow the wagon.

Lacey ran as fast as she could, already gasping for air, her side aching. The wagon was closer now. She ran harder, trying to catch it before she lost the advantage of her shortcut. Fingers spread, she strained to grab the tailgate. Behind her she heard the shouts of the men chasing wagons. Fear gave her extra strength, and her fingers grazed and then clutched the plank. The wood bit into her skin, and the jolting threatened to shake her loose, but she held on desperately. Using all her strength, she pulled herself up, her legs churning in the losing battle. A sharp dip in the land gave her an advantage, and she managed to get her foot on the metal step.

She was not going to be left behind! She heaved her body up, and for a moment she dangled half in, half out of the wagon; then she fell inside. Her breath coming in choked sobs, Lacey dared to peep over the backboard. The men had quit chasing them and were hurrying back to the crowd. Lacey's terrified eyes widened, and a harsh scream ripped from her body.

Her only brother was hanging from a cottonwood tree, kicking helplessly. Even as she watched, he gave another spasmodic jerk; then his body went limp. After that, the only movements were those of the swaying rope and the rejoicing crowd. Lacey knew Billy was dead.

Zeke whipped the horses across the prairie, never pausing to look back to learn the fate of his son or to determine whether his daughter had managed to climb inside. Only when the exhausted horses could go no farther and twilight made the fast pace too hazardous did he slow them to a quick walk.

"Lacey?" he called over his narrow shoulder. "You back there?"

For a while she didn't answer as she digested the fact that he hadn't bothered to ask before now. Finally, in a voice older than her years, she answered, "I'm here, Papa." When he didn't respond she said, "They hung him, Papa. They took Billy and they hung him."

Zeke let the horses slow to a sedate walk, and he stared past their bobbing heads into the darkness.

"Did you hear me, Papa?" Lacey demanded. "They hung our Billy!"

"I hear you." His voice, too, had changed. A hundred years of sorrow seemed to cloak each word.

Angrily Lacey continued. "They would have hung me, too! Why didn't you slow down and let me catch up?"

"If I had slowed up, those men would have had me, too. I was going to come back after you when it was dark. They wouldn't have hurt you. It was me they were after."

Lacey stared at her father's back and felt her childhood die, as well as her respect and love for her father. "You didn't know that," she accused in a low voice. "You were leaving me behind to save yourself."

Zeke glanced back at her. He was frowning, but his eyes were frightened at her perception. "Don't talk like a fool, girl. I wouldn't run out on my own flesh and blood."

Relentlessly, she persisted. "Billy's dead, Papa! He's gone!"

Zeke Summerfield didn't say another word. Lacey tried to get him to answer, but it was as though her father had been struck deaf or mute, so she stopped talking. But her thoughts raced on as she went over and over the unanswered questions. Soon Zeke let the horses stop under a grove of willow trees by a stream, but instead of getting off the wagon, he just sat there, staring at the horses' ears.

"Papa?" Lacey asked uncertainly.

"They're gone." Papa's words were distant and hollow. "Both of them gone and dead. First your mama of fever up at Andersonville, now Billy. Dead and gone."

Lacey crawled through the cluttered wagon and climbed onto the seat next to her father. He was gazing outward with a wild look in his eyes, yet his words were almost whispered.

"The best of the lot—gone. My wife and my only son. I've been given more than I can bear."

"You've still got me, Papa," she reminded him.

"Belle was the best wife a man could ask for. A voice like a choir singing, and Billy, too. They were the ones with talent, her and Billy. I've lost all I had in barely two months' time." He sounded dreamy, as if all this were a lesson he recited from memory.

"I'm still here," Lacey said more firmly. "I can't sing or dance, but I'm your daughter and I'm still alive."

Zeke gave her an uncomprehending stare. "All you can do is sell tonic, and soon you'll be too old to do that."

Lacey sat stiffly. Her feet and hands felt cold, and a hard knot was forming in her stomach. She never cried, but her throat felt tight and her face hot. Papa was all she had left in the world; he couldn't mean the things he was saying. She had suspected that he was weak and no-account for as long as she could remember, but she knew he just couldn't help himself. Mama had been the family strength, the one to make decisions, the one to solve the problems. As far as Lacey knew, all families were like that, never having seen one to the contrary. And now she was the woman. The one to make the decisions and protect the weak—her father.

"We aren't going to sell tonic anymore. It's been nothing but trouble," she surprised herself by saying. "We're going to settle down, Papa, in a real house, and I'm going to go to school. We're going to live like everybody else."

Zeke Summerfield just stared at her. When he didn't contradict her, Lacey climbed off the wagon. "I'm going to start supper. You unhitch the horses." As she unstrapped the pans from the wagon, she planned out loud. "We'll swing wide and avoid towns for the next two weeks or so." Her voice broke, but she kept working, and talking. "That ought to get us out of the range of gossip. Then we'll use the money in the strongbox to buy us a house in some little town where they never heard of the Wonder Tonic." She felt a little better now that someone, even if it was herself, was taking charge. This was what Mama would have done.

She looked back at the wagon where Zeke still sat in the shadows. Using her firmest voice, she said again, "Unhitch the horses, Papa." Silence stretched out. Then he slumped forward to climb off the seat. Lacey breathed a sigh of relief. She had seen him hit her mother for much less than ordering him around, and she had not yet learned Mama's subtle tactics for getting her way without offending him. She supposed he was still in shock, for he moved like a broken man.

Lacey caught her lower lip in her white teeth. She, too, felt disoriented and scared, and she missed Billy terribly, but someone had to be strong. Papa certainly wasn't.

As she took some solace in the mundane function of cooking, she decided to buy whitewash and paint the condemning red and yellow wagon. From now on she would be the head of the family, and they would be like the happy people who lived in real houses that had no wheels.

CHAPTER

1

Lacey dipped her hand into the small syrup bucket and scooped up a handful of chicken feed. Using a sweeping gesture, she scattered the grain in an arc over the smooth-packed yard. A few fat hens waddled in a ludicrous race to capture the feed before the others could get it. Even the red rooster, his tailfeathers greenish black in the afternoon light, entered the race, his voice joining the hens' in a worried clucking. Lacey would have smiled if she hadn't been so tired.

Behind her stood a square sharecropper's cottage, its rough walls innocent of paint. Several of the windows had been broken by the former tenants, but she had covered the openings with heavy paper to keep out the winter cold and the summer flies. For ten years she and her father had lived hand to mouth, moving on when necessary to prevent trouble, for Zeke still, from time to time, reverted to his practice of making and selling Dr. Summerfield's Wonder Tonic. Lacey's pleas and threats had served only to make him more devious. This time, though, she was certain she had reformed him.

They had lived here almost two years—a long time compared to their brief sojourns in other places. The small house was completely surrounded by knee-high cotton plants that stretched for acres. A narrow yellow dirt drive led from the house to the road, but Lacey rarely used it. She worked the fields from morning to night six days a week, and spent the seventh mending and scrubbing clothes and performing all the other household chores. Zeke usually refused to work at all, and to make up for his laziness, she had to labor twice as hard. Otherwise, they would find themselves out on the road again, and a more industrious family would be living in the small shack.

Lacey wiped the grain dust from her fingers and dumped the remaining kernels on the ground. The cloud of red, white, and speckled chickens swirled around her in their eating frenzy, their beaks tapping at her well-worn shoes. Her day's washing flapped on the line she had strung from the corner of the house to the fence that enclosed her tiny but carefully tended vegetable patch. She mentally tallied her savings. Down by the creek in the hollow of a tree was a small canvas sack containing a hundred and forty dollars. Papa knew nothing about it; she dared not tell him. She would use the money someday to buy a place she could call her own. A place she would never be forced to leave.

In the distance, across the broad expanse of cotton fields, Lacey saw a small group of men on horseback. She shaded her green eyes against the sun. They all carried guns, and she saw her employer, Mr. Martin, in their midst. Probably they were going out for an evening of coon hunting.

Lacey went to the clothesline and ran a practiced hand over the sheets. Still damp. The day had been unusually still and humid, as if a storm were brewing. A heaviness weighted the air, causing her to feel restless and uneasy.

Zeke Summerfield came out on the porch and gazed at the riders as he scratched his thin belly. The last ten years had added gray to his black hair and beard and deep grooves to his cheeks. Lacey found herself wondering how old he was. She had been the last of many babies, but only she and Billy had survived infancy.

Billy. She seldom thought of him anymore. The horror of his death seemed to have given a vagueness to his life; to recall him at all was too painful an experience to endure. Looking at Papa, she mused about whether Billy would have remained a hero to her, had he lived. He would be in his mid-thirties now, she guessed—incredible to picture him so old—and likely married and with his own family. Perversely, the thought that he might have followed in his father's footsteps crept in. She decided it was just as well that she remembered him as he had been. Nothing in her experience had endeared men to her.

Papa alone was enough to sour a woman against the male sex. She still recalled the bruises he had given her mother and herself as a child. He didn't dare hit her now. He knew if he did, he would be wearing her heavy iron skillet for a collar. Then there was Mr. Martin, who had a perfectly good wife at home, but who had frequently tried to catch Lacey alone in the barn. She was too clever to be cornered, though. Since her fifteenth birthday, she had become very adept at avoiding men's advances.

Following her father's stare, Lacey watched as the group of men turned into the lane that led to their front door. Lacey's eyes narrowed. They had no reason to come that way to hunt.

"Come in the house, girl," Zeke said nervously.

Lacey glanced at him, then back at the riders. They had no hunting dogs with them, nor were they joking with one another as she might have expected from a bunch of men on a spree.

"You heard me, Lacey. Get in the house." Zeke turned and went back inside.

Icy fingers seemed to brush Lacey's spine as she studied the approaching men. Not one of them was smiling. Slowly she mounted the steps, her hand gripping the rough porch rail. Lifting her head, she waited silently, her eyes now on a level with those of the horsemen.

When they entered the yard, the chickens scattered with

squawking flutters; but Lacey remained motionless, her attention on the leader, Mr. Martin.

"Miss Summerfield," he greeted in terse tones. "Is your Pa home?"

Lacey knew they had seen him from the road. "He is. Is something wrong?"

"I'd rather talk to him."

After a pause, Lacey went to the door and said, "Papa. Mr. Martin wants to talk to you."

"Tell them I went out the back way," Zeke hissed from behind the door.

Lacey turned back to face the men. "I'm afraid you'll have to talk to me," she said with more bravado than she felt.

"Have it your way. There's been trouble in town," Mr. Martin began in clipped tones. "Your pa has been selling an elixir. Some kind of wonder tonic, he calls it. I don't know what's in it, but some folks who paid good money for it are sick now. They say your pa won't give them their money back, because he doesn't have it anymore."

The familiar fear fluttered in Lacey's breast, but she didn't show it. Strange, she thought, how each time was just as frightening as the one before. "A tonic?" she asked coolly. "I haven't seen Papa making a tonic." What she said was true. He was much too wily to let her catch him making it again.

"Nevertheless, he has been," another man snarled. "My wife's mother took some 'cause she'd been feeling poorly, and she's still in bed."

"Was she bedridden before she took it?" Lacey asked defensively. She had never been able to bluff their way out of trouble before, but she always tried.

"Of course not!"

"It smelled like onions and turpentine to me," another shouted.

She wasn't surprised. The last time he was caught, those had been the prime ingredients. At least after the death of the little girl ten years before, he had quit adding foxglove to the tonic.

"What about the others who took it? No one has died or anything like that?" she asked with great trepidation.

"No, but my mother-in-law's sick enough that we thought she might."

Relief flooded over her. To Mr. Martin she said, "I'll tell Papa to quit selling the tonic, but if he says he doesn't have the money to give back, I guess we'll just have to work that off somehow."

"That's not good enough," he scowled.

"You're not saying that we have to leave?"

"That's exactly what I'm saying! I want you out by sundown tomorrow."

Lacey's eyes were as cold as green ice as she met the intensity of his stare. No discomposure ruffled her face; she wasn't about to show fear or dismay. These men were looking for trouble, and a mob fed on the weak and defenseless. "I see. We'll be gone by dark, Mr. Martin." As he turned away, she added, "Give my farewell to your wife." His head jerked back and he met her level gaze. Her innuendo was unmistakable.

With a scowl, he spurred his horse into the side yard, his friends following. Around and around the house they rode at a gallop, sending the hens flapping into the field and trouncing Lacey's garden into the yellow dirt. Lacey sank down onto a straight-back chair and fought to keep her face expressionless. On the last pass, Mr. Martin produced a knife and cut her clothesline, and the clean sheets dropped to the ground and soon were torn and trampled by the iron-shod hooves.

Until they were out of sight, Lacey remained in the chair. Then she slowly rose and cast a long look at her ruined sheets. She went into the house and stood just inside the threshold, staring at her father.

"Don't give me that cold-eyed stare," he blustered. "Martin's lying! I never sold no tonic here."

Reaching for her shawl, Lacey flicked it over her shoulders, still eyeing her father with the same steadfastness she had used on the men outside. Without a word of explanation, she left, letting the screen door bang behind her.

Walking felt good. The brisk pace she set stretched her muscles and eased the tension that made her want to throw dishes and scream like a harridan.

She crossed the field to the creek one last time and went directly to the hollow tree. Since she would never use the hiding spot again, she had no need to take her usual winding path. She reached inside the tree and pulled out the oiled canvas bag that held her life savings. The bag seemed pitifully light for ten years of hard work. For a moment she hesitated and looked across the field at the small house and the lean-to barn that sheltered the wagon. She had almost believed they would be able to stay here.

Resolutely, she struck out toward town, stuffing the bag in the deep pocket of her skirt. She knew what had to be done; she had done it so often.

Her first stop was the livery stable, where she bought two of the proprietor's older horses. Next she had to buy supplies to carry them for several weeks until she could find them another place to live.

As she walked past the hotel, she read a notice out of the corner of her eye. Her steps slowed, then stopped, and she went back. The circular was the sort she had seen several times before. A man named Finias Scarsdale was selling land; he was now residing and doing business here in the Mayfield Hotel. The land was located in Oregon, and he was asking only a dollar an acre.

Lacey read further. For a modest fee, the honorable Finias Scarsdale would also be pleased to procure the purchaser a place on the next wagon train heading west.

An hour later Lacey was on her way back to the sharecropper's cottage. Behind her walked the two horses, and in her hand she carried a bucket of whitewash to paint the wagon. In the pocket of her skirt, where the money had been, was a neatly folded square of paper entitling her to seventy acres of land in Oregon. Zeke Summerfield was waiting on the porch for his daughter's return.

"I was beginning to wonder if you were coming back." When she didn't answer, he continued, "I never did like it around here. The summers are hot as hell, and the mosquitoes could carry off a grown mule. Let's head up toward Pritchett way for a change."

"No," she said, speaking at last. "I'm going to Oregon."

"Oregon!" he gasped. "What in the hell's in Oregon?"

"Seventy acres of land. I own it free and clear." She stopped and faced him. "I'm sick to death of running, Papa. Of not knowing from one day to the next if we'll be chased out of town. I want a place of my own. A real house that belongs to me."

"But Oregon?" Zeke blustered. "Where'd you get the money, anyhow! And what about me!"

Lacey cast him a cold glance. "I said I'm going there. I've worked hard and saved for a place of my own, and now I have it. You can come with me or you can go somewhere else, but either way, I'm not ever going to be run out of town again. We were lucky this time. All we lost were some sheets and a garden. Last time we were burned out. Remember?"

"You needn't take that tone with me," Zeke growled. "After all, I am your father!"

"That's something I never forget for a moment." She matched his glare, then went on to the barn.

She put the horses in the stalls, then inspected the wagon. Although it had been painted numerous times before, the red paint still bled through, and the yellow letters were again faintly legible. Without thinking how tired she was, Lacey pushed up her sleeves and started to paint.

The velvety night of Tocoma, Illinois, cloaked Lacey as she stood in the deep shadows of the boardwalk. Lilting strains of music set her toes to tapping as she watched the laughing couples through the window. The fiddler launched into a spirited reel, and the dancers whooped in appreciation. Tomorrow the wagons would cross the swollen Mississippi River and embark into the wilderness. Everyone, young and old, had come into town for a last taste of civilization.

Only Lacey and Zeke seemed to be missing the party—Zeke because he had somehow got hold of a bottle of whiskey and was sprawled in a drunken stupor on the floor of the wagon; Lacey because they had been chased out of Tocoma in the recent past and she was afraid of being recognized. She stood in the deepest shadows and watched the dancing, her hips swaying now and then with the rhythm as she ached to skip about the floor with the others. Lacey had never in her life been to a dance, but she was sure she could master the steps. They seemed so simple.

The yearning almost got the best of her, and she considered going in. After all, *Papa* was the one the townspeople had been angry with. As she debated, a burly man with red hair danced past the window, and she pulled back sharply. What had she been thinking? she scolded herself. Of course she would be recognized! Even if the people here had no quarrel with her, Papa lay in the wagon at the edge of town, and there was that same red-headed man who had sworn he'd shoot Papa if he came back again.

Suddenly, Lacey Summerfield felt very vulnerable. If anyone glanced at the window or came out for a breath of air, she could be seen. With a sigh, she pulled her shawl tightly around her and turned away. It was time to go back to the wagon anyway, she decided, in case Papa woke up and got rowdy. It wouldn't do to be tossed off the wagon train before they even crossed the Mississippi. She heartily wished she knew where he had gotten that liquor. Probably from one of his new "friends" who felt sorry for a broken-down old man.

The street was short, and most of the buildings were dark

and locked for the night. Only one other showed any signs of life, and it was the saloon, in full swing. Those men who were not at the dance had gone there to drink, to gamble, or to seek what pleasure they might from one of the saloon girls. Tinny piano music floated through the batwing doors as shouts of male laughter drowned the tune. Lacey considered crossing to the other side of the street in order to stay in the shadows, but decided the men inside were too occupied with their fun to notice her passing. She quickened her step to pass the lighted doorway.

And she almost made it.

A gangly man burst through the swinging doors, obviously aided by a large boot in the seat of his pants. He yelled as he fell, colliding with Lacey and knocking her off her feet as he tumbled into the street. Before she could collect her wits, a second man flew past to join the first. Quickly struggling to her feet, Lacey reached down to retrieve her shawl just as a third bumped into her, sending her sprawling again.

Rolling to a sitting position, Lacey glared as the three men stumbled to their feet and began running down the street. Suddenly the doors burst open again, and the tallest man she had ever seen came striding out.

Without seeing her, he put his fists on his hips and grinned after the three he had obviously thrown out. "Had enough?" he shouted. "If you change your mind, come on back and I'll teach you some more manners!" He chuckled heartily and turned to go inside, nearly tripping over Lacey as he did so. "Ma'am?" he said uncertainly. "I didn't see you there. Are you hurt?"

"Get off my skirt," she growled, slapping at his boot.

He hastily stepped aside and solicitously reached down to help her. "I'm sorry, ma'am. I didn't mean to throw those men onto anybody, let alone a lady." He tried to pull her up.

Lacey knocked his hand away. "You only hit me two out of three times. Want to take another shot at it?" She got to her feet and glared at him as she dusted off her skirt and tried to regain some dignity.

"Are you hurt?" he asked again, his deep voice showing real concern.

"No, I'm not," she snapped. "Get out of my way."

"Here's your shawl," he said as he picked it up and tried to shake it clean. "If I'd seen you out here, I would have thrown them through the window instead."

"What?" she gasped. He was smiling down at her. His teeth were white and even in his tanned face, and his dark eyes held a spark of laughter, now that he saw she was unharmed. A thick thatch of tousled black hair fell over his forehead. His shoulders were the broadest she had ever seen, and she was sure he could pick up a whole ham in each of his large hands if he wanted to. Yet his body was lean with hard muscles, and his waist and hips were narrow.

"Do you make a practice of throwing people out of saloons?" she demanded to quell the quickening of her heart.

"Not always. They made some improper remarks to one of the ladies inside, and she took offense. Since she was no match for them, I gave her a hand."

"A lady? In there?" Lacey snorted.

"You didn't hear the remarks," he answered.

Lacey snatched her shawl from his large hands and scrubbed at a corner where the dirt had been ground in. Now she would have to wash it, as well as her dress, and she already had more than enough to do. "If that's the way people are here in Tocoma, I'm glad we're heading west tomorrow."

"You're with the wagon train? So am I. I haven't seen you around camp." His eyes traveled admiringly over her. "I'm sure I would have noticed."

She frowned as she tried to wrap the shawl around her shoulders, twisting it in the effort. "We just got here today."

"We?" He took the shawl from her, straightened it, and draped it around her shoulders. The act brought her almost within his arms. He stopped, his hands holding the ends of the fabric. Their eyes met for the eternity of a second.

Lacey felt her breath catch and her pulse race as if she had been running. Then she came to her senses and yanked the ends of the shawl from him and stepped back. "My father is traveling with me." For some reason she wanted to run, to put as much distance as possible between her and the huge, unsettling man.

"That's an interesting way to put it," he mused. "Usually daughters travel with their fathers instead of the other way around."

"Yes, well, I suppose I'm an unusual woman," she commented acidly.

"I noticed that right off," he said softly.

Again she knew she should run, do something to break the spell he seemed to weave so effortlessly, but she could only gaze up into the brown depths of his eyes.

He looked away as if he, too, had felt something disturbing. "There's a dance going on down the street. Have you been there?"

"I watched through the window, but I didn't go in," she said absentmindedly. His resonant voice held a drawling cadence she found mesmerizing. "Where are you from?" she appalled herself by asking.

"Texas, ma'am," he grinned.

"The whole state? Why is it you people never give the name of a town, just the state?" Her words were sharp to hide the flutter of excitement that his presence was triggering.

"I come from a place I doubt you ever heard of. It's so small that people thirty miles away get lost trying to find it."

"I thought everything in Texas was big," she scoffed, then felt foolish. Even though she was tall, the man beside her towered over her.

"It's still sprouting." Merriment lit his face. "When it's

full grown, that town will be as big as the rest of them. By your accent, I'd put you from the Carolinas. Am I right?''

"Close enough." She had no intention of telling him any more. "Now, if you'll get out of my way, I'm going back to my wagon."

"Don't go yet. It's early, and we won't see another town for a long time. Let me take you to the dance."

"No!" she blurted out. "That is, I would rather not. We have to cross the Mississippi tomorrow, and I want to be rested."

"Begging you pardon, ma'am, but you don't have to swim it. There's a ferryboat."

Lacey's frown deepened. "Get out of my way or I'll call for help."

"That's not necessary. Besides, those three I chased off were the biggest men in there." He stepped aside for her to pass.

As she walked away, he called out, "By the way, ma'am, what's your name?"

Lacey paused, glanced back over her shoulder, and stiffly replied, "Lacey Summerfield."

"I'm Blake Cameron," he told her with a hint of genuine friendliness in his deep voice. "If you ever need my help, you just let me know."

"That's hardly likely, Mr. Cameron," she retorted. "I've been taking care of myself for a long time now, and I'm good at it. Good evening." She walked briskly away.

Blake Cameron stared after her. He wasn't too sure why he wanted to know more about her. Certainly she wasn't his type. He preferred women with dark hair, as a rule, and gravitated toward those with a lusty eye and a rolling hip. This woman seemed to be as proper as a schoolmarm. She had the marrying look about her rather than the bedding look. Blake frowned. After Catherine, he wasn't ever going to marry again.

Still, he thought, the night was dark, and the wagons were at the edge of town. A woman shouldn't be out alone in a border town like Tocoma. As lithe as a panther, he strode after her.

Lacey kept to the shadows, but he followed her easily. She walked swiftly, as if the night held no fears for her. He liked that. Most women wanted him to protect them, and he really admired one who didn't.

When she reached the camp, she mounted the steps at the rear of a wagon that was very different from the others; it looked like a Gypsy wagon he had seen once. She opened a door and paused to look back the way she had come, as if watching for him. The light from inside made a halo of her red-gold hair and illuminated the proud swell of her breasts and the line of her slender waist. Then she seemed to shake herself free of her thoughts and went inside.

Blake stayed for a moment beneath the tree. She was a lovely woman. Her coloring wasn't fashionably dark, but she was pretty anyway. Yet not once had she smiled, and in his experience all pretty ladies smiled. There was something of a mystery about her.

He shrugged. Being a straightforward man, he wasn't interested in mysteries. Besides, there was a saucy brunette in the saloon who wouldn't mind dancing a tune or two. Putting Lacey Summerfield from his mind, Blake strode back toward the town.

CHAPTER
2

Lacey pushed aside the linsey-woolsey curtain that divided her father's side of the wagon from her own; her father had gone outside immediately after breakfast. Unlike the other wagons, this one had been designed as a permanent residence and had a measure of comfort. Lacey had never expected to see anything good about the old medicine wagon, but in it she had slept with some degree of comfort during the long journey through Missouri and Nebraska while the other women complained of overcrowding and aching muscles.

With practiced hands, she made up her bed. Her mother had pieced the old quilts together especially to fit the rectangular shelf that held her bed. When the covers were straight, she folded the bed up against the wall and did the same to her father's. The narrow table where they had eaten breakfast also collapsed flat against a wall when its leg was swung away, leaving her with room to move about.

She raised her eyes to the board concealing the bed that had once been Billy's. It had long since been converted to storage space, but occasionally she still thought of it as it had been. Only the day before, she had seen Papa folding the board against the wall and replacing the toggle pins that held it. His movements had been silent, and when he saw her in the doorway, he had looked uncomfortable. Did Papa still miss his only son? That Billy had been the favorite with both her parents was a fact Lacey had long since accepted.

She reached up and pulled out the pegs to lower the tray. Billy's mattress had been replaced by folded clothing and the few personal items that had been accumulated by Lacey and Zeke. A long time had passed since that shelf had known Billy's weight. She ran her fingers over the smooth wooden frame and up the supporting chains.

With a sigh, she pulled herself from her fancies. Billy was gone, and she had to make the best of her own life. Resolutely, she straightened her folded dresses and cape. Soon the mountains' cold heights would make the woolen warmth necessary even though it was still late summer. Lacey had never minded the cold, though, and after the sweltering weeks on the plains, she was looking forward to the cooler air.

Zeke's clothes were bunched and wadded, as if he had been ruffling through them. Without hesitation, Lacey pulled them straight. As she did so, a tinkle of glass striking glass caught her attention. She lifted Zeke's shirt and stared down at the dozen bottles of Wonder Tonic—labels, elixir, and all. Nestled in the midst of the tonic bottles was a quantity of contraband whiskey—forbidden not only by her, but by the contract she had signed with the wagon master.

Lacey felt all the air leave her lungs. When had he made the tonic? And how had he traded it for whiskey without her seeing him do it?

Nervously, she counted the small containers. An even dozen. When Zeke brewed his elixir, he usually made about fifteen bottles at a time. Lacey thought hard. He hadn't been spending much time with anyone in particular. But not too many days ago they had camped at Fort Kearney, and Papa had made friends with a whiskey-swilling sergeant. Lacey's lips compressed with disapproval.

Gathering the bottles into the fold of her skirt, Lacey

climbed out of the wagon. Anger clouded her mind, and all she could think of was destroying the detested mixture. Her back rigid with fury, Lacey dumped the bottles on the work shelf at the wagon's side and uncorked the first container. Holding it at arm's length, she poured the pale liquid onto the dirt. The strong odor of turpentine and onions nearly gagged her.

When the bottle was empty, she laid it back on the shelf, picked up a hammer, and smashed it. With great satisfaction, she took the next bottle and did the same.

Zeke was several yards away, passing the time of day with the man in the next wagon. The man's wife was ill, and Zeke had every intention of selling him a supply of Dr. Summerfield's Wonder Tonic. After all, now that he omitted the foxglove, there was nothing in the potion to hurt anyone. Zeke had noticed that people generally got well if they waited long enough, and he might as well make a profit as they waited.

The sound of splintering glass drew Zeke's attention. Here in the foothills of the Rockies such a sound was uncommon. Household items were irreplaceable and therefore precious. When he heard the same sound again, he looked around for the cause. The third crash drew him back to the wagon. With growing apprehension he went around back and stared, agape, at the sight of Lacey pouring out his latest supply of tonic.

Her angry green eyes met his as the elixir dribbled to the ground. Without a word she tossed the empty bottle on the mound of glass shards and lifted the hammer.

"No!" Zeke yelled. He lunged at her and grabbed the hammer before she could smash the bottle.

Lacey jerked away and threw the empty bottle at Zeke, causing him to retreat several feet. "How could you?" she fumed with white-hot fury. "How could you do this again?" She yanked the cork from another bottle and threw it at him, contents and all. The bottle bounced off his shoulder and fell, its contents draining out on the ground.

"Now, Lacey," Zeke whined, "be reasonable."

"Reasonable! I told you I would bring you along only if you quit selling this poison! As usual, you went behind my back!" As fast as she could, she uncorked the remaining bottles of tonic and threw them at him.

Zeke stood hunched over with his arms shielding his head and waited for her to run out of ammunition. When the last elixir bottle fell at his feet, Lacey raged, "I've warned you, Papa. For years I've put up with you slipping around and doing things like this, but never again! I'm going to Oregon to make a new life for myself, and you're not going to ruin this last chance!"

"I won't do it again," he wheedled.

"I don't believe you! You've said that for years, and I no longer believe a word you say!" She reached for one last bottle, the large amber one filled with whiskey. Though the wax seal was broken, she still had to struggle to draw out the tightly fitted cork.

Suddenly a large hand closed over the bottle, and some-one said, "Take it easy, Miss Summerfield."

Lacey glared up into Blake Cameron's dark eyes. "You!" she fumed. She had spent a great deal of time and effort during the past few weeks avoiding this giant of a man. He had a way of making her knees feel weak with a single glance, and Lacey hated to feel weak. "Turn that bot-tle loose and get out of my camp!"

"And let you throw that bottle at your papa? I can't do that, ma'am."

Fury made her sputter before she could grind out, "Mind your own business!"

Blake looked at Zeke, who was cowering against the wagon. "Look at him," he snapped at her. "He's an old man. You can't treat him like this."

"He's a snake," she hissed. "A low, mean liar!"

"Don't talk about him like that," Blake growled. "He's your father! He deserves your respect." With ease, he wrenched the bottle from her hands and held it out to Zeke, who clutched it gratefully.

"Respect!" The word nearly stuck in her throat. "You don't have any idea what you're talking about!" She jerked her head back to Zeke. "As for you, when we reach the next outpost, I'm leaving you there!"

Zeke made a whining sound and drew up his shoulders as if he expected her to throw something else.

"That's enough!" Blake roared. "You're not leaving anybody behind! Now calm down."

Lacey turned her fury on Blake. "Mr. Cameron, I'm going for a walk. A very *short* walk. If you aren't out of my camp and out of my sight when I return, I'm going to get my rifle and shoot you!" Her eyes glittered with rage, and her skin had paled to the hue of alabaster.

Turning on her heels, she stalked away through the small crowd that had gathered. From the corner of her eye she saw Zeke stoop to gather the unbroken tonic bottles, still playing the role of downtrodden parent. Lacey was too angry to be embarrassed at having caused such a scene.

She headed for the woods, looking neither left nor right. All her thoughts beat against this latest wrong her father had committed. Didn't he realize they could both be thrown off the wagon train and abandoned in the hostile wilderness? This time there would be no town to run to. She was so furious that tears were coursing down her cheeks. Without breaking stride, she brushed the wetness away with her palm.

The huge trees closed over her and soon shut out the sight of the string of wagons. Still she walked with long strides that jarred the soles of her feet. As if Papa alone weren't bad enough, Blake Cameron had butted in and made things worse!

Blake Cameron! She had been watching him ever since he threw those three men out of the saloon on top of her. He was obviously a shiftless brawler and drifter, though he had had no fights since the train left St. Louis. He was afflicted with an idle nature, also. He didn't even own a wagon, and he slept under the dubious shelter of the wagon master's. Lacey smarted under his rebuke. Blake Cameron was no better than Papa! He hadn't two red cents to rub together and was less stable than an alley cat! How like men to stick together!

Lacey swept branches aside and let them snap back behind her. Her feet followed a downhill slope because that was the most convenient direction to take. When a bush got in her way, she swiped at it with her hand, and when she came to a narrow stream, she jumped it.

As always, vigorous exercise calmed her, although this time it took a while. She tried to put both Blake and Papa from her mind; even a stray thought about either of them aroused her anger again. Instead, she concentrated on Oregon's promise of freedom and a fresh start. She would be a new person there on her seventy acres. No one would have heard of Dr. Summerfield's Wonder Tonic; and Papa, assuming he was still with her, would have no one to sell the elixir to or buy whiskey from. Oregon sounded like an earthly paradise.

Resolutely, Lacey planned her cabin and where she would place a garden in conjunction with it. She would have a stream nearby for washing and drinking water and a chimney that drew well instead of letting the smoke eddy back into the room. Eventually she would even have a wooden floor and an indoor pump.

She and the bear entered the tiny clearing at the same time.

For a split-second eternity, neither moved. Then the bear gave a deep-throated growl and stalked toward her, its dark eyes predatory and sure. Lacey cried out and ran in the easiest direction—farther downhill and farther away from the wagons.

She headed for the dense woods, hoping the narrow spaces between the trees would slow the large bear. Behind her she could hear the crackle of branches snapping as the bear hurtled in pursuit. Too frightened to scream, Lacey looked frantically for an escape. To climb a tree would be useless; the bear would be on her before she scrambled to the first limb, and it could probably climb better than she could anyway, especially with her encumbering skirts.

Bursting through the thick underbrush, Lacey saw a rocky cliff off to her left and headed for it. She clambered up, scratching at the loose rubble as she climbed, hoping to dislodge enough to slow the bear. She could hear its wheezing rumble as it crashed out of the bushes and came after her.

With strength born of true terror, Lacey braced herself and shoved at a precariously balanced boulder. Miraculously, the massive rock shifted, then plunged downward. She glanced below to watch as it smashed into the bear. The animal bellowed with pain and anger and rose up on its hind feet, one of which had been gashed deeply by the boulder's sharp edge. The harsh roar seemed to make the very ground tremble. She had never seen so large a bear, nor one so furious.

Fear lent her speed and she clawed her way higher up the shale rubble. Was that an opening in the rocks? Almost afraid to hope, Lacey scrambled ahead with renewed vigor.

It was. Not deep enough to be a true cave, but more an enclosure formed by a jumble of huge rocks, it was her only hope of escape. She could tell at a glance that it was large enough for her to squeeze into but not big enough to accommodate the bear.

Lacey dived through the opening just as the bear lunged at her. One plate-sized paw caught her leg, tearing through fabric and flesh. Although the impact of the blow momentarily stunned Lacey, she managed to draw her legs in to safety. Inches away the bear's claws, yellowed and hooked like sickles, swiped at her again and again. She watched the bright gush of blood for a moment before she realized it was her own.

Pain flooded over her. A fiery throbbing seared her thigh, and as she looked more closely she found three long furrows in her flesh. Lacey wadded her skirt and petticoat over the wound and pressed as hard as she could to stop the flow of blood.

Maddened by the scent, the bear bellowed again and raked at the heavy boulders as if it would rip apart the mountain in order to reach her. Then the paw was replaced by the bear's snout. Lacey pulled back as the long teeth worried the rock and snapped audibly in the air only inches from her feet.

Suddenly the bear drew its head back, though the air still trembled with its enraged snarls. Lacey felt frantically around in the shale rubble, searching for a weapon as she followed the bear sounds with her eyes. All at once her sanctuary darkened as the bear found the opening in the top of the cave. Lacey screamed as the murderous talons swiped down at her. Her fingers curled around a long sliver of flint, and she struck back at the hairy paw. Amazingly, the walls of her fortress held under the animal's great weight.

The bear's fetid breath filled the small hollow as it struggled to reach her. Furious at being thwarted, the massive beast pounded at the rocks, leaving white scrapes on the granite.

Lacey curled herself up into a tight ball, unsure which opening the bear would choose for his next attack. She gripped the flint so tightly it almost cut into her skin, but she was unaware of any pain as her eyes darted from one gap in the rocks to another.

The animal tried them all. Lacey held her breath and trembled with each new assault, but the rocks held firm. She dared not move far lest she put herself within the bear's reach, but whenever the paws came close enough, she slashed out at them.

Shock was setting in, and a chill rattled her teeth. The beast and the cold rocks made up her entire world. With considerable effort she kept her jaws clamped shut so she wouldn't scream again.

An eternity seemed to pass before the bear stopped digging at her shelter. His growls dropped to a grumble of angry frustration as he paced back and forth, snuffling at all the openings one more time. Lacey held herself rigidly still, in hope he would go away if he had no fresh reminders of her existence.

She heard the rattle of shale and pebbles but couldn't see enough to tell if he had gone. Fire seemed to be pounding in her leg, but apparently the bleeding had stopped. She felt light-headed and dizzy from overpowering fear. Could she walk if the bear had left? She was afraid to acknowledge the thought that she might not be able to move.

Quiet crowded in around her. Not the peace of the woods, but a tomblike silence. Lacey strained to hear, to get some clue as to whether the dangerous beast was gone or only resting nearby. She heard nothing.

She tried to judge the time of day from the angle of the sun, but she was so disoriented that she couldn't tell if it was rising or sinking in the sky. How long had she been gone? Surely not as long as it seemed. It felt as if days had passed since she left the security of her wagon.

Lacey forced herself to wait a few more minutes, then cautiously straightened her cramped legs. The small noise of her movement made her freeze, expecting attack. Still there was silence. Keeping her skirt tight against her wound, Lacey leaned forward. The shale slope came into view and the trees beyond. Slowly she edged closer to the opening. She could see the broken brush now where the bear had plunged into the clearing after her. Picking up a handful of gravel, she tossed it out into the open. It clattered and rolled to a stop. Nothing else moved.

Again Lacey flexed her leg. It moved painfully, but she thought she could walk on it. She had no choice; she must either walk or stay here and die. Carefully she started to crawl from her refuge. Her head, then her shoulders cleared the opening.

She felt rather than heard the bear as it came after her, its huge bulk making the precarious shale shudder. With a cry, she threw herself back into the hole as the bear thudded against the barrier. Its frenzied growls reverberated in the tiny space, and Lacey's screams were loud in her own ears. Knotting herself as compactly as she could, she grabbed a fist-sized rock and pounded at his nose. The gnashing teeth missed her by mere inches. Had he come so close before or were the boulders shifting from his assault? She could no longer tell.

The snarls tapered to rumbles as the bear again paced. His rancid smell filled the air, and Lacey fought to control fear-induced nausea. She had to get back to the safety of the wagons. A hard trembling shook her, and she struggled not to give way to her fear and pain. She had no idea how far she was from the wagons or which direction she had come from. She had to get back soon, for they were to cross the Platte River that day—if they hadn't already gone ahead without her. She again looked up at the sun and wondered if she could possibly have been gone as long as it seemed. Surely the others would come looking for her, but could they find her? She wasn't at all sure they could. She had wandered too deep into the woods, and she had no idea how far the bear had chased her.

The words of the wagon master returned to torment her. If anyone wandered away, he had said at the beginning of their journey, that person would be left behind. Man, woman, or child—it made no difference. He had to consider the good of the whole group, not that of the individual. He had sounded as if he meant it. During the campfire talks, Lacey had heard of a child who had roamed away from another train and had been abandoned. At the time Lacey hadn't believed it. Now she wasn't so sure. Numerous delays had left the wagon train far behind schedule, and many of her fellow travelers had talked of their concern that snow might cut off the crucial South Pass.

Cautiously, Lacey raised her head and peeped through the wide crack where two boulders formed a roof over her enclosure. Twenty feet away the bear lay in concentrated alertness, his eyes riveted to the opening in the rocks. Lacey lowered herself back down and struggled to overcome her brain-fogging panic.

CHAPTER
3

Zeke fastened the collar strap on the harness and frowned over the horses' backs toward the woods. Lacey had been madder than he had ever seen her, and he wasn't looking forward to her return. Still, he thought as he backed the pair into the traces, she had been gone a long time, and the wagons would soon be ready to leave. He fastened the trace chains as his frown deepened.

How in the hell had she found the tonic and whiskey? he wondered. Sure, he had been pretty tight when he put the bottles away, but he thought he had hidden them better than that. Damn her anyway. She had always been more trouble than she was worth.

The lead wagons were angling down toward the murky Platte River. Soon they would start the arduous task of crossing the Platte's sucking mud and unseen currents. Zeke hated everything about the wilderness, and he had been silently cursing Lacey ever since the trip began.

At least, he consoled himself, he had no intention of going all the way to Oregon. Not if he could find a likely-looking settlement. He might even remarry—if he could find a rich widow woman. Thoughtfully, he lashed down the pots and pans that hung on the wagon. Marriage wasn't a bad idea. If he could find a woman gullible enough to let him get his hands on her money, he could woo her, win her, and be gone with the money before she knew which way was up. He smiled deeply in his beard.

Still there was no sign of Lacey. Zeke put his hands on his hips and gazed off the way she had gone. Was she lost? The woods were thick, and it wasn't impossible. His flat black eyes tried to peer through the trees. If she was lost, he could be far away before she found her way out. Maybe she never would.

Zeke climbed up onto the wagon seat. The lead wagons were easing out into the current. He was sorely tempted to drive on and pretend he thought she was inside the wagon. She kept to herself so much it would be days before anybody missed her. But eventually someone would ask about her. Zeke dropped the reins and glared toward the woods. Even in her absence Lacey was bothersome. With a deep sigh, Zeke got off the wagon and jammed the wheel brake in place to secure the horses.

He walked down to the crossing, hailed a man, and motioned to him. As wagon master, Ed Bingham had to be told. "My daughter is missing," Zeke said, feigning deep concern. "She wandered off for a walk and hasn't come back."

"A walk?" Ed asked. "Now?"

Zeke shrugged and scratched his head beneath his old hat. "I told her not to, but she's headstrong and wouldn't listen."

Ed frowned. "That's real bad news, Mr. Summerfield. We're about ready to pull out."

Zeke looked at the wagons that were moving into position for the river crossing. "Well, what do you think I ought to do? I can't just haul off and hope she's with one of the other women."

Ed leaned his weight forward in the saddle and looked at the mountains on the horizon. "You know, that's just what I suggest. She's bound to be around here somewhere. I'll bet she's off in somebody else's wagon swapping recipes."

"I guess she could be at that," Zeke said hopefully.

"If she's not, though, she's as good as dead," Ed finished. "Maybe you'd better take some men and go look for her. Could be she fell asleep or something and lost track of the time. Remember, now, I can't hold back and wait for her. We're behind already. You remember I told you all how important it is to get over those mountains fast."

Zeke nodded and looked as servile as he could. "I've got to look for her, to put my mind at ease. I'll be quick about it."

Ed nodded. "Do what you have to, but remember I can't wait long." Then he relented and added, "One hour. That's all I can do." He pulled his gold pocket watch out to check the time. "Yep, that's all the time I can give you."

Zeke tipped his hat and hurried off to get some men to aid in his search. Soon a dozen of them were combing the woods, calling Lacey's name.

"Zeke, come look over here," a man called out after many precious minutes had already passed.

Hurrying to the small clearing, Zeke first noted the abundance of broken branches at the clearing's edge. Then, unmistakably imprinted in the mud, he saw a huge bear track. Zeke's parched lips thinned. The man pointed at the crushed grasses and bent saplings that indicated the bear's path. He had been moving fast, chasing something. Those with guns brought them to readiness.

Silently now, the men followed the trail. In the softer earth they found the outline of a woman's shoe. Farther on they discovered a shred of blue gingham. Zeke picked it up and wadded it tightly in his fist, blinking at the unexpected turn of luck. Not much farther on, they found a shale slide. Numerous rocks had recently been dislodged, their muddy sides now drying in the sun. Most damning of all, however, was a patch of brownish blood spattered on the rocks. Another print from a bear's paw was plainly visible there, too.

Zeke turned away abruptly. "No need to look anymore, men," he announced in a strained voice.

"But we haven't found her yet," one protested. "She could have gotten away." The man's voice held no conviction.

Zeke pulled a handkerchief from his pocket and loudly blew his nose, being careful not to meet anyone's eye. He didn't care for Lacey, but to end up as a bear's meal was more than he would have chosen for her or anyone else. In a strained voice he said, "You know she couldn't have got away. A bear big enough to leave that track could bring down a full-grown ox." He steeled himself and said, "Where else would the blood have come from? She left the rifle in the wagon, and besides, what woman would be fool enough to try to shoot a bear?"

"Yeah, that's right," one of the men agreed. He looked down at the blood and nodded. His conclusion had been the same as Zeke's. The woman had been attacked by a bear and could not have survived. No one could deny that.

"We ought to find her body," Zeke murmured. "She has to be properly buried. A service has to be said over her."

The men exchanged glances. Awkwardly one said, "Now, Zeke, I don't rightly think it's such a good idea to keep looking. That bear . . . well, he wasn't chasing her for the fun of it."

Zeke stared at him, forcing the man to explain.

"What I mean is, there may not be anything to bury."

All the color drained from Zeke's face, and his eyes took on a glassy cast. This hadn't yet occurred to him: that there might not be a body, at least not anything recognizable as his daughter. Nausea rose in his throat, and he drew a deep breath to gain strength. He now regretted having initiated the search.

"I'm real sorry," the man nearest him affirmed with the others. "Tonight we'll hold a memorial service for her."

"Tonight," Zeke echoed hollowly. "The Lord giveth and the Lord taketh away."

"Amen."

The search party turned and started back toward the wagon train. No one looked up the slope to the place where several large boulders made a tiny shelter, nor did their voices carry over the gusting wind.

Blake Cameron tightened the cinch on his large bay and tested the stability of the saddle. This horse was bad about puffing out his sides as he was being saddled so that the strap would be loose when he relaxed. Once Blake was satisfied the saddle wouldn't turn, he swung up on the horse's back, ready to move out. Having no wagon of his own, Blake was sometimes impatient with the plodding traffic. Without the cumbersome wagons, they would already have crossed the Continental Divide at South Pass.

When Ed Bingham rode up, Blake asked him, "What's the holdup?"

"Nothing," the wagon master answered shortly. The search party was back, empty-handed as near as he could tell from a distance, and he didn't want word to spread. Time was essential, and too much of it had passed. She was probably hiding in someone's wagon to get out of the last-minute work. Ed Bingham didn't hold much with women. Never had.

Blake's horse matched the stride of the sturdy oxen as the wagon train began moving out. "Looks like it could cloud up."

"Yeah, I know. I hope it holds off until we get across the Platte. That river's not to be trusted." Bingham scowled at the gathering clouds. "Besides, I saw some Indians watching us from a bluff yesterday. They were too far away for me to make out what tribe they were from, but there was trouble along through here last year from a renegade named Lame Wolf."

"We'd better get going," Blake said. "We sure don't want any Indian trouble."

"You're right about that," Ed answered grimly. "I'm

not sure we'll be able to try the last crossing until late tomorrow or even the next morning after this delay.'' All that had come of the search for the woman was the loss of valuable time. He hoped Zeke Summerfield would lay into that daughter of his when she showed up. Most likely he had spoiled her all her life.

Lacey raised her head and peered over the top of the rock. The bear was ambling back toward her from the stream, with wet droplets stringing from the thick fur of his muzzle. She licked her parched lips. How long had she been here? Time seemed to have slipped somehow, and she realized she must have been asleep. She swallowed dryly and wished she had some water.

Carefully, she straightened her legs and was rewarded with a stab of pain. Her leg wasn't scratched badly, but it was very sore. She could only hope that exercise would limber her cramped muscles—if she ever got away.

She gazed down the shale slope. Had her father or some of the others tried to find her? Had they given up their search? The slant of the sun told her that night was fast approaching. She wondered if bears slept soundly. She was terrified of leaving the protection of the rocks, but she was also afraid of being left behind by the others. Surely tomorrow the bear would depart in search of easier prey, and she could escape.

Lacey leaned her head back on the unyielding rock and wished she could straighten her body enough to lie down. If she could only get confortable, she could rest in preparation for what might be a long walk. But to do so would put her within the bear's reach.

As the shadows grew darker and became purple smudges on the shale, her thoughts returned to the wagon train. The others must surely have gone on without her. Hopelessness swept over her, and she closed her eyes. She felt utterly alone and abandoned. She would welcome anyone. Even that no-good drifter, Blake Cameron. That just showed how desperate she was. She would even welcome Papa, elixir and all! She shifted to a different position and exchanged glares with the bear.

Blake removed his horse's saddle and laid it under Ed Bingham's wagon. Over it he draped his saddle blanket, hairy side up, so that it would dry. By bedtime it would be less aromatic and could serve as his pillow. He slipped a rope halter over the horse's head and tethered him near the water's edge along with his pack mule and a number of other animals.

Blake crouched beside the Platte and studied it for a while. In the late afternoon sun, the muddy waters were gilded, and a number of sandbars diverted the flow of the broad but shallow river. This part of the river looked no different than the stretch they had passed the day before. It all seemed deceptively safe and easy to cross. But Ed Bingham, who had been this way on several previous trips, had said that pools of quicksand and unsuspected currents lay in wait to topple a wagon or drown horse and rider alike.

Blake's gaze swept farther downstream to the area Ed Bingham had said was the only safe place to make the final crossing. To Blake, though, it appeared even more unlikely. The water was deeper there and seemed wider. But Ed was confident that it was free from pockets of quicksand, and he said that the absence of curling surface eddies meant there were no dangerous currents below. The experienced wagon master had worried about rain; if the water rose any higher, the crossing would be impassable, and that would force them to wait or to go upstream to the next one, and more precious time would be lost. Blake perused the horizon. Were there hostile Indians out there? He fervently hoped not.

Blake stroked his chin and was mildly surprised to find unshaven stubble. He had forgotten to shave that morning. Maybe the day before as well, by the feel of it. He didn't care. Since Catherine's death he hadn't cared about much of anything.

Pushing his hat back, he allowed the memories of Catherine to return. She had been a true beauty, with ivory skin and hair of jet, and with big blue eyes that could melt a man's heart. He had loved her to distraction, and so he had married her. That had been his biggest mistake. Her lily-hued hands stayed soft because they did no work, not even the easiest tasks. Her little pouts and gentle scoldings when she disagreed with him had increased and intensified until she had become a shrew. Her delicate nature then took the course of full-fledged hypochondria. No matter what he did, she was never pleased, never happy. After three years of marriage all the love was gone. She had long since denied him her bed, and it had been even longer since she had given him her body.

For months before her death she had complained of a weakness, a fluttering in the vicinity of her heart. These were only new symptoms to add to the growing list of her chronic complaints. The doctor had privately assured Blake that he could find nothing wrong with Catherine. Even her appetite had not flagged, as evidenced by the fact that her once slender figure had swelled to gross proportions.

Blake recalled the winter day a year and a half before when she had called to him. He had listened to her roll call of complaints, interspersed with her acrid opinion of him as a man and a provider. Then something had snapped inside him, and he had pulled her roughly out of bed.

She should do her share of the work, he had said. At least bathe herself and wash her hair. Anything but lie there and complain incessantly. She had launched into an almost incoherent tirade that left her face flushed and her eyes glassy. Then, suddenly, she had slumped and clutched at her chest. Having endured her histrionics for years, Blake had been unimpressed. He had told her that several of her other attempts to elicit his pity had been more convincing.

No one could have been more astounded than he when she dropped to the floor and died.

Blake had done all he could. He had tried to revive her until her skin was as cold and waxy as clay. Still he hadn't been able to believe it. Catherine hadn't been really sick! She had been malingering all the other times. This time, however, she had not, and she was buried three days later.

After that, things had gone downhill for Blake. He started drinking to blot out his guilt over not having believed her. The small Texas farm he had struggled over went untended, and weeds took over the front yard as well as the vegetable patch. Finally, he had given up and sold everything he owned except his horse and his traveling gear.

After drifting north for a while, he had decided to turn west, so he had signed on with the wagon train. In exchange for carrying messages and running occasional errands, Ed Bingham let him bed down under the shelter of the lead wagon.

Blake looked up at the deep vermilion sky. Sunsets were achingly vivid out here. Maybe because the clouds were so high. In southern Texas the clouds had been closer to the ground. So low sometimes that he had almost believed he could touch them.

The jagged silhouette of umber mountains seemed to spear the great orange sun as it settled lower. From here those mountains looked too rugged to cross. Yet it had been done before. This trail had been used for several years and had passed the test many times. In some places he had seen where wagon wheels had rutted the sandstone a foot deep.

He looked back at the wagons. They seemed very small out here in the Platte Valley, clustered in the darkness like a flock of chickens, with their pale canvas coverings and unwieldy shapes. In numbers, these pioneers felt a certain security. So far there had been no trouble with Indians, and he hoped there wouldn't be, but attacks had occurred before, and they could happen again. He had no desire to have his scalp decorate a teepee.

In the distance he watched Ida May Calvert sashay toward a communal campfire, her wide hips swinging provocatively. He didn't envy the woman's husband. That morning Blake had gone with Ida May to the river to help her get fresh water, and she had practically attacked him. Although Blake was far from reticent about lovemaking, the woman was married, and Blake did have his principles. He had managed to keep her at arm's length and had insisted that she refasten the buttons of her dress. It was lucky for them both that she had complied, because her husband, William, had come charging down to the river, ostensibly to tell her it was time to move the wagons out. Blake had talked his way out of trouble on many occasions throughout his life, but an irate husband was more than he wanted to deal with. He had decided on the spot to avoid Ida May Calvert as best he could for the rest of the trip. From the way she so casually flirted with almost every man except her husband, he suspected she wanted to get caught.

Women, he surmised, were not to be trusted. Not because they were inherently evil, as Ed Bingham maintained, but because they were as changeable as quicksilver. You could think you knew a woman—you could even love her—but after you married her, you might find out you'd never known her at all. He had no doubts that this was William Calvert's predicament, much as it had been his own.

No, he might feel remorseful for not having taken better care of Catherine, and the quandary over whether he inadvertently caused her death might keep him awake at night, but he was glad to be free again. No more shackles of marriage for him, he thought smugly as he watched Ida May cozy up to a man standing at the edge of the group around the campfire. No more recriminations and scoldings. No more efforts to please someone who was determined to be miserable. Now that the initial shock of his wife's death had passed, he didn't even feel lonely. He smiled in the gathering darkness and patted his horse's neck. Perhaps tomorrow he would shave—if he felt like it.

A fair-sized crowd was collecting around the campfire, and he watched curiously. What was going on over there? He saw Zeke Summerfield shake hands with several people who had just joined the group. Everyone moved slowly and aimlessly, as people do when they are unhappy or confused. The woman in the wagon behind the Summerfields' was known to be failing, and she was nowhere to be seen. Perhaps she had died.

Blake strolled back toward camp. He didn't like marriage, but he pitied anyone who lost a loved one. If the man's wife had passed on he should offer his condolences. He looked around for Lacey. She was a strange woman, always keeping to herself. He could almost swear she was avoiding him. That was fine with him, but he did wish she was friendlier. He still hadn't seen her smile, and for some reason that bothered him. He sometimes wished that he could be the one to make her laugh. For her own good, of course.

The low notes of a hymn reached Blake, and he nodded to himself. The woman must have died, all right. Even a fervent preacher couldn't gather that large a crowd from among so many tired people for a mere sermon. Besides, Blake was pretty sure this was not Sunday. The hymn ended as Blake drew near the group. Summerfield was talking in a low and broken voice about the dearly departed.

Blake leaned closer to a man and whispered, "When did she die?"

"This morning, near as I can tell," the man whispered back. "It's purely a shame."

"I guess nobody would deny that." He wasn't so sure, though, that the poor woman wasn't better off. She had seemed to be in pain every time he had seen her.

His gaze swept the crowd. Lacey was nowhere in sight, as usual. To be standoffish was one thing, but this was something else. "Have you seen the Summerfield girl?" he asked the man.

The man looked at him as if he had uttered a blasphemy. "They couldn't find her."

Blake tried to make sense of this. It seemed awfully heartless to refuse to attend a funeral service, even for a woman who could berate her aging father. "Did anyone look for her? Seems like she ought to be here."

Now the man scowled at him with clear distaste. "They looked."

Suddenly Zeke Summerfield stabbed a bony finger toward the back of the group where Blake was standing. "She was a fine and decent person! Not one to be sullied by the sins of the flesh. She had her faults, as we all do, but she was good in her heart. She never lusted."

Blake looked around with interest to see where Summerfield was aiming his remarks. It seemed unlikely that anyone would expect lust from a frail and dying woman. For some reason everyone seemed to be staring at him. Blake turned his attention back to the older man.

"I've seen you watching her, and I know the ways of a man," he thundered, "but she was pure." A madness inspired by his own theatrics leaped in Zeke Summerfield's eyes. "Maybe it was your interference this morning that made her seek the lonely woods! Maybe you're the cause of her untimely death."

People around him began to whisper to one another, and Blake shifted uneasily. Was Zeke Summerfield directing his comments to him? Those were pretty harsh words even for a bereaved man, let alone a mere neighbor. And what was this about her wandering off in the woods? He wouldn't have thought the woman could stand, let alone walk.

A suspicion dawned on him, and he whispered to the man beside him, "Who died?"

"Lacey Summerfield, of course. Who did you think?" The man edged away from Blake.

Blake stared at him in shocked surprise.

Zeke made his way through the crowd, his vision fixed on Blake. Here was a tangible target for his guilt over Lacey's death. Here at last was someone to blame. "Your interference in a family dispute drove my girl to the solitude of those dangerous woods, no doubt to pray for patience and forbearance." He was on a roll, and he planned to play out his hand. Lacey had convenienced him by dying, and since she was dead anyway, Zeke could use this incident to firmly implant himself with the others. He had never been one to let sentiment cloud his senses.

"Your daughter died?" Blake exclaimed. "How did it happen?"

"She was taken by a bear," Zeke declared, his voice cracking. "We couldn't even find her to bury her!"

Blake looked around at the nodding heads. "No disrespect meant, Mr. Summerfield, but if you couldn't find her, how do you know for sure she's dead?"

This was exactly the doubt that had festered in Zeke's mind all day, and he bellowed, "We saw her blood! There was a bear print on the rocks!"

"But no body? A bear wouldn't—that is . . ." He strove for delicacy. "You should have been able to find . . . something, some trace other than just blood."

Zeke shrieked a long drawn-out cry of agony and slumped into the supporting arms of his newfound friends.

William Calvert stepped forth. "You ought to hang your head for shame, to talk to a grieving father like that! You and I both know a bear don't eat bones and all. At least, not the big bones." Zeke whimpered and seemed about to faint. "I was there. I seen the blood and the paw print."

"And you quit looking?" Blake gasped. "You didn't search until you were sure?"

William's eyes shifted downward, and several of the other men moved about uncomfortably. "We were sure she was dead, and we had to get back to our wagons or we'd all be left behind."

"I can't believe what I'm hearing," Blake exclaimed. "You tracked her down, found some blood, and then quit! How much blood did you see?" he demanded.

"A bit. Enough to make a track," William answered defiantly.

"That's all? Just enough to make a track? Hell, I've bled more than that from scraping my knuckles filing a horse's hoof!" He glared at the man with obvious contempt. "When did this happen? Where?"

"This morning before we broke camp. Ed Bingham gave us an hour to find her. We ran out of time, but—"

Blake uttered an expletive that made some of the women gasp. This was the holdup that Ed Bingham had referred to as "nothing." Blake's eyes darkened with anger. "She may still be alive. Maybe she was only wounded." Blake thought about how mad Lacey had been at him when she headed for the woods.

"That's not likely," William Calvert snapped.

Blake's eyes raked the crowd. "To hell with all your theories." To Zeke Summerfield, he said, "I'm going to go back and look. If I find her and she's dead, I'll bury her for you. If not, I'll bring her back."

Something flickered in the older man's eyes. "You can't go back," he said hurriedly. "The snows . . . We can't wait."

"I'll catch up with you. Without a wagon I can travel faster. We can overtake you before you reach South Pass."

"I've misjudged you sorely," Zeke choked out.

"Don't thank me yet. She may be dead."

"Either way, at least I'll know for sure."

Blake turned and strode back to Ed Bingham's lead wagon. By the time he had strapped provisions for several days onto the back of his pack mule, his anger had been replaced by dogged determination. As he was dragging out his saddle and other gear, the wagon master approached with a curious look. "What's going on?"

"I just found out what happened this morning." His anger rekindled, he swung the saddle over his shoulder and walked into the night without further explanation, his pack mule in tow.

Blake's horse snorted and sidestepped at the unexpected shift in routine, but Blake saddled him quickly and eased himself into the cradle. Then he tied the mule's lead rope to his saddle and urged his horse forward. The moon was nearly full, and the rutted wagon trail was easy to see. Without a backward glance Blake headed east. He planned to ride for several hours before stopping for a brief rest where the trail again came close to the river. Then he would continue back toward the campsite.

As he rode, anger welled up in him. The search party had done all they thought they could, but like him they may have stopped too short. He could never bring Catherine back, nor would his efforts have made any difference, according to the doctor, but he felt he should have been able to do more. Now Lacey Summerfield had run off into the woods, mad at him, and couldn't be found.

His horse's hooves thudded against the earth in a steady trot.

CHAPTER
4

Lacey didn't dream. The blackness of her sleep faded to gray and stayed that way. She blinked and tried to bring the interior of the wagon into focus. Then it all came back to her and she realized the pewter-colored walls that enclosed her were the surfaces of the granite boulders. She was cold and ached all over, and even the act of lifting her head caused her pain. Slowly she readjusted her cramped muscles and rubbed the sleep from her eyes. Her wounded leg was sore but usable, she thought. Yesterday's blind panic had abated. If the bear could have reached her, he would already have done so; and since she hadn't been crushed by a boulder falling from overhead, she assumed the rocks were tightly wedged and not a threat.

The inside of her mouth felt like cotton, and her longing for water was far greater than her need for food. Moving slow inches at a time, she peeked out the upper crack in the enclosure. The bear lay sleeping on a flat rock several yards away.

Water was her first concern. She ran her hands over the rough walls of her small cave. Where the large rocks jutted up from the earth, she felt a moistness. It was not much more than a heavy dew, but it was something. She maneuvered around until she could reach the area with a clean part of her skirt and used the soft material to soak up the dampness. She put the cloth in her mouth and let the moisture soothe her dry tongue.

After a while she grew braver and edged toward the cave entrance. The bear lay still, and she was sure he was asleep. As quietly as she could, she eased herself forward. Even the slightest movement dislodged a tiny spray of shale. It would be impossible to slip away unnoticed.

Lacey saw a fallen tree branch amid the rubble. It wasn't long, but it looked stout. She reached for it as the bear opened his small eyes. Her fingers closed around the limb, and she pulled hard to free it and drag it back into the cave.

At first sight of her, the bear came instantly awake. He lunged after her, his yellow teeth clicking on the air where her arm had been. Lacey hurled herself back inside the cave, and as the bear swiped at her, she beat at his paw with the short club.

He snarled and again tried to force himself head first into the crevice. Lacey hammered at his snout and derived some relief from his snorts of pain.

She might be as good as dead, but she wasn't going to give up without a fight. Tearing a strip of fabric from her petticoat, she bound the sharp sliver of flint to the stick. Makeshift spear in hand, she waited for the bear to come close again.

By midmorning, Blake arrived at the riverside camp where the wagon train had stopped the day before. He looked carefully around for any signs of the woman having been back here since the wagons left, then turned his horse into the woods. The search party had left an obvious trail in the leaves, and he knew he would have little trouble following the route they had taken, but whether the young woman had come this way, he was not sure.

He rode quietly, using all his instincts to read the signs. A bent twig here, a turned leaf there. Once, he lost the traces and had to backtrack. Then he came upon the tiny clearing William Calvert had mentioned and saw the bear track. Judging by the way the claws had dug into the ground, the animal had been moving fast. The men had been right about the creature's size. It was likely a grizzly, and that was even worse news.

This trail was easier to follow. Small saplings had been bent aside as the animal tore past. The carpet of leaves had been scrambled and disarrayed by his heavy feet.

Blake cautiously followed the path. He could see why the search party hadn't wanted to tangle with this beast and why they were so sure Lacey Summerfield must be dead. He had heard that grizzlies were half crazy and dangerous in the extreme.

He eased his rifle from its scabbard and checked to be sure it was loaded. If the bear was still around, Blake might need to defend himself on short notice.

His horse picked his way along the edge of a stream and across to the other side. Lacey had done the smart thing, he noted. Instead of heading for open ground or trying to climb a tree, she had stayed in the heavy undergrowth. He hoped this had bought her enough time to find an escape, but he doubted it. A bear could outrun a full-grown man, let alone a woman hampered by long skirts.

Why had he interfered in the quarrel between Lacey and her father? He'd had no right butting into the business of a man and his daughter. He must have been moved by the old man who had looked so helpless. As a result, Lacey had run off, angry and hurt. Maybe she was dead.

The woods ended, and Blake stopped. Ahead lay only a landslide of shale and granite. He must have lost the trail again. He retraced his path to the last clear paw print and tried once more.

Lacey felt as if she had waited for an eternity, spear poised to attack. She knew the flint would never pierce the bear's thick fur and hide, but she thought she had a chance of blinding him. If she had a clear shot, she might be able to stab the spear down his throat and at least wound him badly, if not kill him. Desperation was giving her many ideas, none of which she would have considered if she had been in less danger. But where was the bear?

Slowly, she raised herself to see out. Her head was swimming, and she had to squint to focus her eyes. The bear was not in sight. She eased toward the opening that led to the mountainside, steadying herself as she went. Still she saw nothing. She picked up a handful of pebbles and tossed them up onto the rock above her. They rained down and slid off in a small shower.

Lacey sat back and tried to make sense of this. Had he left? Or was he smart enough to trick her into coming out into the open? Several times he had gone down to the stream to drink, and each time she had felt the agony of the damned. This time she hadn't even heard him leave. Had he been gone long? Then she realized that this was the best chance she was likely to get. Painfully, she pulled herself out of the cave of rocks and into the sunshine, clutching her weapon tightly.

Blake heard a sound in the distant brush and reined his horse and pack mule to a halt. The animals flicked their ears nervously, but he stood his ground. The wind was in his favor, and Blake waited as the sound faded away in the distance. Elk or bear? He didn't want to take any chances.

He picked up the trail and verified that it did indeed lead to the shale slope. He frowned. Until now the woman had used good sense, but in this open territory she was as good as dead. A few yards farther on, he found the bloodied rocks. As William Calvert had said, there was another unmistakable paw mark. But this wasn't as much blood as he would have expected from a kill.

Shading his eyes against the sun, he looked up. There, unbelievably, was a movement—a flash of bright blue. Then before his astonished eyes, a woman crawled out of a jumble of rocks and stood swaying in the afternoon light. She was alive!

Lacey's senses told her she wasn't alone. The bear. He was coming up the hill after her. It had been a trick after all. She staggered on the loose rubble as she turned and struck out blindly.

Blake caught her hand, and Lacey's stick clattered to the ground. She stared up at him. Her lips moved, but no sound came. Slowly, as if her body were melting, she crumpled forward. Blake caught her and eased her to the ground.

"Bear," she whispered almost inaudibly. "Get away."

He looked around. Sure enough, there were bear signs all about. The animal must have had her at bay the entire time. He recalled the rustling he had heard in the underbrush and decided it would be most prudent to leave quickly.

"Can you put your arms around my neck?" he asked as he slipped his hands behind her.

Lacey tried to hold on and balance herself in his grasp, but the world was dipping and spinning. She closed her eyes and buried her face against his throat. A strong pulse beat there, and she felt surprisingly safe.

Blake struggled with the effort to carry her down the ever-shifting fall of rubble. She wasn't large, but she was like a dead weight and he was glad when they reached his horse.

He tried to balance her on the saddle, but she had fainted and the animal was moving restlessly. Blake looked back at the woods and saw the huge bear lumber into the clearing. He tossed Lacey face down across the horse and leaped up behind her. He kicked his frightened horse to a gallop, the pack mule racing by their side.

They skirted the shale slide and put a good deal of woods between them and the bear. When he thought it was safe to slow down, he lifted her and positioned her in front of him. She was weak from exposure and thirst, but aside from a badly scratched leg, she seemed miraculously unhurt. Using his knees to guide the horse, Blake placed his canteen to her lips. Lacey gulped convulsively and opened her eyes.

"The bear!" she exclaimed, looking frantically about.

"It's all right. You're safe. Hold still or you'll fall off the horse."

Lacey stared up at Blake. "You! Turn me loose! Where's the rest of the search party?"

"There isn't one. They looked, but they couldn't find you."

"Then why are you here? I must have lost track of the time. Days seem to have passed." She tried to shrug away from him, but he held her securely in his arms. "I told you to turn me loose," she said more firmly.

"It's hard to balance sideways on a man's saddle, and I don't want you to fall off."

She pushed his arms away and swung one leg over the horse's neck so she sat astride. She clutched the horse's mane and silently prayed that she wouldn't lose her balance. "I can ride as well as you can, Mr. Cameron, and I have never used a sidesaddle." His left arm still circled her to hold the reins, but she saw no way to avoid that. "I'm very thankful that Mr. Bingham waited for me. Otherwise I might not have been able to catch up. Please hurry."

"Don't be too thankful yet. Bingham didn't wait. Everyone gave you up for dead, and they went on without you."

Lacey sat in stunned silence as his words sank into her confused mind. "They left me behind?" she asked in a shocked voice. "Then why are you here? I don't understand."

"Some of the men looked for you and saw where the bear had chased you. They found blood, and they thought it was yours." He glanced down at her leg. "The bear scratched you, but I don't see where all that blood came from."

"That was the bear's," she said absently. "You mean Papa didn't even stay to make sure I was dead?"

"Miss Summerfield, they all thought you were eaten by the bear. They should have looked until they were sure, but your father was too upset at the idea of what they might find."

"I'll bet he was!" Lacey agreed angrily. "Was he with them?"

"Of course he was!" Blake frowned at the back of her head. "You should have seen him at the memorial service. He was half crazy with grief."

"What memorial service?" she asked in frigid tones.

"They held a funeral for you. A lot of people came."

She shifted so she could glare at him over her shoulder.

"Well, they did. Most people would be glad to hear there was such a turnout."

"Not for their own funeral, they wouldn't."

Blake frowned back at her. "In your case I guess the service was a little premature."

Lacey merely made a derogatory sound and glared straight ahead. "So Papa called off the search and let them leave me, did he? Just wait until I catch up with him."

"Miss Summerfield, you're the most unnatural daughter I ever saw. First you tie into that poor old man for drinking an occasional drop of whiskey—"

"Is that what he told you!"

"Then you lambaste him for leaving you behind. You are for a fact the most ornery woman I ever met."

Lacey jerked her head around angrily. "If everyone went on, what are you doing here?"

"I couldn't have left without knowing for sure if you were alive or dead. You wouldn't last a week out here by yourself."

After a few more minutes, they rode into a clearing intersected by a wide stream. Blake reined his horse to a halt and slid off.

"Why are we stopping? Aren't we near the wagons?" she asked suspiciously.

"We won't catch up with them until late tomorrow, the way I figure it. We'll camp here."

She looked up at the sun. It was indeed lowering near the treetops. There was maybe an hour of daylight left. She dismounted on rubbery legs and started to unsaddle Blake's horse.

"I'll do that," Blake interrupted her. "That saddle's heavy, and you've had a hard time."

"I can manage quite well, thank you." Lacey staggered back a step to regain her stability.

"I'm sure you can, but I'd rather tend the animals. Why don't you start supper, if you insist on doing something?"

Lacey went to the pack mule and struggled to untie the cotton rope that bundled the oiled canvas cover. The knot was swollen from moisture in the air, and she had to work hard to get it loose. The saddle would have been much easier, she thought as she untied the pan from the pack.

By the time she reached the stream, she was feeling much better. Her muscles were limbering up, and her head was clearing. She filled the pan in the stream as Blake unloaded the mule and started a fire. Although she detested what the medicine wagon stood for, Lacey found herself missing its conveniences.

After they had eaten their meal and washed the dishes, Lacey sat cross-legged on a blanket, her forearms resting on her knees. She gazed at the landscape, which appeared molten in the glow of the campfire, and said as if to herself, "I'll bet he plans to take my land!"

"Who?" Blake glanced at her in surprise from where he reclined on another blanket.

"Papa! He knows I own seventy acres of rich land in Oregon, and if he can get there first, he'll claim it." She tossed a twig into the fire. "He even has the deed in the wagon. I never should have told him about that land."

Blake frowned at her. "Parents don't do things like that."

"Some do, and he's one of them."

"You know, I've never once seen you smile," Blake said thoughtfully, trying to change the subject. "Do you know how?"

Lacey sat up straighter. "That's a ridiculous thing to say. Of course I can smile. It's just that I see no humor in being abandoned in the wilds and having all my possessions stolen."

"You could be happy that you're outside a bear instead of inside, and that you're safe and full of a good meal."

"You're right, Mr. Cameron," she said after a pause. "I'm behaving very badly. I apologize." Her moss-hued eyes met his across the licking flames. "Thank you for coming after me. I'm not used to having anyone show me such kindness, and I don't know how to accept it, I guess."

"For a start, you could try being more civil. A person would think you'd been fighting an uphill battle all your life, the way you act."

Lacey threw him a searching glance.

"Things couldn't have been all that bad," Blake continued blithely. "You have your father for companionship."

"I gather you have no family?" she said with sweet sarcasm.

"Not anymore. I was married, but my wife died." He paused and studied the fire. "That's why I left Texas. There was nothing to hold me to one spot anymore."

"Admirable. A truly masculine trait."

"I don't know about that," he said, missing her sarcasm, "but I guess you felt sort of the same, since you're here, too."

She sighed and poked with a stick at the fire. "I suppose it was something like that. I want a place where no one ever plowed before. A place of my own."

"You ought to be able to find it in Oregon, and a husband as well."

Lacey looked at him sharply. "I don't want a husband, only land."

Blake leaned on his elbow and studied her. "Why is that, Miss Summerfield? I thought all ladies wanted to get married."

"Not this one." She swung her legs around and lay down, using her arm as a pillow. Reaching behind her, she pulled up the blanket. To prevent any further questions, she closed her eyes.

Blake watched her until her steady breathing told him she slept. Strange, he thought, how vulnerable she looked with her eyes shut and her features relaxed. When she wasn't frowning at him she was a beautiful woman. Her hair had come loose and lay beneath her cheek like a cloud of raw gold, burnished with fire. With her hair unbound she was highly desirable. Blake found himself wondering about her. Had something in her past made her so defensive, or was she just naturally hard to get along with?

He put another log on the fire and lay down in its circle of warmth. The nights here in the mountains were cold, and she must have been nearly frozen up there in those rocks. Yet she hadn't mentioned it. He shook his head in confusion. Every time he expected her to act one way, she did something entirely different.

As usual, sleep came to him easily. His mind, lulled by the familiar chorus of insect voices, drifted into a dream world where people spoke with a soft Texas drawl and the most pressing emergency was a downed fence.

Suddenly he was awake. He saw his horse moving nervously in the unnatural silence. Blake reached for his gun and rolled to a crouching position. Was it Indians? If so, he was a clear target in the firelight. Before he could edge into the concealing darkness, he saw the fire reflect in two eyes well above the ground, and a musty odor wafted to him.

Bear.

Blake reached for a burning log and charged at the eyes, yelling at the top of his voice. There was a surprised grunt, and the eyes vanished as the bear fled from the unexpected assault.

Lacey sat bolt upright, terror pounding through her trembling limbs. "What! What happened!" she exclaimed as she stared around her.

Not wanting to cause Lacey any more anxiety, Blake answered, "Just an animal. Go back to sleep." He tried to pierce the night shadows but could see nothing.

"An animal?" she said testily. "What sort of animal?"

"I didn't see it very clearly," he said evasively. There was no need to worry her.

"I suggest you, too, go to sleep," she commented dryly as she lay back down. "If you spend the night shouting at raccoons and possums, you'll be too tired in the morning for the hard ride we'll be doing. Good night." She flipped over so that her back was toward him. Almost at once she felt guilty. This man had saved her life and was carrying her back to the safety of the wagon train, and she was being extremely impolite. But old habits were hard to break, and Lacey had learned at an early age that if a woman acted too friendly around a man, she was courting danger. No, it was better to keep her barriers up and stay safe.

Blake groaned and threw himself down on his blanket. She was a hard one for sure. Maybe instead of rescuing her, he had really saved the bear. He yanked his cover up and tried to recapture sleep. At last a reedy chorus of night noises resumed, and he dozed.

CHAPTER
5

Blake nudged his horse into the quick walk that was the animal's easiest gait. Thunder rumbled in the distance, and the low clouds seemed to rest on the treetops. This was the rain Ed Bingham had feared. His eyes studied the clouds and reaffirmed that a downpour was imminent. Already the scent of ozone hung in the humid air.

"Why are you out here on a wagon train?" Blake asked the woman who rode in front of him.

"I'm heading for Oregon." Her voice was clipped, and she didn't look back at him.

"I know that, but why Oregon? There's a whole bunch of land a lot closer than that. It's odd for a woman to strike off across the country for no reason. If your papa insisted on going, I could understand, but it seems like you're the one who's set on it."

She continued to ride in silence so he went on. "All the women I know like to live in towns where they can shop and talk to other ladies and find a good man to marry. Don't you like all that?"

This time she did turn her head. "You sure ask a lot of questions. I thought Texans were the strong, silent type."

He grinned. "I don't know what gave you that idea."

Lacey didn't either, so she sighed and firmly shut her mouth.

"In time, of course, Oregon will have towns and cities just like back east. There may be towns there now, for all I know. This is my first time to go there. As soon as the railroad goes through, there will be people everywhere." He was surprised to feel her stiffen.

"I hadn't heard about a train."

"Oh, it won't be any time soon, I guess, but there's talk about putting tracks through someday. Before you know it, you and your papa will have neighbors just as you did before.

"Not me," Lacey responded firmly. "My land is beyond a deep valley on the far side of a mountain. My deed says so. I specifically asked for a remote spot, and I got it."

"Maybe it's remote now, but with the train line will come more people, and that will mean roads and little towns cropping up all around. Why, someday Oregon may even be part of the Union."

"Now you're talking nonsense." Her voice sounded strained.

"No, ma'am. It won't be any time soon, but one of these days it'll happen."

The sounds of the bay horse's hooves were muffled in the long grasses of the narrow meadow, and he pricked his ears back as thunder rolled down from the mountains. All the birds were huddling on limbs close to the tree trunks. Soon a heavy rain would begin, so Blake started looking for a shelter. They could hardly spare the time, but some of these mountain storms were dangerous. Ahead he saw a cliff jutting out of the trees, and that meant the possibility of caves. To keep her from worrying about the pending storm, Blake said, "How did you happen to pick Oregon?"

"It's the farthest away," she replied without thinking. "Besides," she added hastily, "the land is cheap and I didn't have much money."

"What do you plan to do out there?"

"I'm going to farm. I have a supply of seeds to plant next spring. The land must be fertile, since it's never been used. I'm going to live right in the middle of my seventy acres and never see another living soul."

"You plan to plow seventy acres? Just you and your papa?"

"Maybe just me," she reminded him curtly. "Unless Papa changes his ways fast."

"What ways?"

Lacey ignored the question. She wasn't accustomed to talking so much, and she was letting too much slip out. Safety lay in silence.

"You can't begrudge a man a bit of liquor every once in a while," Blake tried to tell her. "There was only part of a quart in that bottle he had. I've known men to drink more than that at one sitting and then go out and brand cows." When she glared back at him, he smiled. "Of course, sometimes they branded the wrong ones, but that's not the point. Your pa's getting on in years, and you ought to be more tolerant."

"Mr. Cameron, you have more opinions on things you know nothing about than any man I ever heard."

"I imagine I know more about liquor than you do, Miss Summerfield."

"I don't care to learn, Mr. Cameron."

"My daddy always said you could learn something from everybody if you kept your mouth shut long enough, Miss Summerfield," he observed blandly.

Again the silence was measured only by the muffled sounds of the hooves and the nearing thunder.

"Once you get there—to Oregon, I mean—where will you live?" The extended silence was uncomfortable, and they had a long way to go. "If you're way up on the far side of a mountain, there won't be a cabin or even so much as a lean-to shed. Where will you winter?"

"I'll build a cabin."

"You know how to do that, do you?"

"I can learn. I can figure out how to do anything if I want to bad enough. After all, men do it all the time, and I doubt many of you built cabins back home."

"I've put up a barn or two. A cabin's not much different. You plan to fell the trees and everything, do you?" His voice was level, without inflection, but she suspected he was teasing her.

"Unless a wind blows the trees down for me, I do."

"You have an'ax, I guess."

Lacey tried to quell her anger at his questions. "Yes, Mr. Cameron, I have an ax."

"The only other question I have is how are you going to stack the logs all by yourself? Up to waist high, there's no trick to it, but after you start building over your head, how will you do it?"

She frowned. This was something she hadn't considered. "I have that all figured out, and I don't want to talk about it."

"I see."

"Besides, there is always the wagon. I can live in it until spring if I have to. It's solid and not drafty like a covered wagon."

"Once the snow covers it, I doubt it will be drafty at all."

"Snow?" Lacey had spent most of her life in the South, and during the few harsh winters she had seen, Papa managed to find a family to take them in until the weather grew warmer.

"Sure. I've heard it snows a lot in Oregon. Be sure to dig yourself an air hole once the snow piles over the top."

She glanced back uncertainly, but his face was perfectly guileless. Uneasily she turned to face ahead. "None of this looks familiar," she pointed out. "Are you sure you know where you're going?"

"Of course I do. I get my direction from the sun."

"But it's very cloudy," she pointed out, "and we haven't seen the sun all day."

"No, but it's there, and I know where it is. I can feel it in my bones."

With a low sound under her breath Lacey deigned to answer. His superior attitude was only typical, to her way of thinking. She almost wished they were lost so she could have the satisfaction of rubbing it in. Hastily she put the unlucky thought from her mind. This was no time to lose their way, no matter how much she would like to prove a point. "You're sure we aren't lost?" she repeated uncertainly.

"Positive." When he saw her trepidation, all the teasing left his voice. "I came through this grove of trees when I was searching for you."

When the lowering skies quit threatening, the first big raindrops spattered against Blake's hat and made penny-sized circles on Lacey's blue dress. Without halting, Blake untied his oilskin poncho from the saddle roll and wrapped it around them both.

The waterproof canvas kept her dry, but it also pulled her back against Blake's hard chest. Lacey gripped the edges of the covering and compressed her lips. This was closer than she had ever been to any man, and the horse's rhythmic sway was rubbing her back against Blake at every step. Abruptly, she sat up, moving away from him.

"Wrap the slicker around you," he instructed. "You're getting wet."

"I don't mind. I like the rain."

"Well, I do mind, and I'm getting wet."

She settled back against him, and he put his arm around her to help hold the front of the poncho together. In doing so, his forearm brushed against the lower portion of her breasts—a sensation she found most unsettling.

The large drops soon became a torrent of smaller ones as the clouds opened in earnest. A rivulet of water poured off Blake's hat in a stream down his back or down hers when he forgot and tipped his head forward. After a couple such mistakes, Lacey was positive she was as wet under the poncho as she would have been without it. She tried pointing this out to Blake, but he ignored her logic and kept her pulled back against him.

Trees finally closed over them, and the rocky cliff just ahead seemed to huddle against the earth under the ominous pewter-colored sky. A jagged spear of lightning pierced the storm clouds and was followed immediately by deafening thunder. Lacey pressed back against Blake's muscular bulk. All her life she had closely guarded her secret fear of thunderstorms. Any fear was a weakness, and when one showed weakness, one usually had a good reason to be afraid.

Blake guided the horse alongside the cliff and inspected the many caves at the base. Finding one large enough, with an overhang to shelter the horse and mule, he reined to a stop and dismounted.

"What are you doing?" Lacey asked. "Why are we stopping?"

"Maybe you haven't noticed," he answered as he studied the opening for recent signs of animal tracks, "but it's raining. Where I come from, we usually come in out of the weather when it does that. Especially if there's lightning close by." Thunder almost obscured his words.

"But we need to catch up with the wagons," she objected.

"Go ahead. Just keep walking west and you'll find them. As for me, I'm getting in out of the weather." He tossed a rock into the shelter's darkness to see if it was occupied. When the rock rattled to the back and nothing scurried out, he turned to the horse. "Excuse me, Miss Summerfield, but it's easier to unsaddle a horse if no one is sitting on it."

"You mean you want me to walk?" she gasped.

"No, ma'am. I want you to go in the cave and get dry. Walking was your idea."

"We'll get too far behind if we wait out the storm."

Blake didn't waste time arguing. He reached up and pulled her off the horse and draped her over his shoulder. Effortlessly he carried her into the cave and deposited her on the dry ground.

Lacey stared at his back as he turned to the animals and led them under the overhang. Slowly she shrugged out of the poncho and looked around. The roof of the cave sloped back to meet the ground where countless seasons of leaves had blown in the open mouth and lodged in the recesses. A pinkish flash of lightning followed quickly by an ear shattering crack made her jump and wheel to face the entrance.

"That was a close one," Blake observed. "It must have hit something nearby." He regarded her pale face and large eyes. "Are you afraid of storms?"

"Certainly not!" she responded, too quickly. "I was only startled by the noise." She helped him remove the horse's gear and build a fire, using the dry debris to catch the spark from his flint. Soon the growing warmth was chasing the chill from the musty air, and a billow of white smoke was pouring out of the gaping mouth to mingle with the rain.

Lacey saw a movement outside, and she stiffened, staring at the thick bushes. Now that she was looking, however, she saw only glistening leaves and falling rain. Nevertheless, she moved uneasily. "I thought I saw something out there," she commented as she strained to pierce the curtain of water.

Blake came to stand by her and looked where she pointed. "I don't see anything."

"Neither do I—now."

"More than likely you just saw a shape in the smoke. A downdraft makes mirages sometimes."

"What I saw was brown, and the smoke is light gray."

"Must have been a tree." He turned away and knelt by the fire. "Some coffee would sure taste good. Do you want a cup?"

She nodded, still not convinced that she had seen only a mirage. She knew a tree and smoke when she saw them.

The storm grew in intensity, showing no sign of quickly passing. Lacey paced the width and breadth of the cave as she glared at the sheath of rain that silvered the entrance. Blake sat stoically by the fire and waited as if he had nowhere to go and all day to get there. Her leg was aching, but she told herself it was because of the long ride. Refusing to give in to the pain, she paced faster.

"You're going to wear yourself out," Blake commented without looking at her. "If you had put all those steps in a straight line, you'd be in Oregon by now."

"Very funny," she retorted. "Won't the rain ever stop?"

"I imagine it will. Always has before." He offered her the only cup. "More coffee?"

"No, thank you." A gale-force wind was whipping the trees and lashing the rain against the rocks of the cliffs. Few minutes went by without a peal of thunder. Lacey's muscles were tense from her tightly strung nerves, and she couldn't have stopped pacing if she had wanted to. As long as she stayed on the move he couldn't see her tremble.

One of her passes into the back of the cave took her to a low ledge. In the process of bumping her head, she looked from the storm toward the rock. Her lips parted in surprise as she discovered several pictures on the flat overhang. "Look! Have you seen these?"

Blake came to her and held a burning tree limb up as a torch. In the flickering light, pale images of stick figures astride horses chased a herd of antelope. Farther down, one group of figures fought another group of lesser proportions, in an obvious battle. Lower on the wall were two squares with wheels and arched tops that could only be covered wagons. Scattered about were odd symbols in white or rust-colored paint.

"What are they?" Lacey whispered.

"Indian paintings."

She whirled to face him. "Indians! Here?"

He nodded. "This seems to be a big hunt, and that one is of some battle. The others are wagons."

"Then they must not be very old! The trail has only been open a few years. Do you think there are still Indians around here?" Her eyes were wide and fearful.

"I've heard there are, but I wouldn't worry if I were you."

"Not worry! Indians are dangerous!"

"Not all of them. Those at Fort Kearney were friendly enough."

Lacey followed him back to the fire. "You're keeping something from me! What is it!"

Blake pitched the torch back into the fire and gazed out at the rain. "Ed Bingham said there had been Indians around here. I guess some of them waited out a storm in this cave, just like us." He smiled at her. "Do you want to draw a picture?"

"No! What Indians? Are they friendly? Why wasn't I told?"

"Calm down. Ed only told the men; he was afraid the women would panic."

"If I had known there were Indians around, I would have stayed close to the wagons! Are we in danger?"

"We don't seem to be," he hedged. "I haven't seen any around here, and those paintings may be several years old."

Lacey clasped her palms together and lowered her head to hide her trembling chin. "Did Mr. Bingham say these Indians were friendly?" Her steady eyes demanded the truth.

"No, he didn't." Blake spoke quietly, but his voice seemed to fill the cave.

"Did he say they are dangerous?" she persisted.

Blake sighed and made a gesture of dismissal. "Quit worrying. There aren't any Indians here."

"Did he?"

"You're about as persistent as anyone I ever saw." Blake ran his fingers through his dark hair before he continued. "He told the men to keep a loaded gun by them at all times and to keep a close eye on the women and children."

"And you let me walk off into the woods?" she gasped. "And Papa didn't try to stop me either!"

"You said you were going for a short walk. How was I to know you would keep going? Besides," he snapped, "I'm not your keeper."

"That's no more than I would expect from a man," Lacey retorted scathingly. "Give me a gun."

"I'm not going to give you my gun. What would you do with it?"

"Shoot Indians, of course. If we're attacked, I intend to fight back."

He laughed. "You'd probably shoot me by accident. I'll handle the guns."

"I can shoot as well as any man. I started hunting with a rifle when I was just a child. I can even shoot a pistol better than Papa. My brother taught me."

Blake cocked his head to one side. "I didn't know you had a brother. Where is he?"

"He died. It was a long time ago." Abruptly she turned toward her present enemy, the storm. Sheets of rain gushed past the cave entrance, and the wind howled like a giant wolf. Twin explosions of thunder made her jump, and she began to tremble visibly.

Blake reached out and touched her arm. "You're shaking. I thought you said you're not afraid of storms."

"I'm not! Leave me alone!" Another, louder clap of thunder proved her to be a liar.

"Come here," Blake said softly as he pulled her into his arms. "You shouldn't be ashamed of being afraid. I don't like storms either." He held her tense body and nuzzled his cheek against her hair. "Only a fool is never afraid. Who told you not to let anybody know when you need to be held?"

She pushed against him. "I don't need you! I don't need anybody! Just leave me alone!"

Blake caught her wrist and drew her back to him. He cupped her face in one large hand as he held her close. "Don't try so hard to be alone, Lacey. A person can't live like that, man or woman. We all need somebody else."

She looked up into his soft brown eyes. He was so tender in spite of his towering size. The dreaded quickening answered in her veins. "I don't," she whispered. "I don't need anybody."

Slowly Blake lowered his head. Lacey jerked away before their lips met, but he gently pulled her back. When his mouth claimed hers, the physical sensations she felt were unlike any Lacey had ever known. His lips moved over hers in a tantalizing caress that made hers part in welcome. His breath was sweet in her mouth, and his warm tongue teased the softness inside her lips and ran over the tiny ridges of her teeth. She felt her head tilt back against his arm, and her body seemed to melt against his. It took most of her strength to shove him away.

She regarded him warily from a distance of several paces. Her entire body was poised to race out into the raging storm if he tried to grab her.

"Lacey," he said in a husky voice, "are you more afraid of me than you are of the storm?" Having a woman so afraid of him was something he had never encountered, and he felt stunned.

"I'm not afraid of anything!"

He gazed into her terrified green eyes, then did exactly what he would have done had she been a frightened animal; he knelt down on one knee and rested his forearm on the other and spoke to her in a voice that could gentle the wildest mare. "I'm not going to hurt you. If it'll make you feel any better, sit over there across the fire." He paused and waited until she had done so. "Why are you scared of me?"

Lacey tried to look away, but his eyes were hypnotic. "You're so big," she finally whispered. "You're strong, and your voice is so deep. I'm not sure I can outrun you—but I will if you try to touch me!" Her voice rose threateningly.

"I'm not trying." Blake sat perfectly still and waited for her to calm down.

"Sometimes men try to corner a woman when they think she's helpless," Lacey said over the crackling fire. "I've had some close calls, and I don't plan to be foolish enough to walk into a trap.''

''You didn't act like this last night. Why now?''

''Last night you didn't try to touch me.''

Blake studied her for a few minutes. ''Have you ever been . . . hurt?''

''No. But I've come close enough to know men aren't to be trusted.''

Blake found her attitude very unsettling. Lacey Summerfield was a beautiful woman, and judging by the way she had returned his kiss for those fleeting moments, she was far from unfeeling. Finally, he said, ''I only meant to kiss you. Didn't you enjoy it?''

''No!''

Blake merely gazed at her as if he hadn't heard her answer.

''A little,'' Lacey mumbled. ''But don't do it again.''

''I wouldn't force myself on you or any woman,'' Blake answered gently. ''If I ever kiss you again, it will be because you want me to.'' He meant every word and his eyes promised her that he spoke the truth.

The wind shifted and pelted rain onto the ledge. Blake moved over and patted the blanket beside him. ''Come here before you get wet.''

Cautiously, Lacey edged deeper into the cave. He had not tried to catch her, and until a few minutes ago, he hadn't tried to touch her. Still, she avoided him and spread out the other blanket to sit on. Instead of reaching out to her, however, he lay back and propped his head on his bent arms. She relaxed a bit more, the danger passed for the time.

''When I was boy, I used to go off exploring on our family's ranch,'' Blake said dreamily, as if nothing had happened. ''We lived in northeastern Texas where there were all kinds of gullies and woods for a boy to roam through. One day I found the entrance to an underground cavern and waited out a storm, just as we're doing now. I never told Mama how big the cavern really was, because she was already upset at me for worrying her so. But that cave was really fine.''

Lacey relaxed a little more. His voice was soothing, and her muscles ached from holding herself so rigidly.

''After that, she made me take my little brother with me on my exploring trips.'' The memory brought a boyish grin to Blake's features. ''He wasn't there to protect me, though. She knew he'd tell her if I did anything I shouldn't. She never will know all the bribery I had to resort to in order to finish my exploration of that cavern.'' His mellow laugh filled their enclosure. ''My brother and I get along fine now, but at the time, I wished I could shake him off my coat-tails.'' He rolled his head to look at her. ''Were there any caves where you grew up, or don't girls go exploring?''

Lacey hesitated. She was irresistibly drawn to this man, but she could never tell him or anyone else the truth about her childhood. Slowly she said, ''There were caves, but I never went in. Billy said they might fall in on me.''

''Billy?''

''My brother.'' She held her breath, but he only nodded. ''My games had more to do with imagination. I pretended I was a princess and that a knight on a charger—white, of course—would someday rescue me from the dragon.''

Blake regarded her thoughtfully. ''Who was the dragon?''

Lacey faltered, then said, ''There are no such things as dragons. Everyone knows that.''

''Maybe not, but everybody ought to believe in them,'' he surprised her by saying. ''As well as princesses in towers and knights on white chargers. A world without dreams would be a bleak place.''

''After a while the dreams become fairy tales, and then only shadows; and that's when a person grows up.'' Her voice held a wistful sadness.

''What was your childhood like?'' he asked offhandedly.

''Oh,'' she sighed as she spun a familiar daydream, ''about like everyone else's. We had a big house with a white picket fence, and I went to school. My mother was still alive then, and she used to sing to me. She and Billy had lovely voices. They sounded like angels.'' Her face became soft and her voice gentle.

Blake watched her. No smile lifted her lips, but there was a gentleness about her that made his heart ache. He didn't believe her for a minute. A girl didn't grow up with a picket fence and an adoring, angelic mother and be terrified of being touched or of showing fear.

Lacey's words trailed away. She had told this tale how many times and in how many towns, to how many people? It was her lodestone, the dream that kept her alive. She had never had a real childhood, but someday, somehow, she was determined to have that house with the picket fence. Her eyes dropped to study the fire. After all these years she had almost convinced herself that in some strange way the tale was true.

''That was in South Carolina?'' Blake asked.

She nodded. South Carolina was as good a location as any, and better than most, since she had never been there. ''We had lace curtains at all the windows and crocheted doilies, all stiff with starch. The floors were covered with thick rugs, and we had a big chandelier in the parlor.'' She rested her chin on her drawn-up knees. She hadn't realized how well she recalled the one fine house she had been inside. It was the one where the little girl had died from the Wonder Tonic, or so those angry people had claimed. Reality surged back over her, and she glanced at him guiltily.

''It sounds as if you had a really nice house,'' Blake said quietly. ''You must have enjoyed growing up there.''

Lacey nodded briskly and looked away. ''The storm is letting up some.''

He curved his neck back to see. ''By morning the rain will be a memory. We may as well spend the night here in the shelter, though. No point in sleeping outside in the mud if we can help it.''

''I suppose. We'll catch up with the wagons tomorrow, won't we?''

"I think so. We still have to cross the Platte." He frowned with concern at the streaking rain.

"That shouldn't be difficult," Lacey replied. "It's wide, but it's shallow and we have no wagon to worry about."

They sat quietly for a while. Then Lacey said in a carefully unconcerned manner, "Are you aware that you called me by my given name a few minutes ago?"

Blake rolled to his side to regard her. "Yes, I believe I did. Do you mind?"

"I guess not," she said, raising her chin coolly. "After all, it seems silly to stand on ceremony when we're here in a cave." Her startlingly green eyes captured his. "Just don't take advantage of it or assume that such familiarity gives you leave to take liberties."

His white teeth gleamed in the firelight. "That's the last thing I would think, ma'am."

She nodded decisively. "Now. What will we do in case the Indians attack us?"

Blake was intrigued. As soon as she felt she was out of immediate danger, she became logical and aloof once more. The frightened girl he had glimpsed might never have been there. "If the Indians attack, Lacey, we will shoot them."

CHAPTER
6

Lacey watched Blake from under the concealing fringe of her eyelashes. He was going about the usual routine of breaking camp, and as he worked he whistled as if he felt happy with himself and his surroundings. This was an alien attitude for Lacey. Her father continually cursed the weather or lamented their impoverished state, then fell into a morose depression and did nothing to change matters. Blake had been up before her, and the aroma of coffee had awakened her. No man she had ever heard of made coffee for a woman.

Under the pretext of folding his blanket, Lacey ran her hand over the coarse wool that had warmed him. It was cool to the touch now, but she fancied she could still feel something of him in the heavy folds. A blush colored her cheeks, and she looked away before he could see it. Here she was a grown woman—no, she thought with cutting honesty, an old maid at twenty-four—and she felt as giddy as a young girl from merely touching Blake's blanket. She tried to rally her usual common sense, but somehow it wasn't there.

He was packing the X-shaped pack saddle, so she ventured a straightforward appraisal. He had already shaved, and his wayward hair was as subdued by a comb as it ever could be. His hands drew her attention, for she knew that people's hands held as many clues to their character as their eyes did. Blake's hands were large and strong, with square palms that looked as if they had done a great deal of hard work. His fingers were at odds with that impression, being long and, yes, almost graceful. The skin was tanned but supple, and veins and tough tendons moved fluidly beneath the surface, giving an impression of both immense strength and immeasurable gentleness.

Lacey's gaze traveled up his lean frame to his face. Beyond a doubt, Blake Cameron was the most handsome man she had ever seen, though he was not pretty, by any means. His broad forehead and clear, dark eyes indicated keen intelligence, but the faint crescent-shaped scar on his cheekbone showed a predilection for brawling. His nose was as straight as a Greek god's, and his nostrils flared aristocratically. She had always thought of sensuous lips—when she thought of them at all—as being thick and rather large, yet Blake's lips were most definitely sensuous and they were perfectly proportioned and apt to tilt upward at the slightest provocation. She decided it was possible that she had equated lust with sensuality in the past. His chin was firm and not a little stubborn—a fault with which she could hardly quibble, as her own chin indicated the same tendency—and was slightly cleft. If she had been asked to describe the ideal man, it would be Blake Cameron.

"Is something wrong?" His words jolted her from her reverie.

"No," she said hastily and turned back to the blanket. She must have been addled to stare at him like that. She rolled his blanket inside her own and tied them with a length of rawhide. He whistled nicely, too, she mused. She couldn't carry a tune herself, but she could recognize one when someone else did.

Blake scattered the dying embers and kicked dirt over them, using the toe of his scuffed boot. Picking up the canteen, he shook it experimentally. "We need to fill this before we leave that creek. I'm not eager to drink mud syrup from the Platte.

"I'll fill it in a minute."

That was another thing she had noticed. He didn't order her to do things, but suggested them. Had she not offered to do it, he would have gone to the creek himself. Blake was like no man she had ever known, and she admired the differences.

Unbidden, her thoughts turned to his kiss of the night before. True, he had frightened her half out of her wits, but he hadn't followed up the advance with an attack. Instead, he had spoken gently to her. Lacey had intended to stay awake until he slept, just in case, but his soothing voice had calmed her to relaxation and then sleep, with the sureness of a lullaby. Trustworthiness was a trait she would never have attributed to a barroom brawler like Blake Cameron.

His kiss still haunted her, but only in the most pleasant manner. She had never guessed lips could be so soft, yet so firm. He had demanded no more than she had given, but her bones felt weak at the mere memory of all her body had wanted to give. Only her ingrained fear of men in general had preserved her chastity, and now her rebellious body was asking if it had been worth it. Lacey frowned. She had better be careful around Blake or he would overcome all her carefully erected defenses, and then where would she be?

Blake picked up his rifle and checked to see if the barrel needed cleaning. He knew it didn't, but it gave him an excellent opportunity to look at Lacey without her knowing it. She was so damned pretty as she knelt there in the dim cave. Her hair was plaited in a single braid that fell over her shoulder and down to her waist in a rope that was as thick as her wrist. A stray sunbeam illumined it to fiery copper and made her cheek and slender neck seem as translucent as alabaster. He admired the way her skin remained pale rather than darkening like leather the way most of the women's had. No doubt that was due to her Irish coloring. He wondered if she had had freckles when she was a child. If so, they had all disappeared. Her face was heart-shaped with a widow's peak and an oval chin, which looked more than slightly stubborn. He liked that. Docile women bored him.

He would have expected her mouth to be narrow and set in downward lines, from all he knew of her sharp tongue, but instead it was sweet in repose. He longed to see her smile and still couldn't understand why she wouldn't. It wasn't that she had bad teeth, because he had seen them clearly when she had upbraided him. In fact, he had had the opportunity of seeing them on several like occasions.

Her eyes fascinated him. They were soft green like the moss that grew deep in the forests at home. They were large and almond-shaped and framed by long lashes of a dark brown. Her throat was gracefully turned, and he had seen a quick pulse beating in the warm hollow. His practiced eye told him she had the kind of body that would look even better without clothes than it did with them.

"I'm going hunting," he said gruffly. He had to get away from her before his thoughts went any further.

"Now? Just when we're nearly ready to leave?" She stared up at him in confusion.

"I won't be gone long. Game is scarce in the open, and I imagine you're as tired of venison jerky as I am. With any luck at all, we'll have rabbit for supper."

Lacey hadn't liked jerky from the very beginning but had learned to tolerate the tough, salty meat. "I'd prefer a rabbit. Or maybe a squirrel."

"I'll see what I can do."

"Will you be long?" She knew very well it would take as long as it took to find and shoot the animal, but she liked to hear him speak.

"I should be back in an hour at the most. Will you fill the canteen and tie the animals where they can graze?"

She nodded and watched as he shouldered his ammunition pouch and rifle. "Hurry back," she said and immediately felt foolish.

"Are you afraid to stay here alone? There's a pistol in my bedroll."

"I'm not afraid at all," she said coolly to hide her embarrassment. "I only want to hurry back to the wagons."

When he was gone, Lacey led the horse and mule down the slope to the small clearing and tied them to two trees, far enough apart so they couldn't tangle each other in the ropes. As she went back to the cave, she gazed in the direction Blake had taken. She was having to make a real effort to remember he was a brawling, shiftless drifter.

An hour. She looked around the cave and wondered what she could do to pass the time. Beyond the opening she could see the silvered surface of the creek, swollen and rushing from the previous night's storm. A bath would certainly be nice. Her last one had been at Fort Kearney, and she had shared it with several other women in the river. Since then she had only been able to sponge off in a washbasin of rainwater.

Her mind made up, Lacey dug through Blake's belongings until she found his cake of soap and a linen towel. As an afterthought she picked up the heavy pistol, checked to see if it was loaded, and slipped it in her pocket. She felt safe with its bulk tugging at her skirt.

The creek was nothing like the turgid Platte. It bubbled and frothed before smoothing into a glassy stillness that meant deep water. Below the surface that reflected sky and leaves, Lacey saw lazy fish idling in wait for a meal. She would have preferred trout to either squirrel or rabbit, but she had no hook and line. A fish meal would have to wait.

Lacey sat on a log and removed her shoes and stockings. All morning her leg had hurt where the bear had clawed her, and just lifting it sent a stab of pain through her. She shrugged out of her dress and draped it over the log, then removed her chemise, petticoat, and bloomers. The cool air tickled against her skin and sent an ache down her leg.

Twisting her leg and propping her ankle up on the log, Lacey examined the three long furrows. On either side of each one, the skin was pink, puffy, and very tender to her touch. The cuts themselves looked raw and angry. She had never seen a wound more serious than the occasional nicks she had received from her paring knife, so she shrugged. It looked bad, but no doubt all large wounds looked this way.

She released her hair from the braid and ran her slender fingers through it. Like molten flame it waved over her graceful body and hung in curling tendrils about her hips.

Her toes found a broad rock at the edge of the smooth water, and she dived into the stream head first. As she bobbed up near the other side, she gasped for the breath the frigid water seemed to have taken away. Invigorated, she again jackknifed under the clear water and skimmed near the muddy bottom. Fish flickered away at her approach, and as she surfaced amid a spray of diamond droplets, her hair streamed around her like a mermaid's. Though the storm-cooled air was much warmer than the water, she dived again, her hair forming a billowing cape of sea-fire.

The cold water eased the throbbing in her leg after a while, as it numbed her extremities. Lacey swam back to the ledge and stood, letting the gurgling current sweep around her waist as water beaded on her skin and dripped from her full breasts. This, she realized, was the first real enjoyment she had known in a long time. Fervently, she hoped her land in Oregon would have a stream with a swimming hole. If it did, she promised herself she would swim every day, weather permitting.

At last she got the pale yellow soap and stood in the shallows to wash herself. The cake was handmade and, though she had to really rub to coax a lather from it, she scrubbed every inch of her body and stood slick and dripping while she washed her hair.

When she was satisfied that she was as clean as lye soap and a good scrubbing could make her, Lacey waded to the ledge and dived into the deep hole again. Soap bubbles rose in a milky froth around her as she surfaced to rub the residue from her skin. Running her fingers through her hair, she let the current finish rinsing it, then padded slowly back to the shallows. She would have preferred to swim longer, but she wasn't sure how much time had passed.

She waded out and dried herself with the linen towel. Her leg looked as angry as it had before, but the cold water had reduced some of the swelling. She pressed the excess water from her hair and straightened the tangles with her fingers, wishing for her comb and brush, which lay in a box in the wagon.

Satisfied she'd done all she could with her hair, she stepped into her bloomers and tied the narrow ribbon that secured them. She longed to wash her clothes as well, but reason prevailed. She had no other dress, and wearing a wet one would be terribly uncomfortable and would make her look truly bedraggled. She might not want to encourage Blake Cameron, but she didn't want to remind him of a drenched cat, either.

She pulled her lawn chemise over her head and was tying its ribbon when she heard a noise. Looking up, she stared around her but could see nothing except trees and bushes. "Hello?" she called out.

Only silence answered, and she shrugged. Chipmunks frolicking among the leaves could sound as big as elks, and no doubt that was the source of the noise.

Her chemise fit her body closely, smoothing over her rounded breasts and peaking out from the cold, erect tips. She had sewn it with narrow lace straps and with lace inserts over the bodice, not because she ever expected a husband to admire her work, but because she took pleasure in pretty things. The same lacework edged her bloomers and petticoat, and all were tied with blue satin ribbons.

The noise sounded again, louder this time. Lacey frowned and glared in the direction from which it had come. "Mr. Cameron! Is that you?" She was already prepared to scold him soundly for watching her bathe. "Mr. Cameron?"

When she got no answer, she reached for her petticoat. If

it wasn't Blake, who else could it be out here in the back of nowhere? Indians?

She pushed her hair back behind her ears and looked around. "Mr. Cameron, don't play games with me!"

Suddenly the bushes parted, and an enormous grizzly lurched into the clearing.

Lacey's mouth dropped open, but she was too stunned to scream. Her terrified eyes took in the matted fur and talonlike claws. As it advanced, it limped noticeably on a badly cut foot. Lacey had no doubt at all that this was the same bear that had cornered her in the boulders. Only now there were no massive rocks to hinder him. He snarled, and yellow teeth that seemed as long as daggers lined his red and gaping mouth.

Slowly, as if moving in a dream, Lacey stepped backward into the stream. Her feet found the wet rocks that threatened to tumble her, and she balanced for a minute, not daring to take her eyes off the bear. Another few steps took her into knee-deep water. The huge beast watched her as if he were enjoying her terror.

Her questing feet found the flat ledge and more solid footing. The bear let out a ground-shaking roar and bounded toward her an all fours. At the same moment, Lacey gave a resounding shriek and dived into the deepest water.

She came up near the opposite bank and shook the water from her eyes as she grabbed at the hairy black roots that lined the steep side. Across the stream, the bear wrinkled his snout in a snarl that showed all his teeth and swiped at her with his enormous paw. Lacey screamed again, not realizing that she called Blake's name.

Bears could swim as well as they could climb trees, and Lacey knew it. Only his reluctance to get wet had saved her so far. She had the horrifying thought that he was playing with her as if he were an enormous cat and she were the helpless prey. Which, indeed, she was. She shrieked Blake's name again.

All at once Blake was there, running into the clearing with his rifle in his hands.

Perversely, Lacey screamed, "Run, Blake! Get away!"

On Blake's arrival, the animal swung his massive head around and lifted his lips in a threatening snarl as foam flecked his muzzle. Blake stopped dead still and jerked his rifle to his shoulder.

The bear, enraged with killing lust, lunged at him, the clearing reverberating with his growl.

Blake fired into the bear's mouth and jumped out of the way. The bear lunged after him, but the giant's momentum carried him past. As he ran to another spot, Blake slapped another cartridge into the chamber. The bear wheeled and reared to its full height. Blake tried to ignore the tremendous size of the bear and again shot into the yawning cavern of its mouth. This time the bear roared with pain, and his head jerked as the bullet struck him, but he wasn't stopped.

Rolling to avoid the paws, Blake again reloaded and faced the beast. This time he waited until the last minute before he fired and dodged to safety beyond the reach of the churning claws. Blood sprayed in long strands from the wounded animal, and his growls were laced with anguish. Mindlessly he lurched and righted himself for another attack.

Without taking her eyes off the drama of death being played out in the clearing, Lacey swam back and pulled herself out of the stream to crouch on the ledge as Blake fired and again evaded the pursuing jaws.

Sobbing with fright, Lacey ran toward the place where her dress lay on the grass. She dug through the folds to find the loaded pistol. Blake shot the bear again and rolled to safety as he shoved another bullet in his rifle.

Lacey's numb fingers closed on the cold metal, and she dragged the heavy pistol from the dress pocket. Gripping it in both hands, she staggered forward, fear making her feet clumsy and her body rigid and cumbersome.

Blake again leveled the rifle at the stumbling beast. He held still, waiting for the best possible shot. The bear charged, his great feet clawing clods of earth in his urge to reach the man. Blake's muscles were tense and straining as he waited, his finger tightening on the trigger.

The metallic click sounded overly loud as the gun jammed. Incredulity appeared on his face, and then he swung at the bear, using the rifle as a club. It connected with the bear's jaw with a solid crack.

Lacey was running. Pistol clutched in her hands, she raced for the bear as it turned back on Blake. Without pausing, she rammed the pistol into the base of the flat skull and pulled the trigger. An ear-shattering blast rent the air, and Lacey was propelled backward as the bear plummeted forward.

Quiet seeped back into the clearing as Lacey levered herself up on her elbows and shook her head to still her ringing ears. A tremendous mound of fur lay in a heap at her feet. Blake was nowhere to be seen.

Lacey scrambled to her knees and clawed at the mountain of hair and muscle as she screamed Blake's name over and over. Desperation and fear bolstered her strength, and she grasped the heavy head by the upper mouth and heaved the animal back.

"Blake!" she cried at the sight of him. "Blake, don't be dead!" She shoved and pulled at the bear's almost immovable mass in order to reach the man who was pinned beneath.

Miraculously, Blake's eyes blinked open, and he gasped air into his flattened lungs. His first view was that of Lacey, half-naked, dragging the gaping jaws away from him. Blake pushed against the matted fur and freed his body and one leg. Putting his foot on the massive shoulder, he and Lacey shoved the bear up enough for him to roll free.

Blake knelt in the grass, hands braced on his knees, and tried to get more air into his lungs as he stared at the glazing eyes of the beast.

"Blake!" Lacey shouted as she hurtled herself at him, tumbling him over. "Are you all right? Are you hurt?"

"Knocked the breath out of me," he managed to gasp as

his arms went around her. "I'll be all right. Let me get my breath."

She slid off his chest but clung to him desperately. "You're not dead? You're not dead?" she repeated over and over as she held him.

"Not unless you kill me now. Let me breathe, Lacey." But he kept his arms tightly about her.

"I was so scared," she sobbed. "It's the same bear that trapped me before. I'm sure of it! He has the same cut on his foot."

"You're not hurt, are you?" he asked in a more normal voice. "He didn't get to you, did he?"

"No, no. I'm not hurt." She held him so tightly she couldn't see his face. "Are you? Did he get you?"

"No, he didn't get me," Blake said with a trace of humor. "He knocked the breath out of me, but I'm all right now." His voice softened. "Thanks to you."

A trembling seized Lacey. "Let's get away from here," she murmured.

He got up and pulled Lacey to her feet, but she was shaking too hard to stand. Without hesitation, he bent and picked her up. Lacey buried her face in the comforting warmth of his neck and closed her eyes. Suddenly she was tired of being strong and independent, and she very much needed someone—Blake—to take care of her.

His long strides quickly covered the distance to the cave, and he knelt to lay her on the leaves that had cushioned their blankets. Her eyes, large with concern, were nearly black in the dim light. A chill still shook her, and he reached over to unbundle the blankets.

"Are you sure he's dead?" she demanded in a trembling voice.

"Positive. You killed him. I didn't think you could do it with a pistol."

"I was right behind him, holding the barrel against his head."

Blake pulled the blankets over her but still lay with his

arms cradling her. "You did that?" he gasped. "You ran right up to that bear and *then* shot him?"

"He was going to kill you!"

Blake stared down at her pale face and gently brushed back a wet tendril of hair. "I never expected you to do that," he whispered.

"I didn't plan to." Her eyes searched his face as if she wanted to remember every inch of it. Her arms were still holding him tightly.

"Lacey," he said softly, as if her name were an endearment. "Lacey."

He touched her face, and there was wonder in his caress as well as in his eyes. Slowly he let his fingers trail over the water-cooled smoothness of her skin and down her throat. She lay still as if she were afraid a movement would shatter the spell. He touched her shoulders, covered only by narrow bands of lace. Her skin was incredibly soft and firm. As his palm slid down the column of her arm, his eyes followed the twin mounds of her breasts that strained against the thin fabric made transparent by dampness. The dusky pink of her taut nipples lured him, and almost reverently he traced his fingers over the firm globe to capture the prize with his palm.

Lacey drew in her breath sharply, but Blake bent his head and covered her lips before she could protest. Tenderly he drank of her sweetness, feeling her untried lips part beneath his in a natural permission. Beneath his hand her nipple grew even tighter, and she arched her back to give more of herself to him. Her hands slid up his back, and he felt her fingers thread through his hair as she learned to respond to his kisses. And he had no doubt that she was learning. Her innocence was evident in the way her tongue met his, timidly, then with more assurance, and the soft moan that held a note of astonishment.

He ran his hand over her ribs to circle beneath her and draw her against him. She was trembling again, but this time he recognized it as passion. She was so slender, so delicate in his arms! He had to hold himself in careful check lest he hurt her with his greater strength.

Lacey seemed to have no such compunction, for she was kissing him with eager abandon as her body moved instinctively against his. She murmured his name in his ear and sent molten lava coursing through his veins.

"Lacey," he whispered as his wanting her approached a need. "Lacey, honey, have you ever done this before?"

"No," she answered gently, her eyes dewy soft with loving. "Never."

Her words gradually filtered through to Blake's brain, and he fought for control. "Never?" he repeated to be sure he had heard her correctly.

She shook her head and pulled herself up to place a trail of fiery kisses along the tender part of his throat.

Blake drew a deep breath and gently unwound Lacey's arms from around his neck. Folding them over her breast, he caressed her hand with his thumb. "Honey, I can't do this to you," he said with infinite tenderness. "Not like this."

She gazed up at him silently.

"Please hear my words," he continued. "I want you. God, you can't know how bad I do want you! But I can't take you like this. Last night you were scared half to death because I kissed you. If I made love with you now, when you're nearly out of your wits over being attacked by a bear, you would never forgive me."

"I'm not half out of my wits," she objected in a small voice.

He took another steadying breath and forced himself to roll off her. "Trust me, Lacey. You're in shock. I can't take advantage of you." He pulled the woolen blanket to her chin to conceal her enticing figure.

"I'm not in shock," she disagreed.

Using all the willpower he could muster, Blake stood, and she sat up to stare at him, blanket clutched where he had left it. "I'm going to go down and get your dress," he said in a carefully measured voice. "Believe me, Miss Summerfield, I won't let this happen again."

As he left, her lips silently echoed his formal use of her name. Then her confused expression crumpled as tears gathered in her eyes.

Blake strode down the slope. He felt proud of himself in the extreme, though he still ached for her. She was not only a virgin, though that was enough; she was also a lady. He knew it was possible that she had no idea at all what went on between a man and a woman. With no mother or older sisters to enlighten her, she was probably a total innocent.

He paused at the clearing and leaned his forearm against a tree. He was no despoiler of virgins, but he wanted her more than he could ever recall wanting any woman. He glanced back at the cave. Even now he wanted to run back and love her until their souls sang. That, of course, was out of the question. He made a strangled sound deep within his throat and decided to carve a haunch of bear meat in lieu of rabbit.

Lacey flicked the scalding tears from her cheeks and glared after him. How humiliating to be turned away like that! True, she was inexperienced, but she was willing to learn. Why, every woman must be unknowledgeable until she had tried it a few times!

The proper part of her tried to convince her that she should be glad he had rejected her and thus preserved her innocence, but another part of her demanded to know why she should be. She had no intention of marrying, and after all these years, she was positive she would never be asked anyway. What earthly good would her virginity do her in the lonely years to come?

She felt overwhelmed by a rare wave of self-pity, but that was preferable to the shame she had felt earlier. Blake might stroll down to the river with Ida May Calvert—she had seen him do so herself—but he shunned *her*. Lacey decided self-pity was better than asking why he would prefer a known slut to herself, so she let the tears come again.

He took his time in returning, she noticed, and when he

did, he carried her clothes in one large hand and the bear skin, tied in a bundle, and a hunk of meat in the other. She reached one arm out of the concealing blanket and snatched her dress and petticoat. Pointing at the meat, she said, "I'm not going to eat that!" Anger had finally replaced pity.

"That's up to you," he said stiffly, not looking at her. He dropped the meat into an empty flour sack and tossed in a bit of loose salt to preserve it until it could be cooked.

Lacey glared at him and turned her back. She yanked the blue gingham dress over her head to cover her bare skin and smallclothes. Then she stepped into her petticoat and jerked the ribbon so snugly it pinched her skin. Readjusting it, she buttoned the dress and smoothed her hair. At least her underwear had dried in the interval.

Sitting on a rock, she combed her fingers through her hair, then twisted it into a bun, low on the nape of her neck. She had lost several of her hairpins, but she made do with what she had. Still she kept her eyes averted, and the silence in the cave was deafening.

Blake finished securing the pans and blankets to the pack saddle and went out to get the tethered animals. Lacey cast a long look at the crushed leaves where she had lain in his arms and felt an emotion that had gone far beyond a mere physical longing. She refused to let her mind so much as shape the small word that now described her feelings for this unsettling man, but she didn't for a moment think it was simply lust.

When he returned, she helped him bridle and saddle the horse and load the pack mule. Still, the silence hung heavy, and neither dared say a word.

CHAPTER
7

Blake led the horse out of the cave and tied the pack mule's lead rope to a tree. Both animals were still skittish from the bear's earlier arrival, and the fresh hide bundled on the pack tree wasn't helping to calm them. Blake mounted and let the bay horse finish his morning ritual of crow-hopping around. When the horse was convinced that Blake was indeed serious about riding him, he flicked his ears forward and stood docilely.

"Come on," Blake called to Lacey as he kicked his left foot free of the stirrup, slid behind the saddle, and held out his hand.

Unless she wanted to walk, she had no alternative but to ride in the saddle with him. Blake had already told her she couldn't ride the pack mule because of the supplies it had to carry. Grasping the saddle horn, she put her foot in the stirrup and let Blake pull her sideways into the saddle. She threw her leg over the horse's neck, and while she arranged her full skirt as decorously as possible, Blake regained the stirrups and reached for the mule's rope.

"Will we reach the wagons tonight?" she asked coolly, her pride still stinging from his rejection of her as a woman.

With a measuring glance at the sun, Blake said, "With

this late start, could be we won't catch up until sometime tomorrow."

"Can't we hurry?" She wasn't eager to spend any more time alone with this man than she had to. Certainly not after he had so blatantly shunned her. She knew she was being unreasonable; by all rights she should be grateful that he wasn't forcing himself on her, but she recalled far too clearly the way his lips had moved on hers and how his hard body had aroused unsuspected fires within her. She had to get back to the wagons so that she could resume her avoidance of him before she did something even more shameful— like kissing him again. She wished each movement of the horse wasn't brushing their bodies together.

Blake tied the mule's rope to the saddle and nudged the horse to a quicker pace. The day was going to be a long one, because Lacey was right there in front of him. Sunlight glistened in the coppery tinge of her hair, and he knew he had only to remove the pins to send it cascading over his chest and hands. Her slender neck seemed too delicate to support the coiled skein, and his fingers longed to touch the exposed skin where short tendrils curled about the nape of her neck. The horse's gait made her supple body sway provocatively, and he wished heartily that she were riding sidesaddle, even if it was more precarious. He shifted his weight and tried to clear her from his mind.

High above them arched shimmering leaves of the dark green of late summer. Now and then Lacey saw a leaf of gold or scarlet, an early herald of approaching fall. Through the openings in the limbs, she caught sight of the gaunt peaks of the craggy mountains. Already patches of snow nestled on the loftier summits. Lacey felt as if she were running in mud against a speeding clock.

"What happens if we don't reach South Pass before snowfall?" she asked in concern, forgetting that she wasn't speaking to him.

"We'll get there. Ed Bingham knows the way."

She paused. "Are you sure we can find the wagons? This

is such a big place, and all the land is so similar through here.'' They were crossing a stream that seemed to be identical to the one that ran past the cave.

''We're heading west. Soon you'll see the Platte River. I cut through the woods to save time.''

''Are you sure you know how to do that?''

''West is west,'' he said stolidly. She would be easier to ignore if she would just keep quiet, and if she didn't smell so good.

A twinge of pain from her scratched leg made Lacey wince. Apparently she had reinjured the leg pulling the bear off Blake. Soon, the wound started to pulse with a dull throb.

As they followed the stream, taking the easiest route through the thick underbrush, the poplars gave way to a forest of birch with chalky trunks marked with black scars. The stream widened to a pond, and Lacey pointed at several piles of sticks mounded on the surface of the water.

''Beaver,'' Blake commented.

Circling the pond, the horse lowered his head to nip at the knee-high grass that grew in lush profusion. Lacey shifted her attention from the jagged mountains to the long meadow and cocked her head to one side. ''What made that trail?'' she asked, indicating the broad swath of trampled grass. ''Elk?''

Blake, too, had been studying the mountains, trying to figure out which notch was South Pass. Her words drew his gaze back to the meadow, and he stiffened. ''Be quiet,'' he said gruffly as he narrowed his eyes and examined the clearing.

''What's the matter?''

''Hush!''

A bird called far up on the hill and was answered by another one deep in the woods. Aside from the familiar creak of saddle leather and the jangle of the horse's bit, there was no sound. Blake leaned over and studied the path more carefully. Embedded in the soft mud beneath the tangle of weeds was the print of an unshod horse. A worried frown knotted his brow, and he turned his animal toward the trees. True, many pioneers rode unshod horses, there being a scarcity of blacksmiths in the wilderness, but this imprint showed a ragged outline, as if the hoof had never been trimmed or filed. Also, there were no wagon tracks, and the trail led north rather than in the direction logical for a group following a map.

Lacey grew very quiet. She, too, had seen the track, and while she didn't have Blake's expertise, she wasn't slow-witted. "Indians?" she whispered as the trees enveloped them.

"Probably not," he lied, "but there's no need to take the chance."

"Don't lie to me."

"Indians," he said after a brief hesitation. "Heading north. I guess there were maybe half a dozen, judging by the width of the trail."

"Can you tell how long ago?"

"They were here since the rain, for sure. With the grass still bent over like that, I'd say we didn't miss them by far." He frowned at the back of her head, unable to see her expression. "You aren't going to scream or faint, are you?" he demanded.

"With Indians nearby? Don't be absurd!" she snapped in a low voice.

"I guess you aren't the giddy sort, at that," he replied as he remembered how she had shot the bear.

Lacey's eyes nervously swept the surrounding bushes. "Are you certain they were heading north? Maybe they were going south and we might run up on them."

"No, the grass was bent the wrong way for that to be true." The denseness of the forest slowed the horse's gait, but Blake had no intention of leaving the thick cover. The slower pace was costing them valuable time, but it was much safer.

For the next hour they hardly spoke, and then only in

whispers. The passage of time had renewed Lacey's confidence, for if the savages meant to attack, they would have done so where the paths had crossed. Instead of stopping for the noon meal, Blake and Lacey ate slices of jerky and dried apples as they rode on.

Lacey glanced distastefully at the sack that contained the salted bear meat. "When are we going to cook it?" she asked.

"Tonight. We will be late eating, but it's safer that way."

"But isn't it easier to see a fire in the dark?"

"A person wouldn't see it unless he was nearby, whereas smoke in a clear sky can be seen for miles."

She thought about this for a while. "You sure know a lot about this sort of thing. Why is that?"

He grinned. "We have our share of Indian problems in Texas. But most of this I learned during our war for independence from Mexico. I was a scout for the Texas army."

"I didn't know that!" She looked back at him.

"That's where I got this," he said, touching the small, crescent-shaped scar on his cheek. "It's a memento of San Jacinto."

"And the Mexican?"

"I'm here and he's not." He grinned down at her.

Lacey faced forward, and her lips held a shadow of a smile. Somehow, knowing Blake had fought the Mexican army made her feel safer, though fighting was fighting, and a part of her was very opposed to violence as a means of settling any dispute. Still, she was glad to hear he could take care of himself.

By midafternoon they angled back to the Platte, and Blake pulled the horse to a stop.

"This doesn't look familiar," she pointed out.

"It does to me. See that rock way up there? The one that looks like a castle?"

She shaded her eyes against the sun and nodded.

"That's where the wagons crossed."

"Well, why are we stopping here? Let's go."

"Do you realize how far that is? Distances can be deceiving out here. If we rode to that rock, we would lose two, maybe three hours. I think we should cross here."

"But if the trail is there . . ."

"We can pick it up on the other side." He dismounted and walked to the river.

Ochre water laden with mud flowed over the shallow bottomland. In places the surface curled and eddied in a serpentine dance, and the rainstorm had glutted the many fingerlike rivulets.

"Why are we just standing here?" Lacey called out to him. "Get on the horse and let's go."

He shook his head. "Something's not right. The water didn't look like this before."

Lacey sighed and tried to control her impatience. "You said the wagons crossed near here. It must be safe."

In deep concentration, Blake frowned at the seemingly turgid river. At length, he said, "Get off the horse and let me ride out to see how deep it is."

She slid off the horse. When her foot struck the rocks, she flinched. The ground seemed to dip under her for a moment as pain coursed through her leg, and she held on to the saddle for support. When the wave of vertigo passed, she went to Blake and stared at the water as he did.

"I don't like the looks of it," he mused as if he were thinking aloud.

"I've never liked the Platte. It has a muddy taste and makes your mouth feel gritty. Let's cross it and put it behind us."

He swung into the saddle and tossed her the mule's lead rope. The horse flattened his ears expressively and edged with a show of reluctance into the water. Blake nudged him forward, leaning over to try to peer into the cloudy water.

Suddenly, the horse plunged downward and his nostrils and eyes dilated with fear as his hooves flailed in deep water. Blake grabbed for the saddle horn as the animal fell, and his feet were washed out of the stirrups by the unsuspected current. The horse held his head high as he fought to stay afloat, but the river was carrying them downstream in a circular motion.

"Blake!" Lacey cried out. She saw the horse bob under, then surface with Blake holding tight to its mane and the saddle. She tried to run, pulling the reluctant mule behind her. "Blake!"

The water was swift, but the Platte was normally shallow, and before too long the horse managed to find a shelf of dirt and scramble out. As soon as the horse reached dry ground, he shook himself like a dog, nearly unseating Blake. Lacey stumbled but kept her balance as she ran to him, with the mule's eyes rolling in displeasure.

"Are you all right?" she demanded needlessly.

"Yeah, just wet. There's a bad current out there." He got off and stood dripping on the muddy bank. "We can't cross here," he pointed out.

"Let's go to that castle-shaped rock and cross where the wagons did."

"It's no shallower there." He regarded the river thoughtfully. "I remember noticing this stretch along here all looked about the same. We might spend hours riding to that spot and still not be able to get to the other side of the river."

"Well, what will we do?" Lacey wasn't feeling well at all, and her leg throbbed.

He looked downstream and caught his lower lip in his teeth as he pondered. "If we go that way, the river may widen out. If it's shallow, the strong current won't be a threat."

"That's out of our way," she objected.

"I don't see another way to get across."

Lacey had to admit that he had a point, so she remounted the horse, and they rode downstream. As Blake had predicted, the Platte widened and the water grew shallower.

"We could cross here," she said when he continued to ride. "Why are we still following the river?"

"Not here." He dismounted, picked up a large rock, and

tossed it onto a sandy hummock that protruded from the water just offshore. The rock landed with a dull thud and sank out of sight. "Quicksand. Ed Bingham told me how to spot it."

Lacey swallowed nervously, her green eyes large and luminous.

"We'll go downstream a little farther." Blake swung up behind her and turned the horse's head to follow the water's course.

After what seemed to be an eternity to Lacey, he again dismounted. "Now what? Is this the place?" The yellow shallows looked as marshy as the quicksand to her.

"I think this may be our best bet." Blake glanced at the lowering sun but made no comment. Instead he untied the lariat from his saddle, looped one end over the pommel, and tied the other around his waist.

"What are you doing?" she asked suspiciously.

"This time we are going to try it a different way. You stay on the horse, and I'll go ahead of you. If you see me in trouble, pull back on the reins and drag me out."

"Drag you out?" she asked. "Trouble?" Her thoughts seemed to skitter out of her grasp like a covey of quail. "Blake, how do you know there isn't quicksand under the water?"

"I don't," he answered with forced cheerfulness. "Just stay on the horse and keep an eye on me."

Lacey's mouth felt as dry as wool, but she managed to nod. Blake fed out the rope until it was taut between his body and the horse. Then, he waded out into the current with Lacey keeping the lifeline tight.

Several times he stumbled, and each time her heart leaped with fear. She could see nothing under the muddy surface; as far as she knew, they could be on the brink of another ledge or perhaps treading on a thin crust over bottomless quicksand. She suspected her imagination was running wild, but she couldn't control it.

Once Blake stopped and tested the riverbed ahead of him

with his foot, then angled sharply upstream. Lacey asked no questions, but made sure the horse followed his path exactly. After what seemed to be hours, but was actually only minutes, Blake waded out of the waist-deep water and heaved a sigh of relief as Lacey joined him on the far side of the Platte.

"Thank goodness that's behind us," she exclaimed. "I wouldn't want to do that again."

Blake studied the snow-crowded mountains where bruised storm clouds were gathering. "Don't feel relieved too soon. We have to cross it again tomorrow."

"What? Why didn't we stay on the other side, then?"

"Ed must have had a reason. The marked trail crosses the Platte twice. I suspect the river loops high to the north, and we would waste too much time following it. Or maybe it has impassable cliffs. At any rate, we should stay as close to the intended trail as we can."

Lacey moved her leg forward so he could mount behind her. "It looks as if it may be raining in the mountains. Or snowing."

"South Pass is supposed to be the last to get snow. We'll make it through." Blake tried to keep his apprehension out of his voice. Snow wasn't as pressing a problem at the moment as the impending rainstorm. The river was almost impassable already, and more water was on the way.

Blake and Lacey made camp beside the river, and Blake built a fire in a hollow between a jumble of boulders. The Indians were on the opposite side of the river, as far as he knew, but he didn't want to chance calling attention to their presence. He rigged a spit from some forked limbs, and Lacey soon had the bear meat browning, along with a handful of dried beans.

While she waited for the meal to cook, Lacey sat on one rock and leaned back on another as she gazed at the faint silhouette of the mountains. "I'll bet if I could see past those peaks I'd be looking straight at Oregon," she mused.

"Oregon is farther north. You're looking toward California."

Lacey turned her head slightly. "I can hardly wait to see my very own land. There will be a stream running through it and a hole deep enough for swimming. I'll build my cabin close to it so I won't have to go far for water."

"Did you have to walk far to get water back home?"

She peered at him through the darkness. "Of course not. I told you what sort of house I lived in. There was a well on the porch and a pump in the kitchen."

"That's right. I forgot." He sat on a boulder below her and watched the firelight lay gilt over her profile.

She leaned her head back on the rock and again looked toward Oregon. "In time I'll have glass windows and lace curtains, and I'll braid rugs to cover the floor—a wooden floor, of course."

"Just like at home?" he asked softly. When she didn't respond, he said, "Lacey, you're going to be real lonely up there on that mountain of yours. Until the railroad goes through, you probably won't have any neighbors."

"I don't care. I like being alone."

"Do you? Have you ever lived all by yourself, day in and day out? I have, and believe me, it's damned lonely. And I didn't have to build a cabin by myself from scratch or live on game until I could harvest a crop."

"Are you saying I can't do it? I won't take Papa with me unless he changes his drunken ways. I told you that. He wouldn't work anyway, and I'd have to do twice as much."

"I wasn't thinking of him. Whatever the trouble is between you two, it's something you have to settle on your own. Besides, maybe he'd rather live in a settlement. Most people would."

"Then what are you trying to say?" Lacey looked down at him.

The fire bronzed her skin and made her slightly parted lips seem rosy in contrast with her white teeth. Her eyes were darker than pine needles, and her hair was ruddy flame.

Blake sat quietly, letting his eyes feast on her. At last he said, "A woman shouldn't try to do all that alone. She ought to have a man."

The crackle of the embers and the sizzling of the meat were the only sounds as silence spun a delicate web between them. Lacey couldn't take her eyes from Blake's. Something seemed to be building between them, and the idea terrified her. She cared for him—far too much—but she couldn't bear the idea that he felt the same. Love was a trap that surrounded two people and blinded them to all kinds of faults. She was afraid to see the expression that lit his dark eyes, even as her heart leaped at the possibility that he might also care for her.

"I don't have a man," she forced herself to say, "and I don't want one. I can take care of myself but not a husband and children as well. It will be hard enough to take care of only myself."

"The idea is for two people to take care of each other," Blake told her.

"I never saw it work that way," she answered pensively. "I don't think it can happen."

"I never saw it either, but I'm sure it can. You just have to put the right two together. It's a matter of proper matching, like choosing a team of horses."

"Well, I'm not a horse, and I don't see anybody clamoring to take care of me," Lacey stated firmly. She was glad that the cool tone had returned to her voice. "Even if someone were, I'd say no. I don't need anybody. I don't want anybody."

Blake sighed. "You're going to get real lonesome up there on that mountain, lady, but that's up to you. As for me, I'm not looking for anybody to take care of. I had my fill of that." A sadness was coming over him, and for some reason her words made him feel bereft, so he said steadfastly, "I'm not ever going to get married again."

"No one asked you to," she pointed out.

"When a man gets married, he's expected to give up

everything from freedom to hard liquor. In return he gets to build fence from dawn to dusk and do chores that should rightfully be shared, and then he has to wait on his wife and listen to her complaining about all her ailments. No, ma'am, I've had my fill of marriage.''

"If that's the way yours turned out, I should think you would have," Lacey agreed.

"That's right. No more ties for me. If I feel like staying in Oregon, I will. If I take it in my head to see California, I'll do that instead. Either way, I've got my freedom, and that's important to me."

"Freedom is important to me, too," she affirmed. "I don't want to be tied down, either. I'm going to sit in the middle of my seventy acres and shoot anybody that trespasses."

Their eyes met and held, and each wondered why the other looked as miserable as he himself felt.

Finally Lacey said, "The meat and beans ought to be done now."

"I guess so." He continued to look directly at her.

Lacey drew a deep breath. "As I said before, I'm not going to eat that bear meat."

Blake realized he was staring at her, and he turned toward the fire. "Yes, you are. We'll have to ride hard tomorrow, and you need your strength. Eating dried beans isn't enough." He cut a slice of meat and put it on his tin plate along with half the beans and handed it to her. "Take it."

Reluctantly she did as he said. Lacey knew he was right but she felt nauseated at the idea of swallowing the flesh of that savage bear. Blake evidently had no such misgivings, however, because he was already cutting himself a chunk of meat, using the skillet as his plate.

Lacey slowly cut off a small piece and put it in her mouth. The flavor wasn't bad, but she had to force herself to chew.

"You aren't going to go all weak and fluttery, are you?" he demanded.

Her chin rose in defiance. "Don't worry about me!" If he

could do it, she could, too. She cut a larger piece and glared at him while she chewed.

Blake nodded at her in tacit approval as a faint smile tilted one corner of his lips.

Lacey ate all he had given her and considered asking for more of the meat just to prove she could, but decided there was no point in being foolish in her pride. Her stomach was rebelling already. She tried to move her aching leg to a more comfortable position and waited with apparent serenity for him to finish eating. She was feeling curiously light-headed and was eager to get the dishes washed so she could lie down. After what he'd said about having to listen to complaints, she wasn't about to tell him of her discomfort.

When he was through, Blake went to the river to get a bucket of water for her to rinse the dishes in. While he was gone she scraped the leftover scraps into a hole and buried them, then started washing the plate and skillet in the pan of hot water.

She had the sensation of being alone now that he was out of sight. No sound came to her, and she felt suddenly very lonely. This was the way it would be on her seventy acres, just as Blake had said. Lacey's hands trembled as she thought about this. Was she doing the right thing? she wondered. But it was too late to undo it. She had spent all her money on the land, and she was over halfway there. She couldn't change her mind now.

When Blake reappeared, carrying the bucket of water, Lacey felt a profound relief.

CHAPTER
8

Lacey awoke with a ringing in her ears and a throbbing fire in her leg. As she got to her feet, the landscape shimmered and danced in front of her eyes, so she steadied herself against a boulder for a minute.

"Is something wrong?" Blake asked as he saddled the horse.

"No. No, I guess I stood up too fast." She blinked and the world stopped whirling, but the morning breeze felt icy on her skin. "It seems colder today. Maybe an early fall is on the way."

"Colder? I was thinking it was warmer than usual. I guess I've been moving around more and got heated up."

Lacey knelt and sliced a piece of the smoked bear meat to put on the sourdough bread. The mere sight of it made her queasy, however, so she hastily handed it to Blake. She ate only bread, hoping he wouldn't notice.

She dreaded getting back on the horse. All she wanted to do was go back to bed and wait for the sickness to pass. A shiver ran through her, and she realized she must have a fever. Also, her leg was really hurting, and she had to try hard not to limp. After her speech the night before about not needing anyone, and his about not wanting to listen to a female complain, she could hardly let him know how she was faring.

Blake drank the last of his coffee and finished the portion she had declined, as well. He washed out the pot and tied it to the mule's pack. All the while his attention was on the building storm clouds. Lacey rolled up the blankets and tied them on the mule. Again the ground seemed to dip and teeter, and she had to struggle hard to keep her face a mask.

"Let's go. We have a lot of territory to cover." He looked back at the bruised sky. "I sure hope that rain holds off until we can cross the river. I guess it would be too much to wish we could find the wagons before we get wet."

Lacey shivered again. The very idea of getting drenched in a cold shower gave her a chill. She felt as if she were freezing as it was.

Reluctantly, Lacey got on the horse and swung her leg over. The resulting pain made her catch her breath and close her eyes tightly. Blake finished tying the mule's lead rope to the saddle and mounted behind her. She grasped the pommel and tried to prepare herself for a day that promised to be much longer than the last had been.

Blake frowned at the lowering clouds. They were drifting down from the mountains, and as they did, they settled closer to the ground. Their undersides were blue-black and rolling, and even as he watched, a finger of ragged lightning jabbed at the earth. "Let's angle away from the river," he suggested. "The wagon trail goes east to west, more or less, so we should be able to find it if we head north. I think we can save some time if we do that, and there'll be no need to worry about those Indians. We're a good bit west of where they headed north. There's almost no chance we'll run across them, so put your mind at ease."

"All right," Lacey agreed. His voice sounded so steady and protective. She was sorry she had lied to him about her childhood. She supposed it was a little matter, but somehow it seemed to make a big difference to her. She hated to lie about anything.

Blake didn't notice how quiet Lacey had become. All his attention was focused on willing the storm to hold off and the trail to appear. Two hours later, he was growing very worried. By now they should have crossed the tracks cut by the wagon's iron-rimmed wheels.

They topped a foothill, and there before them lay a deep canyon. Blake scowled. He didn't recall Ed's mentioning a canyon, and this was a big one.

"Which way do we go from here?" Lacey asked.

Thankfully, he noted, she didn't seem disturbed. A hysterical woman was the last thing he needed right now. Before he could answer, she pointed to the right. "I think north is that way."

"That's east. North is straight ahead." He stood up in the stirrups as if that would give him a better view. "I think I see the trail," he said with relief. "It's over there by that outcropping of grayish rocks."

Lacey looked, but she saw only prairie bordered by a forest on her left. "I don't see it."

"See how the land smooths out there and winds around? I'm sure that's the trail!"

"How can we get there? The sides of this canyon are too steep to climb."

"This way seems easier." He reined the horse around and nudged him to a quick walk around and over the low-growing bushes that covered the rocky surface.

Lacey gritted her teeth as the animal's smooth gait jolted her leg. How could she ever have thought Blake's horse had an easy pace when each step brought her torment? She looked up dully as thunder rolled in the distance. The prairie seemed dusky beneath the clouds and almost vividly hued where the storm's shadows hadn't yet reached. The tempest hovered and growled like an angered monster.

The horse stumbled on one of the fist-sized rocks that littered the way, causing Lacey to gasp. Though Blake gave no sign of having heard her outcry, he slowed to a more cautious pace. The canyon narrowed and flattened, then gaped open again. As far as he could see, the ground parted in a deep yawn.

"Damn!" he muttered in an angry frustration. This was getting them nowhere. The storm was almost upon them, and he hadn't so much as glimpsed the Platte River in over two hours.

They backtracked, and their path became clearer of brush. Blake's eyes searched the far side of the canyon, and this time he was positive he saw the wagon tracks leading west. Yet the deep canyon kept them from reaching their goal.

For another hour they rimmed the canyon. Blake was growing more and more concerned, but Lacey merely sat quietly in the saddle. Then, without warning, the canyon sides sloped outward, and he saw a way down to the canyon floor and across.

He kicked the horse to a trot, dragging the reluctant mule behind them. A stormy day was no time to linger at the bottom of a canyon. The horse broke into a canter, and Blake put his arm securely around Lacey to hold her in the saddle. She made a strange sound and he felt her stomach tighten, but he had no time to talk to her.

As he neared the creek that rushed through the floor of the gulley, Blake noticed that the water flowed from the direction of the nearby storm. Blake pressed his heels into the horse's sides, sending him splashing through the water. Blake angled downstream and was climbing the bank on the other side when he heard the sound he had dreaded. Looking back, Blake saw a wall of water sweep past, swelling the stream to a raging river, full of bobbing tree limbs and gushing torrents. He breathed a heartfelt sigh of relief as the horse and mule climbed the rest of the incline. If he had been only a few minutes slower, they would have been trapped on the other side or, worse, swept away by the flash flood.

Night seemed to have fallen, although he knew it was still

afternoon. The rolling clouds were over them now, and as if they had been waiting for a clear target, the rain descended on the couple with a vengeance.

Blake pulled the mule alongside and fished in the pack for his poncho as the sheets of rain washed over them. Ear-shattering peals of thunder crashed around them. Lacey trembled uncontrollably, and Blake remembered how frightened she was of storms.

Finding the oiled cloth, he draped it over them, pulling Lacey back against him. She was shivering as if she were having a chill, and her teeth were chattering audibly. "Lacey?" he said with concern as he looked over her shoulder. Her eyes were closed, and she seemed unaware of the rain. "Lacey!" He shook her, and she roused slightly.

He had no idea what was wrong with her, but he knew he had to find shelter. Leaving the canyon behind, he headed for the nearby trees.

Lacey lay against him, her face upturned toward the rain. Blake bent over her and cradled her to protect her as much as possible. She curled closer and buried her face close to his bare neck. Blake became alarmed at the heat from her skin. She shouldn't feel so hot when she was shaking all over from the cold.

"Lacey," he said gruffly, "are you sick? What's wrong?"

She weakly nodded and mumbled, "I told you I didn't want to eat that bear meat. Made me sick."

"There's nothing wrong with the meat or I would be sick, too."

"I'm sorry I lied to you," she rambled. "I mean, all those things I told you."

Blake knew her aimless speech was a bad sign. "Oh, hell!" he spit out. "Why in the hell didn't you tell me something was wrong with you?" Lacey murmured a string of unintelligible words and looped her arm around him. "Women are too damned much trouble!" he growled to hide his mounting panic.

The trees covering them broke the slanting panels of rain,

but the storm's winds tossed the limbs in spastic sweeps that lashed the riders. Blake huddled protectively over Lacey, but there was nothing he could do to make her comfortable.

The horse was heading away from the danger of the open plain and deeper into the woods. Blake let him walk. For several hours now he had been almost positive they were lost. The trail he thought he had seen must have been just a natural lay of the land. If the wagon train had come near the canyon, he would certainly have seen some sign of it. They were lost. He now had no doubt.

Blake was a confident man as a rule and had rarely been bested by either man or circumstance, but he was feeling as bewildered as a child. His only thought was to find a safe place to wait out the storm. Then he could think of what to do next. The horse wanted to walk, and that seemed to be as good a plan as any, so Blake gave him rein.

Before much longer, the horse's steps quickened, and his ears pitched forward in anticipation. Blake tried to see what the animal sensed, but even under the trees the rain was blinding. He gave the horse his head and concentrated on keeping Lacey balanced in the saddle and as dry as he could.

After another minute or so, the horse whickered low, and the mule's long ears flipped toward its nose. Blake looked up to see a tiny cabin at the edge of a small clearing. With an exclamation, he urged the horse forward.

He could tell at once the cabin was deserted. The front door was canted to one side on its solitary hinge, and grass grew between the planks of the steps. Still, it was shelter, and behind it was a shed for the animals. He gave thanks for the sixth sense that animals seemed able to tap and rode into the shed.

Lacey clung to the saddle as he dismounted, then almost fell into his arms. "Can you stand up?" he asked as he supported her. "We found a dry place."

She lifted her head and looked around with a dazed expression. "I'm all right," she muttered.

"Sure you are." There was no conviction at all in his

voice. "You just caught a chill from the rain. Stand here while I get the bedroll."

She held on to the side of the hay rick while he unsaddled the animals and pulled some hay down to them. Slinging the bedroll over his shoulder, Blake put his arm around Lacey. She leaned on him for support but made her feet move forward. Again the rain pelted her, but she forced herself to cross the small yard to the house.

The cabin was very old, but hadn't been empty very long. A quantity of wood was stacked inside, probably from the previous winter, and a chair and a bed still stood there. Blake eased Lacey onto the chair and knelt beside her, rubbing her hands between his. "We're fine now," he tried to reassure her. "This must be a trapper's cabin. That, or whoever owned it just packed up and left. See? We even have a bed."

Lacey's eyes met his, and she nodded. The walk across the yard had used up all her strength.

"Sit here," he ordered. "I'll make the bed." He unrolled the blankets on the thin mattress and hoped there were no vermin in it. Most of the trappers he knew were no cleaner than they had to be. Then he went back to Lacey and eased her to her feet. "You have to get out of this wet dress," he told her. His fingers moved over the buttons of her bodice, and she made no effort to stop him.

As quickly as he could, Blake stripped off her dress and petticoat. Her smallclothes were nearly dry, so he left them on her. Lacey swayed, and he caught her before she fell. He carried her tenderly to the bed and laid her down. When he did, her injured leg rolled to one side, displaying the swollen, red flesh beneath the edge of her bloomers.

Blake felt as though he had been kicked in the stomach. Muttering an oath that would have shocked her had she been conscious, he pulled up the leg of her bloomers to see the rest of the wound. The three scratches were infected and obviously had been for quite some time. So far, the telltale red line along a vein that indicated gangrene was not there, but judging from the appearance of the injury, it would not be long in developing.

He drew the covers over her and stared down at her. Why hadn't she told him? He wondered, though, what good it would have done if she had. He had no medicine, and they were lost. Gently he touched her face but drew back his hand as he felt the heat radiating from her skin. For a minute Blake sat in stunned silence, staring at her.

A fire. He needed to start a fire. He got up and coaxed a spark from his flint. Soon a tendril of smoke curled up the chimney, and he gently blew on the tinder until it began to blaze. Food. She needed food.

He ran outside, through the rain, to the shed. The animals glanced up at his hurried entrance but continued chewing the hay. Blake shouldered the pack saddle and carried it back to the house. Lacey lay just as he had left her. He found the sack of meat and the bucket and ran out to fill it with water from the stream.

"Don't panic," he scolded himself as he almost put out the fire with the sloshing water. "Don't make things worse than they are."

He put the water on to heat and sliced meat into it to make a stew. Then he wet a handkerchief in rainwater and went to the bed. Sitting beside Lacey, he tenderly sponged her feverish face. She was flushed with temperature, and when she opened her eyes, they were glassy and dark.

"Don't worry, Lacey. I'll take care of you. Everything is going to be all right."

She gazed up at him but didn't speak. When he started to wipe her forehead, she reached up and caught his hand. Silently, she pressed his palm to her lips and kissed him. "Don't leave me," she whispered.

"No," he said softly as he caressed her hot face. "I'll never leave you, Lacey."

Her eyes closed, and she was suddenly very still. Fear sprang in him as he watched her. Then he pressed his ear to her chest and heard the quick thump of her heart. Relief flooded over him. She was still alive. For a moment he had thought . . .

He pulled back the covers and started sponging her face and neck. The only way he could help her was to bring down her fever. Frequently wringing the cloth in the bucket of cool water he continued his ministrations. He had pulled her chemise up to just below her breasts so that he could mop the blazing skin on her stomach and midriff. His sense of propriety had kept him from undressing her completely, though he couldn't help noticing the fullness of her breasts, covered only by the thin, gauzy material.

When the stew was ready, he lifted her head and roused her enough to spoon the broth down her throat. She managed to swallow and even to protest feebly. This he took as a good sign.

As he laid her back down, he bent over her so that his lips were almost on hers. "You're going to live, Lacey Summerfield. I'll be damned if I'll let you die on me! Fight it! You're going to live!" His voice was angry and commanding, and she stirred uneasily. Gently he pulled her face back and said in a softer voice, "I've looked for you too long, Lacey. All my life. Don't leave me now." He kissed her lightly, then sighed, his face lined with worry.

Leaving the wet cloth on her brow, he pulled the chair over to the fire and ate while his clothes steamed dry. His mind was charging one way and then another as he tried to find a solution to this problem. He was lost. Reason told him they must have been going the wrong way ever since they killed the bear. Otherwise they would have recrossed the Platte long before. Only his stubbornness had prevented him from seeing this sooner. The wagons were gone, and, in all likelihood, were beyond their reach even if he managed to find the trail. Blake ran his finger through his dark hair. There *was* a way out of this. There had to be. It was just a matter of figuring it out.

He rested his forearms on his knees and slowed his thoughts. Ed Bingham had told him a lot about the trail. Ed had been leading wagons over it since the first year it opened, and he knew every hill and stream.

Blake strained his memory for some clue. Then he recalled a conversation he'd had with Ed one night just before Lacey disappeared. Ed had told him about a town that had been settled several years earlier just south of the trail. Ed had not known or had not mentioned why the people had chosen this place to settle, but had said that it was too far out of the way for them to go through there. The town stood on the banks of the Sweetwater River. Blake thoughtfully rubbed his chin. The stream that cut through the canyon bore no resemblance to the sluggish Platte. While it wasn't large enough to be the Sweetwater as Ed had described it; it might be one of its feeders.

Blake took a stick of kindling and drew a line in the dirt floor. That was the canyon. Then he tried to draw the route they had taken. Mostly, they had ridden northwest, so the Platte must be south. He extended the lines and they met. Just as Ed had said, the Sweetwater and the Platte joined. Hope flickered to life. He again studied the lines to see if he had made a mistake. Then he drew in the trail as he guessed it should be. As he had thought, they were nowhere near it. They were, however, quite close to where Ed had said the town was located.

Blake looked over at Lacey. She was as sick as anyone he had ever seen. The town was closer than the wagons and should be easier to find, since the wagons were always on the move. He had to take the risk. Even if he found the wagons, Lacey couldn't be cared for there. Everyone was busy trying to stay alive and outrace the snow. She needed a bed and medicine. Again he studied the map he had drawn. The town was her only real chance.

After he was sure he had drawn it as accurately as he could remember, Blake went back to Lacey's side and resumed sponging her. The hours stretched into darkness, but he kept smoothing her hot skin until at last her breathing became less labored and she slept.

CHAPTER
9

By morning, the rain had swept out of the hills and into the valley, leaving the air crisp and the earth drenched. Blake shifted his tired muscles and again sponged Lacey's feverish face. He warmed the remains of the previous night's gruel and spooned it into her mouth. As she swallowed convulsively, he tried not to worry that her fever had not gone away during the night.

"Lacey," he said softly, "we're going to change our plans." He had no idea if she could hear him, but he continued anyway. "There's a settlement near here on the banks of the Sweetwater. I drew a map last night, and the way I've got it figured, we're closer to it than we are to the wagon train, so we're going to go there. After you get well, we can meet up with another train to Oregon." He hoped he sounded more confident than he felt.

He looked down at Lacey's ashen face. History seemed to be repeating itself. Catherine had insisted that she was ill for so long with her imaginary ailments that, when she did need help, he didn't respond quickly enough to prevent her death. This time, he hadn't been watching Lacey closely enough to tell when she needed help. He should have known that those scratches could get infected. He shouldn't have waited for her to ask for help. And now . . . Fear made anger leap within him. This time the end would be different. He would see that it was!

He bent to take the cloth from Lacey's forehead and was surprised when she reached up and weakly caught his hand. Her green eyes opened, as fever-bright as jewels.

"Leave me," she whispered. "Don't stay behind any longer or you will never find the others."

"Hush," he said gruffly. "I'm not about to leave you behind. Didn't you hear what I said about the settlement?"

"But the wagons . . ."

"Let me worry about that." He covered her hand with his. Her fingers curled like the petals of a flower in his palm, and he noticed how fragile and delicate they were. Tenderness tightened his chest, and he gripped her hand reassuringly. "I'm going to take care of you," he stated firmly.

She closed her eyes and he went outside to saddle the horse and strap the pack on the other animal. Blake turned his attention to the vivid blue sky; such a contrast from the day before. He searched the horizons for a telltale thread of smoke that would signal the location of the settlement, but found no such help. That left him with an important decision: When he returned to the stream that fed the Sweetwater, should he go upstream or down? He shook his head to clear his thoughts; the answer was obvious. Downstream. It had to flow into the Sweetwater.

Lacey roused slightly when he put her on the horse and mounted behind her, but she was too weak to balance in the saddle. He swung her around so her injured leg lay against him, and he slipped her arm around his waist.

Blake felt a tug at the locked door of his heart. Steel determination replaced the worry, and his jaw muscles clenched. He wouldn't fail Lacey as he had Catherine. Suddenly he knew he was going to save her or die, himself, in the attempt. With firm resolution he rode back to the canyon and reined the horse downstream, spurring him to a lope.

The crevasse grew smaller; then the stream widened into

a riverbed as the terrain became steep and crested in a series of wooded hills. The horse sat back on its haunches as loose stones sprayed down the slopes under its pounding hooves. Blake kept up the hard pace, weaving in and out among the trees, keeping the river to his left and in sight. He had learned a lesson from the winding Platte and wasn't about to lose the only guide to the settlement.

The horse, unaccustomed to carrying double weight at such a pace, lathered into a sweat. The pack mule flattened its long ears after an hour's gallop and balked at the speed. Without hesitation, Blake cut the lead rope and set the animal free to follow or not as it pleased. Without the mule in tow, the horse moved forward more easily.

Blake shielded Lacey as well as he could from the branches, but he kept up the straining pace. Time was more important to her survival than his horse or his belongings. When a sheer outcropping of rock barred their path, he guided the horse into the water and half swam, half waded around it.

Lacey lay limp in his arms, only her persistent fever assuring him she was still alive. When he glanced down, he could see her bright hair nestled beneath his chin and her slender form molded against his body. Grim determination kept him going. He was racing against death, and at times he could almost feel it hot on his heels.

The ground smoothed into rolling hills of grass still green from the fading summer. Towering poplars and silvery birches thickened and became woods. The horse was stumbling now and breathing in rasping gasps. The trees slowed their progress, and the branches clutched at their clothing.

Finally the horse stopped, unable to go any farther. He stood, heaving, his legs spread wide and trembling. Blake slid to the ground with Lacey and paused only long enough to pull the saddle and bridle off the horse. He patted the horse and let him go. Leaving his gear where it hit the ground, Blake lifted Lacey into his arms and set out walking through the woods.

When he first saw the cabins he thought they must be a mirage or a trick of the light because they blended so well with the forest and were just as silent. No people walked the wide streets, and he could hear no voices.

Staggering under Lacey's weight and in near exhaustion, Blake stumbled to the nearest house and banged on the door. Only silence greeted him. Frantically, he hurried to the next and then the next. All were empty.

Refusing to believe fate could have brought him to a ghost town, Blake reeled toward a large white frame building near the center of the town where he saw horses with buggies tied to long hitching rails and to nearby trees. He managed to climb the low steps and used the last of his strength to kick open the door. With a resounding crack, the door flew back against the wall.

Rows of startled faces jerked around to stare at him.

Blake shuffled into the room and looked around mutely. His tired mind at last grasped the reason for the town's deserted streets and empty houses. This was Sunday. He was in a church.

A big man near the door scrambled to his feet and took Lacey from Blake's numb arms. His movement seemed to break the stunned silence, for the others then rushed to assist the strange couple.

"Help her," Blake managed to gasp. "Her leg—it's bad." Then he crumpled to the floor.

Blake felt himself being lifted and carried outside, and he turned his head to see about Lacey. The man who took her from him was carrying her easily, and Blake reached over to touch her copper hair before she was out of his reach.

"Take him to my house," the big man ordered. "It's the closest."

Blake braced himself as best he could against the unintentional jostling and was glad when he was deposited in the main room of the house. The man carrying Lacey, followed by several women, walked on into the adjoining room. Blake leaned forward and watched as they laid her on a downy bed. Then the man came out and closed the door behind him, leaving the women to tend to Lacey.

He came to stand by Blake's chair and smiled down at him. "Welcome, friend. Thy wife is in the best of hands. Thee must not fret."

Blake blinked and wondered if he had heard correctly.

"My name is Hiram Gibson. My wife Sarah is the midwife and very clever with the ways of healing. She is with thy wife." When Blake only stared at him, Hiram leaned closer. "Can thee hear me, friend?"

After another moment Blake nodded. "Who are you people? Why are you talking like that?"

"We're Quakers," Hiram said. "I didn't catch thy name."

"Cameron. Blake Cameron." He looked back at the closed door and started to rise. "Lacey's leg is hurt bad. I ought to go to her."

Hiram put a restraining hand on his shoulder. "Leave her to Sarah. She is receiving the best of care. How does thee happen to be here? Are there others with thee?"

"We were with a wagon train. Lacey wandered off and was treed by a bear. I went back after her, but the others couldn't wait. The weather." Even to his own ears the story sounded disjointed and rambling, but he was too tired to embellish it. "I went after her. We killed the bear, but he had clawed her. It's bad. I think gangrene is about to set in. I didn't have any medicine. We got lost. Couldn't find the others."

"God delivered thee to safety," Hiram assured him. "We will care for thee and thy wife and see thee back to health."

One of the young men leaned forward to ask, "Where are thy horses? I will tend them for thee."

Blake nodded vaguely toward the river. "I cut loose my pack mule an hour or so back. The horse gave out about a mile from here."

Several of the men left to retrieve the animals. The others

Hiram banished with a smile. "Let him rest, friends. I will give thee news of his wife as soon as I know myself." He waited until his neighbors had filed out, then removed his black hat and somber coat. "Would thee feel able to eat something? Sarah has cooked a venison roast for our meal. We have more than enough."

Again Blake looked at the closed door. He had only this stranger's word that Lacey was being cared for.

As if the door were a magnet, it drew him to rise and force his aching legs forward. He pushed it open to see three women moving deftly around Lacey. One of the women paused long enough to give him a smile, then continued mixing a yellowish poultice in a stone mortar cup. Another was lifting Lacey's head to spoon a draft between her lips.

Blake was quite relieved by the scene of confident efficiency. Whatever they were doing, it was more than he could do. He pulled the door shut again and went back to the chair by the table.

"Yes," he said finally. "I would be much obliged for food. I didn't take the time to cook anything this morning. We've been riding since daybreak."

"Where are thee from?"

"I'm from Texas, and she's from South Carolina." Blake glanced at the bedroom door. "That's a bad wound. Maybe I should help in there."

Hiram chuckled. "Sarah is in her element. Back home in Indiana, people came from miles around to get her to doctor them. She's as good as any doctor thee will ever see." He heaped two plates with food from the stovetop. "Texas and South Carolina are far apart for courting. Where did thee meet?"

"We met òn the wagon train," he said absently. "We're on our way to Oregon."

"We need more families out here," Hiram said with approval. "All too often the West attracts men who only want to get rich overnight. That kind doesn't build towns. Thee and thy wife were fortunate to meet under such unlikely circumstances and to have a preacher on the train.''

"I guess so.'' Blake was so worried about Lacey that he didn't notice Hiram's reference to a wife and a preacher. He stared with concern at the bedroom door.

"And what is thy line of work?''

Blake turned to the plate Hiram placed before him. "I'm not much of anything right now. Back in Texas I had a farm.''

"I don't suppose thee knows about smith work?'' Hiram asked hopefully. "Our smithy died a month back, and we've not replaced him. Thee could settle here and go right to work.''

"No, no. I thank you, sir, but I'm not Quaker, and this isn't Oregon. As soon as Lacey can travel, we need to head on.''

Hiram passed him a plate of biscuits. "How long has it been since thee left the wagons?''

After a moment's thought Blake answered, "Four or five days. I've lost track of time.''

"Friend, I hate to disappoint thee, but by the time thy wife can travel, thy friends will be long gone.''

This time Blake heard the word "wife.'' Hastily he said, "She's not—''

"I know, I know,'' Hiram interrupted. "Thee doesn't want to delay, but she's in a bad way. It will be days, maybe weeks before she can ride. By then the wagons will be gone, and winter will be upon us. Our autumn is a very short season. It's already late in the year for a wagon train. Besides, we have had a lot of trouble lately from a band of renegade Indians. It would be very dangerous for the two of thee to travel alone.''

Blake chewed slowly and swallowed before he said, "I guess we could join the next train.''

"Thee could, but not before late spring. After last night's storm the passes will already have some snow. No one else will get through.''

"Then we will have to stay here until spring?" He didn't mind, but he knew Lacey would be upset at the delay in reaching Oregon.

"I'm afraid so, friend. It doesn't matter that thee are not Quaker. We have many families here that are not." Hiram hesitated. "I know back east there are those who are not amiable toward my faith. If thee would prefer, I will move thee and thy wife to the house of a neighbor who is not Quaker."

"What?" Religious preference was far from his mind. "I would rather stay here, if there's room." He looked around. The house was small, but there was another door leading off the main room.

Hiram beamed. "Thee are welcome under my roof."

"I guess I could run the smith until someone can take over permanently," Blake said thoughtfully. "I had a forge on my farm and can handle simple things like shoeing horses and repairing cart rims or making nails."

"As the owner of the new sawmill, I welcome a man who can make nails."

"A sawmill? Here?"

"We have even built several houses of planks," Hiram told him proudly. "One belongs to the town mayor, Micah Sloan and his wife, Olive. I'll take thee to see the houses we are building after thee have rested."

Blake jumped as the door opened and the women came out. He stood, his eyes questioning the smaller woman. "Is she going to be all right?"

"She's resting," replied one of the women. "She has lost some blood, but she's young and healthy. The infection is the thing we must worry about."

Hiram gestured to the woman and said, "My wife, Sarah." To her he said, "Our guests are the Camerons, Blake and Lacey."

"No, we aren't—" Blake tried to interject.

"Nonsense, friend, we have plenty of room," the small woman interrupted. "Hiram built this house big for children who have not yet come. It will be good to have that room used.'' She turned to the other women, and after she had introduced them, said, ''I thank thee for thy help. It's not often we end Meeting on such a dramatic note.''

The women agreed and left to spread the word of the new couple. Blake watched helplessly. Everyone seemed to take it for granted that he and Lacey were married. Something in him rebelled, but reason told him it was best this way. The two of them had been alone for days. It would look odd if he told them he wasn't her husband. These were religious people; while he knew nothing at all about the Quaker faith, he decided everyone would be more comfortable if he continued to let them believe that he and Lacey were married. She might be able to travel sooner than everyone thought, and Hiram might be wrong about there not being another wagon train until spring.

Lacey stirred in her sleep and found herself lying on the softest bed she had ever felt. The unexpected luxury pulled her awake, and she blinked up at the whitewashed ceiling. Early morning light streamed through a glass-paned window flanked by simple linen curtains. Where was she? This wasn't the tiny cabin that had been her last conscious sight, nor was it the medicine wagon. Her brain felt muddled and slow, as if she had been drugged.

In confusion, she moved her arm and touched a warm body. Her eyes flew open, and she jerked her head around to see Blake Cameron asleep beside her. Without even wondering how he came to be there, Lacey curled into a ball, put her feet on his back, and shoved him out of bed.

Blake cried out in surprise as he hit the floor and flailed about as he scrambled to his knees beside the bed. Lacey clutched the covers under her neck and matched his angry expression.

''What are you doing in my bed!'' she demanded. ''Where am I!''

''Shhh!'' he motioned with his palms gesturing downward. After a glance at the door behind him, he whispered, "Keep your voice down or they'll hear you."

"Who will hear me?" She looked toward the door, then back at him. "Where are we!"

"I found the settlement I told you about."

"What settlement?"

"I guess you were too sick to remember. This is a Quaker town called Friendswood."

"Quakers?" she repeated, touching her fingers to her brow. None of this made any sense.

"This house belongs to Sarah and Hiram Gibson. Sarah has been doctoring your leg."

Logic was beginning to reassert itself in her foggy brain. "Then why are you in my bed? Good heavens! What must they think of me?"

"Hush, hush!" he hissed. "Somehow everybody in town has the idea that we're married."

Lacey stared at him incredulously. She felt groggy and disoriented but not to *that* extent. "How do you suppose they reached that rather remarkable conclusion?" she said frostily, but in a low voice.

"I carried you into this town, and there was no one else with us. Anybody could tell we had been traveling alone for several days. They just assumed we were married."

"And you let them think that? How could you!"

"Listen, Lacey, maybe you weren't paying close attention, but this is a *Quaker* town. Now, I don't know anything about their religion, but I'd bet all I own that they would take a dim view of a man and a woman traveling together who aren't married."

"We aren't *traveling together*," she ground out. "Not like that!"

"I know that, but I wasn't sure they would believe me. It was far more important for them to take care of you."

She glared at him in disbelief.

"By the time I found this place, you were damned near

dead. Sarah's been spooning medicine down you for two days.''

"Two . . . We've been here two days?'' Her eyes narrowed suspiciously. "And two nights as well? Where did you sleep!''

Blake grinned self-consciously and nodded toward the pillow beside her.

"Here!''

"Well, hell, Lacey, where else could I sleep? They would have thought it pretty peculiar if a husband didn't sleep with his wife. Especially with her so sick. Someone had to be near you in case you needed something in the night.''

"You could have slept in a chair,'' she accused.

"I tried that. No, I really did. A man my size can't sleep in a little straight-backed chair like that. And for that matter,'' he said testily, "why didn't you tell me how bad your leg was! I've worried about you until I was beside myself. Why would you do a fool thing like that!''

"What did you expect me to do? You told me all about how you can't stand having to take care of somebody and how your wife was sick and complaining all the time and how you hated that.''

"She wasn't sick; she just pretended to be,'' he rapped out. "I didn't mean I wouldn't take care of somebody who really needed me. I'm not a monster, for Pete's sake.'' He glowered at her self-righteously. "You worried me half to death, nearly dying like that.''

"I didn't do it on purpose!''

"I know that.'' He paced the room and stopped to frown back at her. "Are you all right now? Do you feel better?''

"Except for my mind being a little fuzzy, I feel pretty well. My leg is still sore, but it's not as bad as it was before.''

"Good. I guess Sarah's medicine was awful strong, because you barely moved the whole two days. Do you know how helpless that makes a man feel? Not to be able to ask if somebody is all right? You lay there like the dead. It was awful, I can tell you.''

The silence drew out between them as Lacey struggled to determine why his words bothered her. At last she grasped the thought and frowned. "Did you take any liberties with me?"

Blake looked shocked. "Certainly not! What kind of an animal do you think I am!"

"A man!" she growled.

He leaned across the near side of the bed, and she shrank back against the pillow. "No *man* would take advantage of a helpless woman! If I wanted to touch you, I wouldn't wait until you were unconscious!" His brown eyes snapped with anger at her unjust accusation.

Lacey's eyes left his and traveled over his bare chest, which bulged with obvious strength, down his lean belly, and lower. "Mr. Cameron," she gasped, "where are your clothes!

Hastily Blake glanced down and grabbed the corner of the blanket to cover his loins. He avoided her eyes as he rose and reached for his pants, which were hanging over the end of the bed.

"Well?" she demanded icily.

"I don't own a nightshirt—never have. If I had known you would wake up first, I'd have slept in my pants.

Her eyes bore into him reproachfully.

"Well, I would have! You can't expect a man to wear clothes day and night, though. It's not reasonable."

Suspiciously, she lifted the sheet covering her and peered beneath it. "Where did I get this nightgown?" She was comforted to see it was long-sleeved and high-necked.

"It belongs to Sarah."

"Who put it on me?" The intensity of her expression dared him to answer wrong.

"Sarah did," he promised solemnly. "I swear it." He held his pants up and added, "Turn your head so I can get dressed."

"It seems a little late for you to think about that."

Blake shrugged and started to drop the blanket. "Have it your way."

Lacey jerked her head away, her cheeks flaming. "You really have a nerve," she fumed to cover the sounds of his dressing. "I never in all my born days met up with a man like you."

"Is that a compliment?" he teased, as he sat on the chair beside the bed. "You can turn around now."

"No! I didn't mean it as a compliment." She frowned at his broad shoulders as he leaned forward to pull on his boots. The fabric of his shirt was drawn taut across the powerful body she had viewed by accident. Feeling excitement well up at the memory exasperated her even more. She pushed herself up in the bed and puffed both pillows beneath her. "The first thing we have to do is tell the Gibsons that we aren't married."

"I sure don't think I'd do that," Blake said, shaking his head.

"Arrangements must be made. You can't continue sleeping in here with me."

"Think about it, Lacey." He sat back and rested his palms on his knees while he regarded her. "I've slept in here for the past two nights. Whatever they will or won't believe happened since we left the wagon train, the fact remains that you and I have shared a bed since then."

Lacey's face paled, and she compressed her lips.

"As I said, these are Quakers. They are very religious, and they're very strict about their beliefs. If you tell them we aren't married, they may run us out of town on a rail. Or worse."

Run us out of town. Her heart threatened to leap from her chest. "They wouldn't!"

"Who knows? I've heard of it happening, and I'll bet you have, too."

"What do you suggest?" *I must stay calm,* Lacey reminded herself.

"Let's leave things as they are for now. You're getting well fast, and another wagon train might pass through before fall. We could join it and catch up with your papa in Oregon. No one here will ever be the wiser."

"What do you mean '*might* pass through'? And why wait for another wagon train? If we don't get on our way, we'll never catch up."

Blake paused, calculating the effects his next words might have. "Hiram says they have had a serious problem with some local Indians and that it wouldn't be safe for us to strike out alone. Ours was the last train that could have even hoped to get through the passes before the snow."

"The last train? Until when!"

"I believe he mentioned late spring," he hedged. At the sight of her chalky face he frowned and stood up to pace like a caged animal. "Oh, hell, Lacey, what else was I to do? I thought they would give you medicine and we could leave the next day. How was I to know she'd give you something to make you sleep so long?"

"Late spring?" She returned to her target unerringly. "Did you say late spring?"

He nodded.

Lacey covered her eyes with her hand and slowly shook her head. "Late spring. This is only September. Look what a mess your lie got us into."

"Not a lie, exactly. They jumped to that conclusion all by themselves. I only omitted a few facts—and then just the necessary ones."

"You lied," she intoned from behind her hand.

"And I guess you've never told a lie?"

She glared up at him sharply from behind her fingers.

"Lacey, think of it as a secret between the two of us. I won't lay a hand on you. I swear it."

"Can you think of one single reason why I ought to believe you? I trusted you, and you lied!"

He came back to the bed and sat down beside her. "Damn it, give me a chance. I made a mistake, and I admit it, but, honey, you were dying. At the very least, I thought you would lose your leg tŏ gangrene. As it is, you'll only have a scar, and maybe a slight limp.''

''Gangrene?'' she exclaimed.

''I had to do whatever was necessary to save you.''

She stared up at him and saw the truth in his dark eyes. ''I'm being very foolish,'' she murmured. ''Forgive me.'' Her voice rose uncertainly, making her words almost a question.

''There's no need for me to forgive you,'' he answered gruffly. ''I made a mess of things, and you've got every right to be mad.''

''No. No, I don't. I behaved like a spoiled child.''

''No, you didn't. If I were in your place, I'd be fit to be tied. You were right to get angry with me.''

''Will you stop switching sides and let me apologize?'' she demanded heatedly. ''I'm sorry!''

Blake's answer was cut off by a perfunctory knock on the door. After a moment, it opened and a small, plump woman carrying a tray bustled in.

''I thought I heard voices. So thee is finally awake. Thy husband was worried to distraction about you.'' To Blake she said with a smile, ''See? I told thee she would be all right.'' The woman carried the tray to the side table and put it down. ''I have broth for thee.''

''This is Sarah Gibson,'' Blake said when he could break in.

''Hello,'' Lacey said uncertainly. She felt very odd to be lying in bed wearing only a nightgown, however high-necked it might be, with Blake in the room and another person there as well. Strange, though, she hadn't felt so shy when only Blake was there.

Sarah took the spoon and lifted the liquid to Lacey's lips. ''Thy husband was worried, with good reason. For a few hours I feared we might lose thee. Blake, Hiram says to tell thee that the search party found thy pack mule and put him out back in the feed lot. Also I looked at thy horse earlier this morning and he is mending.''

''Found the mule? What's wrong with the horse?'' Lacey asked in confusion.

''I cut the mule loose because he was slowing us down,'' Blake explained.

''But everything you own in the world was on that pack saddle,'' Lacey said slowly.

''His horse was badly winded,'' Sarah supplied with another spoonful of broth. ''I doubt he'll ever be good for hard riding again. But if thy husband hadn't ridden so hard, thee would be dead now.'' She smiled fondly at Blake, who was looking uncomfortable. ''We were in the middle of Meeting when he came carrying thee in. I've never seen such a sight in my life. He was worn out. After the men brought thee here to our house, some of them went back up the river and found thy horse.''

''You carried me?'' Lacey whispered as she gazed up at Blake. ''You did that?''

''The horse gave out and couldn't go any farther.'' His eyes met hers in a look that expressed far more than words could have.

''I see,'' she murmured. ''I had no idea. You seem to make a habit of saving my life.''

Blake smiled. ''You did me a favor by shooting that bear. I couldn't lose a friend like that.'' His gaze gave the words intimate cast.

''Nonsense,'' Sarah laughed. ''Friend indeed! Thee is guilty of gross exaggeration if that is all she is to thee!'' She shook her head as she chuckled.

Lacey took the spoon and slowly ate the rest of the broth, but her eyes remained on Blake. She was busy revising her opinion of men in general and of Blake Cameron in particular.

CHAPTER
10

That afternoon, Lacey sat in a chair beneath a large pine in the Gibsons' back yard and watched as Sarah tipped the iron pot to pour the cockleburs into a big colander. "I really do feel well enough to help you dye the yarn," Lacey protested.

"Nonsense," Sarah replied as she poured the strained liquid back into the iron pot. "Thee has been too ill to have recovered so quickly." She took the skeins of wool yarn from the wooden swift and sloshed them in a bucket of cold water. "Besides, dyeing is a tedious job, though not overly hard work." Sarah smiled at her new friend. "Thee can help me stir it."

Lacey knew there was no point in arguing. Although Sarah never seemed to dispute her openly, she was a master at passive resistance. All morning Lacey had followed her about trying to help but had yet to be allowed to lift a finger.

"Thy wagon train was late in passing through," Sarah remarked as she transferred the wet yarn to the iron pot and then swung the kettle back over the low fire.

"We were held up by floods near Fort Kearney. Then there was a week of terrible storms so bad we couldn't travel. Later our wagon master's lead mule went lame. It

seems anyone can be left behind except the wagon master."
She tried to keep the resentment from her voice.

"He does, after all, know the route," Sarah observed.
"It's a hard rule, but reasonable when thee thinks on it.
With so many people in a train, someone is always sick,
lost, or having to fix a broken axle." She picked up a long
wooden paddle and pressed the buoyant yarn under the
water. "Thee is truly fortunate that thy husband was able to
find thee."

A small frown puckered Lacey's forehead. Perhaps this
was the time to tell Sarah that a grave mistake had been
made about her relationship to Blake. "You know, Sarah,
sometimes people are . . . misinformed about a matter.
They assume something to be true when all the time their assumption is entirely false." This wasn't proving to be easy.

"That's so true." Sarah lifted a paddleful of yarn that was
already turning a pale green. As she returned it to the water, she
said, "We had a bit of a scandal here only last year over just
such an assumption." She lowered her voice to a conspiratorial
tone. "There was a young Quaker woman here named Mabel
Bannion. She was flighty, that one. Half the time she wouldn't
say 'thee' or 'thy' and her ways were slovenly." Sarah shook
her head dismally. "We prayed for her frequently. Then last
summer, she started visiting a couple who lived over by the
meadow. James and Lidy Rose Harris, their names were. We
all thought this to be a good thing because, while the Harrises
aren't Quakers, Lidy Rose is as stable and solid as the day is
long."

Lacey watched as Sarah added a small log to the fire to
keep the water heated to a simmer.

"Well, the next thing we knew, Mabel was nowhere to be
seen. Her neighbors said her windows were dark all night,
and it being First Day, anybody would think she would
come to Meeting if she was anywhere about. We thought
some mischance must have befallen her, so we started to
search. Naturally, we went to the Harris cabin first, and
what does thee think we found?"

Lacey leaned forward. "What?"

"Only Lidy Rose. It turned out Mabel wasn't coming over to visit Lidy Rose, but to see her husband." Sarah again shook her head. "They had left together, James and Mabel. Joined a wagon train headed for California, as near as we could tell."

"Do you think they will ever come back?"

"No. Mabel has chosen her path, and now she must walk on it. We Quakers live a simple life, and our rules are not difficult. When Mabel started traveling with a man who was not her husband, she put aside all her teachings and left the faith."

"But perhaps there was another reason for them to leave together," Lacey said quickly. "Perhaps they are entirely innocent of what everyone believes."

Sarah laughed. "Thee sounds like a girl rather than a married woman. When a man and a woman leave their people and strike out together, there is no mistaking what they are doing. Such is the nature of things that, come the first nightfall, they will be sinning."

"Are you so sure?"

"Why else would they leave together? No, Mabel will never be allowed back in the Quaker community any more than James would be welcome in Lidy Rose's bed. None of us would allow Mabel under our roofs. She would be shunned, as she well knows. And if anyone was so moved as to take her in, that person, too, would be shunned for willfully harboring a fallen woman."

Lacey's face had paled. Blake had been right after all. Even if she were willing to risk being cast out of the community, she would bring shame on Sarah and Hiram for having sheltered a "fallen woman." No one would ever believe they were innocent.

"Thee looks distressed. Perhaps it sounds harsh to treat a person so, but thee must remember Mabel did this of her own free will. Besides"—Sarah's voice grew troubled—"her actions have brought trouble to our town. Lidy Rose—

who, by the way, is the sister of our mayor's wife—blames all of the Quakers for what Mabel did.''

''How unfair!''

''Yes, it is. We came west because we were tired of being persecuted for our beliefs. Most of our community came to this place in a mass movement, and we named it Friendswood. Over the past few years, other Quakers heard of us and joined us. Then a few couples of other faiths wanted to settle here, and we couldn't forbid them or we, too, would be guilty of intolerance. Then more came, and now only about half of Friendswood is Quaker.

''Micah Sloan was voted our mayor, and we saw nothing wrong in that. Certainly no Quaker would want to hold public office, and Micah has always been decent toward us, though his wife, Olive, could used a touch more forbearance. Then this happened to Lidy Rose, and she and Olive turned against us and wanted the Quakers to leave.''

''But you and your people were here first,'' Lacey protested.

''True, but now Friendswood is their home as well. There has been no open trouble, but it is well known that Olive Sloan makes the decisions in that family. Micah Sloan is a fair man, but he is easily swayed by his wife and his sister-in-law.''

''What will you do if there is trouble?'' Lacey was all too familiar with being forced to leave town. Sympathetically, she listened for Sarah's answer.

Sarah shrugged stoically. ''We have become accustomed to trouble. We will never lift our hands against them, but neither will we be driven out of this place. It's our home.''

Lacey watched Sarah lift a paddleful of dark green yarn. Her round face was set in stubborn lines though her voice had remained quiet.

''The iron from the pot acts as a good mordant to set the color,'' Sarah said, steering the conversation to a more comfortable topic. ''Look what a deep shade. The cockleburs were a good crop this year. We must simmer this the full hour to set it well, then let it cool slowly." She handed the paddle to Lacey. "If thee will tend this, I will start supper."

Slowly Lacey stirred the yarn as Sarah returned to the house. She had always hated telling even half-truths. Certainly this story about Blake and herself was graver than that, yet she saw no way to correct it without causing even more trouble. She was deep in worried thought as she bent to add hot water to the pot from the other kettle.

Blake pumped the bellows, raising a glow in the hot coals. Using the long-handled tongs, he heated the curved iron horseshoe. Hiram leaned on the workbench and watched, the reins of his horse looped over his arm.

"Thee looks right at home," he told Blake, "Even old Tom, who shod our horses for years, could do no better."

"I've had plenty of practice," Blake told him. "That horse of mine is flatfooted, and I have to keep shoes on him whether he's in the pasture or on the road." He took the glowing metal crescent to the anvil and hammered it flat. Sparks shot out in an arc to the dirt floor, and the horse snorted.

"Has thee been kept busy?"

"Yes, I have. Mayor Sloan was here earlier. His riding horse cast a shoe." Blake gauged the size of the horseshoe and hammered it to a narrower shape. "He seems like a nice man."

"That Micah is. But his wife Olive is a different matter. A Quaker girl ran off with her sister's husband last year, and ever since then she has had a bee in her bonnet as far as we are concerned. Her sister, Lidy Rose Harris, is just as bad. It was a shame it happened, but the girl was the sort to cause trouble somewhere or sometime. I guess there's always one in the bunch like that. We're well rid of her."

Blake made a sound of agreement as he thrust the hot shoe into a barrel of water. Steam hissed skyward, and he held the shoe under the water until it was cool enough to handle. Then he went to Hiram's horse and pushed against its shoulder as he tapped its leg with the toe of his boot. The horse obediently lifted one foot and Blake measured the shoe against its hoof.

When he straightened, he said, "I'm running low on pig iron. Do you expect a load through before winter?"

Hiram nodded. "We get it from a man over toward Fort Laramie. He or one of his sons will bring some over before snowfall. He's running late this year. They may be having more Indian trouble over at the fort."

Blake went back to the forge to match the other front shoe with the one in his hand. "You mentioned before that you've had trouble with some of the Indians here, too."

"Yes, we have. A renegade chief, Lame Wolf, raids us now and then. So far no one has been hurt, but he's a mean one. About half crazy, if thee asks me." He watched Blake widen the shoe on the anvil, flatten it again, then cool it. "Last month he tried to burn some of our houses."

"Did anyone get hurt?"

"One man got an arrow in his arm, but he wasn't hurt bad. We drove four of our horses out of town, the chief took them and left. He hasn't come back. It caused a rift in the town, though."

"How is that?" Blake went to the horse and signaled it to lift its leg. He braced the foot between his knees and started nailing the shoe in place.

"Quakers don't bear arms. The other townspeople thought we ought to take up guns and help kill the Indians. We refused, of course."

Blake let the hoof drop and looked over at his friend. "Did you explain to the others that it's against your beliefs?"

"Sure we did. Olive Sloan had them stirred up, though, and they wouldn't listen. I suppose they didn't like us much more than they did the Indians at that point."

Lifting the horse's hoof to rest on an iron tripod, Blake snipped off the protruding nails and used a tool to flatten the ends against the hoof. "Sounds as if they weren't being entirely reasonable."

Hiram nodded approvingly. "Thee would make a good Quaker. Thee doesn't deal in exaggerations. They were unreasonable, for a fact. I was finally able to get them to see my way, and we sent out the horses. It worked, and no one was killed."

Blake took an iron rasp and filed the rough lip of the hoof to curve into the edge of the shoe. The horse closed its eyes lazily and flicked its tail at a fly. "That sounds like a smart move to me. Maybe when Mayor Sloan steps down, you ought to take a turn at it."

"A Quaker in a public office? Not very likely, friend. We have enough to do just tending to our own business."

Finally, Blake lowered the last shod hoof to the floor and patted the horse's rump. "I wish they were all as easy to shoe as Red. I thought the mayor's horse was going to kick me from here to sundown."

"Some horses don't like what's good for them."

"Yeah, they aren't much different from people." Blake put away the knee-high tripod and hung the rasp and hoof clippers from leather thongs on a nail. "That's it for today. I'll walk home with you." He banked the live coals in the forge, and they went out through the oversized doors. Hiram closed one side while Blake shut the other and slid the bolt into place.

The road wound through the small town, spanned the river by way of a flat bridge, and continued to Hiram's house. Because the town had been built according to the lay of the land and the density of trees, it covered more ground than it would have if the streets had been arranged less haphazardly. As a result, the town seemed part of the woods rather than alien to it.

"Does thee think thee will be moving on next spring?" Hiram asked conversationally. "We would hate to lose a good blacksmith and a friend as well."

Blake looked up at the mountains, which were already assuming the gaudy garb of fall. He liked this place, and he liked the people, but how could he stay if his "wife" joined a wagon train? "I don't know, Hiram. Right now spring seems a long way off." He walked for a while in silence, broken only by the horse's hooves clapping on the hard-packed dirt. "This is the sort of place I had hoped to find, but I don't know how Lacey feels about it. We'll just have to see."

Hiram smiled. Blake could be persuaded. It was just a matter of convincing Lacey. And he knew one thing that no pioneer woman could refuse. "We'll see how it goes," he agreed.

Lacey came out on the back porch as they crossed the yard. She tossed a bowl of water onto the grass and gave Blake a level look that told him he was not forgiven for putting her in this situation. He smiled at her anyway, his teeth white in his soot-begrimed face.

"Hello, Mr. Gibson," Lacey greeted. Then, "Hello, Blake." His name felt strange in her mouth, and she was surprised Hiram didn't seem to notice.

"Thee must call me Hiram," he instructed. "I hope thee won't object to being called by thy first name. We Quakers don't hold with titles."

Lacey smiled, and her face became even prettier. "I would be honored."

Hiram went past her and into the house. Blake said, "You should smile more often. It becomes you."

When she looked at Blake, her smile vanished instantly. "Wash up. Supper's almost on the table."

Blake looked down at his clothes and hands. He must look even worse to her than he had on the wagon train. This bothered him. With a fluid motion, he pulled off his shirt, his muscles rippling beneath his sweat-slicked skin.

Lacey's eyes widened at the unexpected sight of his magnificent body. His damp skin glowed like fine marble, and his bulging biceps were coursed with veins. All in all, he affected her in a way that she found most unsettling, especially when she remembered he had slept beside her in the big feather bed. She turned abruptly and went inside the house. Blake poured water from the well bucket into a basin and started soaping the ashes and dirt from his upper body. When he looked back at the doorway, Lacey was gone. He scowled as he wondered if he had offended her by stripping off his shirt like that. With a groan he sluiced the soap from his body. Embarrassing her further was the last thing he wanted to do.

The meal was well cooked and the food plentiful. Hiram and Sarah, clearly glad to see each other after a day's work, kept up a lively conversation, drawing Blake and Lacey in as much as possible. Lacey stole a glance at the man they believed to be her husband. He had changed from the man she had known on the wagon train. His face was clean shaven and his hair still damp from being washed. His clothes, under Sarah's care, were clean and ironed. But there was also a more subtle difference, one she found difficult to pinpoint. She dropped her gaze hastily before he caught her staring at him.

"Jane Lawson came by this afternoon," Sarah informed Hiram, "and thee will never guess what she told me."

"I'll bet I can. I saw her husband earlier today. Looks like our town is growing come next summer."

"This will be their first baby," Sarah told Lacey. "They have been married over a year."

"How nice for them," Lacey said.

Sarah went on to say, "I must confess I felt a twinge of envy. Hiram and I were wed four years ago, before we left Indiana." Her voice faltered slightly. "The good Lord knows what he is doing, but I had hoped for babies."

"We're young yet," Hiram comforted her with a loving look. "There is still time for a family."

"Of course there is," Sarah agreed quickly. "What of thyself, Lacey? Do thee and Blake hope for children?"

The food turned tasteless in Lacey's mouth, and her startled eyes met Blake's across the table. She was glad to see he appeared as surprised as she felt. Swallowing, she said carefully, "I would like to have children. Some day."

"These matters can't be controlled," Hiram said. "It happens or it doesn't. How long have thee been married?"

"I lose track of time," Lacey said sweetly. "How long has it been, Blake?"

He frowned slightly. "A while. Not long."

Sarah laughed. "Isn't that just like a man? Thee will have to remind him of thy anniversary as well as thy birthday or he will forget them entirely. Hiram is just the same."

Hiram objected good-naturedly, but Lacey knew he wasn't angry at his wife. They seemed so happy together and so well matched. Lacey found herself studying them avidly, for this was like no marriage she had ever seen. They actually appeared to like each other. Of course, her own parents had been ideal for each other. Mama had never objected to Papa selling the tonic, and she had even sung in the show and taught Billy to do the same. But Papa had not been reluctant to hit her, and Mama had kept a hoard of money that she had lifted from the till—as well as from the pockets of the people in the audiences. Was that how it was beneath the surface for Sarah and Hiram?

After the meal, Lacey helped Sarah wash up and then rearranged the damp yarn on the drying rack by the fire. Sarah hummed happily as she bustled around the small room, straightening up for the evening.

The hour passed quickly. Dark had long since fallen, and the sounds of evening came through the shuttered windows. Far away an owl hooted, its mellow notes blending with the other night sounds.

Hiram stood and stretched. "I'm going to turn in now. I've put in long hours today."

Sarah, who had been spinning wool into yarn, also got to her feet. To Lacey she said, "Does thee need anything else tonight? If not, I'm going to bed as well."

"Go ahead. I'm just fine." Lacey had managed not to

think about this moment all day. She dared not look at Blake.

Sarah took one of the lamps, leaving the other for her guests. Hiram followed her into the bedroom and closed the door behind them.

Unwillingly, Lacey faced Blake, who was gazing at her with an unreadable expression. Catching her lower lip between her teeth for a moment, Lacey said, "I guess you can make yourself a pallet in front of the fire."

He sighed. "Now, what would the Gibsons think if I did that?"

"What will I think if you don't?" she countered.

Without answering, he got up, took the lamp, and went into their bedroom and she had no recourse but to follow him or sit in the dark. She closed the door and leaned against it with her hands pressed behind her. Blake sat in the chair and started to pull off his boots.

"You can't sleep in that bed!" she stated firmly.

"Yes, I can. I've slept in it every night since we came to town."

"That was different! I was not conscious."

He tossed his knitted socks into his boots, put his hands on his knees, and looked up at her. "You don't have anything to be afraid of. I'm not going to touch you."

Somehow this, too, sparked her anger. "Do you expect me to believe that?" she asked as he unbuttoned his shirt and shrugged out of it. "At least you could sleep on a pallet in here. Sarah and Hiram would never know." As an afterthought she added, "I was right not to trust you. Look at the mess you got us into! And now you say you won't touch me? Ha!"

"Lacey," he said in a tired voice, "all day long I've hammered iron into different shapes. I've shod horses, made nails, repositioned an anvil that weighs more than I do: I'm tired. I have no interest in ravishing a virgin tonight."

She frowned at him. He stood by the bed, wearing only

his pants. Taut muscles ridged his lean stomach and swelled across his tanned chest. His arms and shoulders looked powerful enough to move a dozen anvils. Again that enigmatic expression covered his face. The dim light from the lantern made his hair a thatch of midnight and his eyes as dark as obsidian, but much softer. Tender, even. Unable to bear the surge of excitement he stimulated in her, she stalked to the window and stared out at the night. He had no right to make her feel so vulnerable.

"If I were you," he said helpfully, "I wouldn't turn around right now."

Angrily, she wheeled to retort and was shocked to silence by the sight of his long, lean body sliding between the sheets. His pants lay on the floor, and she blushed at the right of the hard expanse of thigh and calf. Everything else was mercifully covered by the sheet.

"I told you not to turn around," he reminded her. He flicked the blanket over his leg with an unhurried motion.

"Why did you take off all your clothes?" she demanded.

"It's not comfortable sleeping in them. Besides, you'll have on a gown and I'll be covered by the bedspread and sheet."

"If you won't sleep on the floor, I will!" she stormed. This was really more than she could stand without an argument.

"You can't sleep on the floor or you may get sick all over again. Come to bed."

"I will not!"

"Come to bed or I'll get up and put that gown on you myself."

Something in his voice told Lacey he would do exactly that. With furious movements she grabbed up her gown and yanked it over her head so that it made a voluminous tent with only her head and neck exposed. Her fingers released the buttons of the dress Sarah had given her, and she pushed it down over her hips to drop to the floor.

Blake lay watching her with obvious interest, and she had

to remind herself that he saw only the nightgown and her movements, which bulged it here, twisted it there. Her petticoat joined the dress. She tried to take off her chemise, but the ribbon had knotted stubbornly. After struggling with it for a while, she gave up. She would feel safer with the extra layer of clothing. Pausing, she looked toward the bed where he lay as if he belonged there. The sheet covered only a portion of his deep chest, leaving his shoulders and arms bare. The idea of lying beside him brought a tingle to her body, and she swallowed nervously. Never in her life had she met a man who tempted her as much as he did.

"Do you need some help?"

"Never!" she managed to snap. If she could hold on to her anger, she could keep the other, more treacherous emotions at bay. She thrust her arms into the long sleeves and stepped away from her mound of clothing.

"I can honestly say I've never seen anything like that before in my life," he informed her. "I saw more skin after supper when you pushed up your sleeves to wash the dishes."

Lacey threw him a scathing look as she hung her dress and petticoats on a hook by the washstand. When she approached, he pulled back the covers on her side of the bed. Lacey halted abruptly.

"Aren't your feet cold? Get into bed."

Her feet were icy, but she stood her ground, her heart pounding in her throat. "I'm not coming to bed. I'm going to sleep in the chair."

"No, you're not. I told you I'm not going to touch you."

"Why should I believe you?"

"Because I haven't touched you so far."

"How do I know?"

"Come to bed." He raised himself up on one elbow and leaned over to blow out the lantern, plunging the room into darkness.

Lacey had never liked the dark. Especially in a room that was still strange to her. A draft eddied about her bare feet, and she hurried to the bed. She lay down as close to the edge as she could. It was a large bed, but Blake was a big man. If she moved, she might actually brush against his naked body. Softly she moaned.

"What's wrong? Is your leg hurting?"

"No!"

"Lacey, I'm sorry about all this. I got us into a mess, but I'm not going to make it worse by forcing myself on you. I promise you can trust me. I'll stay on my side, and you stay on yours."

It seemed strange to hear his deep, melodious voice so near her in the intimate darkness. At the same time it was both comforting and exciting. Lacey tried to repress the sensation deep within her that his nearness triggered. "That's fine with me. Just see that you do it," she said coolly. "There's no reason why we can't live through this as long as you keep your distance. There's bound to be a way to get back to the wagon train before snowfall." She glared over at him in the darkness. "I don't want to be married, for real or any other way."

"Marriage is all right for some people," he agreed, "but I don't think I'm cut out for it. Taking care of myself is job enough for me."

"Not everyone wants or expects to be carried on a pillow," she retorted. "Take me, for instance. All my life I've had to take care of Papa. I don't remember a time that he went out of his way for me or gave a thought to my welfare. I wouldn't know how to sit back and let someone take care of me. By the same token, I'm just as tired as you are of having to fetch and carry for someone else. No, if I ever get married, which I won't, it'll have to be to someone who can take care of himself."

Blake looked at her curiously, his eyes adjusting to the blackness. This certainly didn't tally with the tale she had told him about her fine house. "I know what you mean. By the time Catherine died, I didn't want to look after anyone again, either." As always when he mentioned his dead wife, his voice tightened. He looked away. "I'm glad to be on my own. What I can't understand is why you're so determined to go on to Oregon. Friendswood is as pretty a place as any I've ever seen, and we're already here."

"All my money went to buy that seventy acres. I have to get there." Her voice was firm and resolute. "Once I get on my own land, I'll be all right. Nobody can hurt me then."

"Those are strange words for a lady," he mused. "What makes you think somebody wants to hurt you?"

"I was speaking figuratively," she snapped. The last thing she wanted was to let Blake Cameron know that she had lied about her childhood.

Through the wall, she heard faint noises. She could detect the scrape of a drawer closing, the creak of floorboards as someone crossed the room. She heard Hiram say something, and then Sarah laughed, a seductive sound Lacey had never heard her make before. Then there were other sounds and a low moan.

Lacey turned her face toward the darkened wall. "Did you hear that? Maybe Sarah isn't feeling well."

There was a long pause. Then Blake said, "She's feeling fine."

When she heard another purring moan, Lacey sat up. "I know I heard it that time. Something must be wrong."

Blake put his hand on her shoulder and gently pressed her back into the bed. "Take my word for it. Nothing is wrong."

"Then why . . ." Sudden understanding rushed over her, and she was thankful for the concealing darkness. Lacey felt her cheeks flush with embarrassment. Her shoulder tingled where Blake's hand had been. Another sound came through the wall, and this time Lacey had no trouble recognizing it as a murmur of pleasure. She covered her eyes with her fingertips as if this would also deafen her. Sarah and Hiram obviously had no idea how noises carried through the wall. She desperately wished Blake owned a nightshirt, because she was all too aware of his nakedness and his proximity to her. To keep her distance, she tensed her muscles.

Blake moved uneasily and said in a strained voice, "I met the mayor yesterday. His horse is as cantankerous as his wife is reported to be. I hope that horse doesn't cast a shoe often."

"I hope so, too." She struggled for more conversation that would help them ignore what was happening in the next room. "We dyed yarn today. Sarah used cockleburs. Because she boiled them in an iron pot, the dye turned green."

"That horse tried to bite me on one end and kick me on the other. He's mean all the way through."

"When Mama dyed with cockleburs, she used an enameled pot and alum for the mordant. It made the dye a golden brown. I think I prefer the green."

"I'll need to get you a horse before we can leave here. I'm going to buy a new one myself. That bay won't ever be any good for hard riding now that his wind is ruined. He might make a good woman's horse though. An easy gait wouldn't hurt him."

"I think I'll ask Sarah if she has some extra yarn. I'd like to knit her a shawl after all they have done for us."

Both paused to listen, and when the room next to theirs was quiet, both sighed with relief.

A few minutes passed, and then Blake asked, "Are you going to be that stiff all night?" She hadn't moved a muscle.

"I'm not stiff," she denied. "I'm only trying not to crowd you."

"All right. Have it your own way." He rolled over so that his back was to her.

Lacey stared up at the dark ceiling. After he had been still for some time, she finally relaxed a bit. But although she was exhausted, she was determined to stay awake. No matter how still he might be, she was positive that Blake was as aware of her as she was of him. She tried to tell herself that her quickened pulse was the result of distrust, but she wasn't certain that she was being entirely truthful. Before long, sleep overtook her, and she curled into a more comfortable position.

Blake stared toward the opposite wall, telling himself over and over that this was no different from the other nights he had slept next to her and cared for her during her illness. But it was.

CHAPTER
11

Lacey clamped the wooden pin onto the tail of Blake's wet shirt. At once, it billowed in the breeze as did the others on the line. Lacey straightened the worst wrinkles from a sleeve that hung twisted and pulled the collar straight. Handling his clothing in such a familiar fashion gave her a strange but not unpleasant sensation.

She bent to pick up the laundry basket, made of woven willow wands, and tucked it under her arm to rest on her hip. Shading her eyes, Lacey gazed up at the towering mountains. Very soon the snows would start. Had the wagons passed through the dreaded South Pass? She tried to find a dip in the high peaks that might indicate the wagon trail, but they all looked equally high and forbidding.

The wind tugged free a stray wisp of her flame-kissed gold hair, and she pushed it from her eyes as her full skirts blew around her. The leaves of the aspen trees quivered like gold coins in the breeze, and a shower of topaz eddied to the ground. Lacey pulled her shawl tighter and tucked the ends more firmly into her waistband. Fall seemed to have moved in overnight.

She went back up the gentle rise to the house. Although her leg had healed, she walked with a slight limp but she didn't mind. Things might have worked out far worse. She only wished she didn't have to be grateful to Blake. It galled her to be obliged to any man; men weren't to be trusted.

Sarah had already emptied the washtubs and had tipped them up against the house to drain. She looked up as Lacey rejoined her. "Is thy leg giving thee trouble on the hill?"

"Not a bit. It feels as strong now as the other one."

Sarah smiled. "It's healed well. I fear, however, thee may always have a halt in thy step."

"I seldom notice it." She hung the basket on a wooden peg above the washtubs. "Even the scars are fading from pink to white."

"Thee will never be rid of them entirely."

Lacey shrugged. "Who will ever see them, hidden as they are beneath my skirts?"

Sarah gave her a grin such as one married woman shared with another. Lacey felt a blush steal up her neck, and she looked away. She was forever making small slips like that. If she gave herself away now, the shame would be terrible. She and Blake had shared both the room and the bed, and now she had no fever on which to lay the blame.

They went inside, and Sarah held up a small dented pot. "Would thee just look at this? I started to put water in it and found a hole. It's very vexing, as the tinker won't come around until spring."

Lacey saw a glimmer of light through the fire-blackened bottom. "It's scarcely more than a pinprick."

"Yes, but it's large enough to let the water drip right out."

"I wonder if Blake could plug it," Lacey said thoughtfully. "I could take it over to the smithy and ask him."

"Would thee mind? Then I could start the ironing."

"I wouldn't mind at all. The walk will be good for my leg." She felt a leaping excitement over the thought of seeing Blake, and she tried to suppress it.

With the pot in hand, she went outside. She wasn't certain where the smithy was located, but Friendswood was not large. The path she took led her across the stream and curved through the woods past other houses. As she drew nearer the center of town, it broadened and turned sharply downhill toward the river.

Lacey soon heard the distinctive ring of metal striking metal, and she followed the sound to a log building nestled between two large fir trees. Just inside the wide doorway, she saw Blake at work on a plow. He was unaware of her approach, and she slowed to watch him. He had removed his shirt, presumably because of the heat from the fire pit, and his muscles glistened with a sheen of sweat. His midnight-hued hair fell forward over his brow as he struck sparks from the glowing metal. Dust and soot begrimed his powerful forearms and powdered his pants, but he moved with obvious pride. Lacey's head tilted to one side as she observed him. The past few weeks he had shown no signs of drinking or brawling—the two major faults she had identified during their first meeting outside the saloon in Tocoma, Illinois. Lacey was no prude, but after enduring Papa's drunkenness, Lacey had no patience with a man who was given to hard liquor. The hardworking man in the smithy didn't look like a shiftless drifter, either. She wondered if there was a chance—even a slight one—that she had been wrong about Blake.

The wind tossed her skirt, and the movement caught Blake's attention. He looked up, and their gaze met and held. He stood motionless but tense, like a magnificently masculine animal surprised in his natural habitat. Lacey knew she should move or speak or something, but she could only stand staring at him. Finally she managed to break the spell by saying, "I brought a pot to be mended. Sarah noticed it has a hole and won't hold water."

Blake turned and slipped on his shirt out of deference to her and said casually, "Most pots with holes won't." She still stood at the side of the dusty street so he asked, "Will you bring it in here or should I come out there?"

Feeling foolish, Lacey entered the building and held out

the pot. "Can you mend it? Otherwise, she will have to do without it until next spring when the tinker comes this way."

Blake held it up to the light. "That shouldn't be too difficult. I saw a box of tinker's dams somewhere here. I think I can do it."

Lacey watched as he stepped toward the back of the shop. She didn't want to leave, even though chores awaited her at the house. His movements fascinated her, and his slow Texas drawl had made tremors of excitement race over her, as if his voice fed some inner hunger that was never satisfied. Besides, the smithy had all sorts of pleasant and decidedly masculine aromas, and she was intrigued by the blend of steam, leather, and horse scents. She looked around at the dusty shelves of rough planking that held bulky items of wood and metal. A huge anvil was mounted on an upended log that was larger around than she was, and she understood why Blake had been so tired from moving it. Several metal vises were fastened to the top of a work table. At one side of the door stood half a keg of shiny new nails, all with square tops, which Blake had told her he was making in his spare time. The fire pit glowed like a miniature Hades, and the bellows that stoked it was almost as long as she was tall.

"You look at home here," Lacey observed as Blake took down a tin box and rummaged through it for a suitable plug. "I never knew you were a blacksmith."

"I wasn't. Some of this I'm learning as I go along; some I know from having seen real smiths do it."

"I've heard several people say they were very pleased with your work." She watched his hands as he sifted through the metal slugs. They looked powerful enough to grind the dams into steel filings, but they also had been gentle, she vaguely recalled, when he was sponging away her fever at the cabin.

"Look at this," he said, as if he were eager to keep her there a little longer. "Ezra Lawson brought me a broken plow to mend. I was putting it back the way it had been, when I started thinking about the shape." He motioned for her to come to the anvil. "Look at the way this blade curves. If I angle it more this way," he gestured enthusiastically, "it will pull deeper in the dirt with less effort from both the mule and the man. I'm not sure it will work, but it almost has to. What do you think?"

Lacey looked up at him with surprise. In her experience, a man didn't ask a woman's advice. "It looks to me as if it would work." She tried to imagine the blade furrowing into the earth. With the blade turned as he had suggested, it would have a tendency to hold in the dirt rather than repel it outward. "Yes," she said with growing excitement, "I think it *will* work!"

Blake beamed with her approval. "Think of the effort it will save if it does."

Lacey, who had never walked behind a plow in her entire life, nodded eagerly.

They stood close together, their foreheads almost touching. At the same moment each looked up, and their eyes met. Lacey was aware of a hum in her ears that could only be attributed to her thundering pulse. His dark eyes were alight with excitement, and she was so close she could smell the clean scent of his breath. Then, slowly, his expression clouded, and he drew back.

"I guess you think it's ridiculous for me to redesign a plow," he said stiffly.

"No, I—"

"I guess you look at this shop and figure it's all way below you. After all, you're used to lace doilies and fancy houses. I guess you've never seen the inside of a smithy before, have you!" She was so near and looked so pretty that he had to break the spell somehow. Otherwise he would pull her close and kiss her.

"That's not at all—"

"Just never mind, Miss Summerfield. You don't need to pretend around me when no one else can hear. I know you can't see past the soot any more than any other fine lady could. I don't blame you for being the way you are." His cool eyes told her he did blame her, though.

"Stop putting words in my mouth! I ought to know what I think and what I don't."

"And just what do you think, Miss Summerfield?" Blake demanded.

Lacey frowned at him as she tried to formulate her thoughts. She had been thinking how wonderful it had felt when he kissed her in the cave, but surely he couldn't know that. Why had he turned on her? After all, she was the one in the strained position of having to share her bed with a man whose mere voice built fires in her soul, yet she was trying to make the best of it. She, at least, was congenial—a quality she doubted Blake Cameron could even recognize. She was about to tell him so when a shadow fell across the floor.

"Mrs. Cameron," the woman said in pleased tones, "so nice to see you up and about. Good day, Mr. Cameron."

"Good afternoon, Mrs. Sloan," Blake said. "Lacey, this is Olive Sloan, our mayor's wife."

The big, raw-boned woman told Lacey, "Everyone in town knows your name. Such a gallant rescue your husband made. He carried you in his arms until he dropped from exhaustion. So heroic."

Olive gave Blake a proud look as if to say she couldn't have done better herself.

"Your name is very familiar," Lacey said, trying to jog her memory. She was sure Sarah had mentioned an Olive Sloan. Her sister was Lidy Rose. It was all coming back to her. "Your sister is—"

"The one I told you about who drives that spanking bay," Blake cut in neatly. "Remember?"

"Oh, yes, of course," Lacey said hastily. She had almost spoken too quickly. "The bay."

"Lidy Rose sets great stock in that animal," Olive confirmed. "She sent all the way back to Minnesota for him. That's where we're from, you know."

"No, I didn't. Why did you come west?" Lacey asked.

Olive Sloan looked like a very unlikely candidate for a wagon train. She was a tall woman with big bones and broad shoulders, but her attitude was that of a self-labeled aristocrat. Her clothes were of expensive material, trimmed with lace, rather than homespun garments like those that most of the women wore.

"Mr. Sloan saw a great opportunity to be had out here," Olive stated grandly. "We are the pilgrims of the West, you know. The wagon trains are *Mayflowers* taking us to new vistas."

"I guess I never thought of it like that," Lacey said. "Did you, Blake?"

"Nope. Can't say as I did."

Olive gave them her thin-lipped smile. "It's a pleasure to see you in our fair town. Goodness knows we needed a good smith. The last one was a bumbling fool. And you, Mrs. Cameron, are a cultured woman. One can always tell."

"Thank you." She wondered what the woman would say if she knew about Dr. Summerfield's Wonder Tonic. "Please call me Lacey. I would prefer that."

"And you must call me Olive." She looked at Blake. "Has Mr. Sloan been by today?"

"No, he hasn't."

"That man!" Olive said to Lacey, with obvious irritation. "He says he's going one place, and instead he goes to another." She stepped back to the wide doorway and looked up and down the street. Then her black eyes fell on her hapless husband. "Mr. Sloan!" she called out in authoritarian tones. "Come here, if you please!"

Blake and Lacey exchanged glances, their dispute forgotten for the moment.

A thick-set man rode up on a gray horse and dismounted at the door. The animal laid back its ears at the proximity to the smithy and jerked its head when the man looped the reins through the hitching post. "Hello, Olive, Blake." He smiled at Lacey. "And you must be the young lady I've heard so much about. Lacey Cameron."

"Yes, I am," she responded with a bob of her head. "I understand you're the mayor of Friendswood. You have a lovely town here."

Olive sniffed derisively. "It could be better, I assure you. We have an element of undesirables."

Assuming she was referring to her sister's philandering husband and the woman he left with, Lacey tried to look noncommittal and pleasant, both at the same time.

"How is that shoe holding up?" Blake asked the man. "Any problems with it?"

"No, no. Not a bit." The man rubbed his red-veined nose and gestured at the horse, using his hat as a pointer. "That beast is traveling as smooth as silk. I want to hand it to you, young man. You're the first one who has had such good luck with old Charley here. You'll get all my business."

Olive threw her husband a scathing glance. "Certainly he will. He's the only blacksmith in town." She tilted her head and put her hand on her large hip. "Did you remember to bring that iron spider over to be repaired?"

Micah Sloan shifted his weight to the other leg, "No, Olive, I forgot all about that."

She snorted disdainfully and tossed a superior glance at Lacey as if to garner her sympathy. "You had no trouble remembering to socialize with Sam Johnston."

Micah's guilt was clearly spread across his face. "I just happened to run across him down the street, and we were passing the time of day."

"Indeed. Meanwhile you leave me to run all the errands and see to everything around the house. Really, Mr. Sloan, you are a difficult man."

Lacey felt as uneasy as Micah looked. "Perhaps I could drop by your house and get the spider for you. I don't mind at all." She liked the looks of the kindly mayor and hated to see anyone browbeaten.

"Nonsense," Olive answered for him. "You've just recovered from your illness. Mr. Sloan will do it." Her expression told them all that she was sure her husband had less important business than they did.

Lacey averted her eyes in embarrassment. She couldn't just turn around and walk out on them, but she was extremely ill at ease in the face of such rudeness.

"By the way," Olive said, putting her fingertips on Lacey's arm to draw her attention. "I've been meaning to ask you two over for dinner. I know you must be longing for a good meal such as you had back home and some congenial conversation."

Lacey was confused by Olive's statement. Sarah was a good cook, and the dishes she prepared were more plentiful than any Lacey had been accustomed to. "What do you mean?"

"Well, of course I wouldn't know what you ate in the South—your accent does give you away," Olive said with a little laugh, "but you must be heartily sick of all that plain Quaker food. I've heard they don't even use salt! Barbaric! And all that odd language." She laughed and made a shooing motion with her large hands.

"Sarah uses salt, and other herbs and spices as well," Lacey responded stiffly, "and I don't find their language all that odd."

"My dear, you have been sick!"

"The Gibsons are our friends," Blake said in a tone that was deceptively calm.

"But you aren't Quakers, surely. One can always tell by the language, the dress."

"No, we aren't Quakers. I gather there is another church here?" Lacey said.

"Oh, yes, certainly. We're Presbyterian ourselves. Most in Friendswood are. Except, of course, those others."

Blake grabbed up an awl, and with the sharply pointed tool he vigorously reamed the hole in Sarah's pot to a workable size. He snapped in a tinker's dam and tapped the malleable metal much harder than was necessary to spread it over the older surface on both sides. He was tired of holding his tongue and had to fight to keep his anger from getting the best of him.

"Repairing a pot, I see," Micah said with forced heartiness. He could tell the Camerons had taken offense at his wife's cutting remarks.

Olive glared at him for interrupting her. "Which brings me to the other invitation I've been meaning to extend. Mr. Sloan and I would like for you two to move in with us."

Lacey stared at the woman incredulously, and Blake's hammer banged the pot unnecessarily hard. "Move in with you? Whatever for?"

"Why, to get away from those Quakers, of course." In a slightly lower voice, Olive confided to Lacey, "No man is safe around them. My own sister has had proof of that."

Blake had finished flattening the plug, and he handed the pot to Lacey. "Tell Sarah that should hold it until spring, when the tinker comes around. And tell her if she needs anything else, just to let me know."

Lacey took the pot, but not the cue to leave. "Blake and I have no intention of moving, because we are very close to Hiram and Sarah. They took us in and cared for me when I was near death, and that's more than most people would do for two strangers." Lacey knew she should curb her tongue, but she couldn't seem to stop. "And I like Sarah. She's a close friend. And as for my husband, he wouldn't look at another woman." Blake started to speak, but Lacey calmed him by reaching over to touch his arm.

Olive drew herself up to her full height and frowned at them both. "I hope you don't come to regret this decision," she said in a manner that conveyed just the opposite. "It's happened in this town before." She looked at her own husband as if to chasten him for not defending her. "Well, be that as it may, I suppose we'll see you in church tonight."

"I doubt it," Lacey said sweetly. "We're going to Meeting with the Gibsons. Unless of course, you're coming there." She arched her brows questioningly.

Olive Sloan's back was so rigid that her whalebone stays

nearly cracked. "We most certainly will not. Good day, Mrs. Cameron, Mr. Cameron. Come, Mr. Sloan, the day is wasting."

Lacey watched the woman sail grandly out of the blacksmith shop, her husband in her wake. Turning to Blake, she said with a smile, "Do you suppose we're still invited for dinner?"

His anger was quickly dissolved by her jest. "I doubt it. Do you mind?"

"I prefer it this way." She gestured with the mended pot and said, "Thank you for fixing this. It's Sarah's favorite, and I know she'll be grateful."

He nodded. "Are we really going to Meeting tonight?"

"Whether you go is up to you, but I am. Sarah says it's a silent Meeting." Lacey laughed. "She told me these Meetings are always spontaneous, rather than planned, and that they are to meet spontaneously tonight."

Blake smiled companionably at her. "I guess it's hard to gather together the 'two or more' if neither time nor place is set. Yes, I'll go with you." As she turned to leave, he added, "You've got the prettiest smile I've ever seen."

She stopped as if she had been struck. Half turning, she looked back at him doubtfully. Compliments had been rare in her life and had always meant only one thing from a man. But he smiled at her guilelessly and made no move to touch her.

"Will you walk over with me or go by yourself?" she said at last.

"I'll walk with you," he said carefully. "It might look odd if we went separately."

"I suppose." Although she hid it, she felt a surge of eagerness. If she meant to keep him from knowing how she felt, she scolded herself, she had better be more careful. "I'll see you at supper." Their earlier argument was forgotten, and Lacey hummed as she walked down the path to the house.

* * *

After supper Lacey and Sarah put their woolen shawls around their shoulders and, as if on the spur of the moment, announced they were going to the meetinghouse. Hiram said he had been about to do the same as he put on his collarless black coat and picked up his hat. Blake admitted that he, too, was about to go across the way and, together, they trooped out.

The meetinghouse was close to the Gibsons' cabin so they walked, not bothering to hitch up the buggy. Sarah fell in beside Hiram, leaving Lacey and Blake to walk together.

Lacey glanced at the man by her side. He was certainly handsome, she thought as she matched her stride to his. He was the sort of man whom women flocked to as a rule. Of course, no one had approached him in Friendswood, since he was thought to be married, but on the wagon train, more than one woman had flirted with him most shamelessly. She found herself perversely wishing that she knew how to do that sort of thing. He had complimented her, but he must not have meant it. After all, in the cave he had rejected her, and even sleeping beside her in Sarah's wide guest bed wasn't enough to stir him to uncontrollable passion. She had to remind herself that she was glad he hadn't taken advantage of her, but she still wondered why he hadn't. His words of flattery must have been false for his actions had proved that she was unattractive to him. Or was she drawing that conclusion to protect herself?

The meetinghouse was a simple frame structure, one of the first to have been constructed with lumber from Hiram's sawmill. The windows were clear glass with no adornment at all and glowed brightly from the lantern light inside. As Sarah and Hiram mounted the wooden steps, their conversation ended, and all four were silent as they entered the square building.

The pine pews formed a three-sided arrangement. As they filed in, the women took seats on the left and the men on the right. Lacey found herself sitting in the front row, facing Blake across the small open area. Hiram sat beside him and, like the other men, had not removed his hat. Behind them, the walls were whitewashed and unadorned by paintings or decorations of any sort. Nor was there a pulpit or even a lectern.

Lacey's eyes skimmed over the stark walls and unvarnished wooden floor and found nothing on which to focus her attention. She was beginning to see how the Quakers emphasized their aloneness even while they were together. With no religious symbols on the walls or stained glass to study, she was alone with her thoughts.

Once all the people were seated, no one broke the silence. Lacey felt as though she were being watched and glanced up to meet Blake's gaze. His eyes were dark and unreadable, but he seemed troubled, as if he were yearning for something he would never attain. She wondered what it might be, or was it merely a trick of the lantern light?

Blake tried to conceal his thoughts. She was so pretty sitting there in the golden glow. She wore a simple dress the shade of elderberry leaves, and her eyes were the same color. He was sure that dress had never looked so good on Sarah. Lacey's hair was pulled back in a bun like all the other women's, but she wore it more softly around her face, and he kept remembering how her hair spread like angel fire across the blanket when she slept.

There was no point in wanting her. Blake knew that. She didn't want him and made no bones about it. In fact she was determined to hole up on her land and shoot anybody who came near her. She had told him so herself. These weren't the words of a woman who was attracted to a man, nor had her actions given him hope. Except for that one time in the cave when she had kissed him back and made his blood boil with desire for her.

He thought about the long night that stretched before him. Since that first night, she had come to bed more or less willingly, after performing the feat of changing out of her dress beneath the tent of her nightgown, an accomplishment he still could scarcely believe. He supposed she had learned to do that in order to protect her privacy in the cramped confines of the wagon. Then she would lie beside him in the dark, never touching him, and more often than not they would be forced to listen to the lovers in the next room. Blake had no idea how all this affected Lacey, but he was irritable and frustrated almost beyond bearing. He supposed it was different with a woman.

Lacey kept her features smooth and hoped she appeared to be contemplating purely spiritual matters. In truth, her mind was on the big feather bed in the Gibsons' guest room. As soon as the service was over, she would undress and lie beside this man who didn't even own a nightshirt. In the next room she would hear the Gibsons, she was almost sure of it, though of course both Sarah and Hiram would be mortified if they knew it. Lacey couldn't help the odd surging she felt on hearing those murmurs of love with Blake so near. It awakened something elemental in her that she wasn't sure she could control indefinitely. At times, she could hardly resist the temptation to reach out and touch the man beside her. Only her fear of another rejection gave her the strength to stay chaste. This was a new problem to her and one she found irritating.

She noticed the way his white shirt contrasted with the bronzed skin on his neck and the blackness of his hair. He was easily the most desirable man in the room. His hands lay in his lap, but even in repose they looked powerful. Those hands had tended her with gentleness during her illness and carried her the final distance to Friendswood and help. Those were not the actions of an untrustworthy man. Nor would a drifter work so hard in a blacksmith's shop. His manner toward her was always unpredictable: treating her as an equal one minute and verbally dueling with her the next. He certainly didn't act as if he saw her as a desirable woman. Lacey sighed.

Blake memorized the way the light made Lacey's cheeks seem to radiate with apricot softness. He imagined he could almost see a quick pulse in her graceful throat, but of course that must be his imagination, because she was clearly deep in the most reverent of thoughts. Her hands lay demurely in her lap, her long fingers tapering in a delicate curve. She had no business going to Oregon to spend her life as a self-declared hermit. Besides that, carving a life for herself in a hostile wilderness was too hard for a woman alone. She might, in the end, have to marry a dirty fur trapper who would keep her pregnant and hungry. Blake was surprised at the surge of jealousy this thought triggered. He was frankly startled at the idea of welcoming the opportunity to make her his own and care for her. He had thought he was beyond ever wanting to do that for any woman ever again.

Before he had time to convince himself that this was not at all what he wanted, two men farther down in the front row rose to their feet simultaneously and shook hands. This ended the service, and everyone stood to go home. Blake followed Hiram outside as he tried not to think about the night ahead in the big feather bed.

CHAPTER
12

Lacey wasn't in a particularly good mood. Living in such close proximity to the Gibsons after the months of crowded conditions on the trail was wearing on her nerves. Little things were starting to bother her, like the way Hiram talked with his mouth full, or how Sarah wanted each plate and pot on a particular cupboard shelf place that seemed illogical to her. Not that there had been any harsh words spoken— Lacey doubted anyone else felt the strain—but she yearned for space of her own.

Whenever she felt constrained by Sarah's extreme neatness, Lacey experienced pangs of guilt. Sarah Gibson was, without question, the best friend she had ever known. She was as fond of Hiram as she would have been of a brother. That left only one person on whom to blame her irritation: Blake. If she weren't so frustrated by his not caring for her, and if he had not awakened longings and then backed away, she would still be calm and reasonable.

Lacey went out of the house and took the gallon bucket from the peg on the back porch. Down by the stream she could see Blake cutting white oak saplings to make splits for new chair bottoms. He didn't see her as she went down to the water and filled her bucket. She glanced at him sideways. He looked innocent enough as he went about his work, selecting trees about as big around as his forearm. He chose tall ones that grew straight and were unmarked by knobs or limbs below his eye level. Just looking at him caused a flutter in the pit of her stomach.

She tightened her grip on the rope handle and carried the water to a nearby hollowed gum that had been selected and prepared for soap-making. Quietly she removed the make-shift lid and looked in to see that Hiram had, indeed, added the hickory ashes from the fireplace. A drift of gray powder eddied in the breeze.

With all her strength she lifted the brimming bucket above her shoulders and poured the water into the top of the hollow log. The ashes floated up like scum, turning darker and swirling counterclockwise. Lacey put the lid back in place and positioned another bucket beneath the holes drilled in the bottom of the gum. Gradually a few drops of brownish liquid plinked into the receptacle.

Carrying the water bucket with her, Lacey wandered over to Blake. She watched him for a few minutes in silence. "You're doing that wrong, you know," she said helpfully.

He looked up from the tree he was cutting. "No, I'm not."

"I always heard the best white oaks for making chair splits came from deep in coves. These are out in the sunshine."

Blake glared at her. "In Texas we don't have much in the way of coves. We always just used what we had."

"This isn't Texas," she pointed out unnecessarily. She ran her hand over the bark. "These feel brash to me. When you start splitting them, they may be brittle and hard to work."

"Where did you get all this knowledge?" Blake asked sarcastically. "I never heard of a lady cutting trees and making splits."

Lacey evaded his eyes. One winter her family had stayed with an elderly couple to escape the bitter cold of the wagon.

Her mother had cooked and cleaned, and Lacey and Billy had done most of the chores in exchange for their lodging. "I knew an old man once who lived up in the Appalachians. He told me about making splits. He always said the best trees were on the low slopes, in a dark places, and on the north side of the mountain."

Blake didn't look convinced. "This old man, did he live in a cove?"

"Why, yes, as a matter of fact, he did."

"Which side of the mountain was his house on? The north?

"I don't recall," she said defensively.

"My guess is that he favored using trees that grew close at hand. It's more convenient that way." He struck a few more well-placed blows, and the tree toppled.

"I still say these will be brittle. The bark is too rough."

"Well, I've made a few splits in my time, and I've always used trees near water that have kept their leaves into autumn." He gestured at the empty bucket she held. "Don't let me keep you from your work," he said pointedly.

"You aren't. I'm dripping lye out of that gum over there. Sarah and I are going to make soap tomorrow."

"That's a mighty little gum for ashes," he observed.

"I guess you know all about soap-making, too," she said dryly.

"I've done it before. That gum won't hold enough ashes to make it worth your while."

Although Lacey secretly agreed with him, she retorted, "That just shows how much you know about it. If you make a lot at once, it won't get hard. Sarah likes cake soap."

"I never cared whether it got hard or not."

Lacey tilted her head to one side and regarded him narrowly. "Why did you make soap if you had a wife?"

Blake laughed mirthlessly. He couldn't even imagine Catherine doing such a menial chore. "She was always sickly and a fine lady to boot. She wasn't cut out to do chores like that." He had meant it derogatorily toward Catherine, but one look at Lacey's face told him she had taken it the wrong way. "I mean, there's nothing wrong with hard work," he amended. "But some women can do it, and some can't."

"I understand perfectly," Lacey said stiffly. "She was a lady and I'm not."

"That's not what I meant," he protested.

"Very well, Mr. Cameron. I know what you meant. I guess a woman like me couldn't compare with a fine Texas lady."

"Why do you have to take everything so damned personal!" he demanded.

"I suppose it's my low nature," she replied scathingly. "We women who are not ladies have so little else to occupy our thoughts. No teas or garden luncheons, you know. I suppose the late Mrs. Cameron attended her share of such festivities?" She had forgotten that this was exactly the way she had described her own past.

Blake glared at her before he picked up the nearest tree and hauled it over to the water's edge. "I don't want to talk about her."

Lacey watched him cut off the leaves and shove the trunk into the water. She really felt bad about saying all those things. He had undoubtedly loved his wife, and for all Lacey knew she might have been a saint. She was surprised to find herself hoping that Catherine had had clay feet.

Blake topped off the other trees and kicked them into the water to soak until the next day. He secured the trunks with a rope so they wouldn't float away, then straightened and dusted his hands on his pants as he tried to ignore her.

"I suppose I spoke out of turn," Lacey said hesitantly. "I only came over to pass the time of day."

Blake pulled his ax out of the tree stump and continued to pretend she wasn't there.

"That was an apology," she prompted him.

"I forgive you. Now go away."

Lacey scowled. "I must admit I find it difficult to see

what such a fine lady saw in you. Goodness knows, you're seldom even civil.''

"Why do you suppose that is?" he countered.

"Bad temper?" she suggested sweetly.

The growl that came from deep in his throat reminded her of the bear. "Lacey, we are in a very uncomfortable situation here, but we can at least try to make the best of it. I can't see any earthly reason why we should be at each other's throats every time we exchange more than a few words. Can't you at least try to be pleasant?"

"Me? No one has ever accused me of being anything but pleasant!"

"Then I guess nobody ever got to know you very well." He leaned on the ax handle and scowled at her.

"You, sir, are no gentleman!"

He grinned. "Did you read that in a penny novel or did you just make it up on the spot?"

With a choked sound, Lacey turned on her heels and stamped away. Behind her, she heard Blake's deep laughter. It was utterly impossible to talk to him or even to offer him an apology, and his words were particularly galling since she *had* read that line in a book. Besides, he had offended her first by implying she was no lady!

Lacey brushed a tear from her cheek. Perhaps she couldn't trace her family line back to the *Mayflower*, but that gave him no right to talk to her like that. Especially since her blood could be as blue as royalty's for all he knew! She consoled herself that he would never have an inkling of the way she truly felt about him, and in due time she would be safely ensconced on her seventy acres and could put him out of her mind forever. She elbowed open the back door and forced herself to smile to hide her rage. "The lye is dripping," she told Sarah. "Should I go into the woods to look for some ginger leaves to scent the soap?"

"All the ginger leaves must be gone by now," Sarah said. "We'll leave it natural."

"All right." Lacey wasn't at all fond of the natural smell

of lye soap. This was just one more irritation. She instantly felt a familiar surge of guilt. "Here," she said, taking the scrub brush from Sarah. "Let me do that. You're tired."

"Thank thee, Lacey," Sarah said with relief. "I do need a rest. Thee is a good friend."

Lacey set about scouring the floor, her movements almost fierce.

Blake frowned back at the house. He had let her goad him into making her angry—again. How in the world, he wondered, could he feel so protective toward a woman on one hand and so antagonistic toward her on the other? He bent and broke off a sizable limb. Hiding his actions from Lacey by turning his back to the house, he ran his knife through the wood. "She was right, damn it," he muttered under his breath. The white wood had broken into a brittle sliver.

He shoved one hand into his back pocket and rested the other hand on the upright ax handle. Being wrong didn't bother him much. He had been wrong plenty of times before this; what really galled him was that Lacey knew he was wrong. For some reason that bothered him a great deal.

A slight movement across the water drew his attention, and he studied the thick brush more carefully. He saw nothing out of the ordinary, but as he watched, a leafy branch moved in a way unlike the others. Instantly, he was alert, and he keened his eyes as his grip tightened on the ax handle. Now that he knew where to look, he saw bronze skin among the sparse foliage. Before he could decide what action to take, the Indian slipped away, causing only the faintest rustle in the leaf-strewn forest.

He walked backward a few wary steps, his gaze still on the bushes that had concealed the enemy. Then he turned and walked briskly toward the house. Before he reached the door, however, he saw Hiram running toward him down the road, and he veered to meet his friend.

"There's been trouble," Hiram gasped breathlessly. "Carl Odem—he owns the farm beyond the main street— he's been shot. It was Indians."

"Shot!"

"I've come to fetch Sarah. He's been taken into his house, but he can't travel."

"Is he there alone?" Blake thought of the near miss he and Lacey had just had. He had no idea how long the Indian had been looking in the bushes. If he hadn't looked up and seen the Indian watching, one or both of them might be dead now.

"He's a widower, but his grown boys are with him."

As they talked, they strode toward the house. Lacey and Sarah looked up as both men entered unexpectedly, and Sarah's welcoming expression faded after she saw Hiram's concern.

"What's wrong?" Lacey demanded, tossing the scrub brush into the bucket and getting to her feet.

"Indians shot a man," Blake answered.

"Thee is needed, Sarah," Hiram said. "Quickly. It's Carl Odem."

Blake took his gun and bullet pouch off the mantel and shoved a shell into the chamber. His eyes met Hiram's across the room. After a pause, Blake said. "Aren't you going to get your gun?"

Hiram lifted his chin firmly, though his eyes were agonized. "Thee knows I can't."

Sarah hurried to the bedroom to get her bag of medicine and then ran back to join them. "I'm ready."

"Lacey, bolt the front door and the windows and lock up behind us. You'll be safe here," Blake instructed.

"I'm going with you."

"No, you're not. Stay inside."

"Sarah may need me. I'm going." Her tone said that she couldn't be dissuaded.

They hurried down the road toward the center of town. Never had the woods seemed so dense or so close to Lacey. Limbs already stripped of fall's leaves seemed to reach out toward her like skeletal fingers, and with each breeze she imagined an Indian sliding through the brush.

The word had spread quickly. Blake wasn't the only man heading toward the Odem cabin with gun in hand. Even as they passed, some were closing and bolting their shutters while others cast frightened glances from behind their curtains.

The Odem cabin was small and had scarcely enough room for a bed and table, so the yard and porch had become the gathering place for most of the townsmen. Their expressions were all dark. Some looked frightened, but the majority were obviously angry. The sight of the mob sent a chill through Lacey, but she wouldn't allow the details of the memory that triggered her apprehension to focus in her mind. As Blake cleared the way, Lacey followed Sarah through the crowd and into the dark closeness of the cabin. She felt relieved to be away from the angry mob. When her eyes had adjusted to the change in light, Lacey could see the shadowy figure of a man lying on the bed. Around him stood three others, presumably his sons.

"Would thee open the window?" Sarah asked one of the sons.

Reluctantly he obeyed, but he peered out fearfully as he did so.

Sarah knelt beside the low bed and hesitated at the sight of a long arrow protruding from the man's blood-matted shirt. "Carl," she said calmly, "thee knows what I must do?"

Grimly he nodded.

Motioning to his sons and Hiram, she said, "Thee must hold him still while I pull out the arrow. Lacey, wet one of those cloths in my bag with the yellow potion from that vial. As soon as I get the arrow out, press the cloth hard over the wound." She glanced at Lacey's drawn face as she gently tore away the bloodied cloth. "Can thee do it?"

"Of course I can," Lacey stated firmly as she quelled her tossing stomach.

"If you don't need me, I'll go outside and talk to the men," Blake said to Sarah.

Sarah nodded briskly. "They need calming down before worse harm is done." Lacey mutely nodded her agreement.

Blake went out onto the tiny porch, and dozens of eyes were upon him. "Carl is alive," he stated in a clear voice. "He's been shot in the shoulder, and Sarah Gibson is about to take the arrow out." A muffled yell behind him told them that the work had begun.

"It's those damned savage Indians!" a man at the front of the mob yelled. "We won't none of us be safe until Lame Wolf and his band are all dead!"

"That's right!" another chimed in. "We have to kill them before they kill us!"

Blake held up his hand for quiet. "There must be some other way. Has anyone been shot in Friendswood, before this?"

"No, but only because the Indians missed!" a new voice shouted. "One tried to get me down by the creek last spring, but his arrow veered off."

"I suggest we plan what we should do in case of an all-out attack. We all know we could search these woods from now to Sunday and not find the Indians if they don't want to be found. Besides, while we're off in the woods, the women and children are left here, unprotected." Blake paused, then added, "I think we ought to decide what to do if they try something like this again."

The men turned to one another and began talking all at once. Finally, one voice called out over the din, "The town hall is the biggest building in Friendswood. Everybody can crowd into it."

"That's good," Blake encouraged. "It's also in the middle of town, so it's easy for everyone to get to. If there's an attack, we should all go there with our families. Agreed?"

"What if we won't all fit in?" one of them called out. "What if the Quakers get there first?"

"They're people, too," Blake snapped.

"Yeah, but they won't fight! I think the town hall ought to be a refuge only for those willing to shoot back!"

"Does that go for your women as well?" Blake demanded. "Will all your wives kill Indians? Will your children? What about the babies? Can they shoot a rifle?"

"That's different!" somebody else joined in. "They can't be expected to!"

"You're right," Blake agreed. "And you can't expect a man to go against his principles if he's set on not killing! If the town hall is shelter for one, it's shelter for all!"

"Who says?"

Blake shifted his gun to the crook of his arm and met the man's eyes with a level gaze. "I do."

The crowd shuffled and grumbled, but no one was willing to dispute Blake's assumed authority.

Finally, an older man said, "How are we supposed to know when to go there? By the time one of us rides to warn the rest, we'll all be massacred!"

"A bell!" another man shouted. "We need a bell!"

"Yeah, but we can't use the one on the church because it's not very loud. When the wind's blowing from my house to the church, I can hardly hear it. What we need is a really big bell."

"How about it, Cameron?" someone called out. "You're the blacksmith. Can you make us a bell that'll ring loud enough to warn the entire town?"

"I've never made one before, but I imagine I can." He wasn't sure how he'd do it, but between him and Hiram, they could figure out a way. "I'll need iron, though. I know pots and skillets are hard to come by, but if your wives can part with any, bring them to the smithy tomorrow. If you have a plow blade that can't be mended, bring that. The more metal I have, the bigger the bell will be and the louder it'll sound."

The door opened behind him, and Lacey came out. Her face was pasty, and there were red stains on her hands and dress. Blake looked at her in concern and stepped toward her, for she seemed about to faint.

"He's going to live, Sarah says," she called out. "The

arrow came out clean, and he bled freely.'' Her eyes scanned the men's faces. She had hoped her news would calm them, but was relieved to see that Blake had already done so.

Blake turned back to the crowd. "All of you go on home now and tell your women the danger seems to be over for the time. Let them know about the plan and start collecting iron for me.''

Slowly the men dispersed. Having been given a purpose, they had stopped their grumbling. Lacey moved to Blake's side and didn't object when he put his arm protectively around her.

"Are you all right?'' he said gently.

She nodded. "I just didn't know what to expect. Do you think the Indians will come back?''

"Not today. This looks like target practice to me. If they were going to attack, they would have already done so.'' He didn't look at Lacey as he added, "Be careful about going to the creek alone. I saw an Indian hiding in the brush on the other side just before Hiram came to get Sarah.''

Her startled eyes searched his face. "The one that shot Mr. Odem?''

He shrugged. "Who knows? I think he was just scouting, but it doesn't really matter, since they're all dangerous. Just keep your eyes open. All right?''

Lacey nodded slowly. "I'd better get back inside to see if Sarah needs any more help.''

Blake sat on the rough cedar railing and watched her trim body as she turned away. He wanted to protect her, to keep her from even unpleasant thoughts, let alone danger. The idea that the Indian might have been there watching her while she was down by the creek sent a cold wash of fear over him. If anything happened to Lacey, he would die, in part, himself. This revelation astonished him. These were the thoughts of a man in love!

Hiram came out and leaned against the porch post, his hazel eyes scanning the nearby woods. "Carl had a close call," he said in a low tone. "That arrow barely missed a lung."

Blake nodded. "The men out here were ready to go charging off in all directions. If there were any Indians still out there, which I doubt, all they would have to do is pick us off one at a time." He looked up at his friend as he pulled a shred of cedar from the rail. "I know killing goes against your religion, but how rigid are you? I mean, I've known Baptists who could outdrink and outdance everyone else in a bar."

"Killing isn't on quite the same level as drinking and dancing," Hiram said with a wry grin. "I stand firm."

With a sigh, Blake tossed the cedar sliver to the ground. "Will you carry your squirrel gun to and from the sawmill? At least then you'd look as if you were ready to fight."

"Exactly. I can't do that either."

"Hiram, I'm not trying to be difficult, but think about it. If an Indian was about to shoot you, wouldn't you fight back?"

"I've thought about it long and hard," Hiram answered quietly. "Before we came west, I did a large amount of soul-searching because I knew sooner or later the question would come up. No matter how I looked at it, the answer was always the same. A man can back down on a lot of issues and still be a man. In fact, sometimes he has to change his mind in order to be one. But when it comes to killing a human being, I have to stand firm. If I was to shoot a man, any man, it would be the same as if he killed me. I feel that strongly about it."

Blake was quiet for a minute, then asked persuasively, "What if that man was about to kill Sarah?"

Hiram pondered the question for a long time before answering. "Thee has hit on my tender spot. I hope I never have to answer that."

They sat in thoughtful silence for a while, each wrestling with his own feelings and opinions. Hiram broke the quiet by saying, "If it comes to it, I'll stand beside thee and see to thy bullets. I'll even load thy gun. But I will not pull thy gun's trigger.''

With a half-smile, Blake nodded. ''I guess that's all I could ask. I may not fully understand your ways, but a friend never asks more than another is willing to give. Besides, things might never come to a point where either of us needs to fight.''

''I hope they don't,'' Hiram answered fervently. ''I sure do hope not.''

CHAPTER
13

"I don't see why you insisted on coming with me," Lacey said as she ducked to avoid a low branch. "Mrs. Benson walks through here every day and nothing happens to her."

"What Mr. Benson lets his wife do and what I let you do aren't the same thing," Blake pointed out.

Lacey shifted the bucket of flour to her other hand. "But I'm not your wife, and you have no say over what I do or don't do. Even if I *was* your wife, you wouldn't."

Blake didn't respond. He was thinking about the vast difference between Lacey and Catherine. His first wife was afraid to live on their farm, which stood at the edge of a small but thriving town. Yet Lacey had no qualms about walking alone through Indian-infested woods to borrow a bucket of flour. She had many qualities Blake found both irritating and fascinating.

He reached in front of her to pull aside a limb of golden aspen leaves. As he did so, she paused and looked back at him inquiringly. The gold of the leaves was as bright as the fire in her hair, and her expression reminded him of a startled fawn. He held the branch, afraid that she would hurry on her way if he moved. Her slightly parted lips revealed the tips of her straight white teeth, and she seemed to be holding her breath.

"Lacey," he said gently, "why have you been avoiding me so the last few days?"

"I haven't," she answered.

He could see the racing pulse in her slender throat. "Yes, you have. Did I say something to upset you?"

"No." She tried to walk on, but he caught her wrist.

"Then tell me what's wrong. I'm not a subtle man, and sometimes I might say or do things that hurt you, without realizing what I've done."

She wanted to look away, but his velvety brown eyes were too intense. "You're imagining things." Nervously she pulled her arm free and walked briskly down the path toward Sarah's house. Since the day of the Indian attack, she had felt even more uneasy around Blake. When she had seen him take control of that angry mob and disperse the crowd with such ease, he had greatly risen in her esteem. She admired him far more than she wanted to admit to herself and infinitely more than she wanted him to guess. If he knew how she felt, it would give him power over her, and she couldn't allow that to happen. She didn't know why he couldn't see her feelings written all over her face. Certainly they seemed that obvious to her.

For that reason, she had avoided being alone with him as much as possible. She sometimes even went to bed before he did and feigned sleep, or she stayed up very late and slipped into bed after he was asleep. Neither method was satisfactory, however, because every night she was achingly aware of him lying beside her in the dark.

They walked on in silence. Blake couldn't figure this out. She said she wasn't avoiding him, but her actions showed him she was doing exactly that. The only possible explanation was that she simply cared so little for him that she didn't want to be with him. This idea caused him pain, so he pushed it aside, wishing he didn't care for her so much. Because she was a lady, perhaps she wasn't affected by lying beside him every night. Catherine had assured him again and again that true ladies did not experience such base emotions. As far as he knew, that was true. But the closeness certainly had affected him, and his desire for Lacey grew stronger every night.

They entered a small meadow, and Lacey quickened her pace. The yellowing grasses whispered in the breeze, and as her long skirt brushed the tops as she passed, she left a clear trail behind her. Her feet trod on the rustling grass with a noticeable sound.

Blake's eyes darted about cautiously. "You ought to keep to the woods," he told her. "It's safer."

"Quit trying to scare me." Lacey was so eager to get back in Sarah's company and out of Blake's tempting presence that she had been careless, but she couldn't admit that to him.

"I'm not trying to scare you. Can't you just relax once in a while and let somebody take care of you?"

"No, I don't know how."

Blake frowned as he followed her. She really was independent to a fault. "Well, it wouldn't hurt you to at least try."

She stopped so suddenly that he almost ran into her. "Why should I?" she demanded, her eyes the color of a verdant forest. "Can you give me a single reason why I ought to be so weak as to climb up onto a silk cushion and be fussed over? First of all, no one *wants* to take care of me. Second, the West is hardly the place to be a weakling. And third, I can't stand weakness!"

"I'm not talking about weakness. I didn't suggest you become a parasite, and someone might be more than willing to take care of you if you would just unbend a little!"

Lacey stared up at him. "Who?" she demanded.

"Me!"

"You're a drifter. You told me yourself that you may stay

in Oregon or you may head down to California. How could I ever depend on somebody like that?''

''Lacey, everyone has to depend on someone else once in a while.''

''Not me. I'm fed up to the teeth with traveling. I want to settle in one spot and stay there!''

''How could you be tired of it? I thought you just recently left the house you grew up in.''

She looked away and said, ''I meant I was tired of wagon trains. Naturally, I lived in only one house before that. I'm not a Gypsy, you know.'' The lie was growing, but she didn't know how to stop it.

Blake cupped her face in his hands and gazed deeply into her eyes. ''You're as hard to hold as quicksilver,'' he said as if to himself. ''Any other woman would be fishing to see what I meant when I said I wanted to take care of her. Not you. I expect you to wheel and run like a frightened deer.''

''I'm not afraid of you or anybody else.''

''No? What are you afraid of? Yourself?''

She stared at him, hoping he couldn't feel her hammering heartbeat. His big hands sent flames coursing through her, and she steeled herself to keep from swaying toward him. ''I'm not afraid of anything,'' she said, but even she could tell that her words lacked conviction.

''I don't believe you. Only fools are never scared, and you're sure no fool.''

His thumb caressed the smooth curve of her cheek, and Lacey fought to maintain control over herself. ''Does that include you? What scares you?''

''A lot of things. Being alone for the rest of my life. Falling in love with someone who doesn't love me. Telling her I do and taking the chance on having her turn me down—or worse, laugh at me.''

Lacey's breath seemed to be caught in her throat. What was he trying to say? She waited quietly for him to continue.

After a long pause, he said, ''Your name fits you so well. You remind me of a field in the summer. Your eyes can be as green as the grass under the hot sun. Your hair is as fine as rye and as bright as field flowers. You even smell of fresh air and sunshine. Summerfield is a fitting name. So is Lacey. In spite of yourself there's a delicate quality about you, like fine lace. Not that you're fragile or anything like that. Far from it. But you're quality."

"I am?" she whispered.

"Of course you are. Anybody could see it."

The golden aspen shimmered like gilded coins all around them, and the silver-trunked birches towered higher with umbrellas of topaz and flame. A faint breeze scented with the aromas of autumn wafted over them. Everyone and everything else seemed to be eons away.

Slowly Blake lowered his head to kiss her, pausing when they were only a breath apart and watching her until her eyelids closed and her lips parted as if by reflex. Then his mouth claimed hers and tasted the nectar there as she let him mold her body to his. He felt her graceful arms circle him, the covered bucket of flour still gripped in her hand. He tightened his embrace, and she curved to him, as supple as a willow wand.

The passion in her kiss was unmistakable, and it triggered a deeper emotion in him. As in the cave when he had first kissed her, he was overcome not only with desire for her but with the need to protect her as well. As naturally as he accepted the changing seasons, he finally acknowledged a new truth: He loved her.

Blake hugged her to him and buried his face in the cloud of her hair as it came free from its bun. He loved her! Wave after wave of emotion drummed through him, and he was amazed he had not realized it before.

Then the hopelessness of the situation suddenly swamped him. She didn't want him. She had told him so. She kissed him now only because he had overpowered her! Somehow he had again managed to fall in love with the wrong woman.

He released her so unexpectedly that Lacey fell against him. His hands caught her waist and steadied her, but she could feel his soul withdraw from hers. In total confusion, she looked up at him.

"I shouldn't have kissed you," he said. "And you shouldn't have let me! A lady like you ought to know better than to kiss a man that way."

Lacey touched her lips as she pulled away. What had been wrong with the way she had kissed him? True, she'd had little experience, but that could be remedied. "What—"

"No! Don't tell me again about how you want to be left alone or how you don't want anybody caring for you. I know all about it! You think just because I love you, I want to put you in a gilded cage and feed you chocolates and such. Well, you're wrong! You just go to Oregon and live on a mountaintop if that's what you'll be happy doing, but I think you're crazy!" He turned and strode away, leaving her gaping after him.

Lacey ran to catch up. "What did you say?" she gasped, putting her hand on his chest to stop him.

"I said if you want to live on some damned mountain, go do it, if that'll make you happy."

"No, no. Before that!"

"I said I shouldn't have kissed you."

"Did you also say you love me?"

Blake gazed down at her. He couldn't remember ever having felt this miserable. Here was the very woman he had looked for all his life, and she didn't want him. "I may have said that," he admitted. "At any rate, don't let it bother you."

"It doesn't bother me," she said softly.

He was right. She didn't care at all. He shouldered past her and strode on up the trail. A curious prickling sensation had begun behind his eyelids, and he wasn't about to look at her.

Lacey stared after him. Once she started to speak, but she wasn't sure how to say what she was feeling so she closed her mouth again and gripped the bale of the bucket so hard it bit into her palm. Never in her life could she remember anyone, even Mama, saying "I love you." She had never said the words herself. As Blake disappeared into the grove of pines that bordered the Gibsons' yard, Lacey moved her lips soundlessly over the words.

She had no doubt anymore that she loved him. His kiss had made that all too clear to her. But when a man professed love, wasn't he supposed to say it gently and follow it with a proposal, then a kiss? That was how it had happened in every book she had ever read. But Blake had practically snarled the words and then walked off and left her standing alone. How could she possibly trust a man like that?

Walking after him, she frowned. At least she hadn't told him how she felt, but if he had stayed with her she might have. She could be thankful for that.

She slapped a bush out of her way and shifted the bucket to her other hand. So intent was she on building a fortress of anger to protect her dignity that she almost bumped into Blake, who was on his way back to her.

Awkwardly, they stood a few feet apart, staring at each other. Finally, he said, "I didn't mean to walk off and leave you. Why didn't you follow me?"

"I was thinking."

"Lacey, I'm sorry about all that. Just forget it. All right?"

Slowly she shook her head from side to side. "I can't do that. You see, I love you, too."

He couldn't believe he had heard her correctly. "You do?"

"Yes."

He stepped toward her and reached out to draw her close. "Lacey."

"Wait. Let me finish. I love you, Blake, but there's more to it than that. There's trust. Security."

"You don't trust me? How in the hell can you love somebody and not trust him?"

"I don't know. I've never loved anybody before."

"And why wouldn't you trust *me*? Of all the people in the world, I'd have thought you'd trust me."

She looked away from his stricken face. "I don't know how to trust people, I guess. Trust has always been hard for me."

"That doesn't make sense." His eyebrows knitted in confusion. She refused to meet his eyes. "Love and trust go together." He thought a minute. "Do you like me?"

"Of course I do. I just said I love you." Her startled eyes met his.

"That's not the same. Do you like me—as a person."

"Yes, you're my friend."

"But you don't trust me?"

"You're trying to confuse me," she objected. How *could* she love Blake and count him as a friend and not trust him? Yet, if she trusted him, wouldn't she get hurt? She had always told herself not to trust anyone, not to be vulnerable. Skepticism had been her means of survival when Papa had betrayed her over and over.

"No, I'm not trying to confuse you," he said softly. "I just don't understand."

She drew a deep and unhappy breath. "Neither do I." After a moment she added, "We had better get back to Sarah before she starts to worry."

He nodded. "First you'd better put your hair back up." She looked so soft and sensuous with it streaming down her back.

Lacey touched her hair as if surprised to find that it had come down. "Yes," she said absently. "I guess I had." She put the bucket on the ground and twisted her hair into a smooth knot. Enough pins clung in the ruddy masses to secure it. When it was done, she looked over at him.

He made no sound but held out his hand to guide her in front of him. Silently they returned to the house.

When they reached the yard, Blake mumbled something about a chore he had to do in the barn, and then he strode away. Lacey watched his broad back until the double doors swallowed him. He had evoked some very troubling emotions, and she hoped telling him she loved him hadn't been a mistake.

She turned back to the house. Trust. It was her lack of trust that was getting in the way. If what he said about friendship was true, did that mean she trusted Sarah? They were close friends, and Lacey had even volunteered to go through the woods where Indians might be waiting to get the flour Sarah needed so that Sarah could stay safely at home. That was friendship, but did it also include trust? Lacey honestly couldn't tell.

When she entered, Sarah was waiting for her and took the bucket from her hand with thanks. Lacey could tell by looking at her that something had happened in her absence, for Sarah's face was beaming, and she moved with quicker efficiency than usual.

"We have a surprise for thee and thy husband," Sarah told her when she could contain herself no longer. "Hiram came by a few minutes ago and said it will be ready by this afternoon."

"What will?"

Sarah grinned. "If I told thee, thee would have no surprise. But I can say this—it's something thee will like, I'm sure."

Lacey smiled. Knowing Sarah, the surprise could be anything from a litter of puppies to a new source of dye for her next batch of wool. She sat down on the low fireplace stool and started peeling potatoes for the soup pot as she wrestled with her thoughts.

Through the window, she could see Blake standing near the barn door. He was working with an awl on a harness strap, but by his movements she could tell he was upset. Also, he cast more than one angry glare toward the house. All in all, he wasn't acting in the least like the heroes in the books she had read, and she wondered if this meant a lack of truthfulness on his part or lack of experience on hers. She had to conclude that being in love wasn't as simple as the novels had implied.

All through the noonday meal, Sarah and Hiram exchanged secretive glances and covert smiles. Lacey found herself growing more and more curious. After the main course had been cleared away, Sarah brought out squares of molasses cake. Sarah served the ginger-colored dessert on saucers Lacey had never seen before.

"How lovely!" she exclaimed over the delicate pattern of primroses and bluebells on the pale yellow china. "What beautiful saucers."

Sarah blushed. "We rarely use them because they're so fancy, but today is special." She sat back down and picked up her fork. "The saucers were a gift from my friend in Indiana."

"Plain dishes hold food as well as fancy ones," Hiram said stoically. "It doesn't seem proper to keep such plates in a Quaker household."

"They were a wedding gift, and I'll not part with them," Sarah answered firmly. "Besides, my friend who gave them to us isn't of our faith and didn't know any better."

"It must have been difficult bringing them west," Blake observed. "They look as if they would easily break."

Hiram threw his wife a teasing glance. "They rode all the way swathed in Sarah's extra petticoats. She babied those dishes every step of the way, and them not even proper for a simple table."

"Quit pestering me." Sarah stood up for herself. "They aren't garish in color, and whenever I look at them I remember my friend and the good times we had." She touched the painted surface fondly. "I unwrapped them on my wedding day in my mother's front parlor. It was just after we came from Meeting."

"How were you married?" Lacey asked. "I mean, with no preachers to perform the ceremony?"

"We have several leaders in every church," Sarah explained, "but we don't feel they have any greater power to marry us than we have ourselves. After we had sat in silence and thoroughly examined our hearts, Hiram and I stood and held hands and announced that we were man and wife.''

"Just like that?"

"Yes. Then everyone prayed with us, and they all signed a paper saying they had witnessed our wedding." She smiled lovingly across the table at her husband and then looked at Lacey questioningly. "I've heard thy own weddings are different. The bride wears a special dress, and there is music, and the church is decorated with flowers. Is it really like that?"

"I suppose," Lacey said without thinking. "I've never seen a wedding."

"We were married on the trail," Blake interrupted as he gave Lacey a cautioning look.

"I had forgotten," Sarah said. "Where did your marriage take place?"

"Nebraska," said Lacey.

"Missouri," Blake answered at the same time.

Then in the next breath, Lacey said, "I meant Missouri."

"It was Nebraska," Blake said simultaneously. They glared at each other. "It happened pretty close to the state line," Blake amended tightly. "I'm not too sure which side we were on."

"As long as the deed was done, it doesn't matter where thee was standing," Hiram observed sagely. "And all the elaborate fixings aren't as important as how thee feel toward one another."

Sarah looked as if she didn't entirely agree. "Not everyone holds to the beliefs of our faith, Hiram."

"That's true. To each his own." Hiram finished off the last of his cake and leaned back in the chair.

"I suppose after the service, thee moved into Blake's wagon," Sarah said. Then she frowned, "But what became of thy wagon? Thee came to us on horseback."

"I didn't have a wagon," Blake explained.

"So thee moved into her parents' wagon? That must have

been overly crowded for newlyweds," Hiram observed. "I remember how glad I was to get Sarah alone in our own home here."

Sarah threw him a warning look, but Hiram just smiled at her. "Thee was lucky to have had a preacher along on the wagons. Was he of your faith?"

"No," Lacey said.

"Yes," Blake replied along with her.

Lacey tried to lie some more. "We grew up in different faiths."

"Thee have different religious preferences?" Sarah probed with concern. "Is this a problem for thee?"

"Thee is minding their business for them, Sarah," Hiram pointed out.

"Forgive me," she said with a smile. "My tongue is running away." After a moment she added, "I guess thy father was overjoyed at thy marriage. Thee are so well matched."

This time Lacey paused to give Blake time to answer. Unfortunately, he did the same, and silence spun out long. Finally he said, "I guess you could say he never came right out and told me to my face that he didn't want me to marry her."

"Yes, you could say that," Lacey agreed with relief.

Sarah shook her head in disbelief. "How could anyone find fault with a good man like Blake?"

Lacey looked over at Blake and recalled how he had grabbed Papa's whiskey bottle and given it back to him before she could break it. "Yes," she said dryly. "How could anyone object to such an upstanding man?"

Sarah and Lacey cleared away the dishes, but when Lacey started to pour the hot water into the dishpan, Sarah stopped her. "The dishes can wait. Come along. Thy surprise should be ready now."

"What surprise?" Blake asked as Hiram nudged him out the door.

"Thee will see."

Sarah's eyes were sparkling as she untied Lacey's apron

and her own and hung them on hooks. "Thee will be so happy!" she whispered as she hugged her friend briefly.

Brimming with curiosity, Lacey and Blake followed the Gibsons down the path that led away from town. Skirting a stand of juniper and spruce, they entered a grove of birch that grew beside the winding stream. The air was cold with the promise of early frost, and their view of the blue sky was overlaid by the interlaced boughs of red and gold. The ground beneath Lacey's feet was hard, as if it were tensing itself for the long weeks of cold, and their footsteps were whispery in the fallen leaves.

The trees parted, and Lacey saw a tiny cabin nestled near protecting trees in a small meadow. Behind it stood a newly constructed barn and horse pen. To the side was a plot that had once been worked as a garden. In the distance Lacey heard the winter song of the stream.

"I don't understand," Lacey said to Sarah. "Who lives here?"

"Thee does!" Sarah announced triumphantly. "This is thy new home!"

Lacey stopped and stared, first at her friend and then at Blake. He looked as stunned as she felt. Hiram went past them and pushed open the door of the cabin.

"Surprise!" came cries from inside. "Welcome!"

Blake looked past Hiram's grinning face to see a number of the townspeople gathered in the cabin's single room. He looked helplessly at Lacey and tried to signal to her that this was as unexpected for him as it was for her. Her stormy green eyes told him she didn't believe that for a minute. Then Mayor Sloan was pumping his arm, and Olive was granting him her puckery smile, and all his friends were patting him jovially on the back.

"Were you surprised?" Olive queried. "No one gave away our little secret?"

"No, no one gave me any hints." Blake made himself smile as he was pulled inside along with Lacey. A large bed stood against one wall, and a bright rag rug lay on the new floor. A trestle table, also of new wood, stood on the other side near the hearth. Various pots and stoneware jugs sat on the hearthstones, and a small fire was crackling and sending out aromas of cooking.

"We all went in together on this," Olive informed Lacey. "My church group did the cooking and collected the extra kitchenware around town. We knew you had no pots or dishes." She leaned closer. "The largest pot there is from the mayor and myself."

Blake looked around, still unable to comprehend what he saw. His clothes and the ones Sarah had resewn for Lacey hung neatly on pegs at the head of the bed, which was covered with a colorful crazy quilt. On the pine floor, beneath the bed, he saw the rest of his gear, which he had assumed to still be in the Gibsons' house.

"Thee looks stunned, friend," Hiram said with a grin. "Does thee not like thy house?"

"No one has ever done anything like this for me before," Blake said truthfully. "But when did you have time to build it?"

"The truth is, the cabin has been here for a while," Hiram said. "It belonged to someone who moved on a while back."

Olive Sloan, who was standing close enough to hear, snorted. "It was that trashy Mabel Bannion," she informed Blake and Lacey, as well as everyone else in the room. "That's who used to live here, and you may as well know it right off."

"Wasn't she—" Lacey began.

"She ran off with my sister's husband," Olive stated. "That's why Lidy Rose isn't here today. She just wasn't up to it. But she said to tell you she would be around in a few days."

Lacey looked around at the neat cabin. She had never been in the house of a fallen woman. It looked no different from any other home in Friendswood.

"We put in a plank floor," Micah Sloan said in his grand

tones. "Before, it was just dirt. We used lumber from Mr. Gibson's sawmill. The same goes for the table and benches. It's a sign of our growing industry." He hooked his thumb in his coat buttonhole and peered proudly about. "I want to take this opportunity to formally welcome you to our fair town of Friendswood. You, Mr. Cameron, are already a part of our growing community, and I'm sure your lovely wife"—he smiled benignly at Lacey— "will soon be a member of our various sewing circles and the new Women's Club for Social Enlightenment."

Blake stopped trying to catch Lacey's eye and grinned amiably at the mayor.

"I'm sure I speak for everyone," the older man boomed stentoriously, "when I say that if you need help mending a roof or building a bigger barn or adding a new room, just call on the citizens of Friendswood." He cast a fatherly smile at Lacey, whose eyes widened and whose back stiffened at the implications of the need for another room. "Furthermore . . ."

Olive silenced Micah with a glance and stepped forward. Regally she said, "The women of Friendswood welcome you. Drop by at any time."

"Thank you," Lacey murmured, knowing instinctively that Olive didn't really expect her to pop in uninvited.

"Come along, everyone," Olive sang out. "We should leave the Camerons to themselves." She swept grandly from the room, followed by her husband and most of the others.

"Thank you," Blake called after them. "You don't know how much we appreciate all you've done."

The Gibsons held back, and Sarah took Lacey's hand. Fondly she said, "Having thy own place will mean so much to thee. I only wish it was a new place, but thee isn't superstitious."

"No," Hiram agreed, "thee must take no note of the fact it was once the cabin of that flighty Mabel Bannion." He looked around the room and nodded in satisfaction. "It's a tight house, and the roof is sound. Thee will be happy here.''

Blake put his arm around Lacey's shoulders. ''Thank you, Hiram. I know this must have been your idea.'' He felt Lacey tense at his gesture of affection, but he kept his arm in place.

''Not his alone,'' Sarah added pertly. ''A house is important to a woman, as well I know. Before we came here, we lived with my parents and had no place of our own. I imagine Lacey wants her own home as keenly as I did.''

''We're hoping this will encourage thee to stay,'' Hiram said. ''I would be less than honest if I didn't tell thee that was my motive.''

''We appreciate it,'' Blake assured him. ''As for staying, well, we'll have to wait and see what the spring brings.''

''Come and see us often,'' Sarah told them as they left. ''Thee will always be welcome.''

''Thank you,'' Lacey said. ''For everything.'' She waved to the Gibsons as they left.

As soon as they were out of sight, she shrugged off Blake's arm. ''Why did you imply we might stay here permanently? As you well know, that's impossible! I'm going to Oregon!''

''What was I supposed to do? Throw his gift back in his face?'' Blake looked around the cabin. ''This is a nice place. Hiram must have worked hard getting it ready for us.''

Lacey walked around and touched the mantel, the solid log walls, the table. ''A house. They actually gave us a house! I still can hardly believe it.'' She ran her fingers over the smooth pine surface. More softly she said, ''My very own table. I've never owned a piece of furniture before. Not for my very own.''

Blake watched her as she knelt by the hearth to stir the soup that was simmering there. He could almost swear he saw a tear glistening on her eyelashes.

"Well, this is all fine and good," Lacey said in a firmer tone, "but we must be reasonable about this."

"In what way?"

"You will have to move out to the barn."

He stared at her as if she had lost her mind. "No, ma'am. I'm not about to spend the winter in a barn."

She frowned up at him and went to look out at the structure from the window. "It looks sound enough from here. I'm sure you would be quite comfortable out there."

"That just shows how much you know about barns. I'm not moving out of this house." He set his jaw stubbornly. "Besides, the house is as much mine as yours. *You* move into the barn if you're so dead set on avoiding me."

"It's nothing personal, Blake, but it's not a good idea for both of us to live in here. You and I both know it wouldn't be proper." Her nerves felt as tightly strung as piano wires. Surely he could see this was too much of a strain. Being with him in the Gibsons' guest room had almost been her undoing.

"Believe me, Lacey, if either of us sets up housekeeping in the barn, everybody in town will be asking questions. How proper will that be?"

When Lacey looked at him from across the room, he was upset to see her eyes fill with tears. "What's the matter now?"

"Never mind," she answered with a tilt of her chin. "If you have to ask, I don't want to talk about it." One large tear rolled over the curve of her cheek.

He tried logic. "How can I help if you won't tell me what's wrong?"

"It's everything," she said as she managed to choke down a sob. She couldn't cry, especially in front of Blake! She never cried. Not ever. "I can't stay here. My land is waiting for me in Oregon. Buying it took all my savings, and it's mine. She held her head up and her back straight as she gazed unseeingly out the window. "Besides, we aren't going to be able to fool the whole town forever. You saw how we nearly gave ourselves away at dinner. How long will it be before one of us really slips up and makes a mistake we can't fix? They'll all know we were lying, and they'll make us leave town."

Blake went to her and pulled her into his embrace. He held her protectively when he felt her tremble. "There, now, Lacey," he soothed. "Nobody will ever know unless we tell them. Not for sure anyway. Who would ever question it?"

"I hate lying," she said in a choked voice. When he was so kind to her she felt worse than ever. He didn't even know who she really was. If he had known, he would never have said he loved her. The specter of the medicine wagon still hung about her and ruined her life. "If the truth ever comes out, what will I do?" She wasn't referring only to their unmarried state so she added, "Sarah and Hiram would be shunned for sheltering us! I couldn't stand to cause them suffering." She held close to him and tried to pretend he really loved her, just as she was.

He tightened his arms so that she was pressed against him, and he awkwardly stroked her hair, dislodging stray tendrils. "Don't start crying," he said with desperation in his voice. Holding her close was awakening that deep longing in him again, but he couldn't see her so unhappy and not try to do something about it.

"I never cry!" she snapped as her eyelids stung. "I'm just worried about what will happen to Sarah and Hiram if the truth becomes known. Also, I'm afraid you'll want to stay here. Then how will I get to Oregon?"

"Oregon! Is that all you ever think about?" His words were harsh, but he continued holding her close.

"It's my land! Surely you can understand that."

Blake released her and strode out of the cabin. When he returned, he slapped a handful of brown dirt into her palm. "This is also your land! It was given to you out of friendship."

"We can't stay here!" she exclaimed as she clutched the rich soil. "You know we can't!"

Blake sighed and ran his fingers through his hair. "I know it," he admitted in a tired voice. "I just wish things were different. In a lot of ways."

"So do I," she whispered. If matters were as they appeared to be, she would be married to Blake, and she would be a lady with roots securely formed in a fine house in South Carolina. She held out the dirt to Blake. "If you can find a way to get me on a wagon train and to explain my absence, you can stay here."

He took the dirt and tossed it back outside. "I couldn't stay here without you," he told her gruffly. "I wouldn't want to."

"What do you mean?" she asked uncertainly.

"I love you. Remember?" He refused to look at her and instead stared stonily at the front yard beyond the open door. "I can't let you strike off on your own all the way to Oregon. If you're so set on living on that mountaintop all by yourself, at least let me see you all the way there. I'll build the cabin for you and lay out a garden. Then I'll stake some land nearby so I can check on you now and then. That shouldn't crowd you too much. That way I'll know if you're safe or if you need something."

"You'd really do that?"

"Of course I would. And you're just going to have to accept it. Oregon has a lot of land, and you don't have any say over who owns what, so there's no need for you to argue with me. I'm going to own the land next to yours, and that's all there is to it. I have to tell you, though, I would rather stay right here. I like this town, and I like the people. I'm not some old bear who wants to live in the back of nowhere. But if you're set on Oregon, then that's where we'll go."

"It's not just what I want," she objected softly. "We *can't* stay here."

He turned back to her. "Would you stay here if you could?" He gestured at the cabin.

Lacey looked at the four sturdy walls and the furniture. Never in her life had she lived in a house, and she knew the one in Oregon wouldn't be nearly as nice or as well furnished. "Whether I would or not doesn't matter, since we can't."

"You're a grown woman. You can do anything you want to. Would you stay here? With me?"

Her large eyes met his. "We aren't married, Blake, and we can't be."

"Why not?" he demanded.

"Who would marry us? Everybody thinks that has been done already. If we ask the preacher to do it, everyone will know."

His brow furrowed in a frown. This hadn't occurred to him.

"You see?" she said when he had no answer. "We have to leave. Anyway," she said in a tight voice, "you never asked me to marry you, did you? You only asked me to stay with you."

Blake turned away. "You're putting words in my mouth." She made no comment, and he said abruptly, "I'm going to go look at the barn. I have some thinking to do."

Lacey watched him leave before she sank down on a chair and leaned her face on her arms on the table. How foolish she had been to say that to him! She had practically proposed to him. And he had replied by going to look at a barn. Embarrassment brought the tears brimming to her eyes, and this time she couldn't stop them from spilling over.

CHAPTER
14

Blake stayed in the barn a long time as he tried to sort his thoughts. Not being able to marry her had never occurred to him, and this added a new dimension to the problem.

He surveyed his surroundings as though he might find a solution there. The building contained three stalls, each of which opened to the feed lot. On the other side of the central aisle stood a tack room, a tool room, and a lean-to shelter for a buggy, wagon, or plow. He couldn't have planned the barn any better. His bay horse snuffled companionably as Blake poured a measure of feed for him from an old syrup bucket. Blake patted the animal's muscled neck as he continued to ponder this latest predicament. What Lacey had said was true. He knew she would be insulted if he suggested they simply omit the ceremony and live together; ladies didn't do things like that, and besides, he loved her and wanted her for his wife. He chided himself for having done such a poor job of asking her to marry him. She had seemed offended by his approach. He should have been more straightforward. Ladies liked pretty words at a time like that. But then, she hadn't agreed to marry him even if they could, and he wondered about that. Her ideas about love didn't seem to tally with his.

He climbed the steep plank ladder to the hay loft to look around. Even here the townspeople had been generous. A winter's supply of hay—some baled, some in sheafs, according to the practice of the individual farmer—was stacked along the wall. Blake pulled out a bundle and loosened its straw rope binding. After he tossed an armload down the hole in the floor over the manger, he went to the hay door to check the view.

Evening was deepening, and the rims of the craggy mountains were glowing with the aura of sunset. Here in the high valley the forest was already dusky. An owl glided by on silent wings. A light came on in the house, and Blake gazed at it thoughtfully.

From this angle he could see in the two side windows. The room was illuminated like a lantern show. Lacey was kneeling by the fire, putting the final touches to their supper. As he watched, she rose and crossed the room to the bed. Almost shyly she touched the feather pillows, then drew back her hand. She pirouetted slowly and looked again at her new home. Her expression was soft and seemed full of longing, and Blake's heart went out to her. A woman needed a place of her own. Especially a gentle-bred woman like Lacey. But he wondered why she was so awed by the simple cabin. It was clean and tight, but she had grown up in a much finer house. There were many facets about Lacey that just didn't make sense.

Blake watched her trail her fingers across the back of a pine chair. He had seen women do that when they were admiring expensive china or delicate embroidery, but never a plain chair with a cowhide seat. She acted as if she had never been in a house in her life. And, now that he thought about it, how could a lady reach her early twenties without ever attending a wedding? In Texas, marriages were occasions for parties and shivarees that lasted far into the night. He doubted South Carolina was much different, since people were people no matter where they lived. Also, Zeke Summerfield hardly looked the type to own a house with lace curtains and velvet-covered furniture. He might have gone into a decline after his wife's death—Blake had done so himself—but from what Lacey had implied, her mother had died many years before. With a confused sigh, Blake busied himself with the small tasks of rearranging harnesses and equipment.

Later that evening, Lacey sat by the fire and carefully cut her torn blue dress into quilting squares as long as her finger. She never wanted to wear it again and had already bought some gingham from the general store to replace it. Every time she looked at it, she was reminded of the wagon train and the bear.

Blake sat opposite her, his arms crossed over his deep chest, his feet propped against the chimney so that his chair tilted back precariously. He appeared to be daydreaming as he watched the fire leaping in the hearth, so Lacey frequently stole glances at him. The light gilded the planes of his face to molten gold and softened the lines that ran from his nose to the corners of his mouth. His eyes, like his thick hair, were black with ruddy lights from the flames. He had been very quiet and preoccupied since he came in from the barn, and she guessed he was regretting having made his oblique reference to marriage, if it had indeed been that. More and more she was becoming convinced that he had meant something less permanent.

"Did you want to ask me something?" he said, startling her.

"No, no. I was just looking around." She fastened her attention back on her quilting squares.

Again the silence was broken only by the crackle of the fire and the metallic snipping of her scissors.

"I was thinking," she said, grasping at anything to make conversation, "that a row of sweet peas would look pretty along the side of the porch."

He was quiet for a while. Then, "When do sweet peas bloom?"

Her fingers faltered. "Oh. I had forgotten we won't be here that long."

"I might be able to get you some seeds," he said with careful offhandedness. "You could plant them in Oregon."

"I guess sweet peas would grow there," she said doubtfully. "I've never heard. I suppose it would make more sense to plant something useful, though, like beans or potatoes."

"No, it wouldn't," he said softly. "I'll find flower seeds for you."

She looked up to find his eyes on her. His expression, like his voice, was gentle. Her traitorous body quickened beneath his gaze. Silently she chastised herself for melting every time he was kind to her. She tried to keep her voice level as she said, "That won't be necessary." Her words came out clipped and cold, so she tried to soften the effect by saying, "I've heard a horse dealer comes through here early in the spring. Maybe you could trade your horse for another one then."

"I may just decide to keep that old horse."

"But his wind is ruined. He can't carry you all the way to Oregon." Animals were for work, and when they could no longer do their intended job, they were swapped or sold for whatever they might be worth to someone else. Yet Blake wanted to keep a useless horse! Such an extravagance was unknown to her.

"I'll buy another horse," he explained, "but I'm going to keep the bay well. He did me a great service and deserves to retire."

Lacey stared at him openly. Did he want to keep the horse because it had helped save her life? Surely she had misunderstood his motive. "Do you suppose we could swap this cabin for a wagon and team? Maybe somebody on one of the spring wagon trains will want to settle here." She looked around at the first real home she had ever had and felt a keen pain at the idea of leaving it.

"Do you really want to do that?"

She nodded and finally said, ''What else can we do? We need money to get a wagon and mules and to pay our passage. Maybe we can even get some extra money out of it as well, since the furniture is comfortable and the cabin is sound.'' She tried to appear remote and untouched by the idea. ''You can use the money to buy land in Oregon, if you're sure you still want to do that.''

Blake regarded her thoughtfully. ''Do you think we could get money to boot out of this?''

''A nice place like this?'' she exclaimed. ''Certainly we could. Maybe I should handle the trading. I'm good at it and can get top dollar.'' She stacked the squares in neat piles of ten to form her pattern as she talked, not realizing what she had said.

Blake turned back to the fire and studied the molten landscape for answers. No proper lady would know the first thing about bargaining, let alone volunteer to do the haggling herself. Now that he was aware of Lacey's peculiar actions, he could see other inconsistencies as well, like the way she was cutting her own squares and designing her own quilt. He had seen his mother piece many quilts, but she had usually used a pattern shared by a friend or scraps from a neighbor's bag. Lacey was doing it all herself and hadn't even suggested that she might want or even accept someone else's help. And he knew for a fact she wasn't fond of that dress because she had told him so before she started cutting it up—so why make a quilt out of it that would last for years?

Even the way Lacey had washed the supper dishes was odd. She had dried the pieces and put them away almost as if she were caressing the simple tin plates and cups. Afterward, she had wiped the drainboard clean several times and had twice straightened the chairs that were already in place against the walls.

Not realizing Blake was watching her from the corner of his eyes, Lacey continued her reverie. While this cabin wasn't as large as the Gibsons' house, it was much more spacious than the medicine wagon. The thick logs had aged to a silvery hue and looked strong enough to withstand gales that could topple a wagon. The floor was new and still had the golden cast of fresh-sawn pine. She would have a dirt floor in Oregon, at least at first. She gauged the size of the table and chairs. Would they fit in a wagon?

And what about the bed? It had a tall pine headboard with a roll at the top like a cresting wave. The design was repeated in the footboard. It was the grandest bed she had ever seen. The brightly colored quilt that served as a bedspread lay curving over the mounded feather mattress. No matter what else she had to leave behind, Lacey resolved to find a way to take that bed.

Then she remembered that Blake owned half the house and furniture. And half the bed. That reminded her of their pressing predicament, and she glanced at the darkness beyond the windows. They had sat by the fire for a long time, and it was late. Soon Blake would yawn, as she had watched him do many times at the Gibsons' house, and say it was bedtime. Only now they were all alone, and Sarah wasn't in the next room to ensure that Blake wouldn't paw at her as men had tried to do in the past. Lacey felt a prickle of fear. Sarah hadn't been aware she was a chaperon, but Lacey and Blake had known it. She suddenly felt very defenseless, and she didn't like that feeling at all.

When the log on the hearth broke apart, sending a spray of cinders up the chimney. Lacey jumped, her eyes large.

"It was just the log," he pointed out.

"I know that. I'll get another one."

"Don't bother. It's late. I'll bank the embers, and we can go to bed."

"No!"

"Why not? Aren't you tired? It's getting late."

"You go to bed. I'm not sleepy yet," she answered stubbornly.

"Then I'll stay up, too."

Lacey chose a thick log and laid it across the andirons. At once the hungry flames began to consume it. If she could stall, perhaps Blake would be sleepy enough to go to bed and fall asleep before she had to join him. She wondered if she could possibly sleep where she sat. The chair was straight, but she could lay her head on the table. That might suffice for one night, but not for months. She had to think of some way of getting the bed, if not the room, to herself. Blake had said the barn was unfit for people, but Lacey knew better; she had slept in barns more than once and been glad to do it. Tomorrow she resolved to look at the structure herself. After a while Blake stretched as she had known he would and said, "I guess we'd better turn in. I have an axle to repair tomorrow, and it may take a while."

"You go ahead," she said, stifling a yawn. "I'm not sleepy."

"Then why are you yawning? Come on. It's time for bed."

Lacey looked at him testily. "I said I'm not sleepy."

He sighed and stood up to stretch again, his long arms seeming to take up most of the space in the cabin. When he had run his fingers through his hair, he said, "You mean you don't want to share the bed. That's just plain silly, Lacey. We've slept in the same bed for weeks now."

"I realize that," she said without looking at him, "but this is entirely different. Until now we had someone else in the house with us. If I had needed them, I could have called out for help. Here no one would hear me. Besides, I'm not sleepy."

Blake paused before he said, "Is that what you think? That I plan to attack you?"

Lacey avoided his eyes and rose to sweep the ashes back into the firebox. "It could happen."

"I wouldn't do anything you didn't want me to do. I love you." He caught her wrist and pulled her around to face him. "Lacey, let me tell you something you really ought to know. A man has the same amount of strengths and weaknesses as a woman when it comes to loving. I'm no more apt to lose control and attack you than you are to attack me. But if you were willing and we let ourselves go, soon you would be as unwilling to stop as I would. Anything else you may have been told was either an excuse for behaving like a savage or a lie to keep you in line.''

Lacey considered his words carefully before responding. Finally she said, "I don't believe you."

He sighed and released her wrist. "All right. Have it your way. You take the bed. I'll sleep on the floor."

"You will not," she said perversely. If he really loved her, she couldn't take the soft bed. She found when it came right down to it, she wanted his comfort more than her own. The thought was unsettling. "You've already said you have a long day's work ahead of you tomorrow. I'll take the floor."

"I can't sleep on a feather bed while you're lying on the hard floor! What kind of a person do you think I am?"

"A very hardheaded one! Why can't you just be reasonable?"

"Me? I *am* reasonable! Why do you insist on acting like a martyr?"

"Oh!" she gasped, her anger leaping. "A *martyr*, is it! Well, that does it. I wouldn't sleep in that bed with you no matter what. A martyr!" She stormed over to the shelf and grabbed a quilt. With a glare at Blake she carried it to the fireside, flung it open, and spread it on the floor.

"You're the stubbornest damned woman I've ever seen!" he irately informed her.

Pointedly ignoring him, she grabbed a pillow from the bed and lay down on the floor, flicking one side of the quilt over her. In her speed to prove her point she had forgotten to change into her nightgown, and her hair was still twisted into a bun that made an uncomfortable knot on the back of her head. Lacey closed her eyes and pretended she meant to go to sleep this way.

Blake glowered down at her. "You're being foolish. You know that, don't you?"

Lacey ignored him.

"That floor must be uncomfortable as hell. Get into the bed!"

Still she lay motionless, her eyes serenely closed.

"Lacey Summerfield, you're enough to drive a man to drink," Blake informed her. "Are you going to go to bed or not?"

Lacey's only reply was to snuggle deeper under the quilt.

With a groan, Blake crossed the room. He pulled off his boots and threw them over the footboard. "This is your last chance," he told her. "Get up off that floor!"

Lacey kept her eyes closed and her breathing even, though her pulse was racing. Would he pick her up and toss her into the bed? If he did, would he ravish her? Excitement of a most unmaidenly sort surged through her. Now that he had assured her he wasn't going to attack her, she found she wasn't all that unwilling. Certainly if he did, it would put an end to part of the problem. She would have no need to guard herself after that.

Blake blew out the lantern, and she heard his clothes drop to the floor and the bed slats creak as he lay down. Her eyes flew open indignantly. He was actually going to let her sleep on the floor!

Righteous indignation flared as she jerked her head toward the bed. He was lying down and seemed to be settled in for the night. She could see his form in the dim firelight. Grim determination made her turn away. Inconsideration was no more than she should have expected. He was no better than any other man!

In a matter of minutes she heard the slow, deep breathing that meant Blake was asleep. Lacey grimaced. All her bones seemed to be pressing into the hard floor, and she felt a definite draft rising up between the boards. Not only that, but a splinter had worked through the quilt and was pricking her.

She jerked out the splinter and threw it toward the fire. Rolling to her back, she stared up at the beams of the ceiling, which seemed to shift in the yellow glow from the fireplace. In no time, her back had begun to ache and her head was throbbing.

Sitting up, she yanked the pins from her hair and let it fall to her waist. Still Blake slept on. Lacey rose and went to frown down at him. He slept in comfortable oblivion among the billows of down. At that moment she could have cheerfully choked him.

Instead, she jerked her nightgown over her head and fumbled with the buttons of her dress. Why, she wondered, did she have to go through such inconveniences as a dress that buttoned down the back, when a man could just shuck off his clothing and lie down? It was grossly unfair! Blake didn't even wear a nightshirt! If she had to cover herself, he should at least do the same.

She stepped out of her daytime clothes and shoved her arms through the sleeves of her nightgown. It was of heavy flannel and as warm as it was concealing. Again she glared at Blake. After hanging her clothing on a peg, she made a point of kicking the bedstead as she passed, but he didn't even change the pace of his breathing.

Once more Lacey lay down on the quilt. If anything, the floor seemed harder than before. She rolled to her side. The fire had flickered to a brighter blaze, and soon her face felt parched while her back was chilled. She flipped over. Now the light was out of her eyes, but all her weight seemed to rest entirely on her hipbone and her shoulder.

Sitting up, she glared at the bed. There was plenty of room for her. It was every bit as large as the one in the Gibsons' spare room. She had the nagging suspicion that the price for defending her pride would be the loss of a night's rest.

In the bright moonlight beyond the window she could just make out the darkened roof of the barn. No one would ever know if she slept out there. The thought of the mounds of hay seemed almost like heaven. Carefully she stood up and wrapped the quilt around her. She could sleep out there and slip back into the house early the next morning without Blake or anyone else even knowing what she had done.

Lacey quietly went out, pulling the door shut behind her. Instantly a frigid wind whipped her face and made her eyes water. After two steps her bare feet felt frozen, and icy gusts were blowing up beneath the quilt. With determination she hurried on.

Suddenly the muted flapping of wings and a loud hoot sounded just over her head. Lacey turned abruptly and scurried back toward the safety of the porch. Logic told her it was an owl, but some primitive fear assured her it was something a great deal more ferocious.

As she ran up the front steps, she paused. A discarded plank lay propped against the house next to the front door. After a split second's deliberation, Lacey picked it up and hauled it into the house.

Shivering, she padded back to the fire and stood almost on the hearth, as close to the fire as she could get, to let the welcome warmth drive the chill from her. When she stopped shaking, she added a large log that would burn most of the night and again swept the ashes into the firebox to contain the blaze.

She washed her feet and looked back at the bed. When she was a child, they had spent one winter with a large family of boys. There had been no bed for her, so the boys' mother had put her in with the youngest boy, with a bundling board placed down the middle of the bed. The boy's grandmother had insisted the arrangement was more proper than having the two of them sit together on the sofa with no such barrier. Lacey hadn't thought much about it at the time, but now she fell back on the memory. The plank should make an ideal bundling board.

Moving stealthily, she took the board to the bed and eased it onto the mattress. It neatly divided one side from the other and rose up higher than Blake's body. It was perfect.

Since the headboard, like the foot, was solid pine, instead of iron railings like the bed the family had owned, Lacey had no way of securing her improvised bundling board. By sitting carefully on the edge of the bed, her hand behind her holding the board in place, she managed to swing her legs up and lie down, still holding the barrier in place.

Comfort flooded over her. Never had a mattress felt so warm, so soft, so welcoming. The ticking had recently been aired, and it still held the clean scent of pines and sunshine. Lacey sighed with sheer pleasure.

Easing the plank up, she snuggled it against the head of the bed. Putting her hand on the middle and her foot against the end, she managed to keep it upright. She couldn't see Blake at all. He might not even be there for all she could tell.

Almost at once sleep began to claim her, and as her tired muscles relaxed, the large plank fell over onto Blake.

As if this were a common occurrence, he lifted the heavy board and lowered it to the floor. "Good night, Lacey," he said in the darkness, his voice showing no traces of sleep, but a great deal of humor.

She decided it would be more politic to ignore him. She couldn't face sleeping on the uncomfortable floor, and he had promised she could trust him. Nevertheless, she waited nervously, steeled for an attack.

"Lacey, relax."

She felt the feathers shift beneath her as he rolled to his side and propped his head up on his hand. Fearfully she stared at him. The firelight laid a patina of copper over his muscled arms and shoulders and dimly lit his face. She grasped the covers tightly.

He reached out and caressed her river of hair, and the tendrils curled lovingly around his fingers. "Don't be afraid of me. You're shaking all over."

"I'm not," she mumbled. If he grabbed her, she could kick him and maybe get out the door before he caught her. Once she reached the trees, perhaps she could outrun him.

He sighed, and the sadness he was feeling was evident. "Honey, I love you. Don't you know what that means?"

"I guess I don't. Nobody ever loved me before."

"Not ever?" His velvety voice was dissolving her fear, but she was still far from serene. "No beaus? No proposals?"

"Never." She hesitated and said, "I never heard the words before today." He said nothing, so she continued, "In the stories I've read, it's not at all like this. I'm confused." She found it easier to talk to him in the concealing darkness.

His fingers continued to stroke her hair as he said gently, "What do the stories say?"

"Those words are always followed by 'Will you do me the honor of becoming my wife?' Then they kiss."

"Then what?"

"That's always the last page. I guess they live happily ever after."

"There is no 'happily ever after' in real life. People aren't meant for it, and they would die of boredom." His fingers strayed nearer and he caressed her cheek so gently she almost thought she had imagined it.

"This afternoon I wasn't asking that you marry me," Lacey said, hoping the straightforward words would calm her heartbeat. "I want to make that clear."

"I know you weren't." Again his fingers brushed over her cheek, gliding past her ear and down her neck. "Do I really frighten you? Tell me the truth."

"I don't know. You confuse me, and I don't like that. I was a lot more afraid of you when we were fully clothed and sitting by the fire than I am now."

"Why is that?"

His silken voice and gentle hands were playing havoc with both her reason and her caution. She heard herself say, "When you talk to me and touch me like this, all my insides start to flutter, and I don't want you to stop. Not ever." She tried to bite back her words, but they were already spoken.

Blake smiled and cupped her face in his warm palm. "Don't look so stricken, honey. I'm not going to hurt you."

She didn't know what she might say, so she kept her mouth tightly shut and merely gazed up at him.

"Lacey, will you do something for me?" When she didn't answer, he said, "Smile for me. You rarely do, and you have such a beautiful smile."

Although she hadn't meant to do it, Lacey felt the corners of her mouth tilting upward. Somehow he wasn't in the least threatening now.

He touched the curving smile lines at the corners of her lips. "You're a beautiful woman, Lacey, and you should smile often. Has life been that hard for you?"

She nodded and closed her eyes. His tenderness was crumbling all her barriers, and she was sure she was going to cry again. She fought against the stinging tears.

Blake slipped his arm under her and snuggled her head into the hollow of his shoulder. Surprisingly, the act comforted her, and she slipped her arm over his lean stomach. She jerked her hand back when her fingers encountered his bare flesh.

"No, no," he soothed. "Relax and let me hold you. There's nothing to be afraid of."

His steady heartbeat was as reassuring as his voice. In spite of herself, she couldn't help noticing how well her body fit against his, curve matching curve and warmth meeting warmth.

"What is it that makes you so skittish?" he murmured into the silk of her hair.

She wanted to blurt it all out—the years of leaving town just ahead of an angry mob, the men who gave her a job because they thought they could have her body in return, the thousands of small lies Papa told which had trained her from childhood that trusting was a mistake. But she looked up and saw him so near, so loving, and the words couldn't form. He was in love with the woman he believed her to be—a lady with blue blood and a fine lineage. She couldn't bear to tell him the truth and see the veil drop over his eyes. Numbly she shook her head.

Holding her securely, Blake curved his forefinger under her chin and tilted her head upward until their lips met. She was so vulnerable, so gentle at that moment, that he was kissing her before he thought about it. Instead of recoiling as he had expected, she reached out and pulled him closer as she returned his kiss with an openness that left his head spinning.

Her firm breasts flattened against his rib cage, and her body curved naturally into his as their embrace became more passionate. Knowing he must stop now if he was to be able to do so at all, Blake buried his head in her fiery cloud of hair. Over and over he repeated her name in a litany of longing.

"Blake?" she whispered. "Are you about to ravish me?"

Lacey's curiously worded question was so unexpected that it broke the intimacy, and he chuckled. Holding her close, he pillowed her cheek on his shoulder. "No," he answered, "I'm not going to do anything of the sort."

Blake could have almost sworn he heard her sigh in disappointment, but decided he was mistaken. He continued to hold her and tenderly stroke her hair as the minutes glided by on moonbeams and firelight. Finally he felt her relax into sleep.

Still he gazed at the darkened ceiling and watched the fire chase the shadows as he tried to unravel her mystery. He was positive now that she wasn't what she pretended to be. He decided he and Zeke Summerfield were going to have a long and possibly unpleasant talk as soon as he found him.

CHAPTER
15

Lacey awoke slowly, unwilling to relinquish the lovely dream she was having. But dreams being transitory by nature, the visions soon faded leaving Lacey struggling to recall even the essentials of the pleasant experience. She yawned and stretched, and her hand encountered nothing but cool sheets. The night before came back to her with a jolt, and she sat up, ready to flee if necessary.

The cabin was empty, and from the angle of the square of sunlight on the floor she guessed that she had slept late—a rare indulgence for her. She rubbed her eyes to clear her thoughts as she tried to determine whether her recollection of Blake holding her close as she drifted into sleep was reality or just an incredibly beautiful dream. No, she decided, it was no dream. Even in sleep she couldn't have created the sense of security and of being cherished that she recalled so vividly.

She curled her legs beneath her and held Blake's pillow tightly against her chest. The downy feathers still held a trace of his clean scent, and she breathed it in deeply. Resting her chin on the pillow, she pondered her dilemma. He had not forced himself on her, and she no longer worried that he would. All her trepidation resulted from her own impulsive feelings. Blake might be able to keep his distance indefinitely, but she doubted if she could trust herself even one more night. She wanted him as much he seemed to want her, and the worst part of it was that it no longer seemed wrong that they should feel that way.

With a sigh, she fell back on the bed, Blake's pillow lying across her middle, her arms outstretched. What was she going to do? She tried to call to mind exactly what he had said the day before. He had said he loved her, but had he mentioned marriage? The word had never actually been spoken. Maybe he had a far less permanent arrangement in mind. She frowned and embraced the pillow. It really didn't matter. Even if he had proposed on bended knee and written it on the wall in ink, it wouldn't change things. They still couldn't get married.

What she needed, Lacey decided, was a confidante. If she could voice her thoughts and get a response, maybe she could find a way to get around this seemingly insurmountable obstacle. But she could talk to no one but Blake. And Sarah.

Lacey dressed quickly and hastened down the path toward her friend's house. As she went, her mind was in a turmoil. She wished she could explain that the people of Friendswood had made a simple mistake when they assumed that she and Blake were married. If people understood that, everything else could be corrected. After all, she had known nothing about the misunderstanding—she had been unconscious—and Blake was the one who had allowed it to go uncorrected. He'd had her welfare in mind, of course. How could he have known Sarah would doctor her whether she was his wife or not? He hadn't been aware of Sarah's willingness to heal anyone and anything.

But how could she tell Sarah? She couldn't just blurt out that she and Blake weren't married. The situation required more subtlety. She would have to provide some history, but how much? To say that Blake, who had been virtually a stranger to her, had risked his life to save her required some elaboration as well. Her father should have been the one to search for her. To explain Papa, though, meant including the Wonder Tonic and the traveling medicine show.

Lacey set her chin stubbornly. The tonic didn't seem as significant as her lack of a wedding ceremony and, embarrassing or not, telling Sarah about it should help in being able to discuss the real problem. She hoped.

The Gibsons' cabin was in sight now, and Lacey slowed to a more sedate pace. She told herself that she mustn't seem too flustered by all this. She could smile and present it as an amusing though complicated comedy of errors, or perhaps she could tell it in tragic tones and implore Sarah's help— no, Lacey decided, that was all wrong. Maybe a simple statement of the facts would be best. Unfortunately, simple statements, by necessity, lacked subtlety and if this situation needed anything, it was distracting embellishments. The bald facts would make her sound like both a fool and a scarlet woman.

Sarah was in the kitchen when Lacey knocked, and she called out for her to come in. Lacey paused in the doorway studying the domestic scene; Sarah was slicing sweet potatoes to dry for the winter.

"Sit down," Sarah invited. "I'd stop working to chat with thee, but I'm late getting these potatoes put up."

Lacey found a paring knife and automatically started peeling and slicing. The methodical work eased some of her worry, but she was at a loss as to how to open herself up to Sarah.

"Did thee sleep well?" Sarah asked with a warm smile. "Was thee able to find all thy things? We moved them in so quickly to keep the secret, it may take days for thee to unearth everything."

Lacey smiled. "Oh, Sarah, the cabin is wonderful. I can never thank all of you enough for giving it to us. I know you and Hiram thought of it first." The real reason for her visit surfaced, and her smile wavered. "I don't deserve it, though. I really don't."

"Pooh. Thee is talking nonsense. When thee goes home, be sure and take some potatoes with thee. I have more here than I need. Also take some of that fresh soap. Mary Benson made the batch we left at thy house and, while Mary is one of the sweetest souls alive, her soap always turns out soft." With a knowing nod, she added, "Mary tries to make too large a batch at a time."

"Sarah, there's something I want to tell you," Lacey began with trepidation. This was much harder to do than she had hoped.

"Lacey! Is thee in the family way?" Sarah exclaimed. "No, that news would make thee look happy, not uneasy. Blake isn't sick, is he? Did thy horse get out? Hiram isn't here, but I'll help thee catch him."

In spite of her worry, Lacey smiled. "It's none of those things. You'll never guess, so you may as well let me tell you." She picked up another potato and studied it intently.

"Well? What is it?" Sarah asked as she worked efficiently.

"First of all, I mean . . . Well, let me pay you for your extra sweet potatoes."

"I couldn't take thy money, but I'll trade them to you for Blake having mended my favorite pot. But I can tell that's not something that would make thee so nervous. Just what's bothering thee?"

"Sarah," she said, taking a deep breath, "I'm not who you think I am." The words had been very hard to say, but Lacey looked directly at her friend for her reaction.

"No? I could have sworn thee was my good friend, Lacey. Welcome to Friendswood, stranger. Thy twin lives in a cabin near here." Her round face dimpled with her levity.

Lacey solemnly continued. "I'm not the daughter of wealthy parents," she announced in a breathless rush. "I didn't live in a real house until I was fourteen."

"Where did thee live before, then?" Sarah asked in amazement. "How can this be?"

"My father . . ." Lacey drew another breath and said, "My father is a traveling medicine man."

"A doctor?"

"No, no. A medicine salesman. We lived in a red wagon with yellow letters that said Dr. Summerfield's Wonder Tonic." She waited for Sarah's reaction.

"My goodness! I never would have guessed. Did thee see a great deal of the country?"

Her friend's reaction was totally unexpected. Friendliness still glowed in Sarah's blue eyes, and she seemed more interested in the travel than in the tonic. "You don't mind?"

"Why should I? Sometimes the shows are very entertaining." Sarah blushed. "Don't thee dare tell Hiram I've seen one. He would tease me for the rest of my life. Quakers don't abide with music as a rule, but I confess I've tapped my toe to a strain or two." She smiled. "Here we are trading secrets like two young girls."

Sarah didn't seem to be taking this very seriously. Didn't she understand what Lacey's childhood had been like? Suddenly Lacey realized that Sarah didn't and couldn't comprehend what she wanted to say. As the beloved daughter of a dignified Quaker family, Sarah had little in common with Lacey. And if she couldn't tell Sarah about the Wonder Tonic, she certainly couldn't confide in her about Blake. "You don't hold my past against me?" Lacey said as if this had been the entire issue.

"Of course not," Sarah laughed. "Thee has done nothing for me to disapprove of. Olive Sloan might have a field day if she ever heard, but I'm not Olive. Thy secret is safe with me." She leveled her finger at Lacey and arched her brows. "But don't ever let me catch thee repeating what I said about my fondness for music." A smile made her words light.

"Never. I won't tell a soul." Lacey finished slicing the potatoes and said, "I have to go now. There's something I need to do at home."

"Wait. Take some potatoes, and don't forget thy soap.

Here. A cake for both thy pockets.'' She poured potatoes into a peck basket and handed the soap to Lacey.

"Thank you," Lacey said gratefully. "Thank you for being my friend."

"I don't need thanks for that. Get along with thee."

Lacey left with her heart heavier than it had been on her arrival. She couldn't tell Sarah, and there was no one else. Perhaps, she thought dismally, the Wonder Tonic years would be incomprehensible for Blake as well. She felt as if her past were permanently corked up inside her, decaying day by day.

When she reached home, Lacey put the potatoes in a bin in the barn and sat on a bale of hay. Nothing was going the way she had planned. All at once she was tired to the bone with lies and half-truths. With grim determination, she stood up. Maybe she couldn't confide in Sarah, but she had to get her lies off her conscience, and besides, she owed Blake the truth. Before she could change her mind, she set off toward town.

From several houses away, Lacey could hear the metallic twang of Blake's hammer. She paused outside the smithy for a moment to watch Blake fashion a rod of iron that glowed red. When he struck the hot iron, sparks flew, and the tinny sound filled the air. She stood quietly for a few minutes before he saw her. She hoped desperately that this confession would go more smoothly than her last attempt. When he finally looked up at her, she jumped.

"Lacey," he said in surprise, "I didn't see you come in."

"I don't want to bother you if you're busy," she said, almost wishing he would dismiss her.

"I'm not all that busy. Come look." He went to the workbench and pulled away a cloth that had concealed a tall object.

"A bell!" she exclaimed. "You made a bell?"

"It's an Indian-attack alarm. I'm making the clapper now. I didn't have enough iron, so almost everyone in town donated something to be melted down.'' He tapped the shiny side. "I'll bet my horse's old bit is right here.''

She ran her hand over the slick surface. "How did you do it?''

"I made a mold of sand and clay and then poured molten metal into the casting. It took me several tries to get one without cracks, but I finally did it.''

"That's wonderful!'' she said in amazement. "You can do anything!''

He grinned at her praise. "It's not pretty, as bells go, but it's big. I'll bet it will be heard easily past the far edge of town.'' He turned to her. "If you ever hear it, Lacey, drop what you're doing and run for the town hall.''

"I will.'' She frowned at the note of urgency in his voice. "Has there been more trouble?''

"Jake Benson saw a band of braves on the hill south of town this morning. The Indians just sat there and watched him, but Mrs. Benson is a bundle of nerves.''

"I'll go to her.''

"You'll do no such thing! She has Jake to watch over her. Their house is too far out for safety, so they're thinking about moving in closer for the time being.''

He clamped his long pliers onto the metal clapper, which still glowed pale pink, and shoved it into the water barrel. A rush of steam accompanied the faint hiss. "I'd feel better if you stayed close to the house. If there's trouble, I want to know where you are.''

Abruptly, Lacey changed the subject. "I came to town because I want to tell you something.'' She was determined to go through with this, but she suddenly found it as hard to confide in Blake as it had been to tell Sarah. What if he didn't want her anymore once he knew all about her? She wondered if she was being foolish to take the chance.

"What do you want to tell me?'' Blake held up the clapper and turned it several times to gauge its straightness. Then he put the other end into the fire and looked back to Lacey.

Drawing a deep breath, she blurted, "I'm not what you think I am. I'm not a lady."

He grinned. "Sure you are, any fool can see that."

"No. I'm a woman but not a lady." This wasn't going well. "I lied to you."

Blake removed the hot iron. "I know that. You're still a lady, though."

How much did he know? she wondered as his hammering made conversation impossible. When he had curved the end of the clapper into a hook that could be attached to the bell, the noise subsided, and she said, "What?"

"You're trying to say you didn't grow up in an elegant house. I know that."

"How did you know?"

He shrugged. "Little things. The sort of thing you wouldn't notice unless you lived with a person."

"Oh." She plunged on. "I'm not from South Carolina. I've never even been there as far as I know."

"Could have fooled me." Blake looked over her shoulder toward the door as a man entered the smithy. "Hello, Mr. Odem. How's the shoulder today?"

Lacey managed to greet the man and to inquire after his healing wound, but frustration tore at her. She had been so close to telling Blake. Now she would have to gather the courage all over again later on.

Carl Odem gestured toward the horse he led. "He cast a shoe. Think you can put another one on him today? With all this Indian threat going on, I hate to be without my horse."

"Sure thing," Blake said amiably.

Lacey got up to go when Carl settled on the bench by the door, clearly prepared to wait until his horse was shod.

"Blake, I think I'll go on home."

"You're welcome to stay. I'll be through here in a few minutes."

"That's all right. It's time for me to get supper on."

"See you in a little while."

Blake seemed somewhat distant, and Lacey tried to figure

whether it was Carl Odem's presence or the topic they had been discussing that had caused the change in him.

Only one subject could have put that ominous tone in his voice, and that was the Wonder Tonic. Somehow he had found out all about her background, and he was upset.

That night, Blake moved his chair away from the supper table and closer to the cozy fire. Picking up the stick he had been whittling on earlier, he began again. He wasn't making anything, just keeping his hands busy while he thought. The first storm of winter had whistled down from the frozen mountain about the time he had quit work, and snow had been falling for well over an hour. The last time he had looked out, the pale grass, bleached by the fall, had disappeared and the evergreen trees were bowing under the gale-driven snow. The bare hardwoods were clattering like an army of skeletons.

Blake watched Lacey as she washed their dishes. She seemed edgy and ill at ease. Undoubtedly the storm was bothering her. He didn't like to hear the wind blow so hard, either. When it whipped down the chimney it howled like a lost soul. To a woman so fearful of storms, this must be nerve-racking. He was proud to see she didn't give in to it. Lacey was an admirable woman.

Lacey finished and stepped to the rattling window to survey the storm. As hard as it blew, it surely wouldn't last long. An icy gust slammed into the house and blew the chimney's breath back upon itself, scenting the room anew with the aroma of wood smoke. But even that didn't alarm Lacey. She was far more concerned about Blake's silence. What did he know that was bothering him, and how had he learned the truth? How could he have found out? As a gesture of dominion over the storm, Lacey dropped a cup towel to the floor by the door and tapped it along the crack with her toe. Now even that tiny draft was defeated.

Blake still sat stoically by the fire, a piece of red cedar peeling back from his whittling knife. As usual, his unruly black hair tumbled over his forehead, and he wore a warm red plaid shirt of soft flannel. Lacey leaned back against the door. He looked as if he had something to say that was going to upset her.

"Do they have cats in Oregon?" she asked, hoping to evade the subject of his thoughts.

He glanced up but went right back to his whittling. "I guess so. Why?"

"I just wondered. I think I might like a pet. When I was growing up I never had an animal of my own."

"By spring there'll be a litter or two of kittens around town needing a home. You can take one with you."

"You wouldn't mind? After all, we will be traveling together for a while. At least I assume we will. If you're still set on claiming land next to mine."

He sat stroking long curls from the stick. "Get a cat and a dog, too, if you want them." His voice was brusque.

Lacey came over and drew her chair up to the fire. "What are you making?"

"Nothing. I'm just whittling. It helps me think."

She leaned forward, rested her elbows on her knees, cupped her chin in her hands, and gazed into the fire. "I wonder if it's snowing in Oregon. Maybe my land is white now. I hope the stream doesn't freeze completely over. I don't like having to break ice to draw water."

"How do you know there's a stream at all? Maybe there's nothing there but a barren mountain."

"You needn't be unpleasant. Surely if there was no water, the man I bought the land from would have said so. Everybody knows you have to have water in order to survive."

"I've been thinking about that. How do you know this man was on the level? Did he have proof?"

"Well, of course. He had an office set up in one corner of the lobby of the biggest hotel in town. Not only that, he also gave me a deed and signed it with his clerk as witness."

"Lacey, anybody can print up a bunch of deeds. Did he

have a legal document signed by a lawyer you've heard of before?''

''No, he didn't live in that town. He said he was thinking of settling there, though.'' She frowned uneasily. Now that she thought about it, the man *had* been awfully eager to get her money.

''Was there any sort of guarantee?'' Blake persisted.

''Would I have given him all my money otherwise? The deed says in writing that if I'm not happy with the land or if it's already been claimed, I can get my money back.'' A pit of dread was starting to grow in her middle. Saying the words out loud made them sound rather different from reading them in the elaborately scrawled legal language.

''How are you supposed to get your refund? Do you have an address more permanent than a hotel lobby? Or did it say you have to request it from him in person, face to face?''

Lacey's fingers covered her mouth, and she paled. After several long minutes she said in a dull voice, ''You knew all along that I'd been made a fool of, didn't you?''

''I suspected someone might have taken advantage of you.''

''Why didn't you tell me?''

''What could you do? When I heard about this land of yours, we were away from the wagons and miles from civilization.''

''What will I do?'' she asked the hearth. ''That was all the money I had in the world. I feel so foolish!''

''Listen, honey,'' he said, leaning forward to take her hands and hold them in his. ''It's not as bad as it sounds. The land out there is free. All you have to do is stake out a section and file a claim. After you live there for a few years, it's yours.''

''But my money!''

''You were willing to spend it on land anyway. Since we can't do anything about it now, you may as well pretend it went for that. My guess is that you can stake more than seventy acres if you read the fine print in the homestead provisions.''

''I could have used that money!''

''On what? There aren't any stores where we're going. We'll have to be completely self-sufficient for however many years it takes civilization to catch up with us.''

She still felt ridiculous, but having him hold her hands like this certainly helped. *We.* He had said *we* would have to be self-sufficient. Was he still planning on settling next to her, even though he knew all about her? ''But I thought—''

''We could stay here,'' he interrupted. ''Friendswood has everything I'm looking for. Is it that way for you?''

''Blake, you know we can't stay.''

''That's what I want to talk to you about. On the way home from the shop this evening something occurred to me. I've been trying to decide how you'd take it and I'm still not sure, but I want you to sit quietly and hear me out. Do you remember that last meal at the Gibsons', when we made all those slips about our past?''

Lacey nodded mutely. What did that have to do with his finding out the truth about her past? She should have told him herself. A feeling of dread thoroughly chilled her. Lacey braced herself for the inevitable.

''Sarah said something that started me to thinking,'' Blake began. ''She was telling us how she and Hiram were married. Do you remember? She said Quakers don't have preachers. They just announce they are husband and wife and that's it. They're married.''

Lacey's startled eyes swept his face. He was talking about getting married! ''You mean *we* should do that? Is that what you meant earlier when you said 'we'?''

''Lacey, all of Friendswood thinks we're already married.''

''But,'' she stammered, ''we aren't Quakers.''

''We've been to Meeting as often as Sarah and Hiram have, ever since we came here. That must count for something.''

"That's not the same thing!" Hope sprang to her eyes in spite of her contradiction.

He noticed the spark, and his warm smile broadened as he continued. "Back home in Texas, we have a similar arrangement called a bond marriage."

"This isn't Texas," she said automatically.

"I'm still a Texan by nationality, but that doesn't matter. I'm sure the same thing is done all along the frontier. Here's how a bond marriage works. In the less populated areas, there may not be a real church in every settlement, so there are preachers who travel about, weather permitting. If a couple wants to get married and can't or won't wait for the preacher to come to town, they say their vows to each other and have the legal ceremony as soon as it's convenient."

Lacey stared at him. "Is it a real marriage?"

"It sure is."

"And you think it would be a real marriage here as well?"

"I sure do." Blake's face beamed at the acceptance he could see in Lacey's expression.

"We could marry ourselves? Just say the vows and that would be good enough?"

"Honey, if it's not, half of Friendswood isn't married either."

The log crackled, and its resin exploded, sending a shower of sparks up the chimney. Lacey paid it no heed as her mind raced. "I couldn't be any more committed to you if I stood in front of a preacher," she reasoned. "I never joined a church."

"What do you say? Should we do it?" He grinned at her. Now that she was receptive to his idea, he was much happier. "Not too long ago you were set against marrying anybody. This is a permanent step. Are you sure you want to take it?"

She laughed with the unexpected happiness. Her heart was singing at the prospect. "I said that a long, long time

ago—before I knew what loving and being loved was like."
All thoughts of Lacey's past had vanished from her mind.

"Next spring when the roads are clear, we could go
southeast to Morgan. It's a big settlement about two days'
ride from here, according to Hiram, and must have several
churches. We could get married there, and no one would
ever know the difference."

"We could, couldn't we!" Lacey said with another
laugh. "We could tell whoever asked that we were going to
Morgan to buy supplies of some sort. Surely there's something we need that Friendswood doesn't have."

"Then you'll do it? You're sure?" Blake spoke with
tense excitement.

Lacey nodded happily. "How do we do it? I've never
seen a wedding. What do we say?" She gripped his hands
tightly. "Are you sure you have no second thoughts? I must
have heard you say a hundred times that you didn't want a
wife."

"That was before I fell in love with you and before I
thought there was any chance of you accepting me."

"Blake," she murmured at the tenderness in his voice,
"are you really sure you won't regret it?"

"How could I regret it? You're perfect. But first"—Blake
paused while he cleared his throat and took on a more serious expression—"Lacey, will you marry me?"

"I'd be pleased to marry you." Love light shone in her
eyes, and she wanted this moment to last forever in her
memory. "What about our vows? What do we say?"

"We give each other the promises we intend to keep all
the rest of our lives." He reached up and smoothed her hair
where a tendril was curling loose. "Like this: I, Blake
Cameron, take you, Lacey Summerfield, for my wife. I'll
love you and protect you for as long as we live, and I'll
never stray from you."

"I, Lacey," she said, shyly at first but with growing confidence, "take you, Blake, for my husband. I'll never leave
you or give you cause to want to leave me. I'll try to make

you happy all your days, and I'll grow old beside you with no regrets. I'll always love you and want you by me.''

Blake leaned closer and kissed her gently, then more deeply as though this kiss was meant to seal their promises and to etch them indelibly on their hearts. ''I love you, Lacey Cameron.''

He drew back, and their eyes met as their souls touched. Lacey Summerfield was now his wife. His beloved and cherished wife. At last. But now that they had pledged themselves to each other, he wasn't sure what to do next. Sweeping her off to bed didn't seem too gentlemanly, though that's what he would have liked. To sit by the fire and pass idle conversation seemed inane.

Lacey settled his quandary by standing up and holding out her hand to him. ''It's late, Blake,'' she said softly. ''It must be after eight o'clock.''

Blake got up and took her hand and folded it against his chest. Her face was turned up toward his, and he saw love dancing in her dewy eyes. Did she know what she was suggesting? She was such a unique mixture of lady and woman that he couldn't figure out what she knew and what she didn't. Recalling Catherine's hysterics on their wedding night, Blake felt he should ask, ''Do you know what happens between a man and a woman? Did your mother tell you?''

''No, but one winter we stayed with a family in Georgia, and their oldest daughter told me.'' With a smile she added, ''At first I didn't believe her, but she finally convinced me.''

''Good,'' he said with relief.

Putting his arm around her waist, he led her across the room. He turned the lamp to a mere glow that bathed the down bed in pale gold. Sitting down on the edge of the mattress, he gave her an encouraging smile as he removed his boots and socks. Lacey returned his smile and stood waiting.

He pulled out his shirttail and unbuttoned his shirt. Over

and over he told himself to go slow and not rush her, yet the drumbeat of his heart seemed loud in his ears. He tossed the shirt onto a chair.

Lacey still stood by the bed, a smile lighting her face. Blake drew her closer and held her as he released her hair from its constraining bun, the silky tresses gliding through his fingers and curling wantonly about his arms. Feeling somewhat overwhelmed, Blake ran his hand down her back and over her hips. Sweeping her up as he rose, he cradled her for a moment against his chest, then turned to lay her on the bed.

Slowly he removed her shoes and rolled down her cotton hose. He took her slender foot in his hand and held it as he stroked her ankle. She lay still and didn't speak.

Blake moved to her side and pulled her to a sitting position. She complied, and when he bent his head to kiss her, she tilted her chin up to meet him. Her pliant, sensuous mouth opened beneath his, and he slowly explored the silkiness of the inner surface of her mouth before gently nibbling her lower lip with his teeth. As his tongue glided into the recesses of her mouth, he felt her sway toward him with eagerness.

"Lacey," he whispered into her hair as he nuzzled the delicate shell of her ear, "I love you so."

Her smile broadened until he could see the tips of her teeth. The delicate laugh lines at the corners of her lips deepened into dimples.

"I like to see you do that," he told her as their foreheads touched, then their noses. "I want to make you so happy that you smile all the time. When I first saw you outside that saloon, I wanted you to smile even then." He unbuttoned the collar of her dress, then the next button. "But I guess no woman would be too happy at having a drunk thrown on her, let alone three. Even later, though, you didn't smile." He unfastened another button, then another.

Finally he had the front of her dress open, and he gently pushed it off her shoulders. Lacey sat quietly, her legs curled under her and her hair cascading into a pool on the bed. Her chemise was of thin cotton, trimmed with lace, and was threaded with a pale blue ribbon. Beneath the low neck, Blake admired the twin globes of her breasts. Her erect nipples thrust against the fabric invitingly.

"You're so beautiful," he softly spoke.

Rising, he took her hands and pulled her to her feet. Her dress glided to the floor, and a skein of red-gold hair tumbled over her shoulder, partly obscuring one breast. Blake untied the ribbon that secured her petticoats, and they, too, drifted to the floor. Only her thin chemise and bloomers, trimmed in the same lace and ribbons, remained. Beneath these, he admired her long, slender legs with their well-turned calves and trim ankles.

Blake noticed she was unusually quiet, but her face was radiant with a loving smile, and so he proceeded. Taking the end of the ribbon of her chemise between thumb and forefinger, he untied the bow. Her chemise parted obligingly, and one of the straps slipped off her shoulder. The fabric rested on the mound of her breasts.

Blake's blood was coursing now, and he had to use all his effort to remain in control of himself. He lifted the bottom of the chemise and slowly drew it up and off. Lacey shook her hair back from her face but made no move to cover herself.

"God, Lacey," he murmured, "you're beautiful.

Her breasts were full, with rosy nipples. No artifice of corset or stays was necessary to give them lift or cleavage. Her waist was slender, and her hips swelled gracefully beneath his hands.

She was being awfully quiet, and not once had she touched him.

Blake was more than a little curious. She seemed totally unafraid, but she wasn't joining in at all. He took her hands and placed them at his belt, indicating that she was to open it.

Her fingers were cool against his skin and moved clumsily with the unfamiliar buckle, but she released it and unfastened the top button of his pants. She looked up at him questioningly as if asking what to do next. He bent and kissed the warm curve of her neck where it met her shoulder. He heard her breath catch as she rolled her head back to give him access to her throat.

He nibbled kisses over her skin as his hands almost encircled her supple waist. His thumbs caressed her firm skin and edged higher until they stroked the lower curve of her breasts. When he felt a tremor of excitement run through her, he reached around with one hand to stroke her bare back and ease her closer to his body as the other hand rose higher to cup one of the luscious mounds. This time she moaned beneath her breath, and her nipple grew harder against his palm.

Blake moved back to pull down the covers and smiled at her invitingly. Instead of getting into bed, however, she stood there smiling at him. He untied the ribbon of her bloomers and swept both his hands over the curve of her hips, brushing the fabric down and off her body.

She remained before him, and he let his eyes drink in her beauty. He had never seen a woman so perfectly formed. Her skin was cream and rose, and when he touched her, she felt like warm satin.

Blake finished unbuttoning his pants and stepped out of them. Her eyes traveled over him, returning to gaze at his manhood. "You aren't afraid, are you?" he asked tenderly. "I'll be gentle with you."

She didn't answer, but drew her eyes away and up to meet his.

She was being far too quiet, and he felt a doubt creep in. How could a woman kiss as wholeheartedly as Lacey had and yet be so passive at making love? "Are you all right?" he asked.

She nodded but made no sound.

Blake frowned slightly but lowered his head to kiss her again. Their naked flesh brushed, her nipples sending flames across his chest. Then he pulled her closer, and her breasts flattened against him as their bellies and hips met. He moaned at the sensation and dipped his head to the sensitive curve of her neck.

Suddenly Lacey could stand it no longer. She threw her arms around his neck with such exuberance that he fell sideways onto the bed. He gave a startled shout as he fell, and the bed shuddered with their impact. Lacey's lips covered his with a fervor that left him breathless as her leg looped over his in an intimate embrace.

"I'm sorry!" she burst out, releasing him suddenly. "Oh, Blake. I'm so sorry!"

"What!" he gasped as she pulled away from him in the same movement. "What! What happened!"

She sat up and curled her knees against her chest and wrapped her arms around her legs. Miserably she refused to meet his eyes. "I didn't mean to lose control like that," she confessed. "Will you give me another chance?"

Blake looked around, then back at her in confusion. "What are you talking about?"

Lacey covered her toes with one hand and rested her chin on her knees. "I shouldn't have lunged at you like that. I'm sorry."

Blake sat up and put his forefinger under her chin to lift her head. "Lacey, honey, I don't have any idea what you're talking about." To his surprise he saw tears welling in her eyes.

"Don't be kind to me, Blake. I don't deserve it. When you kiss me, my insides seem to explode. I get dizzy, and my heart beats as if I've been running, and I just lose control." She searched his face for any signs of rejection at her confession. "I wanted to be perfect for you our first time."

"Explain," he said.

"Those girls I told you about? They said a man wants a submissive wife. They said when I find myself in a situation like this, I should just smile, be quiet, and lie still. The smile was easy, but you can't imagine how hard all the rest is!"

He stared at her for a moment, then burst out laughing.

Lacey's lips parted in astonishment as he fell back on the bed, still laughing. "What's so funny," she demanded. "I can do it! I just need to learn how. You needn't laugh at me."

"Honey, come here," he put his arm around her and toppled her toward him. "I'm not laughing at you, and submissiveness is not what I want."

"It's not? But they told me all men want that." She lay against him, their bodies again pressed close together.

"They were wrong," he said simply. "I want you to enjoy me. To have as much pleasure from making love with me as I will have with you. That's the only way it's good."

She looked at him doubtfully.

"You're supposed to talk, Lacey, and touch and laugh and do anything else that feels good."

"Are you sure?"

"Trust me."

"What about the pain? What if I don't feel embarrassed and humiliated?"

"I don't want you to feel either of those things. As for the pain, you'll feel only a little discomfort. Soon that will go away, and it'll feel wonderful."

"I don't know about that. Both girls were very clear on that point, and when I asked Mama, she said the same things."

"With an insensitive lover that may be true. Let me show you how wrong they were."

Doubt was written all over her face, but when Blake threaded his fingers in her hair, she kissed him willingly. Almost at once she felt the room dip as he coaxed her to eagerness. She slipped her arm over his deep chest and smoothed the heavy muscles of his shoulder and back.

Blake rolled so that she lay on her back, her hair spread around her like a cape of fiery gold. His dark eyes still held the gleam of amusement. He had said he wanted her to do what gave her pleasure, so she reached up and drew him down to kiss her.

His large hand stroked her lovingly, and she moved beneath him. He caressed her side and moved his thumb over the outer swell of her breast. She remembered the incredible sensation his touch had unleashed before, and shifted so that he had full access to her breast. His fingers found her nipple and gently squeezed and she caught her breath sharply as sparks seemed to shoot through her.

Blake kissed the curve of her jaw and ran the tip of his tongue down her throat and licked experimentally at the tender spot at the base of her neck. Lacey moaned openly and stroked his lean ribs, feeling the constrained power beneath her palms.

His head moved lower, and she experienced a tremor of anticipation as his lips moved over her breasts. Her body thrilled at his touch, and before she could wonder what he would do next, he left a trail of hot kisses over the soft mound of her breast and circled the tip with his tongue. She groaned and knotted her fingers in his hair as he flicked the taut bud and finally drew it into his mouth. The warm wetness of his tongue on her breast was unlike any sensation she'd ever experienced.

Passion flowered within her as he loved first one coral peak, then the other. She had never known such desire as was growing deep within her. All her nerves seemed alive and singing like bowstrings. Lacey arched toward him and gave herself up to pleasure.

Blake's hand moved lower, cupping her rounded buttock and gliding over her thigh. His fingers found and stroked the red-gold curls below her stomach, and Lacey murmured again with pleasure.

With knowing fingers he dipped lower, seeking her most feminine part. Lacey let her leg roll outward to give him more of herself. He stroked her rhythmically as he whispered words of love until he taught the button of her desire to respond to his touch. Only then did he explore her secret recesses.

Ecstasy hammered through Lacey as his lips and fingers

taught her to soar. He moved slowly, drawing even greater passion from her untried body. When she felt as if the flames of love would surely consume her, he knelt between her thighs. One hand still caressed her sensitive breasts as he nudged her thighs farther apart. Guiding his tumid manhood against her, he said, "This may be uncomfortable at first, but trust me. The discomfort won't last long."

Lacey scarcely heard him. A deep need was consuming her, and she knew only that she wanted him to satisfy it. He lowered himself over her, and she clasped his body closer.

Suddenly there was a new sensation that was pleasant, yet at the same time disquieting. He moved with great deliberation as he claimed her for his own, still not rushing her any faster than she was able to accept him.

Lacey moved with him as the experience became more enjoyable and then fulfilling. "Oh, Blake," she sighed as she learned the ageless dance of love. She would have said more, but she had no words to describe what she was feeling.

His powerful hand reclaimed her breast, and his lips closed over hers. Excitement leaped within her as he loved her with expert tenderness. When she was attuned to the rhythm of their bodies, his hand again moved lower and his fingers found the seat of her desire.

"I want you to have all the pleasure along with me," he said tenderly as his hand and manhood stroked her simultaneously.

Lacey moaned as her very soul seemed to burst into flame. A passion such as she had never known or suspected soared within her, and she felt herself being swept into a rapturous spiral. All at once she cried out as she reached love's pinnacle, and she gripped him tightly as wave after pounding wave thundered through her. Her release triggered his own, and Blake leaped with her into the golden flames of love.

They clung tightly to each other while their souls, as one, soared into paradise. Slowly love's fire abated to a glow of complete satisfaction, and Lacey sighed with the joyfulness she felt. The world, which had dissolved in the oblivion of their passion, gradually re-formed around them, and little by little she regained an awareness of her surroundings.

Lazily she opened her eyes. Blake was watching her. His head shared her pillow. A deep, abiding love shone in his eyes.

Silently he touched her face and hair with a gentleness that was almost reverent. ''I love you, Lacey Cameron,'' he whispered.

The woman who never allowed herself to cry, felt tears of happiness gather in her eyes and slide down to the pillow, and she did nothing to stop them. ''I'm so happy,'' she said with a tremulous laugh. ''I love you so much!''

He continued stroking her tenderly as languor overtook her. Still linked in body and mind, they slept.

CHAPTER
16

Lacey was still smiling as she tied the ribbon of her bonnet and slipped her hand through the loop of her reticule. Her eyes met Blake's, and he grinned. There was no need for words between them, for their thoughts still hummed in unison.

"Ready?" Blake asked as he opened the door.

She nodded and placed her hand in the bend of his elbow. They stepped out onto the porch, and their breath formed a thick wreath of fog about their heads. The landscape was altered drastically; a blanket of snow lay around the cabin where before there had been clumps of pine needles and fallen leaves. The snow-laden pines bent under their loads, and the clean-limbed hardwoods pointed with snow-sheathed fingers toward the blue sky.

Blake put his arm protectively around her, and Lacey smiled up at him as they crunched across the porch and down the treacherous steps.

"I love you," she said as they made a trail through the new snow. "Yesterday I thought I loved you as much as I could, but today I love you more."

He chuckled and hugged her. "That's exactly how I feel about you."

Snow clotted the hem of her skirt and tried to swallow her shoes, but Lacey's smile was unwavering. "I used to hate winter," she said.

"No wonder. That wagon must have been colder than the bottom of a well."

"I don't know if it was or not, since I've never climbed down into a well. But it was cold. From now on, winter is going to be my favorite season. I have you to keep me warm and our lovely house to shelter us. Oh, Blake, we're going to be so happy here."

"We sure will," he agreed. "Next spring I'm going to add an indoor dog run and another room. Just in case."

She blushed happily. Although she had always feared pregnancy, she found she wanted to have Blake's children. "What day is this?" she asked.

"Late September or early October. Why?"

"We have to find out exactly so we'll know when to celebrate our anniversary each year."

"Let's say it's October first. That sounds like a good day to start a new marriage."

"That's close enough," she agreed.

Ahead they saw the main road to town and several of the townspeople trudging along toward the church and the meetinghouse.

"Look," Lacey said with a nod. "There's Sarah and Hiram. Let's catch up with them." She looked up at him questioningly. "Do I look any different? I feel as if what I think and feel must be obvious to everybody."

"You look happy, like a woman who is in love with her husband."

They walked faster and intercepted the Gibsons at the curve that led to the meetinghouse.

Sarah smiled at their approach and linked her arm companionably through Lacey's. "Isn't the snow beautiful?" she exclaimed. "It reminds me of winter in Indiana."

Hiram greeted them and pretended to scowl. "It's a sight of work if thee asks me. Earlier this morning I looked out the window and saw a man's head traveling through a deep drift. I hollered out, 'Friend, how can thee walk in such a deep snow?' He yelled back, 'I'm not walking. I'm riding a horse.' '' Hiram grinned at Blake.

"Hiram Gibson," Sarah scolded, "how can thee exaggerate so? And on thy way to Meeting!" Her words were stern, but a spark of laughter lit her eyes. To Lacey she said, "Will thee attend Meeting with us?"

"Yes. We feel more at home there." Lacey looked across the way where the Sloans were gossiping with a crowd of churchgoers. In comparison to Sarah in her simple garments, Olive was as gaily bedecked as a bandbox.

Hiram nudged Blake. "We'll have the collar off thy coat yet, friend." He gestured at his own unadorned lapel.

As the congregation entered the meetinghouse, an expectant hush fell over them. Lacey and Sarah sat together opposite Blake and Hiram. It no longer seemed odd to do so.

After everyone was seated, a young woman stood and said, "I feel so happy to be here in Friendswood that I wanted to tell everyone." She sat down amid the nods and smiles of the other townspeople. Lacey risked a glance at Blake and smiled when he winked at her. After a while one of the men stood and told how he felt moved to express his feelings about forgiveness. Later another woman rose and spoke. Each of the voices seemed to meld with the meditative silence rather than to shatter it, and Lacey was aware of a deep peace within herself, yet at the same time there was a sense of quickening as if she were listening with a sense she'd never used before.

After a time, two of the men stood and shook hands to signal the end of Meeting. Lacey followed the others outside.

The service across the road had ended, too, and the congregations merged as the people started home. Lacey saw Olive Sloan, the mayor in tow, stride out into the road. Her face was red and puffy from the cold, and she looked ready to do battle. Lacey instinctively moved closer to Blake's protective bulk.

Olive almost collided with Hiram, and he nodded to her pleasantly. "Good day, Olive, Micah."

The mayor beamed a friendly greeting and removed his hat to the ladies, exposing his balding head to the elements.

"Hello, Mr. Gibson," Olive said, looking pointedly at the hat, which remained on Hiram's head. "I believe it's customary to remove your hat when addressing a lady."

Lacey and Blake exchanged a glance. Olive was obviously trying to stir up trouble.

Hiram smiled as Sarah slipped her hand beneath his elbow. "Customs vary. As thee well knows, we Quakers don't go along with hat honor."

"If you ask me, it's more a matter of an insult," Olive pursued.

"Now, Olive," Micah tried to intervene.

She pierced him with a reproachful glance. "It seems to me that a man should stand up for his wife. Mr. Gibson has all but implied that he doesn't consider me a lady." A crowd was beginning to gather. Micah looked miserable.

"Thee has it wrong," Hiram said firmly. "I consider thee a lady. However, I will not do homage to thee, for I consider thee my equal."

"Your equal! A man and a woman?" Olive exclaimed.

"I also didn't remove my coat," Hiram added. "If that didn't offend thee, why single out my hat?"

Olive drew herself up to her full height, which was nearly equal to Hiram's. "How dare you talk to me so insolently! Mr. Sloan, do something!"

Caught in the middle, Micah apparently felt compelled to take a stand. "Now see here, Mr. Gibson," he said. "I don't see that it's too much to ask you to doff your hat to a lady."

Hiram's jaw tightened, but he made no angry retort.

Suddenly Blake stepped forward, an easy grin on his face. He slapped Micah companionably on the arm and shook his hand. "It's good to see you, Micah. You too, Mrs. Sloan." He tipped his hat obligingly. To Micah he said, "I've been meaning to talk to you about that open pavilion you were talking about building. The one to be used for town gatherings and socials.''

''Some of us have discussed the plan in detail,'' Micah said carefully.

Hiram nodded, his wary eyes still on the mayor. ''I've started cutting the lumber to size.''

''Wonderful! Micah, I had an idea I want to talk over with the two of you.'' Blake wrapped one hand around each man's upper arm and started edging them away from the crowd—and Olive.

Sensing the release of the tension, those who had gathered to watch the confrontation moved on along toward the warmth of their homes. Lacey spoke a brief farewell to Olive and fell in step with Sarah.

''She's a hard woman, that Olive Sloan,'' Sarah fumed in a low voice as they turned toward home. ''She would like nothing better than to see all of us Quakers run out of town.''

''What she would like and what she can do are two different things,'' Lacey said.

''Are they? We've had to leave so many places.'' Sarah's voice had a catch in it. ''We won't fight. We *can't* fight and still maintain our beliefs. How long can we put up with her persecution?'' She cast a worried glance at Lacey and turned away. ''This town is our home. We don't want to leave.''

Lacey hugged her friend. ''You won't have to. I imagine most people can see through the troublemakers like Olive Sloan.'' Actually she wasn't so sure. She had seen many a crowd set afire by her own father's words, and he had had no religious cause to maintain. All too often, it seemed, people were willing to be led. Which way they went depended on the leader who stepped forward.

They walked carefully across the layer of snow, each deep in her own thoughts. At the fork where the path branched off toward their separate houses, they paused.

''Sarah,'' Lacey said with barely concealed excitement.

"I have something to tell you. I'm so very happy! I just have to share it with someone."

Sarah, who had been worrying about where she and Hiram could go if they had to leave Friendswood, tried to smile. "I thought thee looked unusually happy today."

Lacey caught her friend's hands and glanced about to be sure no one else was near enough to overhear. "We're married!"

"Of course thee are," Sarah laughed as her eyes searched Lacey's face. "What a thing to say."

"No, no. I mean we really are." Lacey laughed and squeezed Sarah's hands. "When Blake and I came here, we weren't married. We hardly even knew each other. Everyone assumed we were husband and wife, and Blake let the mistake go uncorrected. He was afraid I wouldn't be doctored if he told the truth. We know better now, of course, but at the time he couldn't take the chance."

Sarah stared at her as though she couldn't comprehend Lacey's words.

"We fell in love and didn't know what to do. Finally last night we decided to say our vows and have what is called a bond marriage in Texas." Lacey's smile felt tight as she realized it wasn't returned by Sarah. "Blake is a Texan, you know." When Sarah made no reply, Lacey added falteringly. "It was a lovely time, and I wanted you to know. I only wish you and Hiram could have been there to witness our vows."

Slowly Sarah pulled her hands away from Lacey's grasp. Her face was stricken, as if the news had been catastrophic. "Thee have been living in sin!" she exclaimed.

"No, we never touched each other until after our bonding last night."

"Thee slept in the same bed. And in our house!" Sarah pulled her shawl tight and stared at Lacey as if they hadn't ever whispered together by the fireside or toiled to complete a shared task.

"Sarah? Don't pull away from me," Lacey protested, reaching out her hand.

"And to think we gave thee a cabin of thy own! Thee have used us and played us for fools!"

"No, no! We didn't do that!" Lacey's voice threatened to rise along with her level of distress, and she again looked around to be sure no one else was near.

"Take my advice," Sarah said in a tight voice. "Don't let anyone else know what thee has done or thee and thy man will be driven away from here."

Lacey stared at her. "But you're my friend," she faltered.

"It's because of our past friendship that I won't point the finger of blame at thee." Sarah's angry eyes left no doubt as to the present state of their relationship. For another moment she glared at Lacey, then turned on her heel. "I must go now," she stated as she strode off.

Lacey stared in disbelief at Sarah's straight back as her friend walked away. When a shiver of cold brought her to her senses, Lacey turned and ran down the path toward her cabin, stumbling through the snow. Her thoughts flapped inside her brain like trapped sparrows. How could she have been so stupid? She should have known her confession would upset Sarah.

She tripped and fell to her knees and palms and got up with a sob. Her hands stung from the blow, and snow clung to her dress and cape. Lacey brushed ineffectively at the ice clots as she struggled through a low-lying drift. Her heart ached as if it would break as Sarah's words echoed in her ears. They could be run out of town!

Panic seized her. Winter was upon them, and they didn't even have the dubious shelter of a wagon. Where could they go? She wasn't sure they could survive in the harsh elements.

Ahead she saw their cabin. A thin thread of smoke curled up through the chimney from the banked fire in the hearth, and it looked as rich a haven as a castle to Lacey's eyes. She half ran, half stumbled across the yard and up the steps. Flinging herself inside, she leaned against the door and shut her eyes tightly.

Sobs came in broken gasps as she pressed her body against the door. Sarah would almost certainly tell Hiram, and Hiram loved to talk. By tomorrow everyone might know! Why had she shared her news?

Lacey finally quelled her tears and looked around the room. Where could they get a wagon and team? Surely no one would expect them to leave on foot in the snow!

Her panic gradually eased somewhat, and she sat in a chair, still wearing her cloak and bonnet. She wasn't so surprised at Sarah's defection—old thoughts were springing back to life, and among them was her deeply ingrained distrust—but she was appalled at her own foolishness. If she hadn't opened her mouth and let the words spill out, she and Blake could have continued to live here peacefully. They could have gotten married in Morgan in the spring, and there would have been no trouble.

Blake's footsteps and his cheery whistle sounded on the porch, followed by stamping as he knocked the snow from his boots.

Lacey jumped up and cast a glance at the puddle on the floor where the snow had melted off her cape and shoes. She untied her bonnet and whisked off her cape as he came inside.

He grinned. "Why are you wearing your cape and bonnet in the house?"

"I . . . I just came in, and I was taking them off," she faltered.

"Oh? I didn't see you ahead of me on the path." He removed his heavy coat and hat and hung them on pegs by the door. "What are we having for dinner? Got any of that stewed chicken left over from last night?" He bent to kiss her as he walked to the fire.

Lacey turned so his kiss fell on her cheek instead of her lips. What would Blake say when he heard what she had done? Fear again gripped her. He loved Friendswood and would hate to leave it. She used the excuse of hanging her cloak to turn her back to Blake. "There's chicken in the pot on the side of the hearth. I'll warm it."

Blake looked at her curiously as he stoked the fire. "Sarah sure is acting strange. I went by there to see if you had gone home with her, and she barely spoke to me."

Lacey hung her bonnet from its ribbon. "Oh?" Keeping her eyes averted, she went to the hearth, nudged the iron spider into place, and set the pot near the embers.

"Did you two have a falling out?"

"No," she scoffed too quickly. "What an idea!"

He shrugged as she bustled by, then caught her hand and pulled her to him. "I love you, Lacey Cameron."

"Blake, turn me loose if you want me to get food on the table."

"I'm not that hungry all of a sudden. Are you?" He grinned down at her and bent to nibble the spot at the base of her throat.

In spite of her mood, Lacey put her arms around him and held him close. Sarah hadn't confronted Blake, so maybe they would be safe for a while. She tightened her hug almost fiercely and buried her face in his chest. There would be plenty of time to tell him later. For now she decided she had better love him while he still wanted her.

He used the toe of this boot to ease the pot back from the fire and carried his bride to bed.

Lacey wrapped her shawl around her and took a deep breath. No vigilante committee had arrived in the night, and Blake had left for the blacksmith shop as usual. When he didn't return immediately, Lacey had dressed to go out. She dreaded it, but she had to find out if Sarah had spread the news.

Feeling like a martyr walking to her doom, Lacey left the security of her cabin and went toward town. The air was calm and warmer than the day before, and the bright sun had begun to melt the blanket of snow. When she neared the row of buildings that lined the main street, she lifted her head courageously. She had been chased out of town on a run, but she had never slunk away.

The first few people she encountered glanced at her and nodded as they hurried on their way. Lacey mutely returned their greetings with a tilt of her head and kept walking. No one crossed the street to avoid her, and two women even smiled and spoke to her by name. Lacey drew a steadying breath—the first she recalled having taken in several minutes.

At the end of the street was the dressmaker's shop and beyond that, the feed store. These were the gossips' favorite places. In good weather there were always two or more men sitting on the backless benches, swapping tales. The women could be found, rain or shine, doing the same in the dressmaker's shop.

Lacey stiffened her back, lifted her chin, and opened the small-paned door. As she had expected there were two women inside: Olive Sloan and her sister, Lidy Rose. Of all the gossips in town, Lacey feared these two the most.

She nodded to the women. "Olive, Lidy Rose. I see you're out early today."

"Goodness yes, I just had to come try on the gray kersey-mere Mrs. Bastrop just finished sewing for me. Lidy Rose is here for a fitting, too, if Mrs. Bastrop ever comes back from fetching the dresses. I declare that woman would forget her head if it weren't attached."

Lacey's hopes rose slightly. Surely Olive would have either ignored her or lambasted her if she had known Lacey and Blake's secret.

Lidy Rose nodded, making her beribboned hat jiggle. "It's so hard to find an adequate seamstress out here." She gave Lacey a pursed smile. "Speaking of needlework, I saw the quilt you pieced for Widow Robinson. I must say it had fine stitches."

"Thank you, but I can't take complete credit. The pattern

is one of Sarah Gibson's. I only helped quilt it. She had already pieced it." Lacey studied the woman's face to see if she was being led into a trap.

"I guessed as much. The pattern seemed unimaginative and poorly executed. It was the quilting I admired."

"Thank you," Lacey said absentmindedly. Apparently neither woman knew. She silently blessed Sarah for holding her tongue.

"I understand there are plans under way to build a real bandstand," Olive said conspiratorially. "Can you imagine? Soon Friendswood will be as fine a town as any we left behind in Minnesota. Can't you just see the musicales?"

"But there is no band here," Lacey pointed out. "Why do we need a bandstand?" She could hardly believe she was standing here prattling of bandstands when her knees were still shaking.

"True, we will have to make do with fiddles and the like at first, but eventually we will have other instruments." Lidy Rose sounded as shocked as if Lacey had suggested there was no need for the churches.

Lacey frowned slightly. One thing the Quakers were adamant against was the playing of musical instruments, and she had heard one of Sarah's friends say that they considered fiddles the worst of the lot. "It seems to me that a bandstand will only cause trouble," she observed. "Half the town will be opposed to it."

Olive smiled condescendingly. "So what if they are? They can't fight us about it."

"How cleverly put, Sister," Lidy Rose enthused. "They indeed can't fight that or anything else."

Lacey's chin came up, and she set her mouth in a determined line. Sarah might be angry with her, and the friendship might be damaged beyond repair, but Lacey was innately loyal. "I feel I should say good day, ladies. You know the Gibsons are my friends, as are many other Quakers."

"But you aren't of that persuasion," Lidy Rose protested. "You're one of us."

"Am I? I wouldn't be too sure of that."

With head held high, Lacey left the shop. As soon as the door shut behind her, she let out a pent-up breath. None of the Presbyterians knew. That left only the Quakers.

Lacey heard hammering and turned her steps toward the town hall. The large building stood in the center of town and was circled by the road, like many courthouses back in the States. Several men were at work on the long porch, hoisting the cumbersome bell into the square tower that had been built in the roof. The bell's clapper clanged against the iron sides as the massive bell swayed on its journey to the summit, and before long, it was in place.

Two men held the rope while Hiram and another townsman hammered the support into the groove. When Hiram held up his hand in a sign of victory, one of the men ran onto the porch and tugged hard on the bell's rope. Its answering gong made Lacey flinch and the men whoop in triumph. As Blake had told her, the bell wasn't pretty, but it was loud.

Hiram climbed down from the tower and waved at Lacey. He was grinning as he came to her, and his breath made a frosty wreath. "How does thee like our new bell?"

"It's certainly loud enough." She knew by the fact he spoke at all that Sarah had not yet told him.

"We asked Blake to make one that could be heard easily from thy cabin to the Bensons' place. He did a good job. He's a fine man, thy husband."

"That he is," Lacey said with a faint smile. "I'd never argue that point." She hesitated, then said, "How is Sarah?"

"She seems to be ailing," Hiram said with mild concern. "Ever since Meeting yesterday, she's hardly said a word. Just sits daydreaming by the fire, like she does when she's wrestling with a problem. Maybe if thee was to stop by it would give her ease. I know there's things one woman tells another that a man wouldn't understand."

Lacey tried to look pleasant. "Whatever it is, she needs to decide for herself. She knows where to find me if she wants to talk."

"Well, being a woman, I guess thee knows best. Tell Blake I said hello."

"I will." Lacey felt a little better as she walked home. For whatever reason, Sarah was keeping the information to herself. Perhaps everything would be all right after all. But when she passed the Gibsons' house, she felt a twinge of pain; she doubted she would ever be welcome there again.

Later that afternoon, Lacey lifted the wet shirt from the frigid stream and tossed it onto the rough tabletop of the battling board. The strangely warmer wind that had followed the storm was unlike anything she had ever known. At times it was quite gusty, but the most incredible thing was that it was rapidly melting the wet snow. But warm or cold, sun or snow, the wash had to be done. Her fingers stung from the chilly water, but she welcomed the discomfort in the hope that it would take her mind off her troubles. With the short paddle-shaped battling stick, she pounded the dirt from Blake's shirt as she turned it over and over. Rivulets of water coursed over the three-legged table and onto the ground.

She had been working hard since she returned from town and was late starting the weekly wash. She had spent most of her time peeling and slicing the sweet potatoes Sarah had given her. Racks of the dark gold oblongs lay drying in the late afternoon sun. None of her frantic activities had erased or even dulled her anxiety.

She shoved a stray wisp of hair back from her face and dropped the shirt into the black pot of boiling soapy water. Using the long-handled paddle, she pressed the fabric under the surface with the other clothes and swirled them around before going back to battle the dirt from her dress.

Squinting at the sun, she figured she had maybe an hour before Blake would be home for supper. It would take her at least that long to finish boiling and rinsing the clothes. The strand of hair fell again into her eyes, and she struggled to control her anxiety. She should never have told Sarah, but nothing could be done about that now. What was done was done. All she could do was be as good and perfect a wife as she could be to Blake and hope he'd forgive her if they were forced to leave town. If Blake left her because of her stupidity, she didn't know what she'd do. A sense of doom settled over her.

When she realized she was pounding the dress unnecessarily hard, she held it up to see if it was damaged. Critically she inspected the embroidery on the collar and was relieved to find it unharmed. Lacey's thoughts leaped back to the time Mama had taught her to do needlework. During the long days of travel from one town to another, Lacey had practiced her needlework and had developed considerable skill. If there was only one thing Lacey could be proud of, it was her stitchery. But what good was it? She and Blake would need a good team and wagon and provisions for months of travel if the town learned their secret. Suddenly an idea formed. Not every woman in town had the ability or the inclination to adorn her clothes or those of her family, but many had admired Lacey's handwork. Maybe they would be willing to hire her, and if she had enough time, she might be able to earn some money to help buy a wagon and team. But would Blake even want to go with her to Oregon after he learned it was her fault they had to leave? Lacey's heart ached.

She tossed the sodden dress in with the other clean clothes and added a log to the fire. She didn't want to leave Friendswood at all. What she had hoped to find in Oregon she had right here with Blake. But was it hers to keep? Lacey blinked back a tear that tried to form and continued with her chore.

When the clothes had boiled about half an hour, Lacey began ladling them into a pot of clear water. Steam rolled upward as she pulled each piece from the cauldron into the much cooler air. She bent and sloshed as much of the soap as possible from the clothes before putting them into the last pot to finish the rinsing.

Already the sun was balanced on the shaggy treetops and the shadows were long. She plunged her cold-numbed fingers into the rinse water and lifted out the dripping garments. Without wringing out the excess moisture, she draped them over the clothesline Blake had strung up for her. She had spread the large sheets over some nearby bushes. By hanging them up soaking wet, she would have fewer wrinkles to deal with when it came time to do the ironing. A gust of warm wind popped the clothes on the line then died away.

Frowning, she tilted her head. If she had washed the clothes in the morning, they would be dry by now. She decided she would have to plan better next time. It upset her that she was showing so little accomplishment in doing simple household chores. How could she possibly explain her lack of efficiency to Blake? Washing had been much easier when she had only one dress to wear and another to wash.

She tipped the rinse water out of the smaller pots and let it run down the slope. She threaded two long sticks through the "eyes" of the larger pot of boiling water. This was the part she always dreaded because the water was blistering hot and the pot weighed more than she did.

Using all the leverage she could muster, she rocked the pot forward. One of the sticks slipped, and the pot dropped back on the rocks over the fire, sending a wave of scalding water to soak the hem of her dress. Lacey jumped back before she could be burned and held her wet skirt out away from her body. The fabric cooled quickly, and when she dropped it, her skirt fell in clammy folds against her skin. Lacey suppressed a shiver and again tried to lift the pot.

"Here. Let me do that before you get hurt," Blake's voice sounded just behind her. "What are you trying to do?"

"I'm pouring out the wash water." She stepped back as he took the sticks and flipped the big pot over. The soapy water sloshed over the grassy rocks, instantly dissolving the remaining snow in its path, as he upended the pot to drain and stamped out the last of the ashes.

"You didn't have to do that," Lacey told him. "I could have managed."

"I like to help you."

She tried to see his expression, but night shadows obscured his face. "Are you teasing me?" she asked uncertainly. "Why would a man want to help a woman with her chores? It's because you don't think I'm able to do them right. That's it, isn't it?" She was cold and tired and couldn't bear it if he acted sanctimonious. Looking back at the dark windows of the house, she sighed. "I suppose you think I've been lazing around, since I haven't started supper yet. I guess you think I'm inefficient as well as incompetent."

"That never occurred to me." He glanced at the house. "You haven't started supper?"

"I knew it! I knew you'd be angry about that! Well, maybe a Texas woman could dry a bushel of potatoes and wash two pots of clothes and still have time to cook supper, but *I*," she stated, "am not a Texas woman!" With a defiant toss of her head, she marched through the gloaming toward the house.

Blake watched her in confusion for a minute before he called after her, "Nobody ever said you were a Texas woman!"

He looked back at the water-darkened earth. How could he have caused such an uproar simply by helping her pour out wash water? Shaking his head, he went to the barn to clean up for the evening.

Lacey groped her way through the dark house, cracking her shin against the table leg as she did so. From the dying ashes in the hearth, which glowed like a ruddy eye, she ignited a straw, then lit a lamp. How could she have been so careless, she wondered, as to let the fire die? Sarah kept one going all the time with seemingly little effort. Though living in the medicine wagon had been much less convenient, she had developed a routine. In that world she was very competent, but here she couldn't seem to do anything right.

Using a butcher knife, she sliced a salted venison roast into strips for frying. There was no time to boil it, and that meant it would probably be tough. Anger fumed inside her, and salt stung a small cut on her hand where she had nicked herself while peeling the potatoes. Because her family had never stayed long in one place, Lacey had become accustomed to buying most of their food already dried. She had rarely hunted, and Papa never did in the later years, so venison was mainly a memory from her childhood when Billy and Papa had hunted together.

She tossed the meat into a heavy greased skillet and put it on a hearth spider to cook as she stoked the fire back to life. She had once heard her mother talk about a housewife who was so clever she kept the same fire going for years. Lacey decided the woman must have done little else. Her own fire was already fading and seemed to go out if she left it unattended for even a short while.

As she reheated the beans from the day before, she poured hot water over cornmeal to pat out corn dodgers to fry. All this should have been done an hour ago, she scolded herself. Blake was always tired and hungry when he came in from the shop. The least he could expect was for her to have lights on in the house, if not a meal waiting.

Through the window, she noticed the sheets writhing like pale ghosts in the twilight. Her mother had told her that it wasn't a good practice to leave clothes to dry overnight, but she couldn't recall just why. Maybe it was because they might have to leave town suddenly, and if the clothes were out, they might be left behind. She shook her head. Even the ten years of living in sharecropper houses hadn't erased her childhood recollections.

Too late she turned her attention back to the meat. One side was nearly black and curled up in a sure sign of toughness. With an exclamation, she pulled the skillet farther back from the fire. A warning sizzle told her the beans also were scorching. Grabbing the pot handle, she cried out as it burned her fingers. She maneuvered the beans away from the fire and smeared butter on her injury, but her fingers continued to throb. Frustrated tears gathered at the corners of her eyes and threatened to brim over onto her cheeks.

Blake chose that moment to come in and sniff the air. "Is something burning?"

Lacey turned on him with fury. "I don't want to hear one word about my cooking!"

He stared at her in astonishment. What had he done now? "What are you cooking?" he asked in a moderate tone. He had never seen meat in that particular form.

She glared at him. "Venison steak, of course. What does it look like?"

He was wise enough not to answer. "Do you want me to stir the beans?"

"No!" She was determined to do this right, no matter what. She thrust a spoon into the beans and told herself that the burnt odor was coming from some juice that had spilled into the fire. Feeling harassed, she slapped two plates onto the table and gestured for him to sit down.

Again she rescued the meat from the fire, but now both sides were charred to the consistency of saddle leather. Her stormy eyes dared him to comment as she forked a slab onto his plate.

Blake leaned over to silently inspect the offering, then turned his plate to look at the food from another angle. Both sides looked pretty much the same. As he poked at the meat, it rocked along its curled edge. Realizing she was glaring at him, he smiled at her beatifically.

Instead of returning his smile, Lacey spooned a helping of beans onto the two plates. Several of the beans were much darker than the others, and the aroma was not inviting.

"Looks good," he managed to say. "Do we have any bread?"

Lacey jerked her head toward the flat pan on the sideboard where the squares of raw batter lay like little yellow-bricks. A groan escaped her lips. "I forgot to cook it!"

Trying to find something pleasant to say, Blake observed, "At least they aren't burned." He had meant his words to be joking, but as soon as he heard them leave his mouth he knew he had made a mistake.

"Oh!" Lacey slammed down the pot of beans and threw the cup towel at him.

He caught it and tossed it to the table as he stood. "Lacey, I didn't mean—"

"*I* know what you meant!" she cried. "You think I burned your meal. You think I can't cook!"

He looked at the charred offering. "I didn't say you can't cook."

"No, but you *think* it!" She wheeled and grabbed up the skillet she had used for the meat, intending to cook the corn dodgers, but it was so hot it burned her hand. With a shriek, she let it clatter to the floor.

Blake hurried to her and pulled her into his embrace. "Honey, calm down. What's wrong? So you burned a meal. So what?"

"It's not just that," she mumbled against his shirt front. "Our sheets are outside, and it's nighttime, and I haven't had time to put the others on the bed, and I poured soapy water all over my skirt and cut my hand peeling those potatoes, and I don't even like dried sweet potatoes, and I didn't even remember to cook the corn bread, and the meal is too burnt to eat, and I've hurt my hand."

Blake held her securely and tried to make sense out of her words, but something curiously like a sob had obliterated most of them. He stroked her hair back from her damp cheeks and made soothing sounds. He didn't know what else to do, but his stroking seemed to help, because already her ragged breathing was quieter, and she had put her arms around him.

"Honey, don't cry," he said into her hair. "It's just an old pot of red beans and some deer meat."

"No, no, it's more than that. It's your supper! And you've worked so hard, and I didn't even have the lamps lit for you." She looked up at him miserably as she brushed a tear from her face. "I can't do anything right these days! What will you think of me?" She hadn't meant to say that, so she amended it by adding, "And I'm not crying. I *never* cry!"

"Lacey, it's not a crime to cry. Some women do it a great deal of the time. Who told you not to cry?"

"Never mind! If I cry you'll think I'm weak and helpless, and I'm not! I'm really not! I can take care of myself, no matter what you think."

"I sure wish you'd stop telling me what I think," he told her. "I know it's harder out here than it was back home. I didn't grow up cooking over a fire, either."

"You don't understand," she wailed.

"Will you stop crying? I can't stand it when you cry."

She tried to glare at him, but her eyes were glassy with unshed tears and her lip trembled. "I'm not!"

"All right, all right. You're not crying. I was mistaken." He drew her close. "Honey, I don't know what set all this off, but whatever it was, you can stop worrying about it."

She looked up at him doubtfully. Tears clung to her long lashes and made her eyes look large and luminous.

Tenderness welled up in him, and he found himself becoming lost in the green depths of her eyes. "Lacey," he said softly, "I'm going to love you whether you burn the beans or not."

"No, you won't. A woman knows about these things." She clearly remembered Mama saying as much on more than one occasion.

"Sometimes a woman is wrong," he corrected. "I don't love you because of what you can do for me. I love you because of who you are. Do you understand what I'm saying?"

She nodded dismally and wished she hadn't lied to him about her background. She wanted Blake to know the truth.

She wanted to be able to admit to him she had made a mistake in telling Sarah about them. She wanted him to know all this and still love her, but how could she tell him?

CHAPTER
17

The snow melted from the lower slopes and valleys, leaving only the mountain summits with the pristine caps they would wear until the following summer. For the first few days after revealing her secret to Sarah, Lacey was on edge and jumped at the smallest sounds. Soon a week had passed, and still there was no trouble, so Lacey began to regain her confidence.

Now that she was able to think with some degree of detachment, Lacey could see that, by revealing the truth, Sarah stood to lose as much as she and Blake did. Sarah and Hiram had not only sheltered them, but had initiated the plan to provide them with a cabin as well. As far as Lacey could tell, this had been one of the few times the town had acted of one accord.

How ironic, she mused as she stood high on her toes on a chair to turn the drying circles of pumpkin, that she and Blake were given the cabin that had belonged to Mabel Bannion.

Carl Odem had given Lacey the pumpkins to thank her for helping to doctor him when the Indian arrow had pierced his shoulder. She had tried to refuse them, but Carl had been insistent. After slicing them she strung them on poles that

251

Blake had suspended across the rafters. The circles were already nearly dried from the room's rising heat.

Lacey climbed down from the chair and pushed it into its place against the wall. Turning, she saw Blake standing just inside the door, a grin on his face.

"Good heavens!" she exclaimed. "You scared the wits out of me. How long have you been standing there?"

"Long enough to get a good glimpse of your pretty ankles and to see your dress stretch tight when you turned the pumpkin rings."

She smiled even though she gave him an exasperated look. "You ought to be ashamed of yourself. Why are you home so early?"

"All the shops are closing down, and I didn't have much to do."

"Why are they closing in the middle of the afternoon?" When he hesitated, her eyes grew large with apprehension. "Blake?"

"There's been more Indian trouble."

"When? Is anyone hurt?"

"No, everyone is all right. Lame Wolf and his braves rode through the middle of town whooping and yelling, and scared several people, but the Indians are gone now."

"But why would they do such a foolish thing?"

"They were counting coups. When I was a scout for the Texas army, I got to know some Indians who also worked with us. They told me that it's considered a great test of bravery to ride unarmed through an enemy camp. That's what Lame Wolf and his followers were doing."

"Are they that brave or just plain crazy?" Lacey asked as she went to look out the window.

"Maybe both. At any rate, all the shops and stores have closed down for the day, so I came home."

She peered out the window at the flaxen grass that had been pressed flat by the snow. Beyond was a seemingly endless forest, any part of which could hide an Indian. "You certainly are being calm about this," she observed dryly.

"Of course I am. This is the only day we know for sure they won't be back."

Lacey looked around at him.

"Honey, everybody in town is home with a loaded gun waiting for an attack. Crazy or not, those Indians won't be back today."

"I guess that makes sense," she admitted.

She leaned her arm on the window frame and rested her head on her hand. Nodding toward the soaring crags and summits, she said, "I wonder which one is South Pass."

"I never did figure it out. Maybe you can't see it from here. I can't imagine taking a wagon over any of those mountains, or even through the valleys."

"Do you think they made it?"

"Sure they did. Ed Bingham has taken a train west every year since the trail opened. He knows what he's doing."

"Will you mind not seeing Oregon?"

"Nope. Will you?"

"I hope I never see the inside of a wagon again for as long as I live," she assured him fervently, but her stomach tightened with the fear that she might have to do just that.

The winter sunshine glowed on her face, and her position stretched the bodice of her dress tightly across her breasts. Blake watched her with interest, noticing the way her supple waist narrowed under her breasts before curving out beneath her skirts. His eyes traveled upward. Her graceful neck seemed too delicate to support the thick skein of hair she had coiled against the back of her head. The weak sunlight gilded each flimsy strand, and although she had been careful to conceal them, he could see the pins that secured it. If he removed only a few, her hair would tumble down. Experimentally, he reached out and did just that. The bun remained in place but Lacey wheeled to face him.

"Blake!" she exclaimed. "It's broad daylight! What on earth are you doing?"

"We'll draw the latch. Come on." His eyes dared her to

let him love her now, in the middle of the day when anyone might come by.

Hesitantly, Lacey looked up and down the path. No one was in sight, and she frequently passed a day without company. Blake pulled the latch string inside, locking the door, then grinned back at her.

"You know we shouldn't do this," she said as a delicious hunger grew deep within her.

"Why not?" He went to the calico curtains and pulled them closed to cover the windows.

"Well, it would be pretty embarrassing if someone dropped by."

He laughed. "Lacey, you're two different women rolled into one. When you're dressed and on your feet, you're as proper as any lady I ever saw. But when you're stripped down and in bed, well, you're something else."

She tried not to smile as he came across the room, his movements lithe and sensuous, his Texas drawl stirring memories of their long nights of loving. "I ought to be offended, you know. First you call me a prude; then you call me . . . what exactly *did* you call me?"

"You know what I think it is?" he said indolently. "I think it's these hairpins that inhibit you. I've noticed you get a whole lot friendlier when they're on the side table." He pulled the others out and tossed them onto the table, then expertly unwound her hair from its long plait. "There now," he said when her hair billowed around her shoulders. "Aren't you feeling friendlier already?"

She was. His gentle fingers in her hair, as well as the unaccustomed sensation of it lying loose about her was stirring a very elemental need. "You're pretty sure of yourself, aren't you, cowboy?"

"Yes, ma'am. I am for a fact." He pulled off his coat and unbuttoned his shirt as his dark eyes held her in a hypnotic gaze. Casually he tossed the shirt aside and unbuckled his belt.

Lacey's breath came quickly as she watched him undress.

She knew she ought to stop him. If their secret became known, such reckless behavior would make them seem even less proper. With the latch string inside, anybody would know she had to be home. But she didn't even try to hold him back.

He was beautifully made, and just watching him caused the blood to pound in her veins. His skin was smooth, and she already knew it would be firm and warm to the touch. His muscles corded and knotted as he knelt to remove her laced shoes and her stockings. She ran her fingers through the night wing of his hair, and he smiled up at her.

When he stood, she lifted her eyebrows as if coolly questioning what he was up to, though amusement gleamed in her eyes. "You're utterly shameless," she pointed out. "And I'm glad."

Blake pulled back the covers and lay down. "Undress for me," he said. "You've never done that."

Excitement jumped in her, but she said, "I can't do that. Not in broad daylight."

"First the dress," he instructed as if she hadn't spoken. He propped his head up on his arms and waited.

Slowly Lacey opened the buttons that secured the front of her dress. He lay perfectly still. Cool air touched her fever-hot skin as the dress fell open. After a moment's hesitation, she shrugged out of it, demurely turning her back to tease him.

"No. Turn around so I can see you." His voice was soft and silky like the light that filtered through the curtains and the hair that floated over her shoulders.

Hesitantly Lacey faced him again. Her fingers untied the drawstring of her petticoats. She wanted to rip them off and leap at him, but she let them slide to the floor as if she were suddenly shy. Unable to take her eyes from him, she waited. She had never realized how stimulating it would be to remove her clothes in his presence. Her skin seemed to tingle under his gaze.

"Now the chemise," he instructed. His deep voice seemed to reverberate within her.

The sleeveless garment was held together by a slender blue ribbon threaded through gathered lace. She untied the bow, and the sheer fabric slid low over the swell of her breasts. Then it dropped lower still, and her breasts were exposed to his perusal.

She untied her bloomers, and they fell, along with the chemise, to lie among her petticoats. She stood very still, letting him look at her. She was determined to let him call her moves. His obvious arousal told her he was enjoying this as much as she was. She liked seeing his body and having him look at hers, and she smiled as she wondered what those girls back in Georgia would have said about that. She supposed they would label such behavior wanton, but she suspected their husbands would have a different viewpoint if the truth were known.

He held out his hand to her, and she walked the few steps toward the bed.

He drew her down to him, and she lay against his lean warmth. Her heart fluttered fast as their skin met and welcomed the other's touch. Slowly he kissed her, his lips sensuous and teasing. Her teeth caught his lower lip in a love bite that made him look down at her in surprise. She saw hunger leap into his eyes and stored the information in her growing file of things Blake enjoyed.

The tip of his tongue glided over the velvety insides of her lips and along the ridges of her teeth. Lacey met his tongue with her own and tasted the nectar of his mouth. Her hands stroked the bulging strength of his arms and glided down his straight back to cup his firm buttocks. His hand was on her breast, smoothing and caressing, then urging her nipple to aching erectness.

Lacey moaned with pleasure and moved her hips against the swelling shaft of his desire. Without thinking, she let her tongue flick over his hot skin, tasting his neck, his shoulders, his chest as her hand slid between the two of them and caressed the fount of his love. An indefinable utterance came from deep in Blake's throat, and she pulled back, afraid she had overstepped the boundaries.

"Don't pull away," he whispered into the shell of her ear. "I like it." He guided her hand back and let her explore him as thoroughly as he did her in return.

With a fluid movement, he rolled onto his back, drawing her up to lie on top of him. He knotted both his hands in her mass of hair and kissed her until they were both breathless. Smoothly he maneuvered her around until she sat astride his body.

Lacey felt a surging need as the essence of his masculinity touched her most vulnerable places, yet still he held her over him with strokes that sent fire raging through her breasts and plummeting down to feed the inferno that burned deep within her. She moved against him, learning yet another way of pleasing them both. When he entered her, her eyes flew open in surprise and she tried to read his expression. Until now she hadn't considered that there might be more than one position in which to make love.

Blake groaned with pleasure and put his hands on her hips to rock her in a sensuous movement. Lacey's lips parted, and her eyes closed as she gave free rein to her loving. Her hair fell forward in a waving fall that brushed lightly over his chest. Pushing against him, she sat farther back, giving them both greater enjoyment.

Blake raised his head and caught one of her coral-tipped nipples between his lips. Tugging gently, he brought her slightly forward and at his leisure bathed first one bud then the other to throbbing eagerness. When her hair obscured his search, he brushed it back with impatient fingers and continued to stoke her fires to a white heat.

Lacey gasped as her body suddenly seemed to leap to the urgency she had come to expect when they made love. He kept moving within her in the way she enjoyed so well as he drew her breasts to the hotness of his tongue. All at once she cried out as she reached a shattering fulfillment that seemed to lift her careening over all mortal boundaries. Spasms of delight rippled through her in searing waves, leaving her floating in the afterglow of love.

Blake grinned up at the angelic smile on her face. With a movement of his long body, he tumbled her over so that she lay beneath him. He stroked the hair back from her face and kissed the pulse that raced in her temple. Once more he claimed her lips as he began anew the slow, deep rhythm of loving.

Lacey gazed up at him dreamily. His black hair had fallen forward over his tanned forehead, and his eyes were dark mirrors of his soul. Even though she felt languorous and satisfied, her body was reawakening to his.

Without question, she met his pace and to her surprise she started to quicken all over again. She ran her hands over his muscles and felt them ripple and reach to give her pleasure. She moved with him as the ecstasy again built to a fevered pitch.

This time when she reached her summit, he flew with her. In cascading torrents of passion they spun together, before gradually mellowing in a mutual satisfaction that left them breathless with love.

"I didn't expect that," she murmured against his neck when she could speak.

"We've only begun to make love." He stroked her back and shoulders, feeling a tenderness that almost overwhelmed him. At times his love for her nearly filled him to bursting. "Let me catch my breath, and we'll try it again."

"I have a lot to learn," she whispered, her breath tickling his ear. "And I want to know it all—everything that pleases you. I want you so much. I can't seem to get my fill of you. Not just when we're in bed, but at odd times. Like when we're eating supper or when I see you working at the forge."

"Even when I'm all sweaty and grimy?" He grinned.

"You seem to glisten in the light from the coals, and your

muscles look so strong, and yet at the same time, there's a grace about you."

"Me?"

She nodded. "You're like a puma. Sleek and sinewy. Should I be telling you all this?"

"By all means. This is as much a part of loving as anything else. I want to know what you think and feel." A look of total satisfaction illuminated his face. "You aren't the only one who has desires at odd times. The other night when you were taking that jar from the top shelf, for instance. You were standing on a chair and reaching up above your head. You were wearing the same dress you had on today, and it was pulled snugly to the outline of your body. I wanted you so much."

"If I recall correctly, you had me. I didn't get that jar down until the next day." She laughed as she let her hand glide over his powerful rib cage.

"You can have me anytime, too."

She looked up at him in teasing disbelief. "Even at the forge?"

His eyes met hers, and their souls touched. "If that ever happens again, you just say to me, 'Blake, I need a jar off that top shelf.' I'll know what you mean."

"Are you serious?" she asked incredulously.

"You bet I am."

"You'd stop work and come home and make love with me? Just like that?"

"Try it and see," he dared her. "I imagine if the truth were known, half the couples in this town have some signal that means 'Meet me in the bedroom.' "

"Maybe." Her eyes were dancing with delight. "I wonder if you're right."

"Will you try it?" he grinned.

A blush swept her face because she knew she would. "We'll see."

From across the yard came a noise, and then the sound of hooves coming to a stop at the hitching post. Almost at once, they heard steps on the porch and a loud knock at the door. Scrambling out of bed, Lacey grabbed at her clothes. She tossed Blake his pants as she yanked on her chemise. The knock sounded again.

"I'm coming," Lacey called out, her voice muffled by the folds of her dress. "Just a minute." She thrust her bare feet into her shoes and plumped her skirts to cover the untied shoelaces. As she wrapped her hair into a none-too-neat bun, she kicked Blake's boots to him and shoved in the hairpins as she gave him a look that said, See? I told you this would happen.

Once more the impatient knock sounded. Lacey frantically gestured for Blake to move, and she whipped the heavy bedspread up to cover the rumpled sheets. Blake stuffed in his shirttail and grinned mischievously at her as he sat back down on the bed to pull on his boots.

Lacey smoothed ineffectively at her dress and hair as she hurried to the door. Lifting the latch, she opened the door. Her mouth dropped open when she saw the man on her porch.

"Papa?" she gasped.

CHAPTER
18

"What are you doing here, Papa!" Lacey demanded as she stepped out onto the porch and slammed the door behind her.

"Praise be, my child is alive," the man intoned, casting his eyes heavenward.

"How did you find me!"

"I was passing through town and happened to hear a woman mention your name. You know Lacey isn't a common name, and when I described you, she sent me here." He gave her the crooked little smile he usually reserved for his medicine-show audiences.

"Passing through? The snows have already started. Why did you leave the wagon train?"

He smiled again, but his black eyes remained calculating. "Me and the wagon master had a difference of opinion, and I stayed in Crazy Creek, to the west of here."

"If you were in a town, why did you leave?" Her voice remained suspicious, and she made no move to invite him inside.

"Mercy be, child, I've been through several towns since Crazy Creek. No, I've learned my lesson and mended my ways. Behold!'' He stepped aside and gestured grandly at the wagon.

Lacey's mouth dropped open incredulously, and she took several halting steps forward. The wagon was still painted white, but now bright blue letters proclaimed it to be the property of the Reverend Ezekiel K. Summerfield. Fat cherubs hung on to solid-looking clouds and harps that appeared too unwieldy to sound a note. Harnessed in shiny black leather to the front of the wagon were two white horses.

"Papa," Lacey whispered, "what have you done?"

"It's a traveling revival show. I don't know why I never thought of it before. People flock to a show like this, and their purse strings are loose before they leave." He came to her and turned her face around to his. "I never noticed before, but you bear a remarkable resemblance to your sainted mother, rest her soul."

"Quit talking like that!" Lacey jerked free. "And don't you touch me."

"Come with me, Lacey. This broken-down town isn't for you. I'm heading back east. Sure, you can't sing a note, but you look like an angel. I can see you now in a long white robe and maybe something shiny in your hair."

Their conversation stopped abruptly when Blake stepped out onto the porch.

"Mr. Summerfield!"

"You!" Zeke exclaimed. "I thought you'd be long gone by now." He turned to Lacey and demanded, "What's he doing here?"

"He's my husband," she said proudly. "You'd know that if you had bothered to ask about me."

Blake frowned from the two on the porch to the wagon. "Come inside, it's cold out here."

From Lacey's expression Blake concluded that he shouldn't have invited her father inside, but it was too late to withdraw the invitation.

"Blake, Papa was just passing through on his way back

east.'' Lacey's words were terse, and her eyes warned Blake not be too friendly to the man.

''In time, daughter, in time.''

''You're not staying in Friendswood,'' Lacey informed him. ''There will be more snow by next week, so you'd better start traveling.''

''Aren't you even going to offer me a cup of coffee to warm my bones? I'm your papa,'' he wheedled.

Lacey made no move toward the coffee pot, so Zeke helped himself. Blake's muscles tensed, and he started to speak, but Lacey touched his arm and in a whisper said, ''Let me take care of this, please.''

Reluctantly he kept quiet. The last time Blake had seen Lacey and her father together the scene had been very much the same. He had defended the old man then, but now knew Lacey well enough to realize her harshness toward Zeke must be justified. Her papa must have hurt her badly, and Blake fought to restrain himself.

''You've turned into a hard woman, girl,'' Zeke mourned. ''It would pain your mother to see how you turned out.''

''I'm what the two of you made me, Papa,'' she snapped.

A noncommittal grunt came from deep in his beard. Turning to Blake, he said, ''Praise be that you saved her for me. I guess we were all wrong about that bear getting her.''

''There was a bear, all right,'' Blake said gruffly. ''A grizzly. That's his hide on the wall there.''

Zeke studied the huge skin and said, ''He was a big one.''

''Is that all you have to say?'' Lacey stormed.

''It's clear you're all right,'' Zeke defended himself. ''I'm sorry it happened, but you're unharmed.''

''I nearly died!''

''But you didn't!'' Zeke reminded her. He looked toward Blake but wouldn't meet his eye. ''So you're married now. Welcome to the family.''

Suddenly the threat Lacey must be feeling dawned on him. Zeke knew they had not been married before she became lost, and if he said anything around town, there would be trouble for sure. He considered himself married to Lacey, and in the spring they would make their union legal, but Friendswood might look on the matter differently. "Lacey's right. If you're going to get ahead of the weather, you'd better hurry."

"No, I may just stay put until spring." Zeke looked around the cabin. "My old bones complain in cold weather, and, of course, my salvation wagon has no heat."

Lacey's frown deepened. "You cannot stay here."

"Girl, where are your feelings? Can you turn your papa out in the cold?"

"I don't owe you anything!"

Zeke gave her a disgusted look, but he turned to Blake. "How about you? As head of the house you have the last say. Can you turn an old man out in the snow?"

"It's not snowing, and the ground is clear," Blake pointed out with grim determination.

"Our cabin is small. We have no room for you," Lacey stated flatly.

"No room? Why, your dear mother and I raised you and your brother in that wagon out there, and it's not a third as big as this cabin."

Blake could see years of pain and anguish etched on Lacey's normally calm features, and the color had left her cheeks. Her embittered resentment toward her father was evident in her frozen stare. Blake clenched his jaw tightly. The quicker he sent Zeke Summerfield on his way, the better it would be. Damn him! But Blake couldn't afford to let his anger show. The man might talk about his daughter—and her unwed status—before he left town. He had to be diplomatic and handle this with tact. Blake forced himself to speak. "There's dried venison in the shed. You're welcome to take some with you."

"I'm much obliged," Zeke replied, though the look in his eyes belied his words.

"Lacey and I will go get it."

"I'd rather stay inside," Lacey responded as Blake pulled on his coat.

Blake looked at Lacey to see if she would be all right while he was gone and was reassured by her terse nod. This was the woman who had killed a grizzly; she could manage Zeke Summerfield.

When Blake was gone, Zeke wandered around the room. "You've done well for yourself. You've come up in the world. But then, you always were a survivor." He chuckled, and his eyes darted toward his daughter. "I still say you ought to come with me. Cameron can come, too, if he's a mind. You can even have my bed. It's wider, you know."

Lacey's eyes flared at the suggestion. "Never! Blake and I are happy here. Friendswood is our home."

"Friendswood," Zeke tried the name on his tongue. "It has a nice ring to it. Sounds like an amiable place to winter."

"Get out of town, Papa," Lacey warned. "Nobody here knows about the tonic, and I want it to stay that way."

"I don't sell the tonic anymore," Zeke said as he picked up a pin tray and examined it. "I'm a preacher man now. I don't have any use for the tonic."

"How about whiskey?" Lacey demanded suspiciously.

He grinned. "Only a drop now and then. For my health."

"Your 'drops' have always been a quart at a time, Papa. Well, at least you won't find any hard liquor here. This is a very religious town."

"Is it, now?"

"Yes. Half the townspeople are Quakers, and most of the others are Presbyterians." She lifted her chin defiantly. "You won't find many people to 'convert' here. You may as well move on."

"Quakers," Zeke said thoughtfully. "I thought I saw some men in real plain garb."

"You may as well go. There's no way you can turn this to your benefit."

"Now there you're wrong, girl. There's a profit to be

made in every situation. I've just got to come up with the right angle.''

Lacey's back became rigid in her rage, and she reached out to take her pin tray from him before it could find its way into his pocket. As she grabbed it, Zeke caught her wrist.

''You're not wearing a wedding band,'' he observed, narrowing his eye at her. ''Why is that?''

''We couldn't afford one,'' she snapped as she yanked her hand back.

Blake came in and looked from Zeke to Lacey, who was rubbing her wrist. He held out the flour sack of deer meat to Zeke. ''You'd better be on your way. It's not long until nightfall.''

Zeke kept his face a mask, but his thoughts were milling. A man who could afford this cabin could buy a wedding ring for his wife. There was more here than was presented on the surface. He smiled and paused at the door that Blake held open for him. ''I'm much obliged for the meat,'' he said. With a piercing look at Blake and Lacey, he left.

His horses were stamping and blowing in the cold, but he paid them no heed; they were young animals and could stand privation. He climbed up onto the seat and thoughtfully studied the cabin. What was going on there? He knew Lacey better than he knew himself, and she was hiding something. Had she been anyone else, he would have guessed that she wasn't married at all. Not Lacey, however. She was as straitlaced as a spinster aunt.

The wind picked up, and Zeke shivered. Tossing the meat into the back of the wagon, he slapped the reins on the horses' rumps. He had no intention of leaving town just yet.

He drove back to the main street and looked around as the horses picked their way among the frozen ruts. Most of the houses were small and simple, but one was somewhat finer than the rest. It stood next to the town hall and was made of whitewashed planks rather than logs. There were even green shutters at the windows, and the yard looked as if it had been laid out as a garden.

Zeke reined to a stop. Experience in the last few towns had told him to start at the top. "Preacher" Summerfield was in a different class from "Doctor" Summerfield, and he would no longer have to winter in drafty hovels.

He tied the horses at the hitching post and went up the walk and knocked on the door. After a few minutes the door opened, and a large woman regarded him doubtfully.

Zeke whipped his hat off and assumed a humble stance. "Pardon me, ma'am. I'm Reverend Ezekiel Summerfield. I was traveling through your fair town, but my horses are tired. I wonder if you might direct me to a stable for the poor beasts and a boardinghouse for myself?"

"Reverend?" He was dressed like an undertaker, but as she looked over his narrow shoulder, she saw the cherub-bedecked wagon, and her expression became more welcoming. "Come in out of the cold, Reverend Summerfield. My name is Olive Sloan. Fate has brought you to the right place, for I have a room I sometimes rent to passing strangers who I can tell are of exemplary character and breeding. You're more than welcome to it."

Zeke lost no time in entering and gazed about him with interest. A silver butler tray sat on the hall tree, and two silver candlesticks adorned the wall sconces. Beyond her he saw a parlor with a cut-glass lamp and a gold cigar box. He smiled winningly. "I hate to put you out. Would it be any trouble?"

"No trouble at all," Olive assured him. Turning, she called to an unseen servant, "Elly, have Josiah take the reverend's horses around to the barn." She beamed back at Zeke. "Come in and make yourself at home. Shall I show you the room?"

"Yes, ma'am. I'd be pleased to see it."

Olive preceded him up the stairs and therefore missed the leer in his eyes as he watched her wide and rolling hips while she mounted the stairs a few steps ahead of him. He appraised her thoughtfully. He had also learned that rich widows were an easy mark for itinerant preachers such as himself. They invariably wanted to take him in and fatten him up. In the first town after leaving the wagons, he had actually had to marry a woman before she would let him have access to her money. Since then he had figured out ways to get the money without the trip to the altar.

Making his voice as humble as possible, Zeke said, "This is a hard country for a lady such as yourself. I pray the angels have seen fit to spare your good husband?"

"Yes, indeed. Mr. Sloan is mayor of Friendswood."

"How fortunate," Zeke replied, covering his disappointment. He would have to alter his plan somewhat.

"Here it is," Olive said as she pushed upen a door. "It's not fancy, but it is warm." Her tone indicated she expected him to correct her.

Zeke took his cue. "Not fancy, you say? It's a palace! Is the rent high? I'm afraid I have very little money."

"Nonsense. I couldn't charge rent to a preacher. You'll stay here for free, board included."

"That's real decent of you, ma'am. I'm sure the angels are taking note," Zeke assured her solemnly. Looking back at the room, he added, "Why, this room is nearly as big as my daughter's whole cabin."

"Your daughter?"

"Yes, ma'am. Lacey Cameron. She and her husband live at the edge of town."

"You're Lacey Cameron's father? How amazing! She never told anyone she's a preacher's daughter. But why aren't you staying there? Not that you aren't welcome here, of course," Olive added quickly.

"She said they had no room," he answered sadly.

"For shame. Well, you know how it is with young couples. Tell me, Reverend, will you be in Friendswood long?"

"The truth is, I was hoping to winter here. But when Lacey had no room for me, I decided to move on."

"Oh, but you shouldn't! Didn't she tell you? We have had an Indian scare here."

"No!"

"Only this afternoon a chief and a dozen young bucks came riding through town yelling at the top of their lungs. It was dreadful! I told Mr. Sloan that they were likely sizing up our defenses. No, Reverend Summerfield, you can't possibly ride off into the woods with those heathens out there."

"My work lies with the heathen," Zeke intoned.

"But they will shoot you full of arrows. No, no, I cannot allow you to sacrifice yourself."

"But—"

"Not another word." Olive held up her hands and shook her head vigorously.

"Well, if you insist," he said hesitantly.

"I do. Besides, there are heathens enough right here in town to keep you busy all winter."

"Oh?" he asked innocently.

"Quakers!" Olive hissed in an undertone as if the word were soiled.

"Here? In Friendswood?" Zeke sounded properly aghast.

"Right here. Half the town is of that persuasion."

"I have for a fact been led to the right place," Zeke said fervently. "I see my calling true and clear. I've been sent to build a temple and save the good folk from the infidel!"

He dropped to his knees, clasped his hands, and raised his eyes toward the ceiling. Olive, after a startled hesitation, joined him on the floor and closed her eyes prayerfully.

Zeke glanced at her and hid his grin. This was going to be even easier than duping widows. He raised his reedy voice in loud exhortation to the heavens.

Lacey watched the wagon pull out of sight, then turned with stricken eyes back to Blake. "What are we going to do?"

Blake looked past her and out the window. "He damned well better leave town like he said."

"He didn't actually say that. And even if he had, that's no guarantee that he would. I know him. He's looking for a warm place to spend the winter.'' She turned again to face the window.

"Lacey, I just couldn't stand seeing you look so hurt. What in the world happened to you before I met you?'' His tone was fierce as he pulled her to him so that her back lay against his chest and his cheek rubbed her hair.

Lacey stiffened. "It's nothing. It's not worth talking about. Please don't ask.'' She couldn't tell him now. He was far too upset already. "The dangerous thing, Blake, is that he knows we aren't married.''

"Not exactly. I've been thinking about it. All he knows is that we weren't married when you got lost. I'm sure he assumes we got married here in Friendswood.'' Blake had decided to drop the discussion of her past. The more he thought about how the old man must have treated her, the madder he got.

"But what if he asks someone? Anybody could tell him we didn't!''

"If they did, he wouldn't tell them the truth. A preacher wouldn't want folks to think his daughter was a sinner. No, he'll be certain to want us married in everybody's eyes.''

"That makes sense, I guess,'' Lacey admitted. "Still, I don't trust him.''

"Neither do I, honey. Lucky for us he's gone now.''

Lacey didn't dispute Blake, but she also wasn't convinced that her father had left Friendswood. Papa saw a prosperous town here, and he wasn't about to leave before he reaped all the benefits he could.

"By the way, I didn't know he was a preacher.''

"Neither did I.''

CHAPTER
19

Lacey unfolded the intricately embroidered collars and laid them out on Mrs. Bastrop's countertop. Each piece was sewn with tiny stitches, and each was an original design. As the seamstress examined the work, Lacey clasped her hands to steady them.

When the woman made no comment, Lacey said nervously, "I thought perhaps I could leave them on consignment. You wouldn't owe me anything unless they sold. Also, Blake has offered to make me a quilting frame soon. If any of your customers has a quilt pieced and doesn't want to stitch it together, I could do it for her at a very reasonable price."

Mrs. Bastrop pursed her thin lips and peered down her nose through her wire-rimmed spectacles. "Hmm," she said absently. "Actually, these are rather good. This one"—she held up a collar with a motif of daisies and ferns—"would look quite pretty on a dress I'm making for Lidy Rose Harris."

"If Lidy Rose has an embroidered collar, you know Olive will want one, too," Lacey prompted.

"Hmm. Possibly." Mrs. Bastrop studied the handwork. "I think perhaps we could work something out. I don't have time to do fine handwork. The orders for dresses keep me too busy." She shot a searching look at Lacey. "How are you at sewing men's shirts?"

"I can do that," Lacey spoke up promptly. "I have no patterns, but I could finish the clothing after you cut it out." This was the ticklish part; she didn't want the seamstress to think she might set up a competing store, yet she had to sound competent enough to do just that. "I can also design and trim ladies' bonnets."

"And sew dresses?"

"Yes, that, too."

Mrs. Bastrop puckered her lips and drew a deep breath as if she thought Lacey was asking far too much of her. "Very well. I have a dress cut out of claret twill. Will you finish it for me?"

"I would be glad to."

Lacey followed the seamstress to the back room where no one but Mrs. Bastrop was normally allowed to go. Here were the various patterns and the stuffed judys for rough-fitting the garments. Pins littered the tabletops, along with measuring tapes, chalk, and scraps of various materials and laces. Mrs. Bastrop went unerringly through the clutter and found the dress in question.

"As you can see, I've basted the sleeves and bodice. I'd like you to sew them in properly and attach the top to the skirt. It's for Dulcy Harmon. Her oldest boy is marrying the Pilkin girl, and this dress is for the bridal shower next month."

"I'll start on it tonight," Lacey promised, "and I'll have it finished in plenty of time for the party."

Mrs. Bastrop pondered her pattern for a minute, then said, "If you could work two panels, say in roses, using thread the same color as the dress, I could inset them on either side of the front buttons. Could you do that, do you suppose?"

"Of course."

Mrs. Bastrop nodded and gave Lacey a skein of embroidery thread in the same shade of claret. "That will do nicely." She folded the dress and wrapped it, the threads, and the buttons in one package. When she gave the parcel to Lacey, she prompted, "Three weeks, mind you."

"I will. And the collars."

They concluded their business, and Lacey left the shop with a bundle under her arm and coins in her reticule. Her step was light, and she felt happier than she had since her papa had come to town.

News had reached her that he had moved into the Sloans' extra bedroom, and she had seen the two white horses in the mayor's feed lot, so she knew it was true. However, he had made no effort to see her in the intervening week, and she had heard no rumors of his selling the Wonder Tonic.

Nonetheless, Lacey had been constantly on edge since Papa's arrival. Her concern that Sarah might tell someone about Blake and herself had been nothing compared to her worry over her father. All her life his activities had been an embarrassment, and now she had a great deal at stake. She hoped taking in sewing work would help relieve her mind of the ever present worries.

The road led Lacey past the blacksmith shop, and soon she was within sight of the heavy double doors. Her feet slowed, and she drew nearer. In regard for the weather, only one door stood partly open, and inside she could see several men sitting around the glowing coals in the shallow firebox. Blake stood at the anvil, fashioning nails to be used in building during the coming spring.

Lacey drew closer. She didn't want to intrude, but she liked to watch Blake at work. The warmth of the scene framed by the doorway pulled her irresistibly. The men were talking idly, their rough voices rising and falling with an unhurried cadence as they discussed past winters and compared them favorably to the present one.

Blake remained more or less on the outside of the group. Occasionally he added a comment or an observation, but for the most part he seemed content to tap sharp points to the square nails. He had removed his coat, and his blue home-spun shirt was partially unbuttoned, exposing his chest. His sleeves were rolled up above his elbows, and his muscled biceps pulled the fabric taut. As usual his dark hair fell boyishly over his broad forehead and looked as if he had recently run his fingers through it.

Lacey turned to go, but her movement caught his attention. Blake came to the door and motioned to her. "Come on in here and get warm," he invited as the other men rose to greet her.

After a brief hesitation, Lacey went inside. She liked the smithy with its smells of steam and warmed earth and wood. With the second door, the back door, and the windows closed, it had the secure darkness of a cave. The table-high firebox glowed with shifting scenes of fiery design as if the coals had a life of their own. Blake smiled at her as he pumped the huge wooden and leather bellows to intensify the heat. Lacey warmed her hands as she returned the men's greetings.

"We was just telling Blake," one man said, "that we seen those Indians again, me and my brother here. They was just past the old bridge."

"Mark my words, no good will come of it," another chimed in.

"We ought to band together and wipe 'em out, I think. It's just a matter of time before they try a raid on us."

Blake's eyes met Lacey's. "We have a defense plan. You all know that. If the warning bell rings, you're to go to the town hall." Blake's dark gaze held her as lovingly as if no one else were around.

"Do you think there's any real danger?" she asked Blake.

"Can't nobody tell," the first man answered for him. "You can't never tell what an Indian is up to."

Blake said, "I'm not worried, but to be safe, listen for the bell."

"Speaking of the town hall, have you heard about the revival there tonight?" a man asked. "That new preacher fellow is giving a sermon. I plan to go. He's going to be preaching every night this week."

Amid the general assent, Lacey's eyes met Blake's. He

was listening, but he had no intention of claiming any knowledge of Zeke.

"If you're worried about Indians attacking," Blake said to steer the conversation back, "why don't you talk to Micah Sloan about storing food and water in the town hall? Then, if it happens and we have to stay there for a while, we'll be more comfortable."

"Yeah," one of them agreed. "We could put some extra blankets there, too. And more firewood."

Blake smiled at Lacey in a show of confidence. He wanted her to know she had nothing to fear.

She returned his smile, and as she did so she concentrated on her love for Blake. The prickle of fear she had felt at the mention of the Indian threat melted into a joyous peace of mind. So long as she thought of Blake, she felt safe and secure.

"What brings you out today?" Blake asked as he tapped a point onto a nail.

She didn't answer for a moment, as though she were lost in a daydream, then replied demurely, "I was having trouble getting something down off that top shelf at home."

He had picked up his hammer, but her words stopped him in midswing. "The *top* shelf?" he asked as if he wasn't sure he had heard her correctly.

"That's right." Her eyes danced with mischief as she waited to see if he would remember the signal.

Blake tossed his hammer down onto the scarred work surface and swung the bellows back from the fire. "I'm closing up," he announced. "I'd be much obliged if the last one to leave would see that the coals are banked and close the door."

The men nodded as if this were an everyday occurrence. They were too interested in arguing about who should take what to the town hall to care if the smithy closed. Blake put on his heavy leather coat and slipped his arm protectively around Lacey's waist. As they left, he grinned and chuckled under his breath. "The top shelf, you say?"

"Hush!" Lacey glanced back at the smithy. Now that she had actually done it, she was struck with embarrassment. "Someone may hear you!"

He laughed out loud. "They wouldn't know what I'm laughing about if they did hear. That top shelf is giving you trouble, is it?"

Lacey poked him with her elbow and blushed a fiery pink. "You should be ashamed of yourself, teasing me like that." But she added, "Can we walk a little faster?"

By the time they reached the cabin, they were nearly running and both were laughing like children on a holiday. They tumbled through the door, and Blake pushed it shut, pinning her between him and it. His lips found hers, and she breathed in the scent of cold air and pines that still enveloped them both.

"I'm a shameless hussy," she confessed when he lifted his head.

"Damned right," he agreed.

She struggled with the buttons of his coat, and he tried to untangle the frog cording that held her cloak.

"Let's move south," he grumbled, "so we won't have to wear so many clothes."

"If we move far enough, maybe we won't have to wear any at all.

"You really are a shameless hussy," he said approvingly.

She laughed as she tossed his coat onto a chair and tried to kiss his fingers as he worked to untwist the cording. He growled with pretended frustration while Lacey opened the buttons of his shirt and nibbled kisses along his collarbone.

Blake gave up on the fasteners and pulled the cloak over her head without further ado. He could hear her soft chuckle against his skin, and her lips were warming him much faster than the fire in the hearth.

Lacey pulled off his shirt and deftly unbuckled his belt. Blake's fingers were working with the tiny buttons down her back, and she heard him swear under his breath. In response she nipped him and ran her fingernails lightly over his skin.

"Lacey," he said in exasperation, "if you don't want me to rip these buttons off, you'd better quit that."

It only took Lacey a second to decide her dress material was more durable than the thread holding the buttons. She bent to flick her tongue across his coppery nipple as her questing hands found his manhood through the material of his pants. "Go ahead," she dared as her eyes sparkled with devilment.

Blake tried to calm his racing senses. "Honey, don't tempt me. I can't stand much more, and these damned buttons are too small for my fingers."

She smiled but didn't answer. She didn't need to. Her hands were making a reply much more eloquent than mere words.

With a groan, Blake caught her dress and ripped it open. Buttons flew everywhere and bounced off the wall and rolled to the floor. He buried his face in the hollow of her neck and drank deeply of the fluttering pulse under his lips and tongue. His hands caressed her supple back beneath the film of her chemise as she pressed her body against him. When she ran her hands inside his pants and cupped his buttocks to rub her body harder against his, he no longer tried to restrain himself.

He picked her up and carried her to the bed, not even stopping to pull back the covers. Lacey looked at his smoldering black eyes and felt a primal urge of her own. Here was Blake in unleashed passion, and she found it triggered the same response in herself.

With a low cry, she fumbled at the buttons of his pants and tried to undress him. Blake was more direct. He pulled at the ribbon of her chemise and when it knotted tight, he snapped it easily. Lacey gasped with surprise, and he grinned sardonically at her as he ripped open her chemise.

"Blake!" she exclaimed, more because she found this exciting than because she objected.

"I'll buy you another one." He looked hungrily down at her swelling breasts, then captured a proud nipple between his lips. Tugging gently, he stoked her fires to arching eagerness as he loved first one succulent globe, then the other.

Lacey cried out and knotted her fingers in his hair as she gave herself to him in feverish abandon. She was scarcely aware of the yank when he broke the ribbon that secured her petticoats. She wanted him, and her body felt white-hot with her need. He lifted her hips and thrust her clothes down and off the bed. She kicked off her shoes without bothering to unfasten the buckles, and his hands rolled down her stockings as he covered her face with kisses.

Instead of turning him loose so he could undress, Lacey sent flames racing over his neck and chest with her teasing tongue and lips. Blake somehow managed to tear off his own clothes without leaving her, and the bed swayed as he threw himself down beside her.

Lacey rolled on top of him, her tongue seeking his and raking tantalizingly over the soft inner skin of his lips. Her hair came free, and the pins slid to the pillows and floor. Blake knotted the silken strands around his hand and rolled her over to lie beneath him.

Moaning as Blake's other hand kneaded her throbbing breast, Lacey opened her legs to give him access. He came into her with as much eagerness as she felt, and she murmured with the sheer pleasure of their oneness. Moving her hips with sensuous lust, Lacey felt herself already climbing love's spiral.

Suddenly Blake cried out and gripped her tightly, and this sent her over the peak into her own satisfaction. Around and around their souls tumbled and swirled as their bodies thrummed in perfect tune.

"I couldn't—" Blake panted when he could speak at all. "That is, I wasn't able to wait and—"

"Good," she replied with complete satisfaction.

He raised his head to gaze down at her smug smile. "You sure as hell don't act like any wife I ever heard of," he said in awed tones.

"Should I?"

His slow grin answered her. "Hell, no!"

"Then let's do it again," she suggested. "Slower this time."

He laughed and ran his tongue over her delicate ear as his fingers traced the line of her breast. "Woman, you're damned near perfect."

She only smiled and parted her lips for his kiss.

"Blake, I have to go," Lacey said worriedly as she bit off the claret thread and held up the almost finished dress. "Papa has held revival meetings for the past five nights, and I've got to see what's going on there."

He sighed and looked at her with no comprehension. "You're upset, honey. If you go down there you may feel worse."

"But what is he saying?" she fretted. "There's no telling what he may be leading those people to believe."

"You're making too much of this. It's just a revival. I've seen many of them back home. The preacher gives sermons for a week, a few people join the church, maybe there are a few healings. That's about it. I never saw any harmful effects."

"Healings! Is Papa doing healings?" she gasped.

"Most of those people aren't sick to start with, except in their heads. Old Mrs. Hightower went down front and got cured of lung fever. Now, you and I both know that old woman has a new disease each week. She no more had lung fever than I have. Then Frank Murphy threw down his crutch and walked. Hell, I've seen Frank walk without support many a time. He only needs that crutch if he's going to be on his foot for a long time. The bones never set correctly after he broke it. It pains him, but he *can* walk."

"Papa's doing healings!" Lacey's face had paled and she started folding the dress away. "I'm going."

"No, you're not. I want you to stay away from there."

"Why!"

"Right now nobody connects you and your papa, but if you go down there, someone may." Blake had tried once during the week to get Lacey to tell him why Zeke's presence upset her to such an extent, but she had insisted it was the old man's knowledge of their marital status. Now she was going to risk everything by going to see him preach. To Blake this made no sense at all.

Lacey, however, had already made up her mind. She had to know what Zeke was doing that might cause harm to one of their friends. Her nerves were raw, but she couldn't ignore him and hope that this time his actions would be innocent.

"Anyway, that old man isn't hurting anybody. There's no admission fee at a revival. All he can do is talk to the people, and there's no harm in that. If they don't like what he has to say, they won't go back."

"Those healings bother me. And you know he's passing a collection plate. Papa wouldn't do this if he wasn't making money."

"He probably is, but people are putting money in that plate of their own free will."

Lacey put away her sewing and turned to Blake. "I still have to go and see. I need to put my mind to rest."

"I'm asking you not to go." His voice dropped deeper as it did when he was being stubborn.

"Try to understand," Lacey reasoned with him.

"You're going to go down there and get more upset. What if he hurts you again? Like before?"

"He won't do anything to me, but he might hurt someone else. I have to go."

Blake drew a deep breath. "I won't let you."

Lacey stared at him in surprise, her expression getting angrier by the moment. "You won't *what?*" she asked with deceptive coolness.

"I won't let you. You can't go." His dark eyes challenged her, and his stance said he knew he was the boss.

Without further ado, Lacey took her shawl and bonnet from the pegs. She slapped the bonnet viciously on her head and snapped open the shawl as if it were a sheet. Flinging it around her, she said, "Good-bye, Blake. I'll be back later."

"Damn it, Lacey, be reasonable," he fumed.

She stalked to the door and jerked it open.

"There may be Indians out there!" he warned in a dire voice.

She slammed the door behind her.

Bright moonlight lit her way, but the woods were dark and spooky. Lacey wished she had brought a lantern. Soon the moon would set, and she would have to find her way home through the pitch-dark forest. Angrily she ducked under a branch. If only Blake hadn't forbidden her to come, she could have gone back without feeling foolish. But he had, and now she must go or give Blake the idea that he could order her around as he pleased.

She passed several houses whose windows glowed with firelight. Not many people were out. The cold air stung her eyes and made them water, and she almost wished she had given in to Blake.

The town hall was well lit, and even from a distance she could hear the strains of a familiar hymn. She found herself wondering where Papa had learned hymns. She knew he had never been inside a church during her lifetime. She hurried across the town hall's frozen yard and went up the steps.

The revival was being held in the main room, but she could see only people's backs by looking in the windows. Lacey opened the outside door, and the loud song seemed to fill the night air. The sermon was evidently finished, because as they sang, the people were passing a velvet bag. Lacey slipped through the door and merged with the crowd standing in the shadows at the back. Those who saw her smiled when she entered and shifted so she could see the front of the room. When the bag was handed to her, Lacey jiggled it assessingly before passing it along. It was well loaded with coins. She had passed enough hats as a child to figure fairly accurately how much was there.

Zeke spread his arms and beamed beatifically on the

townspeople. "I feel the spirit!" he called out, and they echoed him. "I feel it clear down to my bones!" Again there was a clarion response.

"Come to me," Zeke urged. He walked back and forth on the low platform, a sheen of sweat on his brow. "Come forward to me if you've got a sickness weighing on you. I've got the cure."

Lacey leaned closer so she would miss nothing, but remained sheltered by the shadows near the wall.

A man got to his feet and limped to the front. "Can you cure me?" he weakly pleaded. "I've got rheumatism so bad I can't hardly walk."

"Come forward, brother." Zeke met him at the platform and pulled a bottle of clear liquid from his coat pocket. Uncorking it dramatically, he poured it over the man's head. "Heal!" he yelled as loud as he could. With the flat of his hand, he pounded the man's shoulder and again cried, "Heal, brother!"

The man staggered under the blow, and Zeke used this as an excuse to help him—with great solicitude—to what he called the "healing bench."

"Anybody else?" Zeke called. "Surely I haven't healed everybody here in just five short days! Don't be shy! Come on down here!"

A heavy-set woman got up and moved forward. "I've got stomach trouble. Can you fix that?"

"I can indeed." Zeke whipped out another bottle and handed it to the woman. "This is water from the River Jordan. You take a spoonful a day, and by the time it's gone, you'll be well."

The lady thanked him over and over, and Lacey saw her press a gold coin into Zeke's hand.

A man near Lacey called out, making her jump. "How about me? I've got a lame foot."

Zeke held out another bottle. "Come and get it. Come and get your cure!" The words reverberated in her ears. They were words she had heard so many times before.

When the man reached the front, Zeke said, "A teaspoon a day. No more, no less." He willingly took the coin the man offered.

The cripple limped back to his place, and Lacey edged over to him. "Could I see that River Jordan water?"

Reluctantly, he handed it to her. "Careful now. Don't spill it."

She pulled the cork stopper and sniffed. There was no odor, and when she put a drop on her finger and tasted it, she said, "Water!"

"That's right," the man said earnestly. "From the River Jordan." He took back the bottle, corked it, and put it in his pocket.

No one else claimed any ailments so Zeke started another hymn. As he did, he passed the velvet bag again.

Lacey had seen enough. She eased through the crowd and back out the door. Papa was selling water! If she hadn't been so relieved, she would have been even angrier. It was a flim-flam, but this time it was harmless. Water wouldn't hurt that woman's stomach ailment, whereas turpentine and onions would have.

As she crossed the town hall porch, she met Blake coming up the steps. Cautiously she waited for him to speak.

"You sure are a stubborn woman. Are you all right?" he finally said. He gestured with the lantern. "I'd have been here quicker, but the lantern was empty."

Lacey went to him. "I'm fine, but I was right, Blake. Papa is taking the people's money. He's selling water and telling them it will cure their ills! Plain old water! I'll bet he fills those bottles in the creek behind the Sloans' house."

"Is he charging money for it?"

"No, but he might as well be. Most of the people were giving him money. And he passed the collection plate twice while I was standing there! Who knows how often it goes around?"

Blake frowned. "He shouldn't be doing that, but he isn't forcing people to pay. You've got to remember that."

She took his arm, and they walked down the steps. "Blake, one of the people who bought the water was Abraham Stanley. He has a limp because he cut half his foot off chopping wood. How is a teaspoon of water going to help him?"

"Abraham never seemed very smart to me," Blake commented as they walked in the circle of lantern light. "Just remember. It won't help him, but it won't hurt him, either."

"You don't understand! Tonight it was creek water, but who knows what it may be tomorrow?"

"I knew you'd get more upset if you went to that meeting," he observed sagely. "I was right."

"Well, I *should* be upset! You just don't know what he's up to. Nobody will be hurt tonight, but people have been before!" Blake had to know the truth about Papa. She was ashamed to tell him, but she couldn't carry the burden alone any longer. Taking a deep breath, she said, "At one time he put foxglove in water and sold it as a medicine. Foxglove is digitalis! A mother gave Papa's Wonder Tonic to her little girl who had heart trouble, and that child died!"

Blake stopped walking and faced her. "Do you know that for a fact?"

"Of course I do! Who knows how many others died? We mistakenly went back to that same town, and they remembered us. That's when my brother Billy was killed. The crowd lynched him! I saw it happen!"

"You were there?"

"I was fourteen, but I looked younger, so I was selling the Wonder Tonic to the crowd. When they grabbed Billy, Papa drove off, and I had to run as hard as I could to keep from being left behind." Her breath caught in her throat as she fought to keep from crying. "And do you know that Papa never slowed the wagon? He never even looked back to see if I was in there or to see what happened to Billy. He just drove off!"

"Why didn't you tell me this before!" Blake said in an angry voice. "That son of a bitch was going to leave you to a mob?"

She nodded. "He *did* leave Billy. Oh, Blake, you don't know what it was like. I would find work, and either my employer would fire me for not letting him use me as he pleased, or Papa would start making the tonic again."

Blake walked with his head bent in thought. "I sure wish you had told me all this before now."

"Please understand! I couldn't! We've been chased out, burned out, stoned out of towns. That's why that seventy acres in Oregon meant so much to me. That's why I didn't want to live near a town or around people. Do you have any idea what it's like to be dragged out of your house and watch a mob set fire to it? And not know if you'll be next? I couldn't tell you all these things before. I was too ashamed. I was afraid I'd lose you!"

"Calm down, honey. I won't stop loving you. Besides, he did it, not you."

"I know that now, but at the time I was just a child. I thought I was partly at fault for not watching him closer."

"Why did you put up with it?"

"When Billy died, I was only fourteen. Do you think a fourteen-year-old girl would be safe alone? No one would have hired me or given me shelter, and I would probably have been raped or murdered before I left the first town. Papa's no good, but he was protection of sorts."

"Buy why did you stay with him after you were grown?"

She shrugged. "Nothing else was as bad as when Billy died. I didn't leave Papa then, and somehow I just never did later. Oh, I tried a few times. I'd hitch up the team and drive off. Next thing I knew, he was following me, begging to be let on. I couldn't listen to that, and he drew attention. I had to stop and let him on the wagon."

Blake and Lacey walked on in silence while Blake digested this revelation. Finally he said, "I knew something in your past hadn't been right, but I had no idea it was so bad."

She shrugged. "Everybody has troubles."

He looked over at her and put his arm around her. "Not

that big a trouble, they don't. Lacey, why were you afraid I'd leave? Didn't you trust me?''

"I trust you now," she said simply.

Blake hugged her closer and shortened his steps to accommodate hers.

The road led them past the Gibsons' house, and as they passed, Blake saw Hiram coming out of the barn. "Hello!" he called out. "It's pretty late to be out in the barn. Did Sarah throw you out?''

Hiram held up his lantern and laughed. "Not yet, friend. My cow is calving, and she's having a hard time. Hello, Lacey," he greeted as he came closer to the fence. "It's a cold night for a stroll.''

"We're on our way home," Lacey said uncomfortably. "Are you doing all right?''

"Fine as I can be. I haven't seen thee around lately. I've missed thee." Hiram looked at Lacey questioningly.

"Hiram?" came Sarah's voice. "Is thee out there?''

"Here, by the fence," he said unnecessarily as she was now standing in the barn doorway and could hardly miss seeing two bright lanterns.

Sarah came to him, a smile already wreathing her face. "Have we got company?" she asked. "Who is thee talking to?''

"It's us," Blake answered. "It's good to see you.''

Sarah's steps faltered, but she could hardly turn and go back to the barn. "Hello," she said stiffly.

Lacey drew back defensively, but Blake's encircling arm prevented much of a retreat.

"We ought to get together one evening before long," Blake said, looking from one woman to the other. "Lacey has a new way of making molasses cake that's a joy in this world.''

"Thy cake was already my favorite," Hiram said gallantly. "Maybe thee could give thy recipe to Sarah.''

"Add ginger," Lacey said, scarcely moving her lips. "One teaspoon.''

"Thank thee," Sarah said with equal coolness.

"Sarah has a recipe for rabbit that we like," Hiram prompted. "Come over one night, and we will cook it for thee."

"Thank you," said Lacey.

"Thy cow needs thee," said Sarah.

"She's right," Hiram agreed reluctantly.

"Do you need my help?" Blake offered.

"No, thank thee. I have Sarah, and she's as good a mid-wife as any I've ever seen." He grinned affectionately at his wife.

"We have to go now," Lacey took the opportunity to say. "I'm cold, and the hour is getting late."

"It is for a fact," Blake seconded. "That rabbit supper sounds good, Sarah. We could put a meal together with you cooking the rabbit and Lacey making the molasses cake."

"That's a good idea," Hiram answered for Sarah. "We'll do that."

When Blake and Lacey left, Sarah frowned at her husband. "Why did thee do that?" she demanded.

"Because thee is too stubborn to do it thyself," he answered. "Lacey is thy friend!"

"Thee doesn't know what thee is talking about," Sarah snapped. She looked into the darkness that hid the couple. She missed Lacey sorely, but she was afraid to try to patch matters up. More was at stake here than the Camerons' un-orthodox marriage. She and Hiram had not only sheltered them, but had unwittingly told the other townspeople that Lacey and Blake were married. Guilt over having commit-ted such an act made Sarah too ashamed to change things.

She glanced at Hiram. If the truth became known, they would be shunned, if not actually chased out of town. The memory of what Mabel Bannion and Lidy Rose's husband had done was too fresh. The Camerons even lived in Mabel's cabin, thanks to Hiram and herself. With a low groan, Sarah followed Hiram into the barn.

CHAPTER
20

"Won't you have another tea cake, Reverend Summerfield?" Olive simpered as she offered Zeke a plate of cookies.

"Thank you, ma'am. I don't mind if I do." He took two and sipped his coffee appreciatively as his eyes roamed the parlor. "I must congratulate you. You and Mayor Sloan have done a fine job of making an oasis in the wilderness. Your house is truly magnificent."

"Posh," Olive said happily. "Back home this house would be the servants' quarters." She looked thoughtful, as if she weren't sure her words hadn't placed her in an unfavorable light. "Of course," she corrected the situation, "we had very well paid servants."

"To be sure," Zeke answered without listening to her. He had had time in the past few days to examine the gold cigar box and to ascertain that it was indeed gold and not cheap gilt. Unfortunately, Olive was always with him, and he was having trouble shaking her long enough to see what else in the parlor was of value.

"I guess it won't be long before you can start breaking ground."

"How's that again?" Zeke asked.

"The new temple, I mean. Soon you will have gathered enough donations to begin building it, won't you?"

"Oh, yes, I will for a fact."

"How exciting. You know, Mr. Sloan and I weren't originally of the Presbyterian faith. I'm quite certain your Temple of the River Jordan will come closer to our childhood beliefs. After all, a town needs more than one church." She simpered as she ate another cookie. "Naturally I don't count the Quakers' meetinghouse as a church. They don't even sing hymns."

"Barbaric," Zeke agreed, using one of Olive's favorite words.

"Reverend, there's something I've been meaning to talk to you about."

"What's that, Mrs. Sloan?" He curled his fingers around a silver bonbon dish and lifted it, pretending to balance it idly, while he judged its weight.

"It's your daughter, Lacey. I know she's as good as any woman you'll ever see, being your daughter and all, but as far as I know, she has yet to attend your revival."

"I know," Zeke said in a mournful voice as he squinted to read the trademark on the bottom of the bonbon dish. "It purely pains a father's heart."

"An ungrateful child bites like a snake," Olive misquoted. "I blame it all on those Quakers. Lacey and Mr. Cameron have been going to meeting with the Gibsons ever since they came here."

"I guess I can't do a thing but let her go her own way. We choose our dooms, Mrs. Sloan." On the underside of the bonbon dish, he made out a figure that resembled a bell with faint printing beneath it. "I guess if she saw fit to marry in their church, she feels she belongs there." It *was* a bell, and the printing told him the dish was sterling.

"But they weren't married there," Olive corrected. "She and Mr. Cameron were man and wife when they came here. They were married on the wagon train."

"No, they weren't," Zeke corrected as he turned his eyes toward Olive in surprise. "They barely knew each other."

Olive's eyes grew round. "Barely knew each other? How can that be? What are you saying?"

In confusion, Zeke replaced the silver dish. "Lacey was accidentally left behind, and Blake went back to find her, but they weren't married." Realization dawned on him, and he leaned forward. "You mean they weren't married here?"

"Of course not." Olive drew back and covered her mouth with both hands. "Good heavens! They must not be married at all!"

Zeke stared at her. A preacher with a daughter living in sin wouldn't get much in the way of temple donations. "There's been a mistake, surely! Lacey may be unnatural in her affection toward her devoted papa, but this . . . No, No. They must have been married in the Quaker church."

"I'm positive they said they were married from the very beginning. They lived in the same room at the Gibsons', and then . . . Oh, my! The people of Friendswood gave them a cabin!"

"Now, now, Mrs. Sloan. Calm yourself." Zeke saw that Olive's face was turning deep red.

"We've been duped! The Camerons aren't now and never have been married!" She leaped to her feet. "I'm going straight to Lidy Rose with this. Then we're going to pay a visit to all the women in my sewing circle as well as the Society for Social Enlightenment. Friendswood must know about this!"

"We?" Zeke asked with trepidation.

"You want to come with me, surely! I should think this to be an excellent opportunity to save your daughter from a life of sin."

"Oh, to be sure. To be sure." He, too, stood up hastily. He wasn't nearly as eager to save Lacey as to somehow prevent her from blurting out all she knew about his own past. He grabbed his hat and black coat from the hall tree.

Olive already had put on her cloak and bonnet and was

pulling on her gloves. "Imagine!" Olive exclaimed as she jerked open the door. "Whoever would have guessed they were committing such an appalling act right under our very noses!"

"You're no more astonished than I am," Zeke assured her. If Lacey could be swayed now, why hadn't she given in when old man Martin had wanted her? They could have been spared the trip west.

Olive marched out of the house and down the main street to Mrs. Bastrop's shop. She swept in with regal anger and stopped in front of Lidy Rose, who was selecting new trimmings for her Sunday bonnet.

"You will never guess what I've just learned," Olive informed her sister and everyone else in the shop. "Lacey and Blake Cameron aren't married and never have been!"

"What?" Lidy Rose gasped. "Sister! Are you sure?"

"Ask her father here if you don't believe me," Olive gestured at Zeke.

"I was telling Mrs. Sloan that there must be some mistake. They must have been married here in Friendswood," he said hopefully.

"They most certainly were not!" Lidy Rose corrected.

"They were passing as man and wife from the beginning," another woman said as she sidled over to join them. "I know that for a fact." The women exchanged glances as if this revelation were a direct threat to themselves.

"Mr. Cameron had a wife back in Texas," another said. "He told my husband."

"I heard she died," Mrs. Bastrop said, trying to turn the tide.

"A likely story," Lidy Rose snorted. "No doubt my James is telling the same lie about me. Him and that trashy Mabel Bannion."

That was enough to spark war in the women's eyes. They all recalled Mabel's flirting ways and had secretly been thankful she hadn't latched on to their own husbands. Maybe Lacey Cameron was cut from the same cloth!

"Something must be done," Lidy Rose announced.

"My sentiments exactly." Olive bestowed a nod upon the wretched man beside her. "Reverend Summerfield is willing to join us and insist that she abide by the laws of decency or leave town."

"She ought to be made to leave. The damage is already done," the other woman put in. "They both ought to go. We have young people growing up here, and we have to set an example for them."

"I agree," Olive said. "Follow me!"

The small band of women joined forces and scurried out toward the feed store where a number of men were passing the time of day.

Only Mrs. Bastrop remained in the shop. Her brow furrowed, and she dropped the papier-mâché cherries she held. She had grown fond of Lacey, and she didn't like the look in Olive Sloan's eyes. Hastily she left through the back door.

Sarah was on her way to the general store when she saw Mrs. Bastrop hurrying along. Curious, she stopped to speak to her.

"Sarah, there's trouble," Mrs. Bastrop said abruptly. "Olive Sloan is stirring everybody up."

"Over the Quakers? What have we done?"

"No, no. It's about the Camerons." She looked back toward the feed store, where a crowd was forming.

Sarah drew back a little. "What about the Camerons?"

"Olive is saying they aren't married. It's nonsense, but you know how the town feels about that." She looked back at Sarah's pale face. "I know you're Lacey's friend. Go warn her. I'll run over to the blacksmith shop and tell Mr. Cameron."

Sarah hesitated for only a minute. Then she turned and walked briskly toward the Camerons' cabin.

Lacey had draped the rag rug over the porch railing and was knocking the dirt from it with the broom. When Sarah came into her yard, Lacey started, then stood waiting for Sarah to speak.

"They know," Sarah said without preamble. "The town knows thee and Blake aren't married."

Dread gripped Lacey with icy fingers. "You told?"

Sarah took a step nearer. "No, Lacey. I'd never do such a thing. Olive Sloan somehow found out."

Lacey slowly leaned the broom against the house. "How?" She shook her head. "I don't know. I came to warn thee. Mrs. Bastrop has gone after thy . . . Blake."

"Warn me? What's going to happen?" She put her hand on the rail to steady herself.

"I don't know. There's a crowd gathering at the feed store."

There was a crackling in the bushes, and Blake came running toward them, having saved time by cutting through the woods. "What's going on!" he demanded. "Mrs. Bastrop said there's trouble, and I was to hurry home."

"Olive Sloan knows thee aren't married," Sarah told him. "She's telling the rest of the town."

"But we are married," Blake protested.

"She knows about it," Lacey said stiffly. "I told Sarah the next day after we said our vows."

Blake looked from Lacey to the Quaker woman. "Is that why you two haven't been speaking?" he asked Sarah.

"Thee weren't properly married."

"We're as married as you and Hiram," Blake objected. "We formed a bond marriage. Next spring we plan to have it done by a preacher in Morgan. In Texas that is as acceptable as a regular marriage."

"This is not Texas," Sarah said stiffly, "and thee could have told me the truth before I opened my house to thee."

Blake stared at her before he spoke. "Sarah, I thought that you of all people would understand."

Sarah's eyes wavered.

"You of all people," he continued, "should know about prejudices. We did the best we could." He turned to Lacey. "I love her, and she loves me. We're as married in our hearts as two people can be."

"But not in a church!" Sarah protested. "Thee didn't do it the proper way, in a church!"

"How could we?" he asked her. "The mistake had already been made and was too far gone to be corrected."

"She came to warn us," Lacey reminded him. Her eyes met Sarah's. "Thank you, Sarah. I hear voices. You'd better go before they get here."

Sarah's unhappy eyes looked from one to the other. "I owe thee an apology. I've not been a friend. I was so afraid of what would be said about my letting you stay in our spare room that I lost sight of our friendship. I'm so sorry."

Lacey went to her and hugged her briefly. Tears sprang to her eyes, but she tried to smile. "I understand."

"I don't," Blake said gruffly.

"You've never had to leave your home," Lacey reminded him. "I have." To Sarah she said, "It's all mended between us. Now, go before they get here."

Sarah glanced with unmasked worry toward town. "I'll go get Hiram. Maybe he can calm them."

"Go!" Lacey urged. "Don't let them see you here. Blake and I can handle it." She pushed Sarah gently toward the woods. When she was gone, Lacey held out her hand to Blake. "Come up on the porch."

"Why?" he growled.

"Never meet a mob eye to eye," Lacey counseled. "We'll have an advantage if they have to look up at us."

Olive and Lidy Rose were leading the pack when they emerged into the clearing and started across the yard. Lacey and Blake stood side by side on the porch, not touching, and waited silently for Olive to speak.

"We know about you!" Olive announced angrily. "Your shameful secret is out. What do you have to say for yourselves?"

Blake opened his mouth, but Lidy Rose interrupted with, "There is no excuse. You two are living in sin! This is a God-fearing community, and we won't stand for it!"

Behind them the twenty or so townspeople muttered in

agreement. Olive reached behind her and pulled Zeke to the front. Lacey's eyes widened, but no flicker of emotion altered her composed features.

"Here's your own father," Olive informed her unnecessarily. "A man of the cloth. What will he think of you!"

Lacey's eyes met Zeke's and challenged him silently. Zeke shifted uncomfortably. Finally she said, "I don't think he blames me at all. Do you, Papa." Her words were a flat statement rather than a question.

"Forgive!" Zeke grabbed at the cue. "We must learn forgiveness, and this is a golden opportunity to practice it." He turned to the crowd and waved his arm at the couple on the porch. "There stands my only child—a sinner like us all." There was an objecting murmur, and Zeke amended, "Well, maybe worse than most. Still, a sinner and wallowing in shame."

"No!" Lacey blurted out. "I'm doing no such thing. Blake and I have a bond marriage. In the spring we plan to go down to Morgan and be married in the usual way."

"We have a church here," Lidy Rose stated frostily. "There is no excuse for what you've done."

Blake started forward, but Lacey put a restraining hand on his arm. "Stay on the porch," she whispered. "Don't make them any angrier than they are."

"Repent!" Zeke yelled at the couple in his reedy voice. "Repent and they will forgive!" His black eyes told Lacey she had better grab at this chance.

"I've done nothing I'm sorry for," she replied quietly.

Zeke stared as if she had gone crazy in front of his very eyes. Olive bustled forward, pointed her finger at Lacey, and said, "You're a shameful harlot!"

"She's no such thing!" Blake roared, unable to keep quiet any longer. He shook off Lacey's hand and strode down the steps. "We are more innocent than the lot of you!" He went to a man and poked him in the chest. "Zeb Sikes, you owe me for shoeing two horses and a mule. Esther Wilkes, I saw you out walking with Jake Wheeler, and I doubt either your Joseph or his Betty knows a thing about it.''

There was a flurry of protest and a restless shifting of the crowd. ''Olive, you and Lidy Rose gossip the day away without ever saying a kind word about anybody. As for James leaving with Mabel Bannion, if Lidy Rose treated him the way Olive treats Micah, he didn't leave, he escaped! None of you,'' he growled, striding among them, ''not one of you has the right to speak out against us!''

''Talk to him, Reverend,'' Olive commanded. ''Tell him what sinners they are.''

''Reverend!'' Blake snorted, towering over Zeke. ''He's the worst of the lot. He's no more a preacher than I am.''

''Liar!'' Zeke shouted, fear tinging his voice.

Olive and the others echoed Zeke, their anger kindled brighter at hearing their preacher attacked. Lacey leaned on the porch rail and gripped it fearfully.

Blake grabbed at Zeke's coat pocket and drew out a bottle of water labeled ''River Jordan.'' He uncorked it and sniffed. ''It's water, all right. But it came from the creek behind the Sloans' feed lot.'' He knew he had guessed right when Zeke blanched and snatched the bottle out of his hand.

''How dare you question my honesty?'' Zeke shouted in his best pulpit voice. ''I'm not in the wrong here, you are!'' He raised his bony finger in the air. ''I gave life to that wretched girl, and she has brought an adder into the nest.'' He didn't risk pointing at Blake, but there was no doubt who he meant.

''Run them out,'' a man in back yelled.

''We don't need their kind in Friendswood!'' another seconded. ''Chase 'em out.''

Blake clenched his big hands into fists and hunched his shoulders, ready to fight.

''Blake!'' Lacey screamed. There were too many men for him to fight, and she saw Zeb Sikes picking up a stick to use as a club.

"Here, now," a new voice said in gentling tones. "What's going on?"

Lacey's frightened eyes saw Hiram's strong figure coming through the woods with Sarah beside him.

"Zeb," Hiram greeted amiably. "Esther. Why are thee all meeting here? Have thee nothing else to do?" Although his words were innocent, he obviously knew what was going on, because Sarah looked worried. "I don't see Micah," he observed to Olive.

"He refused to come. And you know why we're here. We've come to run these sinners out of town."

"All of them?" Hiram asked mildly. He moved through the crowd as if at random, but he stopped between Blake and the others. Turning to face the mob, he gently eased Sarah behind him and nudged her toward the porch.

"You're no better than they are!" Zeke accused, shaking the bottle of "River Jordan" water at Hiram.

He caught Zeke's wrist and examined the bottle. "What has thee got here? Is this one of those little bottles I saw thee filling from the creek the other day? I believe it is."

Zeke shoved the bottle into his pocket. "Don't let them turn us from our purpose here!" He tried to rally the crowd, but people were now looking at him uncertainly. "We're here because of what Blake and Lacey have done!" To Hiram he said, "Can you honestly say you didn't know they aren't rightfully married?"

Hiram, who had had no inkling that they weren't until minutes before, said, "Thee is causing a ruckus over nothing. A bond marriage is as binding as a legal ceremony."

"You!" Olive shouted, pointing at Sarah. "You're her friend! Did you know they weren't married?"

"No! She had no idea," Lacey interrupted Sarah's reply. "Neither Sarah nor Hiram, nor any of the other Quakers knew about us!" Her eyes met Sarah's. "She's been my friend, but not my confidante."

Reluctantly, Sarah tried to speak the truth, but Lacey continued. "Olive, you may be able to persecute us, but not them. The Gibsons are innocent and had no idea we weren't married when they gave us shelter. It's all been a terrible misunderstanding, but it's been one you all helped foster.'' She moved to the steps and slowly stepped down into the yard. ''We never said we were married until we realized that you all thought we were. Blake believed it was better to let you think that than to take a chance on us being refused medicine. By the time we realized we couldn't leave until spring, everybody had us wed in their minds, and it was too late to change that.''

She went to Blake and put her hand in his. ''We fell in love and wanted to marry, but how could we when you all believed we already were? So we made a bond marriage.''

There was a moment of silence. Then Olive shrieked, ''She admits it! She says they aren't married and expects us to accept them anyway!''

''Get out of town!'' A woman yelled. ''We don't want you here!''

Lacey gripped Blake's hand but made no move to retreat. The crowd was in an ugly mood, and she was afraid a sudden movement would bring them down upon her and Blake. She could hear Hiram trying to calm them, and Blake was making a warning sound as if he had already found a target for his fists.

''Stop!'' Lacey shouted. ''You want us to go, so we will!'' Blake wheeled to face her angrily, but she said firmly, ''We'll go. If we aren't welcome here, we won't be happy.''

''You're not welcome!'' Lidy Rose screamed. ''Get out of town!''

''Leave by morning or else!'' Olive threatened.

Lacey met her eyes unflinchingly. Slowly she tugged Blake's hand and led him back to the dubious safety of the porch. As she had on other occasions, Lacey looked dispassionately into the face of the mob. The only difference between this one and others was that Papa stood in the front rank and was parroting the yells.

"Lacey, I don't want to go," Blake growled under the noise. "I'm going to try to reason with them again."

"No. They won't hear you." She didn't look at him, but she said in a numb voice, "A mob is the only animal that has no brain."

After a while the crowd grew tired of yelling threats and curses and, since the yard was clean of stones to throw, they dispersed. Only Hiram and Sarah were left standing there.

Hiram turned to Blake and silently offered him his hand.

After a brief hesitation, Blake took it and gripped it tightly. "I'm sorry to bring all this down on you."

"If I could pick a brother, it would be thee. I don't hold thee at fault. Who knows that I wouldn't have done the same, given those circumstances?"

Lacey and Sarah gazed at each other; then Sarah took the first step forward. Lacey hurried off the porch and hugged her tightly. She didn't have the words to express what was in her heart, so she let the tears course down her cheeks as she held her friend.

When they released each other, Sarah said brokenly, "I'll miss thee. I'll not ever have such a good friend as thee."

Lacey still couldn't talk for the lump in her throat, but she nodded hard and squeezed Sarah's hands. "I'll miss you," she managed to say.

"We don't have to go," Blake declared unhappily. "This is our home."

Lacey put her arm around him and shook her head as she gazed up into his eyes. "We have to go." There was no room for discussion in her tone. He held her tightly as Hiram and Sarah quietly walked away.

CHAPTER
21

Lacey made a sack for her clothes by tying together the legs of Blake's extra pants. Into the waistband she stuffed her smallclothes, her hair brush, her two extra dresses, and both her nightgowns. Using his spare belt as a drawstring, she gathered the waistband and knotted the belt.

Blake was less methodical. He picked his clothes from the wall pegs and poked them unceremoniously into his canvas bag. As he did so, he grumbled under his breath and threw angry glances about the dimly lit cabin, and especially at Lacey.

"There's no need for us to go," he stated for the hundredth time.

"You saw the mood they were in." Lacey answered as she had each time before. "If we aren't gone by morning, they will be back—probably with more people to help them."

She looked out the window. "Will you saddle the horse? Dawn is probably only an hour away. I can see a lightening in the sky." She knelt and started nestling one pot inside another to fit on the pack saddle.

"Not that one," Blake objected as she picked up a large cooking pot. He took it from her and strode to the door.

''This is the pot Olive Sloan gave us.'' He opened the door and hurled the pot into the night.

Lacey heard it clang against a tree and rattle to silence. Without a word, she continued packing. She could replace the pot, and Blake had needed to throw something.

''Are you really set on doing this?''

She merely looked at him over her shoulder and turned back to laying the flatware in a cup towel so she could roll it into a bundle.

With a strangled growl, Blake went out into the night. He couldn't understand her. Lacey wanted to stay. She had spent most of the night crying and worrying about where they would go. Finally they had decided to travel down to Morgan, spend the winter, and go back east as soon as weather permitted. They couldn't chance traveling far with winter imminent.

When he entered the barn, a horse snorted, and Blake spoke to it as he lit the lantern by the door. Soft light flooded the interior, and Blake was astonished to see two new horses in the box stall. Not believing his eyes, he went closer.

Instead of his bay with the bad lungs, he saw a young gray gelding and a blue roan. Neither horse was a stranger to him. He had shod the roan on several occasions and had assisted in bargaining for the gray. Both belonged to Hiram, and Blake had spent hours breaking, training, and riding them.

A square of paper was wedged in the grate, and Blake pulled it loose and unfolded it. Hiram had written him a note saying the two horses were a trade for the bay. Blake felt a stinging prickle in his eyes. He hadn't told Lacey, but he had been very concerned that the bay wouldn't be able to carry them both even as far as Morgan. With these horses they would have no trouble at all.

The pack mule dangled his long head over the neighboring gate and nibbled at the corner of the paper. Blake pushed the inquiring nose away and went into the tack room to get the harness.

Left alone in the house, Lacey raised her head and gazed around the room. They had been here such a short time, yet there were memories in every corner. The hearth was where she and Blake had stood when they exchanged vows. The sturdy table had seen meals she had cooked as well as some she had burned and had served as a council table for discussions and a work surface for her sewing. She touched the folds of garnet cloth on the shelf and wished she had been able to complete the dress.

She crossed the room to the bed. Her happiest memories were centered here. As if it were alive, Lacey stroked the polished wood and ran her hand over the billowing feather mattress. She hated to leave it behind.

At last she looked at the bearskin rolled up by the door. Over her objections, Blake had insisted on taking it, calling it her game trophy. She kicked it with the toe of her shoe. That bear had been the source of great pain for her.

Lacey jumped as Blake entered. Her nerves were strung tight from lack of sleep. "I hate to leave our bed," she said reluctantly.

"I'll get you another one."

She looked around the room again. "There's so much we can't take without a wagon. We'll have to start all over again."

"At least we have horses. In exchange for the bay, Hiram brought over the blue roan and the gray gelding I trained for him." Blake looked away and added, "I'm sure as hell going to miss Hiram."

"I know. I'll miss Sarah, too." She bent and picked up the bundle of clothes and gave them to him.

Blake strapped their belongings to the pack mule and tied a roll of blankets behind each saddle. "I guess we're ready," he grudgingly admitted.

"Wait, I have to sweep."

"Now?"

"I won't leave a dirty house. Who knows who will look in here?"

He resigned himself to the wait, knowing this was part of Lacey's farewell ritual. Soon she was finished, and even the porch was clean. She replaced the broom behind the door and closed it firmly. Without speaking, she pulled her skirts back and mounted the roan. She sat gazing at the house, then reined her horse down the path. Night was pearling into gray, and pale blue colored the trees and bushes. The night foragers had retired to caves and trees, and the daylight creatures were not yet stirring. Only the thud of the animals' hooves and their occasional snorts, along with the creak and jingle of harness, broke the silence.

They rode through town, and Lacey looked around at the darkened houses and locked stores. "It's as if we are the only ones here," she whispered.

"This is an odd time, neither daylight nor dark. When I was a boy I thought this hour was much more ghostly than midnight." He looked over at her. "Lacey, you can't run forever. Sooner or later you have to stand still and dig in."

"You don't understand. What if they come back and lynch you, as they did Billy?"

"That was another thing entirely. A girl had *died*. No one was hurt here. The town might disagree about our marriage being legal, but not so much that they would kill us for it."

"I don't know," she disagreed. "A mob will do irrational things."

They rode out of town and past the last of the houses, where a light shown from the windows and the scent of wood smoke hung in the crisp air. It was the tiny cabin where she and Sarah had worked to save Carl Odem's life. She would never have another friend like Sarah.

Lacey nudged the roan to a quick lope. The sooner she was away from Friendswood the better. Blake's horse matched her pace, and the lazy mule had no choice but to comply.

The primitive road to Morgan, carved by the few tradesmen who traveled the route on occasion, dipped up, down, and around the side of the lower mountain. The road was far from smooth, but following it was easier than striking off through the woods. Blake took the lead, and they slowed to a more conservative trot. The ride to Morgan would be taxing, and there was no need to spend the horses.

The road curved down a steep slope and was bisected by a splashing stream. The horses waded through, and Blake let them walk up the slope. He had turned to say something to Lacey when a faint noise drew his attention.

Cocking his head, he stopped his horse and motioned for her to do the same. Now he heard it more clearly. He signaled her to silence as he dismounted and handed her the reins.

Moving cautiously, Blake climbed the steep road and dropped to his hands and knees to peer over the summit. Before him was a band of Indians breaking camp. His heart pounding, Blake studied the scene. There were no women or children or dogs, only men. Bright paint streaked their bodies, and they were talking excitedly as they mounted their horses. It was a war party.

Careful to make no sound, Blake backed down the hill until he could stand and run. When he reached Lacey, he vaulted onto the gray and grabbed the reins, leaning forward to flick them over the horse's head. "Indians!" he hissed. "We nearly rode right into them. Get back to town quick!" As he spoke, he wheeled the gray gelding, almost making it rear.

Lacey needed no urging. She clapped her heels against the horse and leaned forward to send it into a gallop. The noisy stream masked the sound of their hooves and together they raced back the way they had come.

Blake led her to the town hall and dismounted before the horse stopped moving. Leaping to the porch, he swung on the bell rope. At once the bell's harsh voice clanged out the warning. "Get inside," he yelled to Lacey," and take the guns and bullets."

She hurried to obey as the two horses pranced in fright.

The mule broke loose and trotted back toward their cabin, lead rope dangling. The roan also decided home was preferable to being deafened by a bell, so he cantered off in the direction of the Gibsons' house. The gray whinnied in protest, but Blake still held his reins.

Throughout the town, people were jolted from their early morning drowsiness by the alarm bell. Without questioning, all grabbed guns and children and ran for the town hall.

Zeke was eating breakfast when the first peals sounded. He looked from Olive to Micah and swallowed convulsively. "What's that?" he demanded.

"The alarm!" Micah exclaimed, throwing his napkin into his plate and running to the window. "It's the alarm bell!"

Olive rose with a strangled cry.

"Hurry!" Micah shouted. "Let's go to the town hall!" As he spoke, he grabbed his rifle from behind the door and dumped a box of shells into his pocket.

"I'm not dressed!" Olive protested, gesturing at her wrapper.

"Get dressed," Zeke told her. To Micah, he said, "You go on. I'll bring her."

Micah hesitated then left on a run. Their house was closest to the town hall, and Olive could reach safety easily.

As soon as Micah left, Zeke ran out the back way. By the time Olive started down stairs, Zeke had returned. "Get your valuables," he shouted when he saw her on the staircase.

"What?" This wasn't part of the defense plan.

"Get your valuables!" he repeated. "Your jewels! We can't stay here and be massacred! I've hitched my pair to the wagon, and we're getting out of here!"

"But Mr. Sloan . . ."

"We'll stop off and pick him up. Hurry!"

Olive ran to get her jewel box as Zeke hurried to the front parlor. Using the tablecloth as a bag, he scooped up the gold cigar box, the silver bonbon dish and butler tray, and several candlesticks. In the dining room, he snatched all the silver-ware out of the drawer. Staggering under the weight of his booty, he ran to the wagon and tossed it in. As he climbed aboard, Olive bustled out, clutching a large box to her ample bosom.

"Hurry up!" he yelled. The constant clanging of the bell was making him panicky. The two horses danced wildly in the traces.

Puffing with exertion, Olive handed him her jewelry box and clambered up to the seat.

Zeke slapped the reins over the horses' backs, and the wagon bolted forward. He steered between running people and pulled to a gravel-spraying stop at the town hall. "Go get Mr. Sloan!" he commanded.

Dithering with fright, Olive nearly fell off the wagon, scooped up her wide skirts and headed for the steps. As soon as she was clear, Zeke shoved the jewelry box into the back, grabbed his whip, and struck out at the pair of horses. They leaped into a frantic run, spurred on by the whip and the bell.

"Wait!" Olive screamed. "Don't leave us, Reverend!" She ran after him, waving her hand as if to flag him to a stop.

Instead of slowing, Zeke snapped the horses to a run and headed them in the direction of Morgan. He realized his mistake almost at once.

Dozens of Indians, painted garishly with red, white, and yellow, came shrieking out of the woods in front of the wagon. The horses reared, their hooves flailing the air. Zeke cried out as three arrows found him an easy target. He slumped over in death, his weight grinding against the brake lever as the pair reared and plunged.

Blake had seen Zeke leaving and had been too surprised to call out. But when Olive ran after him and the Indians burst out of the woods, he sprang into action. He jumped from the porch to his horse and galloped after her. Leaning from the saddle, he snaked his arm around her bulk and turned the horse back toward the building.

Shouting for the people on the porch to clear away, Blake didn't pause to dismount, but rode straight up the steps and into the building, Olive Sloan still clutched in his grasp.

The door slammed shut behind him, and sounds of screams and yells almost drowned the clatter of the horse's hooves on the wooden floor. Blake dropped Olive and swung down.

Sarah ran to him and he gave her the reins. "Take him to the back corner and try to calm him," he ordered. "Where's Lacey?"

"Over there, with Hiram," Sarah pointed as she led the skittish horse to the least crowded corner.

Blake ran to Lacey. Hiram was beside her, loading the gun as she fired the rifle. Blake grinned at him and took Hiram's squirrel gun. "The bell worked!" he yelled over the sounds of gunshots and whooping Indians.

He picked out a brave on a racing pinto and took a deep breath before pulling the trigger. The Indian tumbled off the horse and lay still.

Lacey, not turning to greet Blake, sighted down the barrel of the rifle and picked off an attacking Indian.

"Your papa is dead," Blake shouted at her.

"I know. I saw it all." She shoved the empty rifle at Hiram and grabbed the one he gave her in return. "That was a damned fool thing you did out there! You're lucky not to be dead, too!" She threw him an exasperated look. "You take care of yourself."

The other women and the children huddled on the floor in the center of the room. Most of them were screaming and crying, or were staring about with glazed expressions of shock. One of the Quaker men had gone to help Sarah hold the horse, and the two of them were struggling to calm the frightened animal.

Blake aimed carefully, trying to make each shot count. There were more Indians than he had expected, but all the townsmen were good shots, and few of the Indians had guns. Now and then Blake heard a scream as an arrow struck home or a thump as one hit the wall by his head. He searched for the chief, Lame Wolf. Blake had learned from the half-breed scouts back in the Texas army that the chief was always the core of an Indian attack—kill the chief and the fight was won.

An Indian jerked his horse into a gallop toward the building, and Blake aimed and shot. The horse went down, but the man rolled free and ran whooping toward the open windows.

Sarah had her back to the open window and was fighting to hold on to the gray gelding. She didn't see the Indian until he grabbed her and was pulling her toward him. His long knife was already raised to stab her when she screamed and managed to pull away from him.

As if by a sixth sense, Hiram heard her above the racket and wheeled to see the Indian lunging toward her again. Without pausing, he snapped the rifle to his shoulder and fired. The Indian, cloaked in blood, fell away, and Sarah dropped to the floor.

He waited to see her stagger to her feet and again clutch the horse's bridle; then he turned to Blake. Their eyes met and Hiram said, "Thee will have to load thy own rifle." Hiram reloaded the gun, aimed, and fired out the window.

"Look!" a frantic cry sounded from the front of the building. "They're lighting a fire!"

Blake risked a quick glance. Out of the range of the bullets, a tall Indian was building a fire. The brightly colored breastplate he wore showed him to be the chief Blake had been looking for.

"They're going to burn us out!" Lacey gasped.

From amid the group of women Olive gave a shattering shriek. "We're going to die! We'll all die!" She hurled herself at Micah, causing him to fire into the trees. "Reverend Summerfield was right! We're all going to be killed!"

Micah turned on her and gave her a ringing slap that made

her stagger. "Either get a gun or get out of my way!" he roared at her.

Olive shrank back to the knot of women and children.

Lacey's eyes were large with fright, but she merely looked at Blake. He lifted his hand and caressed her face. "Hiram," he said, still looking at Lacey, "take care of her."

Before they knew what he was going to do, Blake turned and ran to the prancing horse. In a leap he was on the pitching back and was heading the animal toward the entrance. "Open the doors, Micah!" he yelled as he urged the horse forward.

The Indians were circling the building as Lame Wolf set torches ablaze. Suddenly the double doors burst open, and a man on a big gray horse catapulted into the sunlight. The horse took the steps in an easy jump, his mane and tail flying.

As if in a dream, the startled braves saw the horse's muscles bunch, then lengthen as he landed and stretched into a full gallop toward Lame Wolf.

The chief stared, then grabbed his bow. Only the waist-high fire stood between him and the large man on the plunging horse. Lame Wolf stood his ground and notched his arrow onto the bowstring. Taking careful aim, he waited for the white man to swerve around the fire and offer him a clear shot.

Blake didn't waver. With a Texas yell that had sent chills through enemies from Washington-on-the-Brazos to San Jacinto, Blake set the horse straight at the fire. Through the shimmering heat waves, he saw the chief waiting. Blake felt the horse tense under him and soar into the air, clearing the blaze easily. As his forefeet touched the ground, Blake fired directly between the pointed gray ears just as Lame Wolf released the arrow and fell to the ground.

Instead of hitting Blake's chest as was intended, the shaft had buried itself in his thigh. Blake was too filled with desperate purpose to notice. Lame Wolf, bloodied but not dead, was struggling to his feet and reaching for another arrow as the gray horse thundered past him.

Blake dropped his spent rifle and, as he hauled back on the reins, the animal cut around. This time a bullet from his pistol found its mark before the Indian could shoot, and Lame Wolf died before he hit the ground.

Without pausing, Blake rode at the braves, firing his pistol with deadly precision.

With their leader dead, the Indians were ready to run for the hills. Seeing their advantage, the townspeople started firing again. By the time the last shot was fired, the yard around the town hall was littered with painted bodies. Blake brought the gray to a plunging halt at the steps. Reaching down, he grasped the shaft of the arrow and yanked it out of his leg before he could give it a second thought.

Lacey shouldered her way out of the door and ran to him. Blake held out his hand, but his leg hurt too badly for him to risk dismounting. As the people of Friendswood gathered on the porch, he gazed down at her. "What will it be, Lacey? Do you still want to go?"

She wiped the tears away and then gripped his hand. "No, Blake. I'm through running away. Let's go home."

He grinned and lifted her up to the saddle behind him. Nodding to the crowd on the porch, he turned the horse in the direction of their cabin.

LYNDA TRENT is a pseudonym for the award-winning writing team of Dan and Lynda Trent from Texas. Lynda was a professional artist who began writing to overcome "artist's block." Dan was a NASA engineer who chose writing as his full-time career. Dan and Lynda's favorite pastime is travelling all over the United States searching for the perfect setting for their next book.